THE DOOR
INTO SUNSET

Tor books by Diane Duane

THE DOOR
INTO SUNSET

Tale of the Five
Book 3

Diane Duane

TOR *fantasy* ®

A TOM DOHERTY ASSOCIATES BOOK
NEW YORK

THE DOOR INTO SUNSET

Copyright © 1992 by Diane Duane

This book is printed on acid-free paper.

A Tor® Book
Published by Tom Doherty Associates, Inc.
175 Fifth Avenue
New York, N.Y. 10010

TOR® is a registered trademark of Tom Doherty Associates, Inc.

Library of Congress Cataloging-in-Publication Data

Duane, Diane.
    The door into sunset / Diane Duane.
        p.   cm. — (The Tale of the five ; bk. 3)
    "A Tom Doherty Associates book."
    ISBN 0-312-85184-7
    1. Imaginary places—Fiction. I. Title. II. Series.
PS3554.U233D65   1993
813'.54—dc20   92-42214
                                  CIP

First edition: March 1993

Printed in the United States of America

0 9 8 7 6 5 4 3 2 1

For Anne McCaffrey
who will do *anything* to get people
to move to Ireland

and for Wilma,
who can borrow Hasai any old time

. . . How many heroes gather then
when the Lion wakes again?
When the Eagle leaves the Tree,
how many warriors will there be?

One to give despite the cost:
one to find the one that's lost:

one to wear the maiden's crown,
one to bring the lightning down:

one a shadow, one a fire,
one a son and one a sire;

one that's dead, and one alive:
one that's One, and one that's Five . . .

Rope-jumping song,
Arlene, current 1480 p.a.d.

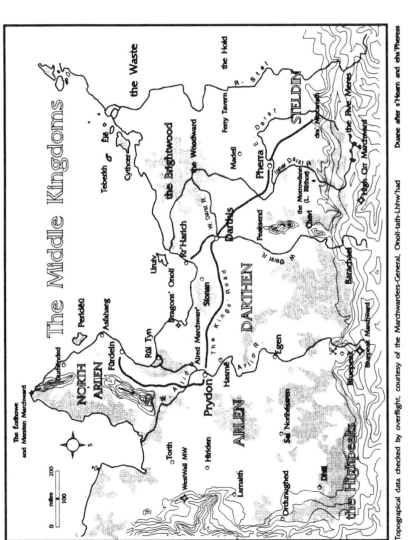

The Middle Kingdoms

the Waste

The Eorlhowe
and Messian Marchward

NORTH
ARLEN

Perideo

Asfaheg

Fordeln

Rúl Tyn

Tebérih   Eie   Cythrer

the Brightwood

Unuty

Dragons' Onoll

Stonan

Alред Marchward

the Woodward

Model

Ferry Tavern   the Hold

R. Stel

STELDIN

Ar'Harlch

W. Darst R.

Darthis

Phera

E. Darst

Inner Darst R.

dro'Morrowfans

The King's Road

Hasmé

Prydon

Torth

WestWall MW   Hinden

Lamath

Ordrunaghod

Diheli

the Highpeaks

Arlid R.

Egen

ARLEN

DARTHEN

Sed Northessen

Bluepeak

Bluepeak Marchward

Arda R.

Peskosend

Chavi

the Morrowfans
(L. Rilthw)

Barachael

the Fíve Meres

High-Qirr Marchward

miles   200
0   100   S

Topographical data checked by overflight, courtesy of the Marchwarders-General, Omolt-tath-Lhhw'had   Duane after s'Hearm and ehs'Phéress

The Battle outside Prydon:
Autumn 1st, 2927 p.a.d.

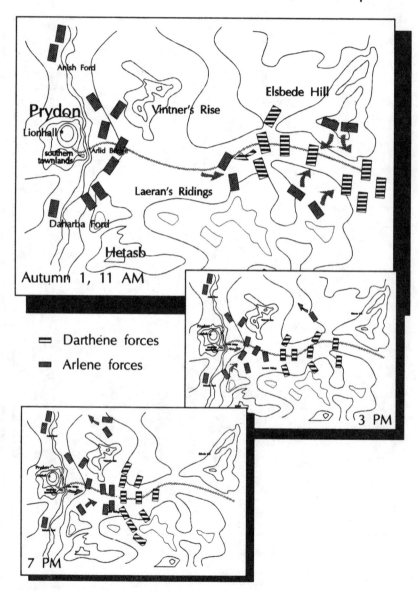

Prologue

What then shall be done to save Thy people? saith Héalhra. Canst Thou not put forth Thy power?

Nay, saith the Goddess: in this I am bound by My own law: this is My creatures' world. My creatures must themselves preserve and master it.

A hard saying, Héalhra saith. Yet shall we do so. How shall it be done?

In the time of thy need, the Goddess saith, shalt thou be overshadowed by My power: thou shalt be filled with My Fire, that hath been long lost to man, and kingship and mastery of the land shall be given thee. A god's power shalt thou have, and with it strike down thine enemy and Mine: great shall be thy glory.

Then when this thing is done shall we go north and found a realm, saith Héalhra in joy: and all things shall go well.

Thou shalt not go, saith the Goddess. For all this there is a price: godhead once so assumed may not be put off. The Saviour of thy people thou shalt be: but no man again. And She looked on him narrowly, and said, Wilt thou pay the price?

Then Héalhra was silent a long while in sorrow. I will pay it, and all shall be as Thou wilt, saith he. But can Godhead yet be sweeter than work, and bread and wine, and love of the body, and sleep after love?

And the Goddess turned away, Her eyes downcast, and made him no answer.

Héalhra his Dreme, 14

The thing that surprised him most about dying was how very much it hurt.

For a moment after he knew he was hit, Freelorn s'Ferrant stai-Héalhrästi had no time to waste on the arrow standing feather-deep in his chest. He was busy doing a magic, the one that would give his land new life from his blood. It was one of the few sorceries a royal person could do without being a king and Initiate as well, and too many lives rode on it for Lorn to let himself be distracted. But in the next moment, as he finished weaving the binding-spell around his fistful of dirt and blood, and would have sagged and gasped with relief, the whole world immediately constricted itself to the size and shape of the alien object sticking out under his collarbone. He would never forget it, he thought – that ashwood arrow, with its peculiar spiral Reaver fletching, and the double-banded tribal hatchmark crudely scratched on the shaft. The striped brown and black fletch-feathers were split where the archer had hastily grabbed the arrow by the fletching in the draw. *A miracle it hit me at all*, Freelorn thought – and then the pain tore him open like a talon from horrified gut to brain.

Consciousness of his surroundings failed him in the fire of pain. He lost the surrounding battlefield, shrouded in unnatural darkness at afternoon; lost the wind and unseasonable snow howling around the friends who had followed him here, as they crouched among the tumbled cliff-rocks, waiting for the attacking Reavers to come and make an end of them. He lost the slender mail-clad woman standing alone in the snow and staring at him in horror, a

13

shadow in her hand; he lost the man behind him who reached out to him in a blaze of blue Fire, crying his name. Only emotion remained to Freelorn now . . . dread of what was happening, loathing of the alien thing lodged in his flesh – both bizarrely replaced, a second later, by shame. How unnatural, how terrible to die! Life wasn't meant to end this way, in blood and anguish. And something else had gone wrong too. It hadn't hurt like this, the last time he'd died—

In the crucible of pain, this moment melted into that one, becoming it. How old had he been – seven, or eight – when the half-broken filly mule panicked in the palace stable and kicked him in the face? He had lain for days, they told him, burning with fever and concussion; not moving, sometimes not breathing. Lorn knew nothing of that. All he remembered were a few long moments of slanting red light – some window full of early evening sky, glimpsed uncomprehending through the brain fever – and then the bright place where he had found himself. At least it had started out bright. Later it had changed.

It changed now. The agony still had its claws in him, but it didn't matter, and Freelorn ignored it and looked out upon the Door that once again stood open for him. Black lintels reared up out of sight into forever; a doorsill carved out of night lay before him. Past the Door flamed endless depths of stars, faint intimations of that Sea that burned beyond mortal light and darkness, washing the long silent Shore where the Dead walk.

Lorn had company at the Door again – the same company as last time, when he had walked here in dream, looking for his ancestor Héalhra Whitemane to demand a miracle of Him. But dreams didn't really count. This was the second time he had done the true journey to the Door. It was getting to be a habit . . . a dangerous one, even for a king. You could make the trip one time too many, and not come back.

That had actually been his intention on his first trip, after the mule-kick . . . when he found the Other standing in the Door, and complained bitterly to Her that he didn't like the place where he'd been sent, and wanted to come back home. She had told him he wasn't finished, and had made him go back . . . and since She had never let him have his way before, he hadn't been surprised. What did surprise him, now, was his companion tugging at him from behind, pulling at the hand he was trying to loosen from its grip, and saying the same kinds of things She had said before—

Lorn, no!!

It disturbed Freelorn that She wasn't here. Though Her dismissal last time had been swift and bitterly disappointing, he longed for another sight of Her. Or had it been a Him? The memory grew vague as he grasped after it. Power, that he *did* remember, and a joy that would break the heart and heal it, both at once. That joy had been part of what convinced him to go back the last time. He had been promised more of it—

Lorn! You have things to do!

—and the promise had been kept. But this time his business was with Someone else. Last time he walked here, he'd come to ask his ancient Father the White Lion about the whereabouts of Hergótha the Great, the kings' sword of Arlen. But the Lion had fobbed him off with demigodly hints and riddles, and then Freelorn had become involved and distracted in business of Herewiss's. That was what came of trying to get work done in dreams. Now, however, he was not going to be distracted. He took another step forward – tugging along the one behind, who wouldn't let go – and cried into the void, *Father? Where are you?*

Here, the answer came. *I heard you were looking for me.*

—and for once things were working right, for it wasn't Héalhra his line-father, the ancestor of all the kings of Arlen, who answered: it was Ferrant his blood-father. Ferrant was simply there, leaning on one lintel of the Door, his arms folded, gazing at his son with humorous calm. It was utterly like his father to be so casual on

15

Death's literal threshold. But then his father was seven years dead.

Later, if he made it back to life, Lorn would weep at the memory of this moment, of the calm regard of a ghost. But here, in the shadowy place between the world's reality and the soul's, he was as matter-of-fact as his father. Slowly he pulled his hand quite out of the grip that held him from behind, and said, without preamble, *Why didn't you Initiate me before you died?*

Because it would have killed you, Ferrant said.

How? Why? I was ready!

If you have to ask, Ferrant said, *explaining it wouldn't help.*

Freelorn had to laugh at that; it was his father's exact turn of phrase, remembered from a thousand childhood arguments. *A lot of good that does me now!* he said. *Father, don't you realize the trouble Arlen's in? Seven years now there's been no king on the throne but the bastard who bought his way there and hunted me across the Kingdoms after you died. The royal magics that keep the Shadow bound are going to pieces for lack of maintenance! Darthen's queen and I just bound the Dark One again, but the rope is rotten – I won't have a king's whole power to use until I'm Initiate! You were the only one in Arlen who knew the rite – and you died before you told me! For our people's sake, and Darthen's, what do I do now?*

What I will tell you to do now, Ferrant said, looking serious.

Freelorn listened with all of him.

What I did, his father said, *and my mother, and her mother and grandfather before her. Make it up as you go along.*

Father!!

His father looked at him with a tired but compassionate expression. *For all the generations I was ever told of, each king or queen who took a son or daughter to Lionhall for the Nightwalk at day's end has pointed that prince or princess at the door of the Hall, and said to them, 'Our Father bids you make your way through old Night to the morning, unguided and alone, as He did'*. And then the king or queen leaves, and comes back in the morning, to be greeted at the door by a new ruler-Initiate, or else to carry out the corpse. *There's no other way.*

You mean the original rite's been lost?!

His father said nothing.

Father, Freelorn said desperately, *if I die in the Nightwalk, the land dies with me, and all our people starve! My people! I can't afford to take the chance! What do I do? Give me a hint!!*

His father looked at him gravely.

Go to Arlen, and learn the rite.

But Eftgan's army won't be ready for—

I said nothing of armies. Go to Arlen, alone, and become Initiate.

But they'll kill me if they catch me!

His father shrugged.

Freelorn was chilled by his calmness. For a little while he could say nothing. What finally came out was, *I miss you.*

But you miss Hergótha as much, said Ferrant, and there was a ghost's lean smile on his face.

For the first time, Freelorn became aware of still having a body, there so close to souls' country; his eyes began to burn. *Why did you have to die?!* he cried.

His father said nothing.

I can't stay here much longer, Freelorn said. *You know that no-one rules Arlen without Hergótha. I need it, and you had it last. Where is it?!*

His father gazed at him, and shook his head.

I'll deal with you later, Freelorn said, and turned away.

Yes, his father said, *you will.* And he was gone.

Freelorn rubbed his eyes briefly, then turned back to Herewiss and found him gazing at him with an expression anguished and helpless. Immediately he went to him and took Herewiss's hands. *Come on. You didn't really think I was going to leave you, did you?*

Wordless, Herewiss pulled him close and simply held him for a moment. *We've got a lot of work to do, and not enough time to do it in, and no way to tell how it's to be done,* Freelorn said. *So let's get to it.*

Together they turned away from death's Door, back towards the battlefield.

Lorn rose up to find that a miracle had happened. Not so much that he was still alive. If you're willing to live, and your loved is the first man in a thousand years to control the blue Flame of Power, dying of a mere arrow through the heart is a difficult business. As they came back to consciousness of the world again and helped each other sit up in the snow, Herewiss merely reached out and touched the arrow; and shaft and barbed point and the place where they had gone in all vanished together in a flicker of Flame. Lorn spent a long moment looking down at his chest, still somehow expecting to see feathers.

Then someone else crunched over to kneel in the snow beside them, and they looked up. It was Segnbora. She was mail-clad still, though the mail had a great rent in it, with a healed wound at the bottom. If she had before been alone on the cliff's edge, she wasn't any longer. Over her loomed a huge thunder-winged shape, burning in iron and diamond. And as for the long sharp shadow in her hand, now it was a shadow set on Fire; it streamed and burned like a windblown torch with the blue Flame she had pursued so long. The suddenly empty battlefield made it plain she had done something that had saved all their lives. But her expression, that of someone who has found her heart's desire, made such an undertaking seem prosaic and small.

'You've got it,' Freelorn said. *'You've got it!'*

Much babbling followed – explanations, and cries of delight as Lorn's other friends, his little personal army, five strong, came out of their hiding-places in the rocks and rejoiced. Only half an hour ago hope had been dead: Herewiss's Power crippled, all of them doomed to quick

18

deaths on the stricken field or slow ones by torture. Now it was all changed. Even the Queen of Darthen was sitting up again, healed in an instant of her own wounds by knife and arrow: and the low midsummer sun was coming out again, leaning golden towards evening. At such a time, anything seemed possible. The seven were already speaking of the throne of Arlen as if it was a thing achieved. And in the middle of them all, silent, there sat Lorn: one small mustachioed man, now suddenly brother to queens, companion to Dragons, and the most wanted man in the Middle Kingdoms . . . wanted primarily by the Power that had taught all Creation death.

Freelorn thought wistfully of the days when he could have died with a clean conscience . . . then got up, brushed the melting snow off him, and once again started to work on becoming what he had been trained to be, a king. He did it reluctantly. Sooner or later kingship would kill him, as it had killed all his line from Héalhra down to Ferrant.

It now only remained to see how long he could make it take.

1

'It hath more the look of a collar than of a
crown,' said one who looked on.

'Ay,' quoth the young King, 'but if a collar,
'tis for my throat, not thine.'

Darthene Tales: 'Of Bron the Young'

The morning after the second Battle of Bluepeak, Freelorn
found himself suddenly awake in bed, gazing up at the
ceiling with the feeling that the past seven years had never
happened, were all a dream. Under the covers, he was as
warm as he might have been on any of those early days, in
his bed strewn with furs and velvets. Outside the room's
unseen windows were sunlight, and city noises, and on the
sill, brown sparrows chattering. This was Prydon, certainly. His father was the king, and he himself the prince,
and everything at peace. A very odd, very bad dream, it
had been. He lay there purposely not remembering it.

Then he noticed that there was a crack in the ceiling;
and though his bedroom ceiling had a crack in it, it wasn't
this crack. Regretfully he closed his eyes so as not to see:
but it was too late, the crack was in his mind as well, and
widening. For one thing, he was in bed, a real bed with a
mattress, and good lawn sheets, and no bugs. How many
years now had it been since he had been safe in any place
with a bed? Hundreds of nights spent in the wet, in the cold,
with only stars or clouds for ceiling, remembered themselves to him. No, it had all happened. Especially the bugs.

Lorn opened his eyes again. The walls were tan instead of white, and there were hangings where bare marble should have showed, and black wood bedposts instead of his own teak, and a light quilted cotton coverlet instead of his velvet one. Well, it was Midsummer after all. But most of the coverlet was on the other side of the bed. He turned his head to that side. There was a man-size, man-shaped lump on the other side of the bed, wrapped in eight tenths of the covers as if in a cocoon. *He's done it again*, Freelorn thought, resigned.

Herewiss was snoring. Freelorn turned over on his side and looked at what he could see of his bedmate. Precious little: the top of that curly dark head, and closed eyes, and a nose. The coverlet was wrapped tight around everything else. It was the old story: you could nail a blanket to the bed, but by morning Herewiss would have all of it. *How does he do it?* Lorn thought. It was an old pleasant habitual thought, meant to keep him from thinking something else.

Like the crack, the thought asserted itself anyway. *This man*, Lorn thought, *last night this man took on the greatest created power known, and held his own against it. For hours. This snoring lump, this blanket thief, this bit of flesh and bone and blood. My loved. Herewiss.*

'Herewiss,' he said quietly. No response; when his loved slept, he slept sound . . . and certainly today he had excuse. 'Dusty,' he said, the old nickname – when they had played together, years ago, Herewiss had seemed to think that the way a prince got to be one with the land was by carrying as much of it as possible on his person. 'Nnff,' Herewiss said, shifted position slightly, and snored louder.

There was another name, of course. Freelorn did not feel quite comfortable with it yet, though it was his alone to speak. Herewiss had found that Name with his Fire. All his Power was bound up in that one word, all his intent, his destiny, his whole self: that much Lorn knew from his own old studies. It made him nervous. Names, some ways, *were* their owners. And this name was a dangerous one, too great for a man. Even for a hero in an old story, such a name would have raised its wearer to glory, and then doomed him.

Unfortunately, this was no old story, but a new one. Asleep beside him, snoring, lay the vessel of a magic that had been busily making the impossible old legends come true for several months, and showed no sign of stopping. Lorn let out a breath. His own names, his outer ones, were no safer or easier to live with. Lately he was feeling as if they followed him around and tugged at him for attention. 'Freelorn stareiln Ferrant stai-Héalhrästi', said the one: so that there stood both his blood-father and line-father, looking over his own name's shoulder, reminding him of royal descent and royal responsibilities – neither of which he had handled well for the last seven years. Or 'Freelorn of Arlen', the short form, even more annoying because he was not enough 'of Arlen' right now to set foot there without an army at his back. And worst of all, what Eftgan called him: 'Lionchild'. It was a courteous, affectionate nickname, recalling her Line's old kinship to his. Eftgan was very courteous. Lorn wished to the Goddess she would stop it.

And the name 'Freelorn' itself . . .

He propped himself up on one elbow, looking at Herewiss. Herewiss snored on. Freelorn took a breath and whispered that other Name that made him so uncomfortable. It was short, but it made a silence around it. The snoring stopped. Blue eyes looked at him, suddenly wide awake. Then they smiled. 'Lorn,' said Herewiss, muffled, half his face still under the covers.

'Morning.'

'Thank you for not saying "good".' Herewiss stretched, and pulled the coverlet over his head. 'Why do you always have to wake up so early? We had a battle all day yesterday, can't you sleep in just for once?'

Freelorn was rescued by a knock on the door. 'The Queen's compliments to you, gentlemen,' said a voice outside, sounding entirely too cheerful; one of the chamberlains, no doubt. 'Her Grace is fasting this morning, but breakfast is being served downstairs.'

'I want a bath,' Herewiss muttered from underneath the covers.

'Our regards to the Queen,' Freelorn shouted at the door, 'and we'll be down as soon as his highness here has had his first bath of the day. Come on, get up.' He started laboriously to pull the covers off Herewiss. 'I want one too. I refuse to be the only one who smells bad at this coronation.'

'My Goddess, I forgot.' Suddenly the covers were everywhere except around Herewiss, and he was fumbling for a robe. 'Where's Khávrinen??'

'Under your clothes, as usual . . . You do this oh-Heaven-where-is-it business every morning. Sometimes I think you should sleep with that sword.'

Herewiss looked sidewise at Freelorn with the expression that meant some terrible joke was being smothered, and then went back to searching. 'Under that tunic, the white one,' Lorn said.

Herewiss straightened up, clutching a nightrobe around him. The free hand held Khávrinen. Superficially the sword looked like just another hand-and-a-half broadsword, obviously amateur work though of good material – grey steel with an odd blue sheen. But in the hand of the man who had forged it in terror and blue Fire and his own blood, it blazed – the blade burning inwardly like iron at white heat in the forge, while blue Flame wrapped up and down the length of the sword from point to hilt, about the hand that gripped it and the arm that wielded it. Right now that Fire licked and wreathed leisurely as weed in water, mirroring Herewiss's calm state of mind. But Freelorn had seen it when Herewiss was angry, or exerting himself. Then lightning came to mind, young gods wielding thunderbolts against the powers of darkness, defeating them – or being defeated. Freelorn swallowed, thinking again of the impossible becoming possible. It had been a close business, yesterday. The Shadow, the darkness cast sideways from the Goddess's light, was surely annoyed with them all . . . and especially with this bit of flesh and blood that leaned Khávrinen safe against the wall, and yawned and rubbed his eyes.

'Come on,' Herewiss said. 'The Queen may have to fast, but we don't. Are you going to lie there all day?'

Freelorn got up, put a robe on and went out after his loved.

They went down the hall together and found even the palace living quarters unusually noisy. Children, the princes and princesses indistinguishable from the many other children of the household, were running in all directions, squealing, chasing pets, chasing one another; harried-looking chamberlains were chasing some of the children with clothes, or carrying bundles, messages, laundry. At the corner of their own hall, where it turned right, there were several children, all dressed in hose and buskins and tunics of dark-blue linen, clustered together and staring around the corner at something. Freelorn looked at Herewiss. Herewiss shrugged, sneaked up behind the children, and peered around the corner with them. Lorn followed suit.

Down at the end of the hall was this floor's bathroom, and no-one was waiting to use it . . . most likely because of the darkness lingering like a fog around the hallway's end, half-hiding the bathroom door in a tangle of shadows that smelled of hot stone or metal. Looking straight at the darkness, one saw nothing; but avert the eyes slightly, and in the shadows something moved and glittered smokily, massive and indistinct.

One of the children, perhaps six years old, pert-faced and blond, looked up at Herewiss and Freelorn with an expression half annoyance and half great interest. 'What's *that?*' he said.

Herewiss shook his head. 'Nothing . . . just magic.' He looked down, noting the shade of the child's hair, and the White Eagle stitched small above the heart of the

25

midnight-blue tunic. 'One of your royal mother's relatives. We'll get her out of there. Shouldn't you be having breakfast?'

'I have to go first.'

'*You* want to get in there and play with the plumbing,' Herewiss said. 'If you have to go, prince, then use the privy. The other way. Hurry up or you'll wind up standing behind all the tall people and not see any of the Hammering.'

The prince groaned loudly, and looked over at Freelorn in a bid for sympathy, but Lorn shook his head. Sighing, the princeling went off with his two friends.

'Some things never change,' Lorn said.

'Seems that way. Come on.'

They headed for the bathroom. From inside the door, as they approached it, came sounds of singing; a single strong contralto, nasal but true, and surrounding it, a chorus of approximately fifty voices from highest soprano to profoundest bass. Freelorn recognized the tune as a Darthene drinking song, but the words were in no language he knew. The smell of burning stone was strong around them as he knocked on the door and shouted, 'Are you decent?'

The singing stopped, and the contralto voice laughed. '*Eh'ae-he,*' it said, '*ssih esdhhoui'rae ohaiiw!*'

Freelorn sighed and pushed the door open. The bathrooms in Blackcastle were justly famous for their spring-fed plumbing, a masterwork of engineering, sorcery, and blue Fire. The water came up from the ground naturally hot, and not even sulphurous; pipes guided it where it was wanted and spilled it out into tubs huge enough for any king, or any eight of his friends. The walls were decorated with bas-reliefs depicting the Goddess creating the sea-creatures, the windows were cunningly baffled to prevent drafts even in winter, and the floors were impossible to slip on. It was a dream of a place. The tub closest to the northern windows had a carved screen pulled in front of it . . . not that this was really necessary, for there the shadows were thick as night, and among

26

them lay the very end of a massive tail scaled in what looked like black star-sapphires above and rough grey diamond below. The tail twitched like a thoughtful cat's, and fierce rainbow flickers slid up and down in the spear-length, double-curved diamond spine at its end.

'You're talking Dracon again,' said Lorn, as Herewiss came in behind him and shut the door. 'Say it in Darthene. And how can you wash in the dark like this?'

'I said, yes, I'm decent, but come in anyway. And it's not dark here,' said the contralto voice. 'Not to me, anyway.'

'Well, it is to us,' Herewiss said. 'Lighten it up, or we won't be able to see the dirt! Good morning, lhhw'Hasai. Lorn, which tub?'

'*Yl'thienh, rhhw'Hhirhwaehs; u rhhw'Fvhr'ielhrnn.*'

'Oh, right, 'morning, Hasai. That one, Dusty. Here's the bathflannels.'

Laughter filled the room, not all of it human. 'Dirt? On *you*? The six-baths-a-day man?'

'*Ssha*, 'Berend, or I'll turn you into something vile.'

'I'll do it myself and save you time. Can't be late for the Hammering.'

'What are you wearing?' Freelorn said.

Water splashed. 'A bath flannel.'

'No, to the Hammering, you dolt!'

'All you ever think about is clothes,' said Segnbora, with infinite, affectionate scorn. The shadows thinned and she came out from behind the screen, wrapped in a flannel big enough for a blanket, and dripping. There was almost more of the flannel than there was of her, Lorn thought. She was a slender thing, wiry, narrow as a swordblade and with about as much curve; delicately featured, with deep-set eyes in a face with a sharp look about it. Her hair was slicked down from the bath, and even the wet couldn't hide how it was coming in silver at the roots.

Lorn had to turn his head and smile as she sat down on a nearby bench, holding the flannel most carefully around her. On the trail Segnbora had been all business, never caring whether anyone saw her undressed, or whether she saw anyone else that way; there were more important things to worry about. But evidently old habits reasserted themselves when she came back to civilization. She reached under the bench for another flannel and began to dry her hair. 'The full kit,' she said. 'Formal surcoat, and Skádhwë. My presence there may confuse some people . . . and this morning, it may be wise to cause all the confusion we can.'

'And Hasai?' Herewiss reached for the soap-ball and knocked it into the bath. He began to fish for it.

'We shall be there if we're needed,' said the chief of the many voices that had been speaking out of the shadows. Eyes as wide as a man is tall looked at them from the remaining darkness, burning with cool silver fire. 'Now that we are becoming human, it would be pity to miss our first bout of your kind of *nn's'raihle*.'

'Give me that soap. He keeps using that word,' Freelorn said to Segnbora, 'and you keep giving me different meanings for it. A dance, a family argument, a word game – which is it this time?'

Segnbora shrugged and scrubbed at her hair with the flannel. 'It can be any of those for a Dragon,' she said. 'It's choice; but there's a whole family of ways they make choices, and to them the way we do it looks similar a lot of the time. Though the motivations are different. We're choosing a queen – or rather, she's allowing her people to exercise their option to get rid of her. We can dance with her, as it were, or else get rid of her and find another partner. But to we Lhhw'hei, the important thing is the dance itself. The changing of partners is incidental; the choice matters. Not what it is, just making it.'

Freelorn's gut turned over inside him. Last month Segnbora had been a new but trusted friend, a perfectly normal failed Rodmistress and sometime sorceress. Just another person. Now suddenly she had an extra shadow, and an invisible escort of what might be thousands, and odd overtones to her voice that had never been there before. *We Lhhw'hei* . . .

'Anyway, I'm worried.' Segnbora threw the small flannel away, shaking her hair out and running her fingers through it.

Herewiss, his hair full of lather, stopped scrubbing for a moment and looked at her. 'Foreseeing? Or just a bad feeling?'

'Foreseeing. And underhearing. Careful, that soap's going to get in your eyes. Someone out there is thinking *very* bad thoughts about the Queen. And even though I'm in breakthrough now, and I can hear people thinking from here to Arlen, I still can't hear details in this mind at all, or even identify the source.' She looked in bemusement at a straggle of her wet hair, and flicked it up with a finger. For a moment Segnbora had a curling halo of blue Fire. Then it went away, and her hair was dry. 'Do you hear anything?'

Herewiss frowned a moment, then shook his head. 'Not even the bad feelings. If it's on the fringes of even *your* ability to perceive at the moment, that argues some powerful shielding. A sorcerer of considerable ability . . .'

Segnbora looked disturbed, and Herewiss did too, as he ducked to rinse the soap out of his hair. 'I can't see why, though,' Segnbora said. 'Surely any sorcerer now knows that we're at open war with the Shadow . . . if not yet with anyone else. Working against the Queen and her forces in that war can only ensure *everything* going to pieces sooner or later. Famine everywhere, whole nations dying . . .'

'If that's the case,' Herewiss said, wiping his hair back and the water out of his face, 'whoever has chosen the Shadow's side has to have been offered something that makes the chance of starving to death with the rest of the country, or being hanged and drawn and nailed up as a traitor, and possibly even rejected by the Goddess after death, look worth taking. That scares me.' He reached for a sponge. 'What was the foreseeing?'

'I saw light down in the Square. A flicker of it, very fast. Two flickers. A still one, golden light; and then a quick one, more silver, I think. Lots of people standing around,

29

but none of them reacting to anything in particular. They might not have seen anything, if it was an arrow or a crossbow bolt . . . or perhaps it was symbolic. You know how foretellings are, sometimes the message is abstract even though the image seems concrete.'

'And the gold was Dekórsir? The Queen's Gold?'

'Truly I couldn't tell. Though—' Segnbora looked up over her shoulder. *'Mdaha?'*

'Your foreseeing is not like our remembering-ahead,' said the Dragon, in a slow uncertain basso scrape of song . . . one voice alone, not the usual chord. 'We see the you-who-are-part-of-us . . . not the others associated with you. At least, not usually. We—' He paused, that single voice slipping into silence for a moment. *'I* see you in the sun, with your talon drawn. You stand quiet. Suddenly there is a movement from behind you, someone pushes you aside—' Another pause. 'Nothing more,' Hasai said.

'So someone's going to attempt Eftgan's life this morning,' Freelorn said. 'At least we have warning. But what can we do?'

Herewiss finished scrubbing, dunked again. 'Keep it from happening . . .'

Freelorn looked at him. 'Oh? You can't do anything, you're Darthene nobility . . . and you count as a guard, under that ruling, when was it? Sometime in the 1400s. You're one too, by that rule,' he said, looking at Segnbora. 'If either of you move to help her, she has to give up the throne by default.' He paused. 'That leaves me . . .'

'And how if this whole business is a blind to get you out in the open so that someone can send *you* to the Shadow?' said Segnbora. 'Lorn, there are some methods of killing too quick for even the Fire to prevent. You were fortunate, yesterday . . . or rather, the Goddess seems to want you alive for something. I wouldn't do Her the discourtesy of throwing Her gifts away.' Segnbora stood up. 'Besides, there are a few others of us . . . eh *mdaha?'*

Those silver eyes looked grave. *'Sdaha,* we are

Dracon . . . we cannot become involved in the business of humans.'

'Oh really? The way you refused to become involved at Bluepeak last night? You melted a hole half the size of Darthis into the valley, getting those Reavers off our backs.'

'We were protecting our *sdaha*. No such situation obtains here. Besides, by virtue of the *sdahaih* relationship we *are* you . . . so we would not be allowed to intervene on Eftgan's behalf anyway, if you are honouring the intent of this law as well as its letter.'

'Dammit,' Segnbora said, knotting her flannel around her, 'we are. And a lot of good it'll do us, Dracon or human, if we wind up with a dead queen.'

Herewiss got up out of the bath, dripping and scowling, while Freelorn scrubbed meditatively. 'What time is it?'

'Half eleven,' Segnbora said. 'The Forging's at noon.' She headed for the door. With her, around her, a rumbling uneasy darkness moved, half hiding her.

'See you downstairs,' Segnbora said. The door thumped shut.

Freelorn watched Herewiss towel himself off, still scowling.

'*Can* we stop it?'

'We'll find out,' Herewiss said.

The Great Square in Darthis might have been great when the town was young. These days, as the centre of ceremony for a city of ten thousand souls, it was inadequate . . . especially when three quarters of them tried to squeeze into it at once, as they had today. It was hot, too, on such a summer day, the morning after Midsummer. The only shade was under the huge old blackstave tree in the centre of the Square. But no-one stood there, even though there seemed no-one to keep them away from it. Cool in the shade, in a level spot among the great humped roots and cracked paving blocks, nothing stood but a small flat anvil and a stool. No-one

31

went near the spot. Sweet-sellers and roast meat-sellers and ice-sellers and people with chilled wine and new whey and barley-water and buttermilk went about hawking these to the sweating crowd, and there were plenty of buyers; but no food or drink kept anyone's attention for long. All eyes returned at last to the anvil, and the stool, and the tree.

It was, of course, not just any blackstave tree, but *the* Blackstave, the Heart-Tree of Darthen, own brother-tree to Berlémetir Silverstock which stood in the Kings' Grove near Prydon, and from which the White Stave of Arlen had been made. Queens and kings had been crowned under the Blackstave – both Arlene and Darthene, in the older days when no kingship was complete that had not been solemnized in both countries. Kings had occasionally also been hung from it – once, in the Fell Reign fifteen hundred years ago, and then again three hundred years later: at which time the new King of Darthen, Bron, had made a vow that no such thing should ever happen again. 'If a king is a bad one,' said Bron, 'then his people should have a chance to do something about it before any more blood is shed than his own.'

So Bron went out in the summer morning and sat down under the Blackstave, unarmed, without any guard, and proceeded to hammer out his own crown out of soft gold; and his people watched him in astonishment, having heard the proclamation that the King had caused to be published. From now on, once a year – the date became Midsummer later on, adding more excuse for celebration to the holiday – every queen or king of Darthen must forge their crown anew in public. They might bring no guard with them, nor might any subject make to protect them save with his or her own body. And anyone who had a grievance against the king or queen might make it good on the ruler's body, right then. The ruler might protect himself, but only with his own body. No revenge might be taken on any attacker, directly or indirectly. If a king died, his successor took up the forging . . . and hoped to survive it. If a queen lived, then she was queen for another year, and no assassin or plotter might expect to survive any attempt on her royalty; they had had their chance. A ruler who broke the rules forfeited the throne. One who tried to forego the Forging was exiled.

No-one killed Bron, but then he early showed signs of being a good king, and his children kept to the tradition he had started. Since that time, three kings and two queens had been killed by angry subjects, and some nine or ten had been roughed up and given a good talking to. All the others had beaten out their crowns, and gone inside Blackcastle afterwards, and heaved long sighs of relief. One never knew, on that warm morning, what past sin, or real or imagined slight to a person or political faction, might walk out of the crowd with a drawn bow.

Freelorn, looking out of his room's window at that crowd, felt an itching between his shoulders at the thought. There had been some talk in Arlen, a few hundred years back, that the same custom should be adopted there. It had never happened, and he was relieved. He had enough trouble working his courage up to the point where his knees no longer knocked before a straightforward battle, where there were clearly marked enemies and some specific issue to fight over.

He tightened his belt around his surcoat, looking down into the mass of sweaty, noisy people, crying children, hawkers, silent shapes on horseback, and the glint of weapons in the crowd – a spear or two, a few slung bows, a few swords, many knives. All casually worn, to be sure. Many people wore such on their daily business, even in town, for pride and looks and fondness of the weapons themselves as much as for protection. But those people on horseback . . . He recognized clearly several faces of lords prominent among the Forty Houses, the Darthene lower cabinet. Hiliard, in the tenné velvet: how could anyone wear velvet on a day like this? And over there, a blue surcoat semée of white martlets; Nerris of Devenish, from Arrhen-Devenish up in the north. She had reason enough to be annoyed with the Queen, what with the public reprimand about the taxes. And several other people, escorted or just quietly standing in the crowd, all of that party in the Houses that had been most critical of the Queen lately for her actions. *What should she be doing, for pity's sake?* Lorn thought, hitching his belt up and fastening the loops to it from Súthan's sheath. *Sitting still while Cillmod raids her granaries and her western borders? They're so afraid of war they'll do anything to avoid it, even unbuckle their belts for that damn usurper . . .*

Lorn turned to hunt through the mess of clothes at the end of the bed, and after a moment came up with the knife tossed in among them. He had been holding it for the day until Eftgan should ask for it back; it was the One Knife from the Regalia of the Two Lands, the razory black-bladed knife with which Eftgan's blood and his had been shed yesterday. He paused to do something that he doubted had been done to most sacred implements: balanced it across one finger to check how far forward the knife's balance-point was. *Not too bad. Two full turns, probably, depending on the range. . . . Up the sleeve, I think.* He hunted about one of his jerkins for the broken leather thong that was in its pocket, and used the thong to snug the knife in place well above his elbow and out of sight. *Good . . .*

He took a moment for the mirror, a plate of polished steel fastened to the wall. Freelorn made a wry face, looking at his clothes. This Lion surcoat had got him in trouble every time he'd worn it recently. But Eftgan was going out on a limb for his sake; he had to do the same for her. He brushed a last bit of lint out of the folds. Black surcoat, white Lion passant regardant, standing and looking at you stern and patient, with the silver Sword held up in the dexter paw. *Lionchild*, he thought, uneasy as always . . . then smiled a bit, grimly, determined to like it for once. This surcoat was getting tight: or maybe he was putting on some size across the shoulders. Unusual. *Wonder if there's enough seam to let it out a bit . . .* And

Súthan shifted softly in the scabbard as he moved. He glanced down at it with a habitual mixture of great love and great annoyance. *We've been a long way, we two. But why, why aren't you Hergótha?! I'd trade you for Hergótha like a dented pot if I had half a chance.*

From outside the window came a peculiar whirring sound, the reflected noise of the clockwork in the northern tower of Blackcastle as it ground into position to strike noon. Freelorn slipped out of the door and pounded down the stairs to the tunnels that led into the courtyard.

In the doorway full of hot light he paused, just behind the guards, peering out to see if he could see anyone he knew, Herewiss or Segnbora or any of his own people. None of them were in sight. As he stood there, eyes in the throng crowded up by the doorway glanced at him, noticed the device on his surcoat, and lips began to move. *King it out*, Lorn thought to himself, and stepped out into the crowd as if his stomach weren't wringing itself like hands. People made way for him, a touch uncertainly, and glances fastened themselves to him and prickled under his skin.

Above him, noon struck, the slow deep notes falling heavy in the close courtyard. Lorn kept walking, looking for a good spot to stand. The Midsummer sun bore down on the shoulders of the black surcoat like a hot weight, and Lorn began to regret his undertunic. But without it he would itch, and the silver embroidery would rub him raw; and he could hear his father telling him, when he was twelve, 'Kings don't itch, and they don't squirm. It's not dignified. But they're allowed to sweat; no-one minds that.' *We'll find out today*, Lorn thought, making for the tree.

And a stray arrow? Idiot.

He stopped right at the front of the crowd, ten feet or so from the anvil, and stood quietly with his arms folded, feeling the eyes bite into his back. It was peculiar. He'd been stared at often enough before; but today it was really bothering him. If only there were someone else he knew in this crowd—

Abruptly he saw one: right across from him, on the other side of the tree, the Queen's husband, Wyn. Wyn was not a tall man, but didn't need to be. He was one of those people who seem to be about twice anyone else's height even when kneeling, with the face of a handsome hawk. Wyn was a wine merchant, and had a reputation for being a calm man – which made it interesting to consider the five-foot-long, unsheathed, two-handed broadsword he was leaning on, as casually as if it was a pruning hook. He met Lorn's eyes with a slight twitch of a grin.

Freelorn returned the half smile, but didn't move otherwise. He casually looked over the people standing behind and around Wyn, wondering why their glances were bothering him so today, trying to conceal it. Just a crowd of city people, dressed for holiday: broad ladies in bright dresses, men in breeches and embroidered shirts, here and there a surcoat of some son or daughter of hedge-nobility; the flash of silver, the glitter of eyes; whispers, murmurs, chatter, the happy shouting of a little girl near the front waving a toasted sausage and getting its grease all over herself and her smock and the skirt of the lady next to her, who turned and—

You go first.

No, you.

He refused to turn around. 'Kings don't turn to overhear things,' his father had told him in that same severe session so long ago, which had ended with Freelorn arguing the point and having his bottom warmed. 'Kings wait till the speaker comes round to face them in courtesy.' But it was hard not to turn, especially when the voices seemed so close behind him that they were nearly in his own head. And truly only the slightest difference in tone kept them from seeming as if they were in his own voice: one of them quicker, lighter than his own tone, with faint, odd harmonies weaving around it; the other with the touch of drawl that he almost knew better than his own voice anyway. *That* voice he had heard before, this way. But never before in broad daylight, in a crowd like this. Only

36

in the dark, in the silence, and only a few times lately – in moments when outer voices failed, and words ran out, and his heart heard the other's overflowing heart whispering *My loved, my own, o my loved* . . . until the urgency of their bodies built to strike the sweetness through with lightning, and leave them both gasping and blind. This was not that slow, deep warmth, but something brisker, more businesslike . . . though in its own way just as personal, just as fierce—

Freelorn swallowed. *Underhearing.* It was the commonest of the othersenses . . . and something he had never had a problem with until recently, until Herewiss's Fire burst free. Lorn gripped Súthan's hilt and began to understand the piercing of eyes, the threatening pressure of minds he wasn't sensitive enough to hear. But all his reading on the subject had never hinted that the sensitivity might be catching— *Well, never mind it now! They're about to do something. Be ready for it.*

I'm not ready, I can't feel who—

—Neither can I. No use waiting. Go!

Is she ready?

Yes. A third voice, drier. *Let's play out our hand.*

All this in a second's flicker. And because Freelorn had not turned around, he saw the darkness draw itself together on the far side of the courtyard, by the postern door; saw day slide back defeated from a growing patch of night, in which darker shapes moved, and voices chanted slow warning in a choir of muted thunders, while many eyes gazed out, glowing like those coals of which gems were said in lore to be the burnt-out cinders. People backed away hurriedly from that darkness, all but the smallest children, who stared at it in calm fascination and had to be pulled back.

Out of that dark came walking a slight slim form in black, wearing a long formal surcoat, tenné-brown, the arms on it the undiffered arms of a Head of one of the Forty Houses: lioncelle passant regardant in blood and gold, holding a sword. Unsheathed in her hand the woman

37

held a three-foot splinter of pure night, black enough to have been broken off death's own Door. And so it had been, for this was Skádhwë out of legend, the sword Shadow, won and lost in the ancient days by Efmaer, Queen of Darthen, and newly recovered from Glasscastle beyond the world's bourne. For a thousand years and more that sword had not seen the light of day. Now the Midsummer sun fell in vain on its blackness, and around the length of it blue Fire wreathed, curling upwards in quick fierce flames the colour of deep twilight at their hearts.

Segnbora pushed her silvering hair back out of her face, where a breeze had blown it, and paused just out of the Blackstave's shade. One hand in her pocket, she leaned casually on the Shadowblade . . . and then looked down in understated surprise as the needle point of the shadow calmly slipped downwards into the cobble it rested on, as if she had chosen to lean on a cheese.

Segnbora pulled the sword out of the stone and stood straight with it, looking around the crowd in cool assessment. So did the larger pair of eyes in the darkness about and above her, silver with a cast of blue.

I think we have their attention, Segnbora said, and her amused bespeaking seemed to Freelorn so loud in the silence that the whole crowd should have heard it.

No agreeing answer came – just another movement over by another of the gates, the south gate that led out into the marketplace. There was less motion in the crowd this time, but more sound; a gasp that turned into a whisper that became a murmur, and then a cry that many voices took up, unbelieving, astonished: 'Fire!' And so it was: for here, sauntering casually, nodding and smiling at people, came a tall broad-shouldered man all in white – the white of the Brightwood surcoat, with its Phoenix in flames, and the white Cloak of the Wood's ancient livery, now only given to lords of the Brightwood line, or the Queen's own knights. The man had a hand-and-a-half broadsword resting on his shoulder, and the Flame of Power wound and wreathed about it and streamed away behind, harsh, hot-coloured and clear, the pure fierce blue of a Midsummer noon or a Steldene cat's eyes. 'Fire,' they shouted after him, unbelieving, astonished, delighted, 'Fire!' Millennia, it had been, since anyone but women had wielded the Fire. And the last two men to wield it, more than two thousand years ago, had had to become gods to do so, and died of it. If the Goddess Herself had walkcd in from the market square, it would probably have caused less amazement. After all, *everyone* saw *Her* at least once before they died. But *this* . . . !

Lorn watched the crowd push back and forth and reel and shout at the miracle that walked through them. Herewiss slipped free of the crowd, about halfway between Freelorn and Segnbora, and slid Khávrinen off his shoulder and set it point down on the cobbles before him, folding his hands about the hilt. His glance flicked left to Segnbora; she tilted her head at him, the slightest nod.

Herewiss turned to Freelorn, gazed at him, binding them all together into a united front, a gesture to whomever or Whatever watched. Freelorn returned the look.

Dusty, I've been meaning to ask you— But he was jolted out of concentration as the trumpets on the walls sounded a sennet. The Queen came out.

She came in a plain shirt and breeches of bleached linen, and wearing boots, like any other countrywoman with a morning's yardwork to do in hot weather. The shouting in the crowd quieted at the sight of her. Eftgan d'Arienn, like her husband, was short, though no-one under any circumstances could have called her small: an oval-faced woman, with a sweet expression and short-cropped blonde hair. Her close-set blue eyes and sharp nose sometimes made her look to Freelorn rather like a small, inquisitive bird, a chirper like the wren. But her voice always broke the illusion. It was the pure North Darthene drawl, like Herewiss's, reflective and cool, and the mind behind the

39

blue eyes was hard and deep and missed little. That was no surprise, since she was a Rodmistress as well as a Queen, trained in the Silent Precincts. Indeed, she had been marked down to succeed one of the Wardresses, till the death of the heir, her brother, had brought her out of the Silent Places to Blackcastle. But Eftgan's Power would do her little good here and now. She was without her Rod, the focus of her Power, and forbidden to use the Fire for her defence in any case. Eftgan carried nothing but a leather bag, which she dropped by the anvil with a clank and looked around her.

Here and there in the crowd a hat or bonnet came off; many bowed, those on high horse as well as those standing. Eftgan bowed her head briefly to them. 'Lords and friends,' she said, the old words, 'today I must know your will with me. Before the Goddess, I tell you I've done my best for you this year past. Here while I make my crown, you shall make plain to me whether my best has been yours as well. Our Lady defend my right, and yours; and see Her right done, for the land's good and in the Shadow's despite.'

'Be it so,' the crowd murmured; and the Queen nodded again, less formally, and turned around to sit down at the anvil, on the stool. She rummaged in the toolbag and came up with several small hammers, and a punch and hand riveter. Then from the other bag she produced the gold, a small fat ingot that she turned in her hands for a moment and gazed at, watching the way the sunlight fell through the moving leaves and caught on it, glancing bright.

The crowd fell quite silent. Eftgan picked up one of the larger hammers and began working on the ingot. The crown didn't have to be ornate – just recognizably circular, something that would go on the forger's head. Some kings had practised in secret and had then astonished everyone with how little time they spent turning a block of gold into a band. But Eftgan looked unconcerned with speed. She sat there, a little hunched over, pounding the ingot flat, the ringing of the hammer muted as it hit the gold, brighter when it missed or bounced and hit the anvil. She didn't look up at the people around her; not a glance for her husband, for her children peering between the people in the front rows, for Herewiss or Segnbora, and certainly no glance for Freelorn, right behind her.

He slowly began to gnaw on the inside of his cheek, an old nervous habit. Here they all were, in force, but what could they really do? Herewiss and Segnbora and Hasai were effectively helpless. Oh, perhaps anyone who moved against the Queen would have their mind wrung dry for information at a later date – but a lot of good that would do Eftgan if she fell. The heir to Darthen was presently twelve years old, busily eating an apple some feet away from Herewiss, and staring at Khávrinen . . . and it seemed unlikely that Wyn, his father, would be made regent if something untoward should happen. The Forty Houses were nervous about Arlen's recent aggression, and would welcome an excuse to back away from the 'dangerous' course of confrontation that Eftgan had been steering. Some other regent would be chosen, someone more cautious, and in that caution Darthen and Arlen would founder together—

—and the shriek and motion across the courtyard brought his head up with a jerk, blood jumped in him, he flushed—

—and felt stupid, because it was the broad lady in the bright skirt, bending down to do something about her daughter, who had had the sausage stolen out of her hand by a small brown furry dog that had wriggled out from behind them. The young girl was crying and trying to hit the dog, and the people around them were beginning to chuckle as their shock passed. Eftgan glanced up sidewise from her work, grinned, looked down again.

—and too suddenly for shock Lorn found himself looking at that woman as well as at Eftgan – looking at the woman with two other sets of eyes, seeing her as it were from two different angles. And he saw, as those other eyes did, how the gesture that had begun as a straightening of

41

the woman's skirts, now ended with one of her hands bringing up from under the volume of them a small cocked crossbow—

From behind he felt someone push him aside, but it was not him, it was Segnbora feeling it. She wheeled, but he didn't have time for her vision. The crossbow was up and aiming. At the same time, as if someone else was doing it, Súthan was out of the sheath, and Lorn took the sword two-handed. The crossbow quarrel flashed brassy gold with noonfire as it flew at the Queen. Súthan met it. Something sharp stung Lorn in the cheek; he flinched, eyes tearing with the pain.

Shouting broke out in the crowd. Across from him, Segnbora was standing quite still and glancing from the startled young man who had just bolted from behind her, trying to see better, to the woman with the crossbow, as the people in the crowd around her grabbed the bow from the woman's hands and seized her. The little girl was crying louder than ever, not understanding the sudden anger.

Light glanced off something silver, and again Lorn saw it with an extra pair of eyes as the knife flew. It flew wide, though, and clattered on the cobbles under the tree, and the well-dressed man who had thrown it from behind Herewiss turned and tried to shoulder his way through the crowd. Lorn was in no mood for it, and in even less of one when he glanced down at the odd feel of Súthan in his hand and found the sword missing the pointward third of its blade. He dropped it, pulled the One Knife from under his sleeve, and was about to take it by the blade and throw it when someone tapped him on the shoulder. 'Never turn toward the shoulder you're tapped on,' his father had said long ago: 'always turn the other way instead.' And Lorn did, and so was able to put the One Knife quite accurately into the upper right lung of the pretty young woman who had been about to stab him in the kidney.

She doubled over and went to her knees, and the people behind and around her, who had seen what she'd tried to do, looked at Freelorn in shock and made no particular attempt to catch her. He felt inclined to agree with them. Lorn turned around for a second, amid the angry shouting, to look at Eftgan. She glanced up, hammering away, and glanced down again – not looking particularly surprised, as if she had seen what had been happening with the same multiple vision Freelorn had briefly experienced.

And then there was a growl, and the furry brown dog stopped being a dog, and Eftgan looked up again, very surprised indeed.

Screaming began among the people closest. Shape-change could be decorous, or ugly, depending on the original mass of the sorcerer, the size of the shape one intended to take, and the amount of power and time one expended on controlling the change itself. This sorcerer was in a hurry. The dog literally exploded out of itself like a firework, skin and blood mingling horribly, and grew huge in a screaming, stretching tangle of sinew and naked muscle. A breath later, a tatty-pelted thing half like an ape, half like a wolf, and the size of a carthorse, was springing at Eftgan. She leapt up, horror plain on her face, and nothing but the hammer in her hand. She threw it full and hard in the monster's face.

It staggered back, shook the blood from its dented brow out of its eyes, screeched horribly, and jumped at the Queen again, slavering, its claws unsheathed and ready.

The sun fell into the courtyard. Terrified, the crowd pushed frantically back from the skin-scorching heat, from the wild swirl of fire knotting about the twisting, horribly howling shape halfway under the tree. The Blackstave's lowest branches charred, their leaves writhing into flame. The thrown hammer, fallen to the cobbles, puddled into slag and ran like rainwater between the stones. Then the fire went out.

Where the shapechanger had been, a flat pile of ash was starting to blow about on the red-glowing rocks. More ash, in tiny flakes, drifted up out of the courtyard on the hot air that stank vilely of burnt bone and meat. Standing beside the pile of ash was a creature that looked like a horse, except that its mane and tail appeared to be made of flame, and its eyes glowed a hot amber, merry and wicked. It looked over at Herewiss.

He looked shocked, and chagrined. 'Sunspark—'

'Just because I don't take baths,' the fire elemental said, 'is no reason to leave me out of things.'

It turned to Eftgan, and smiled at her, as far as a horse can smile. 'You're welcome,' it said.

'Thank you,' she said; 'so are you.' And she sat back down at the anvil, and picked up another hammer, a smaller one, and went back to work on the gold.

Until she was finished, no-one moved, and no-one said anything, particularly not the woman with the crossbow nor the man with the knife, who were being held, not lovingly, by the spectators. The girl who had tried to stab Freelorn lay groaning on the stones, not bleeding much; Lorn had been careful, knowing Herewiss would want to talk to her. Now Lorn simply stood there and breathed hard, holding the recovered hilt-shard of Súthan in his hands. When he was finally called, a tall wide man standing next to him in the crowd had to nudge him to get his attention.

'Arlen?'

Eftgan was standing with the gold in her hands, hammered out and riveted, a rough-looking circlet perhaps an inch wide. Freelorn went to her. They exchanged a rueful glance as he sheathed his broken sword. Then she held Dekórsir out to him. 'If you would do me the honour, brother.'

He took the circlet from her. She looked out and around, at the crowd, who stirred and murmured. 'The gold is forged,' she said, 'and by this token I am your Queen indeed, and I will be your good lady and defend you from those who would do you harm, as you today have defended me.'

The silence grew around them again. Freelorn lifted up

the circlet, and carefully set it on Eftgan's head . . . then tried to straighten it, and found this hopeless. It was quite crooked, and a poor fit.

'You'll never make a jeweller,' he whispered to her. 'Stick to queening.'

She smiled at him like sunrise.

And more loudly, for the crowd to hear, he said: 'Take your crown, Eftgan datheln Arienn ie kyr'Bort tai-Éarnësti, and wear it well, and bear it well; for like the Goddess our Mother, you have wrought your own burden.'

The cheering started, and built. Freelorn looked around the crowd with satisfaction . . . until his glance lit again on the shapes on horseback, and the shapes that stood, the shapes that held their peace and watched the common people shout. It occurred to him that a crown might make a queen, but it would not make her secure.

'Of your courtesy,' the Queen said to the people closest in the crowd, 'give over those folk you're holding to our guards, and let them be held to wait our pleasure. That one may need the surgeon as well as the household's Rodmistress: have them called. Does anyone here know that woman with the child? Good. Sir, I'd be glad if you would go with the little one and see her lodged in Blackcastle and properly treated. I wouldn't have her frightened by this confusion, it's no fault of hers. Arlen,' the Queen said, to be heard, 'did that knife mark you at all?'

'A scratch only, Darthen,' Freelorn said. 'Yet I confess to you that I'm getting tired of being hunted like a hound, even in this your own town. I weary of having the battle carried to me by Arlen's usurpers. That was why I came out in the open at last, and came to you. If nothing's going to change—'

'No fear of that. Enough of skirmishes,' said the Queen, and reached up to adjust Dekórsir, which was sliding sideways on her bright hair. 'Let us have a war.'

45

2

There is little to choose between the pen and
the sword. Too often, both write in blood.

Gnomics, 1216

Early sunlight lay in a long warm parallelogram on the
polished basalt tabletop. The soft scratching noises of a
quill underwrote the airy silence of the room whenever the
several voices there fell quiet.

'And you found nothing at all?'

'Of course not. That poor woman has no memory of
anything from the time the dog took her daughter's
sausage to the time she found herself being held. It was the
sorcerer, the shapechanger, who was controlling her.
Probably he passed the crossbow to her in town, on the
way to the Hammering.'

'So this man was controlling not just her, but the other
two with the knives as well? Isn't that terribly difficult?'

'It's not difficult at all. It's just that the backlash from a
direct-control sorcery is horrible – a human mind isn't
meant to run more than one of itself. Also, the undis-
charged energy of the controlled mind snaps back at you
like a misdrawn bowstring when the spell finally breaks. If
the poor fool could have survived such a violent shapechange, he'd have the Shadow's own headache right now –
if the backlash hadn't actually killed him outright. I have
to wonder what kind of hold that creature's master had
over him.'

Eftgan took a long drink out of a cup of barley-water

and lemon. 'I am dry as last year's bones,' she said, putting it down. 'That's so good.' Lorn watched her push back from the great table, put her hands up behind her head and stretch. The room was one of the informal dining rooms attached to the royal suite, a high-ceilinged tower room. On the table a collation had been laid out for the Queen to break her fast. She had help; Freelorn's people Dritt and Moris and Harald were there, as were Wyn, and Torve s'Keruer, the Chastellain of Bluepeak. The Queen was sitting happily in front of the wreckage of half a cold roast of beef, picking at the remains of it as the mood took her. Herewiss was sitting at the far end of the table, writing busily, while Segnbora looked over his shoulder.

'I just wish we had him alive,' Eftgan said. 'No shame to you, Sunspark, you did what was necessary.' She glanced at the fireplace, which though it had no wood in it, still had a fire.

The fire looked back at her, ironic. 'I try.'

Lorn dunked a bit of roast beef in a bowl of horseradish sauce. 'It would have been nice to have proof from his mind that Cillmod sent him. Or more correctly, Rian. That would have been cause to declare war right there.'

'Oh, I have reason enough. And we know that sorcerer was a tool of Rian's, and Rian knows we know. No problem there. But the question now becomes, what the best courses of action are for us.' Eftgan took another drink. 'If we're going to have a war, we have to consider our own force in arms, and whether we have enough people to beat all the mercenaries Cillmod has on his pay-roll. There's also the problem of the loyalties of the Four Hundred . . . but with the crops as bad as they are now, those are wavering. And finally,' Eftgan said, beginning to play with a pen-knife that lay near her, 'there's the question of Cillmod's master-sorcerer. Rian is definitely not just a man acting from political expediency. He's a disguise of the Shadow's, or rather, he's become one.'

'If that's a question at all,' said Moris from down the table, 'it should be answered with a horse, a rope and a tree-branch. No-one becomes a tool of *that* one without agreeing to it.'

'Bloodthirsty creature.' Eftgan looked at him affectionately. 'Mori, the agreement to evil isn't always so clear-cut and conscious as the old stories would have us think. But that's not our problem right now. What we have to do somehow is tempt the Shadow in him out of cover – and then strike It down. My job, most likely . . .'

There were uneasy looks around the table. One might speak lightly of disposing of the Shadow – especially if one came of Eftgan's line – but the execution was likely to be more difficult. Even Segnbora, related to that line and using a life's worth of repressed Fire, had managed only a temporary solution at Bluepeak.

There was a faint click as a quill was tossed to the tabletop. 'Well,' Herewiss said, from the table's end, 'let's see how this sounds.'

Parchment rustled. '"Eftgan datheln Arienn ie kyr'Bort tai-Earnésti, by the Goddess's good gift, by descent from the Eagle, by gift of her people, and by the might of her hand Queen of Darthen, Princess of the Harichel Isles, Lady paramount of the Brightwood, and Maintenant of the Old Kings' Road: to Cillmod stareiln Kavannel, styling himself sharing-son to Ferrant stareiln Fréol stai-Héalhrästi, and sitting in the throne and place of the Rulers of Arlen: greeting and defiance—"'

Freelorn sat up straight in his chair. 'Wait a moment! "Styling"? I thought we had proof that he was one of my father's children. No-one not of the Lion's blood can go into Lionhall and come out alive . . . and he did that.'

Eftgan smiled narrowly. 'So he did, but Lorn, that's not proof! Or, mean-minded creature that I am, I can refuse to accept it as such. If I don't explicitly contest Cillmod's use of that style and dignity – with which he's been making free – he could use the omission to argue that I should be supporting *him*, on the grounds of prior and present possession of the throne. It is Our official position that *you* are the only Lion's Child available.'

'Suits me. Go on, Dusty.'

'"—sitting in the throne and place of the Rulers of Arlen: greeting and defiance.

'"Having seen by many sure signs that your lordship means no good either to Darthen your neighbour, nor to Arlen over which you now hold sway; as by the looting and burning of Our granaries near Egen, and by the many returns of Our messengers from your domains with neither yea nor nay to Our frequent suings for calm on Our borders; and as by the most recent and lamentable bloodshed in the fields of Bluepeak, where We did adventure Our royal person for the maintenance of the Great Bindings whereto should be your chief concern, and for Our pains were set upon by mercenaries in your hire, and in the same treachery and ambush were rudely advertised of your dangerous alliance with the Reaver folk from over mountain; and chiefly moved by the late cowardly and treacherly attempt on Our life, made by your tool and instrument, which attempt was by the Goddess's good humour brought to nothing; We are minded to make an end once for all of these troublings of both your folk and Ours, which have since the time of Lion and Eagle been bound as one land and lordship in heart, though two in name.

'"Wherefore, setting aside with trembling that Oath which Éarn Silverwing Our forefather swore with Héalhra Whitemane the father and protector of Arlen, I Eftgan, Queen of Darthen, do declare and proclaim the land and lordship of Darthen to be at irreconcilable war with yours; till that you be cast down from that lordship, and the throne and Stave of Arlen restored to their rightful master, that is to say Our well-beloved brother Freelorn stareiln Ferrant stai-Héalhrästi, called Lionchild, now honoured guest in Our domain and raising force for your present undoing."'

'Good,' Segnbora said under her breath, looking grimly satisfied. 'That'll give him something to think about.' For a moment, great fierce silver eyes burned behind and high above her in agreeing grimness.

'*Ssha*, 'Berend.'

'"And he and We do most heartily provoke and defy you to meet Us in clean battle outside the city of Prydon where you now hold sway, on the First of Autumn of this year, with as many of your coin-bought defenders as you shall see fit; where we shall make to prove on you and them that you are a foul usurper, a traitor to Arlen's people, to the Lion Whose rightful rule you feign to wield, and to the Goddess in Whose Name and stead a ruler must steer Her land. Even now, that this outpouring of blood might be prevented – and indeed, commanded by the Goddess to offer Her mercy even to those whom mere fallible mortality would judge undeserving of it – We offer you this alternative: to release the mercenaries in your pay and retire the Arlene regulars to their used postings, and to set your borders at peace; to deliver up to Our pleasure, in a tenday's time, one Rian stareiln Heisarth; and for your own part, to be over mountain, over Arlid or over sea within the same tenday's time, never to return to Arlen while breath is in you."'

'Not likely.'

'Dritt . . .'

'"But should you refuse this alternative, then Fórlennh and Hergótha Our swords are turned irrevocably against you, and red war is yours until you die. Consider well your choice; and the Goddess guide it for Arlen's sake, and yours. An end to Our words. For to ensure that these letters fall not into the hands of those who mean Our lands no good, we have entrusted them to the hand of Our loyal friend and subject lord Herewiss stareiln Hearn stai-Eálorsti kyn'Éarnësti, Prince-elect of the Brightwood and a lord-member of the Comraderie of the WhiteCloak. These letters given under My hand in Sai Urdárien, that is Blackcastle, in My city of Darthis, this first day of Summer in the second year of My reign, being the two thousand nine hundred twenty-seventh year after the coming of the Dragons. Eftgan as't'Raïd Darthéni."'

'Dear Goddess,' Eftgan said. She leaned back in her tall

carved chair and stared at Herewiss – a wry look. 'Hark to you! What makes you think I can spare you for a vacation in Arlen?'

'Who else could you send,' Herewiss said, 'that you could count on to get there, and stay there, without being murdered?'

'Me,' Segnbora said, from down the table.

'Be still a moment,' Freelorn said. 'I didn't forget you. Eftgan, it's perfect.'

'*You* put him up to this, did you? Later for you, Lion's whelp. And what makes either of you think I want to go to battle so soon? I was thinking of next spring—'

Freelorn reached out to the parchment and glanced down over it at the slightly tilted vertical lines of Herewiss's fat neat cursive. 'Queen, why throw away a perfectly good famine? Springtime – when people will have barely survived a long bad winter – isn't as good a time to get them to fight as the autumn, when the winter's before them and looking horrible. Besides, this business needs to be settled before the spring planting. Maybe you have better news of Darthen, but from what I've seen of Arlen in the past year, it can't bear another year of drought. We need this winter's snow.' He began curling and uncurling a corner of the parchment. 'Otherwise you know what's coming as well as I do, if you think of it. In a year, maybe two, rule in Arlen collapses, and the refugees spill over into Darthen, in desperation, to keep from starving. The Reavers come over the invasion routes that haven't yet been closed, and can no longer be held, and over a few seasons wipe out the few who've managed to survive that long. In the end . . . nothing. Waste land; the Shadow will kill off even the Reavers when they've served Its purpose and exterminated us.' He smiled, an unhappy look. 'And then who's left to help the Goddess run the world?'

Eftgan chewed her lip. 'Autumn it is, then. But my forces are scattered right now, and diminished in numbers after Bluepeak.'

Freelorn shrugged. 'I don't see how we dare wait much longer than the first. If we have to campaign much south of Prydon, the weather starts becoming treacherous around then.'

'True . . .' The Queen leaned back and put her boots up on the table. 'I still hate to be raising forces around this time of year. The wheat needs my attention: it's no time for the Queen to be playing with armies . . .' She sighed. 'But you're right, it can't be helped. And it must be settled quickly. I haven't the resources to make this war twice. Herewiss, the last I heard, the Brightwood could field about three thousand people on short notice.'

'Closer to thirty-five hundred now, Queen. But do I take it correctly that you agree to my embassy to Prydon?'

'Oh, well, since Lorn seems to have this all planned out . . .'

'That part was my idea,' Herewiss said. 'Someone has to see what the terrain looks like . . .'

Eftgan looked at him cockeyed. 'And so you earn your name.' Freelorn saw Herewiss go slightly pale. Earning one's name was not always a safe business. And 'herewiss' in the Darthene meant 'battle-wise', and was used of tacticians or generals. 'All right,' Eftgan said. 'I can use, shall we say, a military attaché in Prydon. But Lorn, I want to know that you understand what you're doing. First, Herewiss is not exactly inconspicuous. A man with the Fire—'

'Yes, a man with the Fire. Good. Let them see what they're up against. Let them test him.'

The Queen sat back, looking thoughtful. 'Lorn, there's also the minor business of your relationship with him. They know that you two are lovers. They would know that he would be spying out the place for you, even if we hadn't sent them defiance. And if they can find any way to do him harm . . . they will.'

'I know,' Freelorn said.

After a moment the Queen looked down. 'Very well. Continue.'

52

'Don't think me cruel,' Lorn said. 'You agreed with me that it was time we stopped letting the battle be carried to us. What we have to do is walk right into the Shadow's den and pull It by the beard – then stand up against the worst It sends, and afterwards, crush It. Rian in particular is an unknown quantity. We need to know what he can do, *now*. And the best way to find out is to wave Herewiss in his face.'

'He can't refrain from me,' Herewiss said. 'Power tests Power, always. And in this game as in any other, some advantage rests with the side that moves first. So . . . I go draw Rian out.' Khávrinen in its sheath was leaned up against his chair; the Fire about its hilt burned briefly higher, as if fuel had been thrown on it.

'And not just Rian,' Freelorn said. 'Some ways, Herewiss is our banner – a symbol to the Shadow of all Its plans that the Goddess is destroying. It will definitely respond to his presence in Prydon.'

'It'd respond to mine, too,' Segnbora said from down the table. 'Look, you two, you don't dare waste me! I'm in breakthrough right now, and my Power's running high, but it won't be so for ever. A month, maybe – then I'm no more to you than any other Rodmistress.'

'Oh, somewhat more . . .' said a voice that spoke without sound; and that end of the room did not so much grow dark, as seem to have been that way for a long time. The air there smelled of burning stone, and there were eyes in the dark again. 'Yet I would not care to be wasted, either; my *sdaha* and I may be of some small use to you.'

Eftgan smiled. '*Lhhw*'Hasai, I had thought to ask you two—' Hasai laughed in the Dracon fashion, a sound like a small lake boiling over. 'However many of you there are, then – I had thought to ask you what you felt you could do best in this campaign.'

'We'll go ask the Dragons for help,' Segnbora said.

Those silver-burning eyes looked at her calmly, but there were misgivings in them. '*Sdaha*, we are guests in this world: refugees, here only by the mercy of the

53

Immanence. Your kind was here first. We have long been careful to keep our intrusion in your lands and lives to the barest minimum. We do not become involved with humans.'

'Oh really?' Dritt said, dryly. There was some muffled laughter up and down the table as Segnbora and her mindmate looked at each other.

'I told you, *mdaha*. You're going to get that response everywhere we go. And about time.'

'So you think, indeed. But will *lhhw'Hreiha*, the DragonChief, think so? What involves one Dragon involves us all.'

'Then it's already too late,' Segnbora said. 'We're going to have to confront the *Hreiha* as soon as we can and get her approval.'

'Neither will her approval be as easy to come by as a king's,' Hasai said. 'She speaks for our whole kind: in her person she lives all our lives, all our "deaths". Her decisions affect not only what we will be but what we have been – the *sdahaih* and *mdahaih* alike, what you call the "living" and the "dead". She may feel she needs time to make the decision. The last decision so major took a hundred circlings of the sun or more. Then there were many bouts of *nn's'raihle* to confirm it, and the Master-Choice at the end of the process . . .'

'That would put it into next year,' Freelorn said. 'We can't—'

'Lorn, that would put it into the next century.' Segnbora was smiling, but the look was rueful. 'We'll just have to try to rush things a bit. And if she doesn't approve . . .'

'One does not go against the *lhhw'Hreiha*.'

'One does if she's about to get us all killed, *mdaha* . . .'

The room was still for a while, as silver eyes and hazel ones rested in each other, considering. 'You are my *sdaha*, my living self,' Hasai said. 'But life is intemperate; I must keep you from reckless choices.' The room grew full of what he meant – the presence of a terrible weight of years,

54

of other Dracon souls and lives, now inextricably part of Segnbora, and intent on keeping her self and their selves in the world.

Segnbora nodded slowly. 'Yes, you must. But *I* have to keep you from refusing to make any choice at all. Outliving the problem is no solution to it.' And she gazed at the Dragon and would not look away. The hair rose on Lorn's neck as mortality, fierce and frail, and immortality, weighty and blunt as stone, leaned together and strove in the suddenly blistering air. Then the heat was gone, and there was unity; but it was troubled.

'You are my *sdaha, dei'sithessch*,' Hasai said. Segnbora looked down. 'We shall try occasions with the Dragon-Chief. We shall lose this battle, and perhaps save your kind and mine. But I'm of you, *sdaha*.'

Segnbora stared at the table with an expression abstracted and afraid; but she still wore a curl of smile.

'What do you see?' Herewiss said, quiet-voiced.

Segnbora's eyes came back to the present. She looked up. 'Nothing clear,' she said. 'I'm nearsighted, yet . . . Sticks. Stones.' She shook her head. 'Loss. Something found, and lost again . . .'

Eftgan glanced at Freelorn. 'So that settles them,' she said. 'Herewiss goes to Arlen with Sunspark. Segnbora goes in company too, though a bit more quietly. I go with an army and arrive on the First of Autumn; and there we all join forces, and take what adventure our Lady sends us. How are you going, Lorn?'

He swallowed. 'Alone. I've been told. I have to go to Arlen to find my Initiation . . . and Hergótha and the Stave as well, I hope. If I survive, I'll meet you afterwards. There's no other way.'

No-one said anything immediately. There was something about the silence that suggested some of them thought even the battle might not be a final solution. Lorn breathed out, and went on. 'I'll start somewhere southwards, and work north. They won't be expecting that, either; they'll expect me to rush into things headlong, as usual, the straight way along the Kings' Road. Or else to try the midland route near Osta, as I did the last time.'

'You're going to have to disguise yourself,' Eftgan said.

'I know.' He smiled slightly. 'This place seems to be crawling with Rodmistresses and people with Fire. I should think you could come up with something.'

Eftgan nodded. Freelorn glanced over at Herewiss and found his loved looking at him with the strangest brooding expression, one that seemed to say, in astonishment and (most startling to Lorn) discomfort, *At last, my loved is a man indeed . . . !* Freelorn strained for the underhearing that had been troubling him all morning. It refused to come, and he turned away to look at Eftgan, troubled at heart.

'Good enough,' she said. 'Go your ways, my dears. We'll talk more on this after dinner, with the Council. But I think we shouldn't wait more than a few days to start.'

People got up, one by one, and headed out, while Freelorn sat still and studied the table.

'Lorn?'

He looked up. He and Eftgan were by themselves. A lark sailed singing past the high window, up into the blue air, till its song was lost.

'In seven years, nearly,' Freelorn said, 'I haven't been alone.'

Eftgan sighed, and got up. 'When you're a king, as far as people go, you're alone all the time,' she said. 'Did you think She gives kingship away for free?' She patted him on the shoulder as she went by on her way out. 'But stay with it, my brother. It has its moments.'

Like that one just then, with Herewiss? he thought, as she left.

For several minutes Lorn sat there, and then got up and went out to see about his disguise.

In the grate, from the fire, eyes looked after him.

3

I think I love you,
and the problem
is the thinking.

d'Kaleth, *Lament*

There is a story that when the Maiden was making the world, She purposely dug the bed of the river Darst in a nearly complete circle around Mount Hirindë because She felt that the only thing needed to make its already splendid view perfect was water. As in other such stories, the truth is likely to be as complex as She. Mistress of the arts of war as well as those of peace, perhaps She was also thinking of the defensibility of such a hill, seven eighths surrounded by a river a mile wide, full of treacherous shoals, and stretching out into great flats of wetland and bogland that would eat any attacking force alive. In any case, Darthis has never been taken by any foe, and the view is still unparalleled in the north country, particularly by moonlight.

Lorn stood there leaning on the low parapet of the Square Tower, the highest one in Blackcastle, looking south across the town to the dull hammered-pewter gleam of the river, and the marshes rough and silvery under the first-quarter moon. It was late, an evening a week after the Hammering. Under him the town was a scattering of streets dim in cresset-light, clusters of peaked roofs, the broad broken part-circle contour of the city's second wall, long grown over and through with houses; here and there a tallow-glass or rushlight showed in a high window. The occasional voice, a shout of laughter or a snatch of song, drifted up through the cool air, coming and going as the wind shifted.

He swatted a hungry bug that was biting him earnestly in the neck, and looked out past the marshes, south, where patchwork fields and black blots of forest merged and melted together into a dark silver shimmer of distance: no brightness about them but a faint horizontal white line, the Kings' Road, its pale stone running east in wide curves and vanishing into the mingling of horizon and night. *It would be nice to be going that way*, he thought. That was the way to the Brightwood, among other places. Four or five times he had ridden that road, sometimes with his father, on visits of state to the Wood . . . and later on his own business, for Herewiss's boyhood home was there. A long time ago, that first visit with its arguments, its snubs, the standoffishness that shifted unexpectedly one night into friendship between a pair of preadolescent princes.

Lorn laughed softly at himself. He had thought Herewiss ludicrously provincial when he first saw him – a dark, scowling beanpole in a muddy jerkin, taciturn and scornful, and overly preoccupied with turnip fields: a 'prince' living in an oversized log cabin, with a tree growing through its roof. What Herewiss had thought of *him*, with his fancy horse and his fancy sword and his fancy father, Freelorn had fortunately not found out until much later. There probably would have been bloodshed.

As it was, Lorn looked back at the memory in astonishment and wondered how he could ever have felt that way about Herewiss. He had been no prize himself. His princehood had just begun to mean something to him – 'and too damned much of something!', he could still hear his father growling, at the end of one memorable dressing-down. Lorn had succeeded in alienating just about everyone in the Brightwood on that first trip, including the one girl whose attention he had desperately been trying to attract. Crushed by a very public rejection, which had ended with pretty little Elen picking him up and dumping him headfirst into a watering trough, Lorn had bolted into the Brightwood, looking for a place to cry his heart out. Around nightfall he had found a place, a clearing with a nice smooth slab of stone, and sat down there and wept because no-one liked him.

Now he looked back for the hundredth time in calm astonishment at the circumstances that had brought Herewiss to find him, rather than the Chief Wardress of the Silent Precincts . . . for of course that was the spot he had picked to cry on: the holiest of altars to the Goddess in perhaps the whole world, at the heart of those Precincts where no word is ever spoken by the Rodmistresses who train there, so that Her speech will be easier to hear. There Herewiss found him, and befriended him, almost more out of embarrassment than anything else, and got him out of there before they both got caught. And the friendship took, and grew fast.

Look at him, the thought came, in a rush of affection, sorrow, unease and desire, all run together in a bittersweet dissonance of emotion. And that second set of vision came upon Lorn again, so that he saw himself from behind, through Herewiss's eyes as he came out on the tower's roof. It was uncanny and disturbing. For what Herewiss saw wasn't just a dark shape leaning on a parapet, but a much-loved embodiment of intent, and old pain, and warmth, and strife that would lead to triumph: a figure incomplete and annoying in some ways, but also heroic and sorrowfully noble—

The underhearing slipped off, leaving Lorn uncertain whether to laugh in affectionate scorn or cry with frustration. *That's not me!!* he thought. Nonetheless he said nothing, and held still until his loved had joined him. They leaned on the wall together, shoulders touching, looking out southward to where the fields melted into silver-black sky.

'When I first met you that time,' Lorn said, 'were you trying to grow a moustache?'

Herewiss began to laugh. 'After fifteen years, you ask me that now?'

'Well, I was just remembering, and all of a sudden I remembered this thing on your lip.'

Herewiss laughed harder. 'Oh, Goddess. Yes, I was. I'd been working on it for months. But then you arrived, and you had one, so I shaved mine right off.'

Lorn chuckled. 'And then Elen told me to grow it back or she'd have nothing to do with me,' Herewiss said. 'So I did. I doubt there was much of it there when I found you, though.'

'There wasn't. It looked like dirt. In fact, I thought it *was* dirt.'

Herewiss grinned wryly. 'Wonderful.'

'Well, you and dirt were never far apart,' Freelorn said. 'Farm boy.'

'City brat,' Herewiss said in a poor imitation of a thirteen-year-old's scorn. 'You might like dirt too if you touched it occasionally.'

They both burst out laughing, and Lorn slipped an arm around Herewiss's waist as Herewiss dropped one about his shoulders and hugged him. 'I was packing,' Herewiss said. 'What do I do with this?'

He nodded off to his right. Lorn glanced over. Sitting on the parapet was their lovers'-cup, the grain of its plain turned wood showing silver in the moonlight, the carved leaf-pattern around the edge indistinct and shadowy. Freelorn was surprised. 'All these other times we've travelled, you usually carry it . . .'

'All these other times, I haven't been anyone particular. Things have changed . . .'

I know, Lorn thought, remembering that odd look a week ago at the table, and wondering for the hundredth time what to do about it. 'But what are you going to drink out of?'

Herewiss shook his head. 'Better you keep it. It would be remarked on . . . and the less attention is drawn to you while I'm in Arlen, the better. Don't you think?' And he laughed once more, just a breath of sound this time. 'Lorn, don't look that way. Do you think there's *any* cup I drink out of, that I don't think of you?'

Freelorn shook his head slowly. 'It's the same here,' he said, and the roughness down in his throat surprised him as his voice caught on it. 'Anything in that?'

Herewiss handed the cup to him. 'Brightwood white,' he said. 'My last for a while. My father won't send it to Arlen any more.'

'That's a shame,' Lorn said.

'It's your fault,' Herewiss said. 'He stopped trading with them right after he found out that Cillmod was trying to have you killed.'

Freelorn was astonished. 'He did that for me?'

Herewiss looked at him in affectionate scorn. 'He *loves* you, you idiot. After all these years, haven't you got it through your head?'

Freelorn lifted the cup and poured out a quick libation to the Goddess over the edge of the parapet. 'Well, here's to him, then. And Her.' He drank.

Herewiss peered over the edge. 'Better hope She wasn't standing under that.'

'And to you,' Lorn said, his voice catching on that rough spot again as his eyes met Herewiss's in the dark. He drank again, and handed his loved the cup.

'Lorn,' Herewiss said, and drank. The underhearing spilled over again: the cool fire of the wine, held in the mouth for a moment, savoured, to catch that flint-touch of sharpness that always reminded the taster of the scent of green leaves just after rain . . . but the taster wasn't Freelorn. All this came mixed with a trembling along the limbs, as Herewiss thought of leaving Lorn tomorrow, leaving him all alone, watching him head towards Arlen and not being able to do anything to protect him. Not wanting to *need* to protect him, truly. But still, one wanted to make sure that things went right . . . And overlaying all this, a dull mourning, a feeling of simply missing Lorn, missing him even though he wasn't gone yet: the

61

premonition of the ache that would set in as it had in separations before – the silence on the far side of many a conversation, the emptiness in the next place at table, in the curve of his own arm . . .

It was too hard to bear, the other's pain and his own both at once. *Don't make it worse for him*, something said inside Lorn. 'Dusty,' he said, and Herewiss only drank again and looked south.

Lorn said that other Name, too softly for anyone but Herewiss and the one Other Who knew it to hear.

Herewiss looked at him, bowed his head. 'Yes,' he said.

'You never told me the Fire was going to rub off,' said Lorn.

Herewiss turned the cup around and around on the parapet. 'You might have suspected it would,' he said. 'I wasn't sure, so I didn't say anything. But you know they do it on purpose, in the Precincts.'

Lorn nodded. 'Eftgan and Segnbora were paired that way for a while, weren't they? So that when they shared together, Eftgan's Fire would wake Segnbora's up.'

'That's right. Didn't work, or course.' Herewiss drank. 'Too deep a blockage, and too much power, in Segnbora's case. But normally it works.' He shrugged. 'Theoretically, anyone with the threshold amount of Fire, more than that spark that everyone has, can have it awakened by someone else already focused. Now here *I* am . . . and one of the things She told me was that I was to be a catalyst, to start to spread Her Fire around again, and among men as well as women.' He breathed out, hard. 'Apparently it's working, even with just that slight spark. I don't know why I was surprised. She knows what She's doing.'

'Dusty,' Freelorn said, with great feeling, 'I don't want the Fire. I don't even want the underhearing, particularly. It makes me walk into things when it hits.'

Herewiss looked for help at the sky. 'Nine tenths of the human race prays to have the Fire restored to it, and *you* don't want it—'

'The other tenth are all Rodmistresses,' Freelorn said,

'and sometimes they don't want it either! I can't control this, I don't have time to learn how, and if it gets me in trouble—'

'I can't block it,' said Herewiss. 'It's involved with the parts of your mind where intuition and hunches live, and if I tried meddling with those, I might just as well chop off your arms and legs and send you to Arlen in a cart: you'd have as much chance of surviving the next couple of months.'

Freelorn took the cup back. 'I know, I know.' He drank about half of the wine at once.

'And the only way to stop the Power waking up any further—'

Herewiss fell silent. Freelorn looked at him. 'We won't be doing much of that for the next couple of months, anyway,' he whispered.

'Don't remind me.'

There was silence for a few minutes, as they passed the cup back and forth.

'I wish you could come with me.'

'Even if it meant—'

'Dusty, it's just, just that . . . I don't want to be a god.' Freelorn looked south. It was easy to fantasize the presence of mountain peaks white in the shimmer of moonlight on the edge of the horizon, even though Bluepeak was hundreds of miles too far away. 'Everybody I know is turning into one, all of a sudden. I always wanted you to have your Fire, you worked and suffered and struggled so hard for it, you couldn't be *you* without it . . . but I thought everything else would stay ordinary. Now your Power's slopping over on everything it touches. And there's so much of it. The mountains down south aren't shaped the way they used to be, because of you.' He laughed. 'A month around you and Segnbora picks up Skádhwë, four thousand Dragons and enough fire for any fifty Rodmistresses. Pretty soon Dritt and Moris and Wyn and everybody else are going to break through and catch Fire just from breathing your used air.' The laugh had a

63

slightly desperate sound about it this time. 'And where does it all leave me, when I want to stay the way I am? Can the *you* that you are now, love a mere mortal?'

Herewiss looked at him for a few seconds in silence, and then lifted the cup and looked at him over the rim.

'I don't know,' he said. 'Let's find out.' And he drank, and gave the cup to Freelorn.

'I have to finish packing,' Herewiss said. 'Come to bed?'

'In a while.'

Herewiss nodded, hugged him one-armed, and headed down the stairs.

Lorn leaned there and looked south for some time, while his mind settled. He had been looking for words to tell Herewiss what was bothering him for days and days; now he wasn't at all sure that the words he'd found had been the right ones. Underhearing didn't do you much good when it only went one way. It would be nice if loving was what he had thought it would be when he was young and stupid: perfect understanding, perfect union, effortlessly arrived at. But there was only one lover from whom that could be expected . . .

His gaze dropped again to that white road, running east into the night. Nearly four months ago, it had been. He and his people and Herewiss had been hot on the trail of the old Hold in the western Waste, a place surrounded by disquieting legends, but nonetheless a place of which Herewiss had had great hopes. It had been mildly surprising, but not specifically unusual, to find a small inn on the river Stel, at the borders of the Waste. After days out in the wild, they had been grateful to stop there for a night. They were all short of money, and had wound up striking a typical travellers' arrangement with the innkeeper. One of them would share with her, that evening, by way of settling the scot. There had been some argument over who would get to do this . . . for the innkeeper was utterly beautiful; dark-haired, green-eyed, a tall queenly woman full of wit and merriment. Segnbora had finally won the draw, and had gone upstairs after dinner, grinning faintly, to the genial hooting and encouragement of the rest.

Harald and Lang had stayed up a while by the fire to drink, but Lorn had preferred to go straight upstairs to that astonishing luxury, a room of his own, there to revel in a bed with no-one in it, especially no-one with more legs than he had. Later, of course, he would sneak into Herewiss's room, or the other way around. But sometimes when you had been travelling with other people for a long time, it was a great joy to slip away and listen to the silence for a while, and watch the moon come up, and not have to worry that the pursuit would find you more easily because of it.

He did that. A soft spring moon, full and golden, outside the diamond-paned window; the wind in the apple trees, snowing their petals gently on the ground and drifting them about in a kindly mockery of the season past; a jar of wine that he had appropriated from the kitchen after helping with the dishes – and the innkeeper had scowled at him as if he was a naughty boy, and then winked and gestured him out; a chair and table by the window, with one warm rushlight burning like a star in the dim room, and the good bed with its clean linen, inviting him – not just now, but later, when he was just tired enough – it all conspired to produce such a perfect peace as Lorn had not felt in years.

And then there she was, in the doorway, gowned in white and dark-robed as if about to retire, and leaning in to peer at him like a mother checking on a child staying up late. Lorn had left the door open for the breeze, and at the sight of her he was glad he had. She came in and sat with him by the window, and they began to talk.

To this day he remembered so little of what was said. They talked about everything under the sun – histories and how they part from the truth; and old legends and stories told to children in Arlen, and how they differ from those told eastward in Darthen or south along the Stel;

what to do about clubroot in a cabbage field, or about a cavalry charge; and endless other things. And whatever she spoke of, she did so with such knowledge, and such love . . . and sometimes with great sadness in her face, as if she felt herself somehow responsible for a famine here or an unhappy ending there, so that Lorn would have done anything to ease her sorrow if he could. But it always passed into other talk, into memory, or merriment, or sweet or sober joy. And it was not until long after the rushlight had burnt out, and the moon had slid softly up over the roof and out of sight, that Lorn realized that the moonlight had not left her, but still rested on her, golden, when everything else lay in starlight or shadow.

Then, at last, his heart thundering in his ears, he knew Her. Then he understood clearly how poor a word 'queenly' had been, yet a word that would have to do, for the One in Whose name all kings and queens ruled – the One Who comes to every man and woman born, once before they die, to share Herself with them and have them know that they are loved. She pushed aside the cup that they had finished between them, and reached out and took his hand, and lifted it to Her lips.

'Dearest son of Mine,' she said. And the voice was his mother's.

A long time, She held him through the weeping. And when it was done, and She was Mother no longer, but Bride—

'You're up late,' said a voice right by his ear.

Freelorn jerked upright and slapped his left hip with his right hand, uselessly, for Súthan was not there any more, and it was a good question whether it ever would be again. The Darthene mastersmiths said its metal was probably too old to reforge successfully. He glared at the source of the interruption. Beside him on the parapet was a North Arlene hunting cat – or at least it would have been, if hunting cats had pelts that glowed a dull grey-dusted orange like coals in a banked fire, and black-irised eyes with pupils that were slits of molten yellow.

'Is there something I can do for you,' Freelorn said, breathing slowly to quiet his heart, which was now pounding for different reasons, 'or are you just looking for something to burn, as usual?'

'Herewiss is wondering where you are,' said Sunspark.

'Mmf,' Freelorn said. His feelings about Sunspark were mixed at best. But this much he knew, that he didn't want a fire elemental as a go-between . . . especially when that fire elemental was sometimes Herewiss's loved. Not that he was precisely jealous, of course, but— 'Tell him I'll be down in a few minutes.'

'He didn't send me,' Sunspark said, tucking itself down in a housecat-by-the-hearth position on the parapet. Only its tail hung down over the edge behind, and the tip of it smouldered as if thinking about bursting into flame. 'And do your own errands, mortal man. I have one master only, and you're not he.'

'Look,' Freelorn said, upset by the coolness in its voice, and unsure why he was upset, 'wait a moment. I'm sorry. You startled me, that's all; sometimes people are rude when they're startled.'

Sunspark blinked slowly. 'The way we burn things when we're startled?'

'I guess so.'

'Well enough. But you people do about fifty other things when you're startled, as well; I wish you would make your minds up.' And it sighed, so genuinely human a sound that Freelorn felt for it. Sunspark was studying to be human. Sometimes this was funny, but sometimes one came away after a lot of time spent 'helping' with one's hair singed for the trouble.

'Different reactions from different people,' Freelorn said. 'We're all one people, but not one kind, like elementals. I take it you just heard him, then. Underheard him.'

'I always hear him. How not? He's my loved.'

'There's more to love than just hearing.'

'I know,' it said. 'Compassion. He is teaching me.'

67

If the look in Sunspark's burning eyes was affection, it was of a dangerous sort, and Lorn wasn't sure he wanted anything to do with it. *Something else slightly out of the ordinary*, he thought. *I'm in a threesome with a brush-fire* . . .

'You're not, indeed,' Sunspark said, and lazily stretched out a paw, flexing the claws; they burned white-hot. 'You're interesting in your own way, but you're most unlikely to master me as he did. And I doubt I'll ever give love save where I'm mastered. This much I'll say, though, for your sake, since he loves you: I would not have him in pain. Please watch what you do.'

'I'm trying,' Freelorn said, surprised. He had never heard Sunspark say 'please' before.

Sunspark gazed out over the town, calm, or not noting the look. 'So I heard. It's well; for otherwise, king or no king, I would certainly have you for nunch.' It tucked the stretched paw back in again, serene. 'Most of all, I won't have him tamed; so watch your heart, for it was trying, just then.'

'What?' He looked at it, too alarmed even to be angry for the moment.

'Oh, you're trying to tame him, all right,' it said. 'Who should know the symptoms better?' It regarded him with dry amusement. 'Many another has tried it with me, and wound up as cinders. And what about you? Will you have a pet? Or be loved freely by something dangerous? You may die of it, but you won't mind the death, not afterwards, when the love is a hundred times greater.'

Freelorn began to shake. It was hard to tell whether Sunspark was speaking allegorically, since its kind didn't handle life and death as humans did. Herewiss had had problems of this sort with Sunspark before, and had taken a long time to convince it not to simply kill people who were bothering him. 'You sound sure of yourself,' Freelorn said at last.

'I know what worked for me, and for Herewiss. It should work for other humans, but Herewiss keeps complicating it with explanations.' It laughed gently. 'If I come to understand *why* our loving works for him, that will be enough for me. And the sooner, the better. No use wasting time.'

'Why not?' Lorn said. 'You won't die any time soon.'

'*He* will,' said Sunspark.

Lorn was shaken. 'And what was it that worked for you?'

Its voice was soft, and even puzzled, as if even now it didn't understand the answer. 'Fight with all your power, to the death, and lose the battles, first. Learn defeat. Then you get everything. Win, and lose it all.' It shook its head slowly, and sat up, stretching fore and aft, cat-fashion. 'If I had won,' Sunspark said, reflective, 'he would be ashes on some south wind, and I would have been free . . . of this.' It gazed down over the parapet, towards the lower towers, in one of which Herewiss lay. 'Free of him, of love, and fear, and death . . . free of you mad creatures.' To Freelorn's amazement, it turned and bumped its head against his shoulder, and the touch was warm. 'Mastery is better,' it said, muffled, 'even if I'm on the wrong side of it.'

Very slowly Lorn put a hand up to stroke the burning pelt. It was like hot velvet to the touch, and Sunspark shivered in response. 'Maybe it's unlikely,' he said to it, rubbing the good place behind the ears, 'but it might be interesting anyway, to try to master you, and find out firsthand what the Dark you're talking about.'

One eye opened and looked at him. 'So it might be at that,' it said, sounding amused. Then it straightened up. 'He's waiting for you,' it said, and leaped off the parapet, dissolving into a streak of fire that struck outward into the night.

What have I got myself into? Lorn thought, and sighed, and went down to bed. In the morning, he would ride for Arlen.

4

They who say we are made in the Goddess's image,
they say true. For She made the world, yet in
the heat of Her creation forgot the Shadow of Death
that lurked, waiting Its chance: and unthinking
She bound it into the world, and now rues Her doing.
And we, like Her, make works that we fancy shall
last for ever, but leave this or that great matter
out of our reckoning; and then rue the mistake
after. Here, though, we come at last by Her mercy
to differ. For the mistakes we make, we can set
right: She, never. All the hosts of man must come
to the Last Shore before She may end the world and
begin anew. Yet though we may set our mistakes
aright . . . how often do we so? And in this the
Shadow's laughter may be heard. In our pride and
blindness is Its only hope . . . and the means by which
the likeness between us and Her is made complete.

s'Lehren, *Commentaries on the Hamartics*

Dead tired, wrung out, held safe and close, he would have
thought that this once he was safe from the dream. He
found out otherwise.

It started as innocently as they tended to – one of those
strange, slightly frantic, funny dreams in which good
friends and people you've never seen before all rush
around on bizarre missions that make perfect sense while
you're dreaming, and none whatsoever when you wake.
He remembered wading a muddy river in company with

Herewiss and Lang. Where the rest of his people were, he couldn't imagine. A while later in the dream, he remembered that Lang was dead, fallen off the trail over the Scarp near Bluepeak. But in the dream, Lang's appearance was some kind of good omen, so he let it pass: they were too busy to bother with small business at the moment, it would wait. Then suddenly they were in an inn somewhere – so he thought, anyway: a small crowded room full of shouting people. No, not shouting – singing. Over the singing, as if he had his head bent to catch an intimate conversation quite nearby, he could hear two people talking together softly.

'What was the problem?'

'Dear one, I seem to be pregnant.'

'That's news! Will you be all right?'

'For a few months, at least. But—'

And then a pause as he realized this was not an inn at all, but some kind of cave, in which some sound was echoing and hissing so that it sounded like many voices talking at once. It might be the sea, outside. That would make sense, for he could smell salt air. He headed for the shadowy walls of the place, hunting a doorway, while the voices began to argue.

'Wait a minute! What do you mean, *you're* pregnant? *I'm* pregnant!'

'That's ludicrous! What have you been doing to get pregnant?'

'The same thing *you* have!'

Lorn began to laugh quietly to himself as he went, because it occurred to him suddenly in the dream that one of the two people arguing was male. He walked on, into the stony shadows, and then began to wonder whether he was going in the right direction. The seacrash was dwindling away into silence.

He paused, stood still, feeling nervous. The last sound faded away, leaving him standing in silence and darkness.

Moonlight there was, lying faint in long parallelogram-shapes upon the patterned floor. He went by it, touching a

71

familiar doorframe here, turning a corner there, now knowing surely where he was going, for he had walked these pillared halls by night and day for sixteen years of his life. The old almeries and chairs and presses looked at him calmly as he went by in the moonlight, and the stairway up to his old room spread itself broad for him, though he couldn't go up there just now. He had other business; they were waiting for him. He found the great curtained archway in the white marble walls that led to the hall he was looking for, the place where they were waiting. He put out his hand to touch the embroidery-stiffened velvet of the curtain, feeling acutely the touch of the gold wire under his fingertips. He moved to push the curtain aside.

And then he heard it, that low awful moaning sound, and barely had time to turn and flee before it burst out from the curtains behind him – the pale thing. He had seen it often enough before, it had been chasing him seemingly for his whole life, and he didn't need to turn to know what it looked like. He didn't even need to turn to see it. Fleeing, all his attention fixed ahead of him as he ran pounding down the tiles and looking for some place to hide, he could still see it clearly coming behind him, with that same doubled vision of the Blackcastle courtyard. A huge thing, scabrous, pallid, with a shape that never stayed the same for long, but flowed and changed like some glowing corruption. But mostly it had a broad pale body – of a deadly paleness, like something leprous – and long soft grabbing arms, and a wet white toothless maw that drooled pus and slime, and huge chill vacant eyes like sick moons that refused to stay in one place like eyes should. He ran, he ran, but it did him no good – it never did. It would get its claws into him and his blood would run with its corruption, he would feel the poison stink of its breath in his face as it lowered its mouth to his and—

—the door, oh blessed Goddess, there was the door out into the garden! He ran for it in horror, tugged at its iron handle, it was stuck, hammered helplessly at the oaken, iron-nailed width of it, then yanked again in crazed desperation as he heard that evilly longing moan behind him. This time the door flew open, so fast that it hit him in the mouth. He gasped with the shock, flung himself sideways and through—

—and found something worse. The sky was red, red like blood, long streaks of blood across a black like death, and the taste of blood in his mouth, and something screaming through thunder, the end of the world. There was his choice. Flee out into that, and die; or stay and face the pallid thing that hunted him, that he heard coming up behind him, that reached out for him even now and wrapped its great soft horrible arms around him and turned him around by force and held him, held him till he screamed for help, any help, even death would be better than this, and he struggled, wild and desperate, as its mouth came slowly down—

Lorn was sitting up in bed, panting. The room was dim, but the moon was long since gone; the light coming in the window was the beginning of dawn, all rose and grey. Herewiss was not in bed, and all the covers were wrapped around Lorn for once. He couldn't think of any time when he had ever wanted them less. In left-over loathing he struggled out of them, kicked them away, and sat there in the bed naked and shivering.

The door opened hastily, and Herewiss came back in, in his robe, dripping. 'You shouted!' he said, and hurriedly sat down on the bed and reached out to Freelorn. 'Are you all right?'

'No.'

'That dream again.'

'Yes.'

Herewiss sat silent for a moment. Then he said, 'You're overwrought. We're *all* overwrought. That's all.'

'Tell me about it,' Freelorn said softly.

Herewiss reached out to him and held him, held him hard. 'I don't want to leave you either,' he said into Lorn's shoulder.

Freelorn hugged him back. 'Let's not start again.

They're going to be waiting downstairs for you before too long, and I need to say goodbye to them. And we need to be brave and strong and certain for them, and all the rest of the idiocy.'

And who's brave for you? he quite clearly heard Herewiss's heart cry out. *Oh, Lorn, I can't do it just now, yet you need me—*

It would have been too easy to agree with that. But he thought of Sunspark, and watched what he did. 'Come on,' he said, thumping Herewiss's shoulder, and then reached down to hold up one sodden sleeve. 'One last bath, huh?'

'It's a long way to Prydon,' Herewiss said, sounding rueful.

Lorn pushed him out of the bed, and got up himself, looking for something to wrap around him. 'Go on. I'll catch up.'

Freelorn found his own robe and his razor, and started to go after – then paused for a moment, juggling the razor case thoughtfully.

'Are you coming?' Herewiss shouted from down the hall.

Freelorn considered and discarded several possible responses. 'Coming?' he finally shouted back. 'I'm not even breathing hard.'

He headed out, following the laughter.

Breakfast was a hasty affair. The Queen had appointments in the south that afternoon, and she needed time to prepare the sorceries of the Kings' Door, the single permanent worldgate in the human part of the Middle Kingdoms, for the single step that would take her and her assistants a thousand miles. There were also other considerations. Those heading west to Arlen needed an early start to make sure that they would be at the Red Lion, the first staging inn along the Kings' Road, by nightfall. Freelorn would not be able to see them on their way, for the Queen didn't want him going out of Blackcastle without her.

'We are going to encourage some misconception about your whereabouts,' Eftgan had said to Freelorn the day before. 'Since you're going out of here disguised, I am going to do a shapechange on one of my own people and have it seem as if you're still here after you're gone. It won't fool the worst of the powers we're dealing with, or not for long. But it'll create confusion in Arlen, and that's all to the good.'

So Freelorn came down to breakfast rather behind Herewiss. Their farewells were made, in private as usual. Now Lorn was ready for the rest of them . . . but nervous on other counts. Herewiss would be taking Moris with him to Prydon as an 'equerry' and eyes-behind, but no-one else except, of course, Sunspark. Segnbora was going alone with Hasai, for quicker movement; Dritt and Harald were riding out south and east with messages to the nearest of the Darthene lords on whom levies were being settled. Lorn hated to see his people split up so. They were used to working together and covering for one another. But they would manage well enough.

At the top of the stairs that led down to the small side hall where breakfast was laid out, Lorn paused. There they were, his little group, finishing their meal. He headed down the stairs. One by one his people caught the sound of his step, and looked up to greet him: and stared.

Herewiss looked at him in shock. 'What have you done with your moustache?!'

Lorn stared back. 'It fell in love with a passing caterpillar and ran off. What do you think? I *shaved* it, for pity's sake.'

He looked at Eftgan, who was gazing at him over a cup of cold mint tea with approval. 'And I wouldn't mind finding a barber and having my hair cut shorter, later on.'

'That was wisely done,' Eftgan said, and everyone looked at her. 'Well,' she said to them all, 'I'm going to be putting a shapechange on him. I had thought I would make it a cleanshaven seeming anyway, to confuse matters as much as possible. But not even the best shapechange would be any good if someone happened to touch his face and find a caterpillar there.'

Laughter broke out, and Lorn went to the table and helped himself to a small trencherbread and a stoup of cider. Herewiss, picking up seconds of fried bread beside him, looked closely at Lorn and then laughed and said, 'You look really strange.'

'Well, thanks kindly.'

'No, I just meant I'm not used to seeing your upper lip . . .' He looked curiously at Lorn. 'You look older.'

'I thought it would go the other way.'

Segnbora came up beside them and looked at Lorn. 'It's pale,' she said. 'It'll look better after it tans.'

'I hope so. I hope I can get used to how it feels. Naked.' He rubbed it.

She smiled, in the offhand manner of someone who has something else on her mind. 'Lorn, I'm glad you came down before we had to leave: I have to tell you something. No, Herewiss, stay. Listen—'

'He's pregnant,' Freelorn said suddenly.

'No, *I'm* pregnant, but—' She stopped. '*What??*'

Both she and Herewiss stared at Freelorn. He sighed. 'Sorry. I think I overheard you. Underheard you. Hasai is pregnant, right?'

Segnbora looked at Herewiss. 'What have you been doing to him?!'

'Nothing unusual,' Herewiss said. 'It's just crossover. *You* of all people might have expected it.' And then he blinked. 'What do you mean "no, *you're* pregnant"??'

'Uh, I am. That's why I wanted to talk to you, Lorn. You're definitely her father. She's almost two months—'

'"*Her?*" A girl?'

'I'd be a pretty poor hand with the Fire if I couldn't tell that much, even this early,' Segnbora said. 'I would have said something earlier, but I wasn't sure. Before I broke through, I thought the stresses of picking up Hasai and the *mdeihei* had just thrown my flowering off schedule. Then these past few days, I was too busy to notice the "strangeness" right off . . . I've gotten so used to having other lives inside. But now I know.' She smiled.

'A little girl!'

Segnbora smiled.

'Wait a minute,' Herewiss said. 'Hasai is *male!*'

Segnbora glanced at him, a helpless comic look. 'They don't handle these things the way we do,' she said. 'If the *sdahaih* part of a Dragon is pregnant, the rest of them are likely to get broody too, if many more of them are female than male. Most of my *mdeihei* are female . . . Hasai's line is famous for it. It falls most intensely on those most recently *mdahaih*. That's Hasai.'

'Where are they all this morning?' Freelorn said, looking around as if expecting the breakfast room to go suddenly dark.

'They're off discussing it. And teasing Hasai, I'm afraid. I'm going to have to have a few thousand words with them.'

Herewiss looked closely at her. 'Are you all right? Can you ride?'

'Ride?' She laughed. 'I intend to *fly*. But I suspect the Dracon parts of me are going to affect this pregnancy. It may be a while before I come to childbed. Even now she's not as far along as a two-month's child would normally be.'

'A little girl!' Lorn said softly.

Segnbora put her plate down, pulled him close and hugged him. 'I just wanted to make sure you knew that I'll be taking good care of her,' she said. And in his ear she said, 'Not every day I get to cart a princess of Arlen around the countryside, after all.'

Freelorn was becoming more confused than he had ever been in his life. 'Look,' he said, 'whatever – just take care of yourself, all right?' He put out a hand to touch Segnbora's face.

'I will,' she said, her eyes gentle. 'My liege and my dear friend . . . you do that too. None of your famous last stands while you're travelling, hear? We need you alive.'

Lorn nodded.

'And you too,' she said to Herewiss. 'Don't start playing to the groundlings for no reason. Save your Power; you're going to need it.'

Herewiss smiled, took her hands, kissed them. 'They're getting ready to go,' she said, squeezing his hands, and turned away.

Freelorn looked at Herewiss. 'I hate these goodbyes.'

'The hello will be long,' said Herewiss, 'as usual.'

After a few minutes they went out into the courtyard outside the hall. It was mostly empty, so early in the morning. Freelorn went from horse to horse, saying goodbye to Dritt and Harald and Moris.

Finally he stopped by Sunspark. It was saddled and bridled, but the bridle was for show: the elemental could have munched up any bit ever made if the notion took it. Lorn patted its neck, and Sunspark looked at him out of eyes that were fierce, but not afire.

'Take care of him,' Lorn said, under his breath.

'I shall,' it said as softly: 'I shall indeed.' And it nipped him in the shoulder.

Without thinking, Lorn punched Sunspark as casually in the nose, and as hard, as he would have punched his own Blackmane. Sunspark started straight up, came down again in a great clatter of hooves, showing eye-white and with ears laid back flat. It started to rear . . . and then settled down, putting its ears up again. 'There really *may* be some interest in this,' it muttered to him as Herewiss came over and mounted up.

'I should hope so,' Lorn said. He looked up at Herewiss but said nothing.

Herewiss smiled back at him, and said the same nothing.

Eftgan turned away from her own farewells to Moris and Dritt and Harald. 'Our Lady go with you, my dears,' she said. 'Look for us about thirty miles west of Prydon on the eighty-sixth of Summer. I'll keep in touch with you as I may.'

'May She ride with you too,' Herewiss said, and nudged Sunspark, and rode out of Blackcastle's courtyard, down towards the winding streets of the town. The others followed, some of them leading pack-horses, and last of all came Segnbora, walking, with Skádhwë slung at her side. She punched Lorn cheerfully in the shoulder, and followed the others' echoes down into the mist and quiet of morning.

Lorn went up to the tower room to finish his own packing – so he told himself – but paused a long while at the window to watch them out of sight: the little party with their pack horses, heading west on the road, and the single small figure that walked straight south from the road into the fields. The pack horses vanished first in the mist, which was just now lifting.

He sighed and shifted his glance to that one small figure out in the green. In the middle of a field it paused a moment, and something seemed to happen to the light about it. The tiny shape grew taller, spread arms that grew to be black-webbed wings, leaned forward to let the great expanse of tail balance the huge head and length of neck. The rearing shape, burning golden and green even in the misty light, acquired a shadow that streamed out behind it and then reared up as well, a black shape, paling to silvery grey beneath. Both of them spread wings and rose up, without even flapping – simply soared up through the mist, almost to the tower's level. Together they leaned upward, folded their wings back from the great hawk-spread to a narrower dart-shape like that of a stooping falcon, and shot out of sight, upward and westward, like the wind.

A little girl . . . Lorn thought.

'So we keep hearing,' said Eftgan, in the doorway. 'Lorn, are you about done here? The barber's waiting for you, and we're needed down south fairly soon.'

Lorn nodded and went with her. 'I had a thought,' he said, 'of a way you might be able to help me.'

Eftgan looked at him with her eyebrows up. 'You mean *besides* the armies?'

He smiled crookedly. 'I would like some pots, please, a good assortment, some of them used and some new,' Freelorn said. 'And a pack horse to carry them.'

Eftgan nodded thoughtfully as they walked. 'True,' she said, 'a man on a horse, alone, with no reason to be wandering around in the country, is likely enough to cause comment. But who pays attention to one more travelling tinker? You'll want some tools, as well.' Then she burst out laughing. 'But, Lorn, do you *know* anything about mending pots?'

Now it was Freelorn's turn to laugh. 'A friend of mine taught me a thing or two. Herewiss didn't do *only* swords, you know. In fact I think he would have achieved Khávrinen sooner, if the Brightwood people hadn't kept nagging him to weld their pan handles back on.'

'Well enough, then,' the Queen said. 'I'll see what I can find.' She sighed. 'The kitchen staff probably won't mind losing some of their old pots, since they're always nagging the Chief Steward for new ones . . . And I'll speak to the stablemaster about a pack horse.'

She glanced out of a window at the morning as they went down a flight of stairs. 'It'll probably be pleasant for you, seeing the old haunts,' she said. 'Your fostering-country. I had heard that you had had another daughter, down that way, when you were younger.'

'She died right after she was born,' Lorn said. The pain was so old that he could almost be casual about it. 'There was something wrong with her heart, I was told. That's all I really know about it . . . I was a long way away when it happened.'

Eftgan nodded as they headed towards the stairs to the royal apartments. 'Well,' she said, 'somehow I think this new one is going to be all right. And my congratulations! I just hope she's not born speaking in tongues, like her mother. Here's the barber. Come straight upstairs when you're done: the Door's almost ready. I'll have your things sent for. And the pots.' She went off looking amused.

Half an hour later, after what he could have sworn was the loss of three quarters of his hair, Lorn walked up that narrow stairway. He was briefly distracted as he glanced up at the decorated ceiling. It was tiled in an odd lattice-pattern, with many tiles painted to resemble holes bored in the ceiling. But the breath of cool air coming down to him told him that some of those holes were real . . . the right size for shooting poisoned darts through, or for pouring boiling water. This central tower of Blackcastle, its keep, was the oldest part, and dated back to just after the time when Eálor Éarn's son had been attacked by assassins in his own house. Those assassins had not come off well, though they thought they had caught Eálor unarmed in his rooms. Their timestained, dusty skulls were nailed up neatly on the wall of one of the castle dungeons, and the big fireplace poker which Eálor had snatched up to ward them off had been made the battle-standard of Darthen, Sarsweng by name. But since that time, the Darthene royal family had taken steps to make sure no-one came at their quarters who wasn't welcome there.

'Anybody home?' he called as he came almost even with the landing. The door at the top was ajar, but there was no guard there that he could see.

'No!' shouted someone, and began giggling wildly: a blond head stuck itself around the corner of the door and stared at Freelorn with big mischievous green eyes. It was another of the princes, Goddess knew which one. There were five of them, most fairly close in age, all blond like their mother, and two of them were twins. Lorn had never been able to keep them straight except for Barin, the heir and eldest.

'Come on up,' Wyn shouted from somewhere back in the apartments. Lorn went through the door as the prince, in a plain grey smock well decorated with lunch, scampered away into another room.

The royal apartments were of the same black basalt as

everything else, but the stone here was dull-surfaced rather than polished, as in the newer parts of the castle. Big windows opened out on the morning from the central hearth-room, and rather beaten-up furniture was scattered around. On one couch the twin five-year-old princes were snoozing at opposite ends, one with his thumb in his mouth. The other had his head pillowed on the side of a large dog with long silvery fur.

'In the back, Lorn,' Eftgan called. 'The middle door.'

He walked through the rooms down a hall that led into the heart of the keep. The middle room's door stood open and, past the big canopied bed in it, so did a low door bound with huge bands of bronze. A key with an ornate finial almost the size of Lorn's fist stood out of its lock. Freelorn padded across the thick dark carpet, past the three-year-old prince, who was playing with a resigned-looking tabby cat, to this inner room. There Eftgan was sitting on a stool, and Wyn behind her, rubbing her neck while she sat half bent over, leaning elbows-on-knees and panting like a runner who's just run a course.

A short distance away from them, outlined against the dull stone wall in a thin line of bitter blue light, was the Kings' Door. It looked as if someone had taken Khávrinen or Skádhwë and used the sword to cut straight through the two-foot-thick stone as if through a loaf of bread into the outside air. But the view through the tall rectangular hole was not one of the city from about a hundred feet up, as it should have been. On the other side of the opening was a great stretch of green country, hilly, with a far prospect of snow mountains in the background, and sheep grazing calmly thirty feet away. Off to one side were several grooms in the livery of the Darthene royal household, and a number of horses, Eftgan's Scoundrel and Freelorn's Blackmane among them. Fastened to Blackie's saddle by a leading-rein was a small shaggy brown packhorse, laden with pots and pans.

Lorn shook his head in quiet amazement, his hair

ruffling slightly in the breeze that poured out through the opening. Though with Eftgan's help he and his people had used the Door before, he had never actually seen it in its own place. If a ruler was apt enough at sorcery or Fire, its doorway could be made to manifest briefly in other places, as Eftgan had obviously just done to let the horses be put through from the courtyard.

'If this thing weren't so convenient,' Eftgan said, between deep breaths, 'I would close it, I swear I would. Using it costs me more than almost any other wreaking I do. But if I did shut it, I would lose the best escape route in the place. Too many people try to kill kings in their beds . . .' She looked up at Lorn. 'What do you think?'

'About closing the Door? It seems a waste.'

'Lorn, I meant what do you think about your *face*.'

He shrugged. 'I'm used to it by now, I suppose.'

Eftgan's expression was wry: she glanced at Wyn as she straightened. 'Did you ever see a man with such a sense of humour? Or lack of it. Lorn, go look in the mirror.'

Bemused, he peered around the edge of the little room's door and glanced at himself in the mirror over the clothespress. Except it wasn't a mirror. It was a window, and some stranger was looking through it at him. Blond, a south Arlene perhaps, with that southern, heavy, rough cast of feature, ruddy-complexioned, slightly husky of build. And then he realized that the other man's clothes were the same as his—

The breath caught under Freelorn's breastbone for a moment, then got loose again. He touched his face: the blond man did the same.

'How long have I looked this way?' he said, his voice coming out oddly. It was deeper than usual.

'Since you left the barber's.'

Lorn went back into the room of the Kings' Door. Eftgan was on her feet now, stretching, putting her clothes in order. Her sword already hung at her hip. Wyn now handed her a poker, about three feet long, half its length encrusted with diamonds driven into the black iron.

83

Eftgan hefted Sarsweng, gazing idly at the flash of its gems, then looked at Lorn. 'Does it suit you?'

'Very well,' he said. 'What if I want to take it off myself?'

Wyn brought Eftgan a leather strap. She wound several turns of it around Sarsweng, slung the poker over her shoulder, and fastened first one end of the strap, then the other, to her baldric. 'Four elements combined with your own blood,' she said. 'Boil a pot of muddy water and use it to wash: that's one way. Just beware. Once it's off, it needs me or another Rodmistress to put it on again.'

She kissed her husband. 'I won't be too late,' Eftgan said. 'Don't forget to sit in on Balan's lessons today.'

'I won't,' Wyn said. 'Don't forget to look into that business with the vineyards.'

'I'll do that. Come on, Lorn.' Eftgan turned away, through the Door.

He followed her. At first there was no feeling of doing anything more than stepping through a doorway. Then pressure built up in his ears, he swallowed, and they popped. He walked over to Blackmane and took his reins from a groom, who bowed to him casually, and headed back the way Lorn had come.

He watched the other groom join his fellow, stepping through the Door. Then it was gone, and the breeze from it gone as well. Eftgan mounted up. Lorn took just long enough to make sure that everything he needed for the trip was packed in his saddle roll. He paused to look over the packhorse too. 'His name is Pebble, the groom tells me,' Eftgan said over his shoulder. 'Will these do?'

'Your cooks are right,' Lorn said, examining one holed kettle. 'You *did* need new pots.'

Eftgan chuckled. 'There are some newish ones there as well . . . it seemed as if a mixed bag would look more natural. Tools are in the canvas bag there. Mount up, Lorn, and let's get going.'

He got up on Blackmane, and they rode south. They were in high country, not yet mountainous but soon

84

enough to be that way – the Southpeaks reared up in the distance, low, blue, and misty in the morning. The land about was not much good for farming: the bones of it showed through the ground, mostly slate here, giving way to granite. Ferny-looking bracken was everywhere, both last year's dried growth and this year's new. There were sheep on some of the nearer hills.

Eftgan was cantering along beside Lorn, looking around her with a slightly preoccupied air. For some time Lorn said nothing to her, and after a while the mountains distracted him. They were distant, but even from here he could see the banners of cloud that streamed away from them, torn like tattered veils by the high winds. 'What do you make of that?' he said finally.

Eftgan glanced up. 'Ah,' she said. 'Well . . . the other day, Herewiss destroyed one of those mountains. You remember.' There was mockery in her tone, but it was kindly. 'You don't take away a whole mountain without changing the weather pattern that's used to living around it. It's going to be unsettled down in this part of the world for a while now.'

I am consorting with gods, the back of Lorn's mind said to him in uncomfortable echo of the morning's conversation. *And gods won't stop at changing such as me: they'll change the bones of the world if it suits them . . .*

'That is what prompted this meeting, I think,' Eftgan said. 'Various people became uncomfortable at the occurrences of the past few days. In any case, the meeting is fortuitous . . . if the cause is what I think.'

She paused, as if for breath. Lorn thought at first that he understood the cause: they were climbing a steepish hill, and Blackmane was working at it, his chest heaving in and out like a bellows. Scoundrel, walking beside him, was making light work of it all as usual . . . but then he was carrying a load a third lighter again than Lorn's gelding was.

Freelorn clucked at Blackie and urged him up to the top of the hill. 'So what am I supposed to look at—'

85

And he saw, and the breath went out of him as they paused there on the hillcrest, waiting for the escort to catch up with them.

The party waiting for them numbered about thirty. Their horses were small, barely more than shaggy ponies. That was what first gave away to Lorn just who it was he and Eftgan were meeting. The waiting group's clothes confirmed the judgement. They wore no trews or breeches, but the strange long undivided shin-length garment that he had come to know since he was young – a garment that was tied up between the legs with another band of cloth when the people wearing it needed to move quickly, as in battle. Bows in cases hung by the sides of the horses, and crude curved swords in rude sheaths. He could see how poor the sheaths were, barely more than tree-bark strapped together with leather thongs. He had no desire to be so close, none at all. Not three days before, he had had one of these people's arrows a span deep in his chest.

'What are we doing meeting with *Reavers?*' he said to Eftgan, under his breath.

She paused for a moment, then rode down the other side of the hill as the escort caught up with them. 'They're here, in my land. Anybody in my land is my business.' She eyed him, a rather challenging look. 'Besides . . . Cillmod seems to have been talking to them. And when is the last time *we* did any such thing?'

Lorn shook his head. Historically, there had never been much use in talking to Reavers: the few who had tried had died without finding anything out. The Reavers came from over the southern mountains, in the summertime, through the passes, they tried to take people's land, they were driven out, always with terrible losses, and after a respite, they always came back. Not every summer, by any means. But most years you would hear of burnt crops somewhere, of land overrun and won back with too much blood. It was rare to know anyone from the south who had not lost friends or family to the Reavers, or who did not hate them with the same resigned and impersonal hatred one usually reserved for plague or root-wilt. People tended not to think of them as really human, and this was easy, for their languages were as strange as their ways, and they died rather than remain captive. There was some discussion as to whether they even knew the Goddess. Just now they had invaded in greater numbers than ever before, and been driven back again more conclusively than when the first alliance of Arlen and Darthen had done it. Yet here they were again . . .

Lorn looked down the hillside. This party didn't look particularly threatening . . . but where there was one Reaver, there were a thousand more, sooner or later. 'How long have they been here?'

'No more than a day or so. The circuit Rodmistress for these parts sent me word. They've done nothing, threatened no-one. They've just waited here.'

'Waited,' Lorn said.

'Yes.'

'Do we have an interpreter with us?'

'I can manage that,' Eftgan said. '"Samespeech" is one of the first things they teach you when you master your Fire. How our guests will find it—' She shrugged. 'We'll burn that bridge when we come to it. Meanwhile, you have your own face back until we part. I think you may need it.'

They rode on down the hill without further words exchanged: but Eftgan slipped Sarsweng from its carry-sheath and laid it across her saddlebow. Lorn looked more closely at the group of Reavers awaiting them, as they drew closer. They were much of a size, but there was one man among them who was smaller than the rest, sharp-faced, with fair hair tied up in a tight knot behind. He looked faintly worried.

Lorn stopped his horse close enough to be polite and not to need shouting, but fairly well out of spear- or sword-reach. Beside him, Eftgan pulled up and nodded politely at the strangers, all of whom shifted uneasily at the movement, as if expecting it to be some kind of signal for attack.

It took a moment for the rustling to die away. When it did, Eftgan said, 'The Goddess's greeting to you, strangers, and my own with it. What brings you into my country?'

This time the start that ran through them was much more pronounced, and Lorn found this understandable. He clearly heard Eftgan's voice asking the question in her drawly north-country Darthene. But at the same time he heard it inside him, *under*heard it, in Arlene of a perfect Prydon-city accent – his own, in fact. Yet it was still her voice. All the Reavers flinched and stared at one another like scared children, except the small man at their head. The set, wary look on his face apparently needed more than this surprise to unsettle it.

'What do you mean by "your country?"' the man said. The words of the strange language, as they came out, sounded surprisingly light and lyrical – but then Lorn had never heard Reavers do anything but scream unintelligible battlecries before.

If the response surprised Eftgan, she showed no sign of it. 'All this land is in my care,' she said, 'from these mountains to the sea far to the north, and from the great river to the next great river eastward. I see to it that the ground bears fruit for beasts and men, and that the people who live in my country have enough to eat, and that they are safe in the places they live, and that justice is done them. I have sworn to die rather than fail in any of this. And even if I do die, the Goddess who gave me this responsibility will hold me responsible still. I have Her to answer to. So I speak of the country being "mine", and the people who make their homes in it call me theirs: their Queen.'

The looks of concern and bewilderment that passed across the Reaver's face troubled Freelorn considerably. Didn't these people even know what a ruler was? *And what if they don't? How are we going to explain to them that this is* our *land, and we would thank them not to invade it every summer—*

'You speak of seeing that your people have enough to eat, and being safe,' the man said. 'I know that work myself, and do it for my own.'

'For all the people like you, everywhere?' Eftgan said. 'Or only these with you now?'

'These and others,' the Reaver said. 'As for the great many others, I am only their eyes, and their lips to speak, if any can be found who understand.'

Eftgan nodded. 'What words would the others speak, then?'

The man cocked his head to one side. 'Those who move on this side of the mountains,' he said, 'seem to have a new arrow to their bow.'

Freelorn nodded too, then, and nudged Blackmane a few steps forward, closer to the man on his shaggy horse. Only a few steps: the man looked at him, alarmed, and moved in his saddle. 'The arrow,' Freelorn said, 'is mine.'

The man was still staring at him, an odd unsettled look. 'If when you speak of a new arrow,' Lorn said, trying to match the man's own old-fashioned, poetic idiom, 'you mean that the mountains moved to aid us, rising up and falling at our behest, when they never did so before, you speak of something that was my doing. Or if you speak of the fiery shadow that rose up from the battlefield east of here, some days ago, that arrow was mine as well. It is my bow they were set to. And more arrows will fly yet.'

He paused. The man just would not stop staring at him. 'I belong to the land westward beyond the river,' Lorn said, 'as this lady belongs to the lands hereabout. It is my lands you have come to, as to hers. And so we ride together to meet you.'

The Reaver took a deep breath, like someone steeling himself to do something that terrified him, and nudged his own horse with his heels, heading him toward Lorn. Lorn sat there, fairly terrified on his own behalf, and cursed himself silently for not having even a knife ready to hand at the moment. But he held his ground.

The small man stopped right in front of him and just to

one side, close enough to touch and to examine minutely. The shaggy skin thrown over everything; the roughspun cloth of the overtunic; the peeling, crudely tanned leather of the sword fittings and tack. And slung by the side of the horse, the short quiver of Reaver arrows – with the rude hatchmarks by the fletching, two rings, crossed, and red paint rubbed into the scratches.

Lorn stared at the arrows a moment, then looked up into the face of the Reaver. It was pale with fear, and the knuckles of one of the man's hands were strained white where he clutched the reins. The other hand lifted, now, reached out tentatively to Lorn, touched him gingerly on the chest where the arrow had gone in; then prodded. Again, harder.

Then the man said, rough-voiced, fearful, 'You are alive. You are one of Them. The Gods.'

Oh, Lady! Lorn thought, distressed. He breathed out, met the man's eyes, shook his head – *but does that even mean the same with them as it does with us?* 'No,' he said. 'The – arrow – that I loosed . . . it struck yours aside. That's all.'

The Reaver looked from Lorn to Eftgan. 'I have never seen such a thing,' he said. 'They said your people were accursed, and would rise from the dead to haunt us.'

'We do not do it often,' Eftgan said, 'and never without the Goddess's leave.' Her voice was light, but she slid a sidelong look at Lorn. *They?* she said, bespeaking him.

Yes. 'I have things to do,' Freelorn said to the Reaver, 'and could not let your arrow stop me.' He worked hard to keep his face quiet, for sitting here and bald-facedly taking credit for Herewiss's miracles made him guilty. 'There are people in my land past the river who would deny me my right to care for it. I am on my way to take back my own from them.'

A look of suspicion went across the Reaver's face. 'They told us,' he said, 'of the wicked one, the child of the beast, that was cast out, and fled for seven years, and would try to return.'

90

That set Lorn back for a moment. *Child of the beast, indeed*— He thought of his father's dry wise humour – and then of Héalhra's statue in Lionhall, all cool wisdom, and passion ready to strike, but controlled – a symbol for a person who had become more than any mere beast, more than any mere man before or since.

Beside him, Eftgan sat impassive, waiting. 'You seem to have been told many things,' Lorn said, finally, 'and it must be hard to know what to believe. But more can be said than what you have been told. For one thing, I have no desire to kill you all.'

The man's eyes narrowed. 'What of the mountain that fell on our people?' he said. 'What of the shadow and the fire, that made day of night, and opened the earth, so that it swallowed a thousand great companies of my folk? Child of the beast, you lie. We came the great journey, hungering, from the snows, and death is all you had for us. Death is all you have ever had!'

Freelorn shook his head, to have something to do to cover up the fact that his hands were shaking. *Hungering. Could it be something so simple as that? It's cold enough in our southern lands, hard enough to grow anything: how is it for them?* But his anger was beginning to get the better of him. 'As for the mountain, that was a door that had to be closed,' he said. 'Hungering you come; what of *my* people, then, whose fields you set afire, whose cattle you drive off or kill, whose houses you burn, with my people in them? By that door you have come a thousand times. Now it is shut, and my people in that part of the world will fear you no longer! But as regards Britfell field,' Lorn said, 'if you send a messenger back to your own side of the mountain, you will find that your people are not dead. Sent back to your own countries, and well away from our own, yes. But the Goddess bids us not kill, when it can be avoided.'

The Reaver's eyes were still narrowed. 'That too could be a lie,' he said.

Lorn reached up, pulled down his shirt to show the healed scar, looked up again and met the man's eyes and held them. '*This* was not,' he said. '*I* came back. Your people went by another road. But they live. Send, and see.'

Fear and anger were fighting in the Reaver's eyes. '"Your own" – what gives you right to keep all the good for yourselves, to shut us out for ever? Our beasts have little, our children die; here the grass is green and the sun is warm, so why must we die and you live? Rather than that I will make *you* die – or perhaps I will not, myself, but my sons will, and their sons – and then those who are left will yield up the green places to *us*, and we will have our share—'

Lorn's heart was beating fast with anger and fear. *And so we are no further along than we were before. Back to driving them out, killing them, being killed, the fields burning—*

—and the image came to him; riding out in this part of the world with his father, a long, long time ago. Far south-eastern Arlen, the green fields of it in the summer, stretching miles and miles to the foothills of the mountains. But nothing *but* grass would grow there, and the green fields were too far away from any settlements to support the sheep that could have grazed there – by the time they were walked back to civilization, all the fat would be walked off them and they would be lean and ill. 'It'll be many years before this part of the world has enough people living in it to make it *worth* living in,' his father had said, 'and nothing we can do about it but keep the land safe for the Goddess, and wait Her time—'

'Listen to me,' Lorn said to the Reaver, his voice so calm it surprised even him. 'What you say has truth about it. Why *should* we have all the green country?' Out of the corner of his eye he saw Eftgan's eyes flick towards him. He made no sign. 'In the south and east of my own country,' he said, 'there is empty land that my people cannot use, for it's too far from where most of us have come to live. Tell me if it's as I think, that you do not sow fields, to grow grain? You only pasture sheep and cattle?'

'Grow – grain?' the man said, bewildered again.

Oh, Goddess, thank you— 'Never mind,' Lorn said. 'Those empty lands I told you of: they are wide, none of my people live nearby. Once I have my own back, I will give them to you.'

Eftgan shifted in the saddle. Lorn ignored her.

'Give—' the man said.

'You and your people may be there, as many of you as can be supported by your horses and sheep and cattle,' Lorn said. 'That land is wide. You must promise that your riders will not come into the settled lands where my people are. But that land will be yours to move through, yours and your people's, always. And should you become hungry, if the land fails you, we will find other ways to help you.'

The Reaver looked suspicious again, but this time the fear seemed to be ebbing out of his eyes. 'If this is a true offer,' he said slowly, 'those for whom I speak would help you take back "what is yours". Even the others never made us so fair an offer.'

The others? No, later— Lorn breathed in, breathed out, shook his head. 'No. Forgive me, but you must return to your own place for the moment. Or if you like, remain here, but help no-one. I and the – others – must settle our own affairs without the help of strangers.'

The Reaver chieftain was silent for the space of a few breaths. 'And you,' he said to Eftgan, 'do you also say this?'

'At another time, I may,' she said. 'For now I say that what my brother promises, that he will perform, and that I will help him perform, inasmuch as I can.'

The Reaver looked at them both for a long few moments, his face grim, but no longer angry. Finally he nodded. 'This must be thought on,' he said. 'I will send, first, to see what is true about our own people. Should I and my comrade-chiefs find you truthful . . . then here we will stay, and wait.'

Eftgan nodded at that. 'I will send you a messenger in some days, if I may, to see how you are getting along.'

The Reaver bowed in the saddle – a quick gesture, but courteous enough – and turned his pony and rode off. His group gathered around him, and followed him away.

Eftgan and Freelorn watched them go. Eftgan was shaking her head. 'This has been one of my more interesting mornings in this world,' she said. 'Lorn, you asked him some of the right questions, and I was able to see some interesting answers in his head. They don't understand the idea of owning land at all, I don't think. They don't understand houses, or being tied to one place – and as you found, they don't understand farming. No wonder they never looted the fields, only burnt them. To try to make the people settled there move away, I suppose, so that the land could be returned to grazing, which the Reavers understood.' Eftgan shook her head. 'These people . . . are as we were, a long time ago, after the Darkness fell, but before the Dragons came . . .'

Freelorn nodded. 'Now all I have to do is win my kingdom back,' he said, 'and give a third of it to them . . .'

'Yes,' Eftgan said, throwing him a peculiar look, 'I doubt my people would be happy with the offer, either. Better you than me, brother. Nonetheless, it was an offer that needed making – and if you had not, I think I would have had to. He was quite right; we have no right to our plenty while they starve. Sometimes the Goddess speaks to us unusually clearly . . .'

Eftgan tugged at the reins and turned Scoundrel back towards her own people. Lorn followed her, musing. 'Hunger,' he said. 'Did we ever seriously consider that as a reason that they kept coming back again and again? Or did we always prefer to think that they were just a herd of bloodthirsty brigands?'

Eftgan shook her head. 'It would certainly be easier to get people to fight them if a ruler pretended not to know otherwise. Whether any other Darthene or Arlene kings or queens have had such suspicions . . . it's hard to tell. But *we* do, now.'

He nodded. 'You ought to head home,' he said to Eftgan – forced himself to say to her – and reached out a hand. She took it, slid it up the forearm so that they gripped each halfway up the other's arm; the warrior's grip, or the king's.

'Go safe,' she said, 'and go always with Her.'

'She's always here anyway,' Lorn said. 'As for my half of it—' He shrugged. 'I'll do what I can. Meantime, you be careful too. And if you hear from Herewiss—'

Eftgan said nothing, just nodded, then turned and rode away to her waiting people.

Lorn turned his back on her, and nudged Blackmane with his heels. 'On the road again, my lad,' he said, and let the gelding take his own way through the bracken and the jutting stones, eastward, towards the low hills and the distant Arlid. In a soft clangour of pots, Pebble came pacing after them on his lead rein. Lorn only turned once, after a while, and saw the flash of something diamond-hafted held up under the noon sun. Lorn waved in that general direction, unable to make out figures distinctly. Another flash, blue this time, and then the only light left was the everyday light of the sun on the heather and the stones.

He turned again, and rode east.

5

Iha'hh irik-kej ahaa taues'ih ohn taue-stihé hu.

The only thing more to be feared than a great
desire is that same desire come true.

Dracon proverb

'I plan to fly,' she had said, so offhandedly. Being more
than half-Dragon, these days, she thought she might as
well. Now Segnbora flew, and shook her head at her own
naivety, for she had never thought it would be so complicated.

How many times in the old days, when she had merely
been a sorceress, did she look up at birds and think, *What
a marvel to do that. And how easy it looks.* And so it did; a
flick of the wings, the wind to bear you up, freedom to
soar. Well, freedom there was, now, but not in the shape
that she had ever expected. There was a strange body to
manage, with its own habits and prerogatives. Well, not
exactly strange; no Dracon body would ever be strange to
her, inside or out, now that she was 'outdweller', *sdaha*, to
Hasai.

She glanced over at Hasai as she soared. They were
flying slowly, for pleasure's sake. Rushing would not
profit them in the slightest at this point, and there had
been little enough time to fly for pleasure since she had
broken through into her Power. Hasai was in slow-flight
extension, his wings at full spread, not moving. A Dragon,
Segnbora had found, rarely needed to move its wings

except when landing, to brake – an old habit, even that not entirely necessary. Using the wings to push against air was the least part of flying, for a Dragon. Once upon a time, back in the dim times on the Homeworld, when Dragon-kind was young and inexperienced, it had been the most important part. But now, for most of their flying, Dragons propelled themselves using forces that the world itself bred in its turning – invisible lines that stretched north to south, as well as other lines more local, and more tenuous but more powerful forces that started where the air gave out and had to do with the sun, and the moon and the other worlds that went around it.

Other worlds, she thought, shaking her head slightly. There was soft laughter from some of her *mdeihei* in the background. They found it mildly funny that the humans of the Middle Kingdoms didn't even know about the other planets in their solar system. Segnbora had not even known what a solar system was, until Hasai suddenly became her *mdaha* and changed almost everything in her world.

Nor had she known about what flying took; but she was learning, in short order. She had a chorus of hundreds of breathy, rumbling, echoing voices singing in the back of her mind, now; all Hasai's linear ancestors, all of them *mdahaih*, 'indwelling' – physically dead, but nonetheless alive inside her, and vocal – and all commenting in intricately interwoven melody on her skill, or lack of it.

She sighed a soft chord to herself and looked over at Hasai again. He had an eye on the countryside below them, seemingly watching the patchwork fields and clumps of forest go by. 'Where are we?' she said to him.

The *mdeihei* sang amusement. Hasai ignored them and made a picture in her head, a map on a large scale, showing her Arlen and the bulge of the North Arlene peninsula, the winding course of the Arlid River through it all, and a tiny, tiny bright point that was them, a specific height above the earth – all in scale. It still astonished her that Dragons could imagine such *large* things. But then they were none too small themselves.

'You'll learn to do it soon enough yourself,' Hasai said. 'There is Aired Marchward, see, there not too far from Prydon.'

'Another hour,' Segnbora said.

'At this speed,' Hasai said after a moment. He was still having trouble with the human idea of hours, the 'divided day', as he called it; but having Segnbora as *sdaha*, he was getting the idea quickly enough.

'There are no human MarchWarders there, are there . . .'

'None,' Hasai said. 'The *rhhw'ehhrveh* have been dwindling away, in recent times. When we first came, the Dwellers at the Howe thought it would be good to know humans from youth, and live with them, to see what kind of world this was and how we might live in it best. And indeed some humans sought us out. But the human MarchWarders' houses have not prospered, by and large. Some said this was because our minds were not meant to work in the same way, and we damaged the humans by living and associating with them.'

There was a rumble of agreement from some of the *mdeihei*; Segnbora could feel others, back in the deeps of her mind, looking on silent and uncertain, an uneasy shifting of shadow and subdued gemlight. 'The only Marchwards that have *rhhw'ehhrveh* as well as *lhhw'ehhrveh* any more are High Cirr and dra'Mincarrath,' Hasai said. 'No point in going down there just now. The Warders at Aired have ties with the DragonChief; our energies are better spent there, I think.'

'All the same, I should like to meet one or two of the *rhhw'ehhrveh*,' Segnbora said. She was curious about what it must be like to have learned the ways and language of Dragons slowly, over a childhood, instead of suddenly, over a matter of days, as she had. What could it be like to be a companion to Dragons, but still human? She started to make a wry face at the thought that any days of simple humanity, for better or worse, were behind her now. But her Dragon's face wouldn't do it, and simply dropped its jaw in the gesture that meant humour, and invited another Dragon nearby to enquire as to the source.

Hasai, being *mdahaih*, didn't need to enquire, but dropped his jaw as well. 'How are you doing?' he said. '*Sdaha* or not, that form can't be quite comfortable for you yet.'

She snorted, a shrug, felt the cushioning of an updraft increasing under her, and stretched her wings out a bit more to get the best out of it. 'Learning,' she said. 'This is a lazy body.'

'Lazy!' Hasai said, and laughed, in an indignant basso profundo rumble like a distant earthquake.

'Very lazy! You saw that, just then. There's plenty of sun even with the cloud today, no need to use anything but force to fly; but come any updraft stronger than a sneeze, and "aha!", says the body, "a chance not to have to work!"'

'Why waste energy?' Hasai said, putting his wings out more fully as well, and absently gaining some tens of ells of altitude, so that Segnbora had to grasp force and pull herself up beside him again. 'See that?' Hasai said. 'You had to work to catch me up. And I did nothing but add some extension. *You* simply have this idea that flying is work, or ought to be. You're going to have to get rid of that, if you're to be a Dragon in truth, and not some kind of hybrid . . . as the gossip will have it if we're not careful.'

Segnbora cocked her head at Hasai. 'What's wrong with being some kind of hybrid?' she said.

A long low rumbling chord of protest went up from some of the *mdeihei*. 'Oh, be still,' Segnbora said, annoyed. 'When I want your advice, you lot, I'll ask for it.' The *mdeihei* might be wise with the accumulated wisdom of thousands of years, but they also tended to be conservative – too much so for Segnbora's taste, sometimes. 'New things are happening here, and none of you have had a new idea since you were last *sdahaih*! So listen to *this* end of history for a change, and see if you can't learn something!'

A shocked silence fell within her, for the *mdeihei* were not used to being told off by one *sdahaih* to them. The *sdaha*, the physically alive Dragon at the 'near' end of the ancestry, was supposed to be properly submissive to the *mdeihei*, and appreciative of their advice. *Well, about time they learned that I don't intend to handle things that way*, Segnbora thought. '*Sithesssch*,' she said to Hasai, who was laughing softly, 'hybrid may be the word that fits, whether we like it or not. Are the Dragons, the *live* dragons, really likely to find it so much of a problem?'

Hasai laughed softly, being amused himself by the sudden silence, but did not answer directly. He tilted his wings off leftwards, banking suddenly, and Segnbora did the same and followed him around and downwards. 'One of our line was at the last *nn's'raihle*,' he said. 'You remember.'

Segnbora looked back into the dark place at the back of her mind, the 'cave' where the *mdeihei* lived, and saw burning red-amber eyes looking back at her, the Dragon in question. 'Ashadh, of course,' she said, and reached back in mind and folded Ashadh's dark wings and star-ruby hide around her, and lived in the memory again. Against a night sky all torn with flying moonlit cloud and fitful stars, the mountain-shape of the Eorlhowe reared up, and its stones were washed with Dragonfire as two bright shapes at its base circled one another in stately dance – or dance that looked stately until the claws flashed out to tear. The old Dweller-at-the-Howe leapt, talons out, flaming, and was met halfway by the slender, big-winged form that seized him about the throat and let him thrash and struggle. Then a vicious flurry of motion— Nothing but Dracon talons can rip a Dragon's stony hide; but rip it will. Llunih, the old Dweller, came crashing to the ground, and then came the fire. A moment later his body was ash and charred bone, he himself was gone *mdahaih*, and Dithra d'Kyrin was *lhhw'Hreiha* in his place.

Part of Segnbora wanted to shudder at the matter-of-fact way the Dragons assembled there took it all. But

Ashadh, who had been there, and the parts of her mind that were beginning to think in the Dracon fashion, saw nothing at all unusual in this. Llunih had begun an argument, and had been unable to prove his case beyond reasonable doubt. His dance had been insufficiently complex, his song too simplistic; and one with a more subtle argument had found the heart of his error, and ended it. That was the way Dracon logic perceived the change in leadership. The fittest, the wisest, came inevitably to lead. All Llunih's knowledge passed to Dithra, and all his power as DragonChief.

'And the argument,' Segnbora said to Hasai, 'was about whether it might not be wiser to cast the human MarchWarders out of the Wards altogether . . .'

'So it was.'

'So weird mixtures of Dragon and human are unlikely to be welcome when even plain humans aren't. I thank you for the memory, Ashadh,' Segnbora said, and Ashadh slipped free of her, and bowed and veiled himself in shadow again.

'Dithra was always a hard reasoner,' Hasai said, as he straightened out his line of flight again, passing by a great bank of thundercloud on one side, and Segnbora matched him. 'Now that she is *lhhw'Hreiha*, nothing has changed in that regard. And she has the power of the office to make her feel that much more certain of her opinions. Dangerous enough, that situation. But the DragonChief's certainty is not entirely a matter of her own strength of character. Much of it comes from the *mdeihei* – not only her own, but those of all the rest of Dragonkind. She knows the Draconid Name, the Name by which the Immanence called our people when we were first made, passed down through all these years from Chief to Chief. Every *mdaha* is *mdahaih* to her, as well as to its own *sdaha*.'

'Even you,' Segnbora said.

'Even I,' Hasai said. 'At least, so it ought to be. I—' The human personal pronoun was coming easier to him of late, and Segnbora was not sure whether to be pleased at this, or alarmed. '—I am no longer quite what I was even a few "tendays" ago. But for the moment, my connection to the *Hreiha* feels as it did. I remain, as before, one of her memories – if a living one – as I am one of yours. She can call me up at will, live in my life as you lived in Ashadh's just now, and dismiss me when she pleases. Any Dragon-Chief might do as much, of course. Not that a *Hreiha* tends ever to *do* much of anything . . . except when in *nn's'raihle*, as you just saw. She will argue for or against what concerns her – and one in possession of the Draconid Name can "kill" the *mdahaih* as easily as the *sdahaih*.' *Rda-é* was the word he used, the active verb form of the rarely used Dracon word for permanent death. It was the only time Segnbora had ever heard him use it in connection with himself or any other Dragon. Even *mdahhej*, the death of the physical body, only meant shifting one's mode of living in the world. To go *rdahaih* was to become nothing, to be utterly destroyed: or to die as humans were considered to die.

She shook her head. 'And you think we might be on the wrong side of the argument from the start . . .'

Hasai sighed, a long single note of uncertainty and concern. 'We will not be able to tell until we start having it,' he said, 'and by that time, it will be too late. But the signs don't seem good.'

They flew in silence for a while. Segnbora cast an eye down on the fields, now shading from the green of late-planted barley and oats to stands of yellower corn as they began to come out of the wetter lowlands of southern Arlen into the drier country to the north. 'Do you think it would be wiser to stay out of the argument entirely?' Segnbora said. 'Is that what you're trying to tell me?'

'I think perhaps we are in the argument already,' Hasai said. 'Already a Dragon has interfered in human affairs . . . as you pointed out.' He sounded rueful. 'Anyone *sdahaih* to me has only to live in my memories to discover that.'

'Such as the Dweller.'

Hasai shrugged his wings in agreement. 'Word will have come to her by now, from other sources. Sd'hirrin and Lhhaess, the MarchWarders at Aired, keep a close eye on the doings in Prydon since things changed seven years ago; and they are close in the counsels of the Dweller because of it. Also, they are related. They come of Dahiric's line, as does she.'

Segnbora sang a low note that was as close as a Dragon came to a sigh. The Worldwinner's line were not directly descended from Dahiric, of course, since he had died at the end of the Crossing, scarcely more than a dragonet. The line was collateral, descended from other children of his parents, most of whom had borne the same livery of green scales and golden underbelly. And an oddly high percentage of Dwellers had been of his line—

Then Segnbora shut her jaws with a snap, and looked over at Hasai. He was looking at her with an odd expression somewhere between amusement and unease. 'Yes,' he said. 'I was going to ask you why you had chosen that particular livery to embody in when you flew. Some might call it impertinence. Especially Dithra.'

Segnbora shook her head, a totally human gesture which the *mdeihei* derided good-naturedly in the background. 'It seemed natural,' she said. 'I don't know. It happened accidentally, the first time—'

Fire rose in her throat, the closest Dracon equivalent to blushing. 'When you first became truly one of us,' Hasai said, 'and got me with child. Yes.' He looked sidelong at her, tilted sideways, and abruptly dropped beneath her, doing the first quarter of a most precise hesitation roll, so that they briefly flew belly-to-belly in what for Dragons was a slightly naughty gesture. 'Well, we shall assume that the Immanence had a hand in it, and say no more. And let those who say "hybrid" look to their own liveries, none of them so noble as mine, or yours. As for the rest of it—' He righted himself and sang the same sighing notes Segnbora had. 'We shall make ourselves known to Sd'hirrin and Lhhaess as best we can, and answer their questions.

Sooner or later they will discuss us with the Dweller. We cannot just fly up to the Eorlhowe and melt our way in, after all. We will be sent for. And then—'

'We try to survive, and get help for Lorn,' Segnbora said. Suddenly it sounded less likely than it had in Blackcastle.

'Yes,' Hasai said, gazing ahead of them. Another thunderstorm reared up there in their path, towering upward in piles of blinding white until it flattened out into a tattering anvil of grey a thousand yards higher. 'And meanwhile,' he said, grasping force and folding his wings back for better airspeed, 'we *live*.' And he shot straight ahead into the storm, vanishing into the threatening whiteness as if through a wall.

The cloud flickered abruptly from inside – a hotter white within the chill dead-white of the mist – with the crash of provoked thunder following a second later. Segnbora's jaw dropped in a smile; she folded her wings, sank the claws of them into the forces of the world, and like a second arrow fired from the same bow, followed him in.

She already knew what Aired Marchward looked like, for various of her *mdeihei* had been there on business, or socially. The Arlid this far north was an old gentled-down river like the Darst, slow and oxbowed, bending on itself again and again in loop after loop, detouring around many small hills. One bend of the river held a particularly high hill in it, tall and conical, grassy-sloped, with a cracked stony head where even the grass gave out in a slope of grey granite and scree. Down at the hill's foot, above the river, was a great dark vertical rift in the hillside, some ten or twenty ells wide. Water trickled down to the river from it from some spring inside the mountain, and growing things made a green tongue trailing down the watercourse from the hill's open mouth.

They circled the hill several times, knowing they were watched, letting themselves be well seen. There was nothing in the world that was big enough to be a threat to a Dragon, of course, but all the same old traditions established on the Homeworld had to be observed. For creatures who might live some thousands of years before dwindling away into the final silence of the oldest *mdeihei*, courtesy was all-important; and for a species that had come so close to extinction, survival was more important even than courtesy.

Segnbora gazed down at Aired with interest. For some reason, those of her *mdeihei* who had visited there had done so in winter – perhaps to avoid too many humans seeing them. All their memories of that part of the Arlid valley were of a river frozen and buried under snow, a mere curving hint that water lay underneath, mostly traceable by where plants and trees were not, and by the faint dark scratch-lines of frozen reeds upthrust through the snow. But now birds perched and sang in those reeds, and the water glittered, and warm sun and cool shade slid over the hillside.

'I think we've seen enough,' Hasai said. 'Let us go down.'

Segnbora tilted her head in agreement. Together they planed down, matching movements without effort, being *sdaha* and *mdaha* after all, but still with some care, with the turns of wing and limb that said they were on joint business, and in agreement with one another. This was another of the matters of being Dracon that Segnbora was still handling with some care: movement, and its many complex meanings. She might talk lightly to Lorn of *nn's'raihle* being dance and argument and legislation all in one, but there was a bit more to it than that. Dragons had not always had speech. In their earliest days, there had been only movement as sign of intention or desire. Sung language might have been invented since, and then later yet the speech of the mind discovered – but the older mode of communication had never been supplanted by them, only augmented. *Nn's'raihle* itself came originally of that oldest tongue, the speech-by-dance, *ehhath*; the acts of

105

love were conducted in it, and the acts of death. Segnbora was new to it, despite all her *mdeihei*, and consciously kept her motions and positions in *chhath*'s older and more classical modes, just for safety's sake.

They landed with little fuss – a quick flare of wing to keep it elegant, and then a leisurely fold of the webbing to say that their business was important, but not instantly so – at least not by Dracon standards. Segnbora looked over at Hasai; his spines were all roused forward, an indication of general good humour. She wasn't nearly so certain herself, but she roused spines back at him regardless.

He dropped his jaw, then turned away and sang greeting at the cave-opening, a long low simple chord. Then they waited together. Segnbora did her best not to rustle.

There was movement inside the cave, and then a head put itself out of the opening, scattering rainbows in the sunshine from scales of the deepest blood-ruby Segnbora had ever seen. Eyes the same colour as the stars in the sapphire upper scales, a fierce glowing crimson, looked at them both with some interest.

Hasai shrugged wings and bowed his head in the greeting-mode that matched what he had sung; casual respect. Segnbora did likewise.

The other Dragon returned the gesture with an interested flick of wing added. 'Be greeted,' she said, the song winding around her words speaking of a bored host glad of visitors. 'Come in, if you will.'

'Gladly,' Segnbora said. The other Dragon – Lhhaess, she knew from her *mdeihei* – gave her a considering look as she turned back towards the cave, having noticed the 'thumb' spine to Segnbora's right wing, the 'false primary'. It was a black too deep for any normal coloration, and doubtless looked odd with the rest of her green-and-gold livery. Segnbora merely tilted her head a bit to one side, to acknowledge the look, and followed their hostess in.

The inside of the hill was not as dark as it might have been. There were crevasses high up in the hillside, which had been quite effectively hollowed out and reinforced by melting the remaining stone into place, and long shafts of light came down to strike on the bare smooth floor. The other MarchWarder, Sd'hirrin, lay curled there in one shaft of light, and rose courteously to greet them; a Dragon of unusual size, almost a quarter again as big as Hasai, and liveried in star-amethyst and onyx, with violet-burning eyes.

'Sd'hirrin,' Hasai said, 'well met again.'

Sd'hirrin looked at Hasai mildly. 'Surely we have not met,' he said. 'Perhaps our *mdeihei* have.'

'Oh, no,' Hasai said. 'I came here last some ninety rounds of the sun ago. Surely you remember; it was after Dithra took office.'

Sd'hirrin and Lhhaess looked at each other, then back at Hasai again. 'That was Hasai ehs'Pheress,' Lhhaess sang, surprised. 'Doubtless you are of collateral line, but—'

'There *was* no collateral line,' Hasai said, and dropped his jaw. 'You know that. My dam and sire hatched no other egg after me, and I never mated. At least, not before casting the last skin.'

The two MarchWarders looked at Hasai most dubiously. He had used one of the more casual idioms for physical death.

'Hasai ehs'Pheress went *mdahaih*,' Sd'hirrin sang, with overtones that said he thought perhaps some game was being played with him, and he didn't care for it. 'I have *mdeihei* in common with his line, and word spread—'

'So it should have. And I did go *mdahaih*. Indeed, I almost went *rdahaih* instead; it was a close thing. But I found a *sdaha* at last. Or she found me.'

The MarchWarders looked at Segnbora, now. Sd'hirrin's look was suspicious, as well it might have been, as he looked at a Dragon he had never seen before – and almost all Dragons knew almost all other Dragons on sight, there being few enough of them in the world. But then his look, and Lhhaess's, went back to Hasai in bewilderment.

'You are too much here to be *mdahaih!*' Lhhaess said, sounding slightly indignant as well as confused. 'You are physical!' The word she used was *dav'w'hnesshih*, there-enough-to-bite, one of the words used only of Dragons or other living beings still in their original bodies. And indeed, standing there in the downpouring noon-light from the cracks in the hilltop, Hasai was quite physical enough to cast a shadow, which no *mdaha* should have been able to do, no matter how vigorously he was manifesting.

'*Auhé*,' Hasai said, shrugging one wing, 'it's my *sdaha*'s fault, I suppose. She has never been one for following tradition; some days I despair of her.'

Segnbora caught the sidelong look in Hasai's eye. She stretched her wings up and bent her head down somewhat lower than Hasai had, the properly respectful gesture of a younger Dragon among elder ones – but with a slightly insouciant sidewise tilt to her head which indicated, youth aside, that her and the others' relative ranks would have to be worked out later. 'Segnbora d'Welcaen,' she said to them. And then when she saw Sd'hirrin opening his mouth to say that that hardly sounded like a Dracon name, Segnbora shrugged out of the Dracon form as if out of a cloak, letting go the Firework that had been holding it in place, and stood in her own shape again. Skádhwë was in her hand, flaming blue: she sheathed it, watching with satisfaction as the Dragons gazed at her in astonishment.

'The Goddess's greeting to you, Lhhaess, Sd'hirrin,' she said; 'and my own with it.'

They stared at her, and then their heads swung as one to Hasai.

'You have gone *mdahaih* to a *human?*' Sd'hirrin said.

'It cannot be done,' Lhhaess said. But she was looking at Segnbora with less shock, now, and more curiosity.

'I took what life the Immanence sent me,' Hasai said mildly. 'It does not seem to have served me so badly.'

'I thought it couldn't be done, either,' Segnbora said, 'at least not and leave me sane. But it's been done, all right. I found Hasai going *rdahaih*, but he passed to me instead, and all his *mdeihei* with him. Which is going to eventually raise some questions for the *Lhhw'hei*.'

Sd'hirrin folded his wings right down, the gesture of a Dragon trying to show no outer reaction while it consolidated its thoughts. But Lhhaess said to Segnbora, 'We'd always thought that only a Dragon of one's own line could accept another as *mdaha* that way . . . if not an egg-child, at least a collateral relative . . .'

'We may be more alike than any of us thought,' Segnbora said.

'That can't be so—!' Sd'hirrin began to say, standing suddenly and spreading his wings right up to full extension in discomfort. But Lhhaess turned to him and said, 'Whether it can or not, what's come of our hospitality? For shame.' To Segnbora she said, 'Have you eaten and drunk? We have none of the kinds of things humans use, but we could find something in a short time, I think—'

'I took sun with Hasai on the way here, thank you,' Segnbora said, and smiled a bit at Sd'hirrin's nonplussed expression. Dragons lived off light, which they drank through the webs of their wings: it fuelled their Dragon-fire and helped them fly . . . and no mere sorcerer, no matter how talented, could change his or her body to such an extent as to eat sunshine. It would be one more thing for Sd'hirrin to think about. 'Perhaps we might go out and bask later. But business first.'

'What business?' Lhhaess said.

She had thought for a long time about how to best phrase this, and Hasai had been little help to her: Dracon protocol was mostly about temporizing. 'The business of Arlen. Being here as long as you've been, you can't help but have noticed the difference between things as they are the last seven years, and things as they were when there was a king in the land.'

'I have seen some thirty kings and queens here,' Sd'hirrin said. 'I saw Freolger fall off his horse, that great

109

fall that caused so much trouble with his ministers; I saw Faran the Seafarer go sailing away with her fleets that never returned, and Laeran the Young at the gates of Torth, hammering them down. I have seen kings hanged, and queens laid low by the plague, and enough bad times before that these look not so much different to me.'

'Then you should look harder,' Segnbora said. 'Sd'hirrin, all your years are impressive enough, but don't think to weigh down a mere human with awe of them; my *mdeihei* are as old as yours. You and they may both have seen the Worldwinning, but whether it's made all of you any wiser, who's to say? What *I've* seen is how time passes, or seems not to, for a Dragon who listens too closely to the voices of the past. Their advice will be no help to you against the trouble that's coming.' She took care to speak in the Dracon precognitive tense, the future certain, in which one could not lie, but could only speak truly about what she foresaw. She had seen the forthcoming trouble often enough now, in her own dreams, made sharper by her newfound Fire and Hasai's way of seeing the future whole, in terrible broad blurred glimpses marred only by being filtered through her too-human perceptions.

'What trouble?' Lhhaess sang, sounding disturbed.

'You've seen. The land doesn't bear much more than grass; the weather is misbehaving; the armies move; pestilence is rife, people are starving. And where *are* all the people who should be living here?' Segnbora said to Sd'hirrin. He had folded his wings down tight again. 'This was pastureland, once, and farm country. The hedgerows are still here, but not much else. Trees grow up through the barns; the herds are gone; the roads are all gone to grass. Where has your Wardship gone?' She used the oldest word, from the Homeworld, *lhhw'auviuh'thaeh*, life-guardian. 'Dragons settled here as MarchWarders to guard the *rhhw'hei* from the Dark, so it's always been said. Doing nothing about the forces that drive them away is a poor way to guard them!'

'Precipitate action is dangerous—' Sd'hirrin began. But

Lhhaess moved uneasily, and Segnbora knew that the argument that she and Hasai had had so often had been staged here as well. She was glad of it.

'Oh come,' Segnbora said. 'In a language where the words "to do" and "to be" are the same, that's a poor excuse. The Shadow is moving, Sd'hirrin! The same Shadow that fathered your old enemy the Dark, three thousand years ago, and killed half your people coming here: the same that snuffed your star out and sent you on this journey to begin with! Did you really think you would lose It in the dark? It's followed you here. It lives here as It does everywhere else in the Universe, right out to the place where even the stars' light can't flee from It any further. It tried the obvious moves, and lucky for you, they failed. It attacked you when you first came; the Messenger came and saved you. For a while. A scrap of the Dark lived to attack you again, and M'athwinn ehs'Dhariss of the Worldwinner's line killed it again; but she warned you that Its day was not done. Are you deaf even to your own people's prophecies? She said, "Its subtleties are many, and Its end is not yet". And that's all true. The Shadow has given up obvious attacks on this world. Now it attacks through humans. It's the Shadow that moves Cillmod's armies and policies. And you look aside, afraid, not wanting to be involved. For Its own defence the Shadow has inflamed your old fear of doing some harm to humankind – and so made certain that by inaction, you will!'

Sd'hirrin looked troubled, and subsided, but said nothing. Lhaess spread a wing out, a thoughtful look. 'Tell us then, *raihiw'sheh*,' she said, 'what you would see done.'

Segnbora smiled a small thin smile. 'Advocate', Lhhaess had called her, the name for one proposing an argument in *nn's'raihle*: the one who takes the prize, or pays the price, on winning or losing. 'To stop the famines and the wars at their source,' she said, 'the royal magics must be re-enacted by a properly enthroned Initiate. Arlen needs its king again. Before I became *sdahaih*, I was bound to the man who should be king; Freelorn, old King Ferrant's son. I'm bound to him still. He is moving to take back his own. But he'll need all the help he can get, for the Shadow sees the spoiling of Its plans in him, and wants him dead by any means. The forces of Darthen are moving to war against Arlen for the breaking of the ancient Oath. No war against them would work if the Dragons were with them – humans hold Dragons in such awe and fear. The threat of all Dragonkind roused would be something to give even the Shadow pause.'

Sd'hirrin and Lhhaess looked at him and were silent for a while, conferring in underspeech, Segnbora thought. At last Lhhaess said, 'You know we can give you no aid without the DragonChief's leave.'

'Neither of us would have asked any such thing,' Segnbora said.

'But eyes are of use,' Hasai said, 'and ears that hear others' songs.'

Sd'hirrin sang a brief chord of amusement. 'News there is in plenty,' he said. 'That we would give any Dragon that asked.' He looked slightly askance at Segnbora.

'Then let us stay a while,' Segnbora said, 'and hear the news. Hasai has been by himself a long while, away from the company of Dragons. I would be glad to hear what Dragons who aren't *mdaheih* to me sound like; new song is always welcome. And in time . . .'

'In time,' Sd'hirrin said. 'There is a great deal of that.'

Segnbora had thoughts on that subject. But she kept them to herself.

They spent some days there, talking to the March-Warders, hearing the news and telling it. What Hasai had said was true enough; Sd'hirrin and Lhhaess had been watching Prydon and all of northern Arlen closely, with something of the fascination of a small child watching a busy anthill. They gave them endless news about troop movements in and out of Prydon, all of which Segnbora passed on to Herewiss by mindtouch each evening. That at least was of interest. There was an ingathering going on, slow but steady, and some four thousand men were now quartered in Prydon who had not been there earlier in the summer. But when the Warders ran out of troop movements to report, all the talk turned to family histories, whose *mdeihei* knew whose, and who won what obscure argument however many years ago. For the first few days or so, it occasionally seemed to Segnbora that Dragons had never done anything *but* argue. She itched to be about something more productive, but Hasai kept quoting her the old proverb, '*Rrrh'n heih hw'haé ae-sta mnenhi'thae*'; 'water melts the stone just as well as Dragonfire does'. 'The fire is a good deal faster,' Segnbora would mutter at him. But she knew he was right.

She spent most of her time at Aired in Dracon form. It helped her to patience, since time flowed differently when one lived in a Dracon body – both more slowly and more intensely. It also meant that any hunger she might feel could be assuaged by lying out in the sun or flying above the cloud cover, drinking sunfire rather than raiding the bag of provisions that was all she had brought with her. And it meant that she could work on her *ehhath*. Her dance was still too stiff, her song-conversation too formal, and she knew it; but over a few days' chatting with Sd'hirrin and Lhhaess, Segnbora began to loosen up and feel herself more competent. She also started to become better at judging a Dragon's personality from its style of *ehhath* – useful knowledge, for Dracon faces are immobile, and personality and mood communicated themselves through *ehhath* more than any other way.

And then the morning came when she looked up into the hot blue sky and said to Lhhaess, who was basking nearby, 'We have incomers,' she said. 'Quite high up; they're just into the blue. Another black. And someone in Dahiric's livery . . .'

'With a black?' Lhhaess rose up and put her wings in order, gazing up into the sky herself. 'That would be

Hiriedh ehs'M'harat, then, in the Worldwinner's colours. And the black is probably Aivuh ehs'Rrhndaih.'

Segnbora shuddered all over as the *mnekh'eiea*, the ahead-memory, came over her – the sort of precognition that Dragons took for granted, and which had been plaguing her since she first became *sdahaih*. As usual, it brushed the hard-edged present aside as effortlessly as wind scattering dry leaves. Suddenly she found herself sitting beside a stream, in long grass, in her human shape. On one side of her was Hasai, and on the other, a dragon scaled in star-emerald and topaz. The other was bending down beside her and singing, low and distressed, 'I wouldn't have anyone else know of this, *aihesssch*: it's an embarrassment to me!' Segnbora heard herself say, lightly, 'It's our secret, then, Hiriedh.' But in the memory she knew she herself was distressed too, frightened of something that seemed about to happen, rushing toward her, inescapable; a huge and threatening change—

—and the memory was gone, and Segnbora would have breathed out in unnerved relief, if Dragons breathed. She looked over at Hasai, and he looked back unconcerned. He had not seen what she had.

Her *mdeihei* rumbled in the background, a sound of vague upset. Segnbora ignored them. She had heard that rumble every time over the past few days that some curious Dragon came to look over the strange half-human-half-Dracon creature, or creatures, staying at Aired. Quite a few Dragons had come and gone, in every size and livery that could be imagined. Some had been polite and inquisitive, some had been astonished, some outraged; some had peered and stared, and talked over their heads, as if Segnbora and Hasai had been beasts in a zoo. If the past couple of days had done anything for Segnbora's concept of Dragons as a species, they had changed it from a vague sense of great numbers, great age, and obscure nobility, to a concept of many individuals, some better or worse than others, and all simply and unpredictably Dracon. At first her own interest in the individual personalities had outweighed the personalities' reactions. But now she was bored with it all. And at the same time, curious: for many of the Dragons had showed an odd combination of fascination with them, and what looked like much-repressed fear. *Fear of what?* Segnbora had wondered, and wondered again now. *We're no threat. Yet there was always that look about them – of a Dragon remembering-ahead, remembering something that will harm it some day.* The same sort of ominous memory, actually, as she had just had . . .

Segnbora put the thought aside for the time being, for there was no use trying to deal with *mnekh'eiea* while other things were busy happening. She got up and put her wings up in the proper gesture of welcome, and glanced over at Hasai. He was wearing the same manner, but there was something uneasy about the curve of his tail. She sang a soft chord's worth of sigh and turned to greet the visitors as they landed.

One of them indeed wore the Worldfinder's livery, like Segnbora's, but not quite so vivid in colour – the paler colour of summer grass rather than spring's. That was the Dragon of her memory, Hiriedh, and she threw Segnbora an odd look while settling her wings. The other, Aivuh, like Hasai, went in black star-sapphires and rough grey-white diamond underneath, his spines and fangs all diamond; but the eyes were the same pallid golden colour as Hiriedh's, and looked at the two of them with cool assessment.

Lhhaess and Sd'hirrin came forward to meet them and make introductions, and this was done with all necessary courtesy as far as the naming of names went. Hasai gave Hiriedh a bow of surprising depth when he was introduced, making Segnbora wonder where they had met before. But he was keeping his thoughts to himself at the moment, and that made her wonder too.

Aivuh was looking Hasai over with that same considering look in his eyes, glancing from Hasai to his shadow under the sun. There was no return of Hasai's bow, nor any for Segnbora. 'It's as we heard,' he sang in a voice surprisingly light and soft for his size, which was almost that of Sd'hirrin. 'You are *dav'w'hnesshih* indeed.'

'My solidity,' Hasai sang back, rather dryly, 'seems to have become a favourite topic of late. It may come of going *mdahaih* in a younger world. Or to younger *sdeihei*.'

'Llunih went *mdahaih* so,' Hiriedh said, in a light voice much like Aivuh's, 'and could never manifest enough to cast a shadow, let alone bite or be bitten – not though it was the Dweller herself he went *mdahaih* to.' She looked over at Segnbora again. 'I rather think your *rhhw'ae* here has something to do with it. Some one of their magics, perhaps.'

Segnbora dropped her jaw slightly. *Your 'humaness' here*, Hiriedh had said, using the courtesy form of the species-pronoun that Dragons applied to human beings. Unfortunately the pronoun was nearly the same as the one Dragons used for inanimate objects and animals. 'We have a few magics of our own, it's true,' Segnbora said, singing as dry and slow as Hasai, and bowing moderate respect; if others were rude, that didn't mean she had to be. 'As you will have noticed from the doings down by Bluepeak Marchward, and the changes in the mountains there. But no, not in this case; I doubt sorcery or even Fire could have managed what Hasai did by himself. I assumed he simply wanted to *live* . . . more than is usual for Dragons.'

The word she used was *iuh-kej* – the term for life in its active sense, doing rather than just being. There were Dragons who felt using the word too freely, or without qualification, was in bad taste, and the look Hiriedh turned on Segnbora now seemed to indicate she was one of these.

'How would you know what is usual for Dragons?' she said coolly. She had not settled herself, as even Aivuh had, but was pacing slowly up and down the stones near the riverbank, her tail wreathing and working slowly.

She ignored them again, but the pacing was making her twitch. She started to pace too, paralleling Hiriedh. *At*

116

least it's something to do while I think . . . 'One doesn't have to count one's scales to know if one has a hide,' Segnbora said, keeping the response cool herself. 'Only look at me, Hiriedh.'

Hiriedh did, and looked away again, as if seeing something most unpleasant. 'The sorcerers of the *rhhwhei* can do such things,' she said, her tail lashing now, 'changing their shapes to those of birds or beasts, or even other humans – taking their shapes and voices. There should be no difficulty for a talented sorceress to manage being a Dragon for short periods—'

Segnbora laughed out loud, a long triple-toned hiss, and kept on pacing, closer to Hiriedh now; she matched the other's tail-lashing with good-natured curves of her own. 'If I were just a talented sorceress,' she said, 'I might manage a short period of such change, yes, before having to take to my bed for a month. An hour of this, two hours, would kill me. And no amount of mere sorcery could give me this.' She dropped her jaw wider, smiling harder in the Dracon manner – but the dull, reflected glow of Dragon-flame was clearly visible way down in her throat. 'What must I melt for you, Hiriedh? Or must I do something less subtle?' She stretched her neck out towards Hiriedh's lashing tail; her jaws snapped hard as the tail whipped out of her way – just.

Segnbora paused, her neck curving around to keep her gazing at Hiriedh. She kept her jaw dropped down in good humour. '*Dav'w'hnesshih* indeed,' she said, 'and not just Hasai, either. But I think I don't need to prove what my fangs are made of. I am Dracon, Hiriedh.'

Hiriedh paused, then started pacing again. Her wings were starting to cock upward in the forward-spread mode of one threatening, or meaning to threaten, with the terrible razory wing-claws. 'That must yet be seen,' Hiriedh said. 'Shape is not everything. Surely you have been human enough, of late, when you wish to be.'

'Old habits are hard to break,' Segnbora said. 'And the Goddess made me so: it would be discourtesy to throw that self away completely, seeing that She spent some years on it.'

Hiriedh was pacing closer. Her jaw was dropped open too, now, and Dragonflame showed as Segnbora had showed it; but the position of her wings made the smile a threatening, scornful one. 'Then you admit you cannot be Dracon,' she said, 'for even humans raised with Dragons all their lives cannot master our language, or even the voice with which it's spoken. They cannot see time as we see it, or the world.'

Segnbora shifted her pacing into a slow circle around the other, as Hiriedh had begun doing. It was surprisingly taxing to have to interact this way with someone who was going to be close enough friends with you, some time sooner or later, that she would be telling you her darkest secrets; especially when she was hostile and suspicious now, not having had any of the same ahead-memories. But *mnekh'eiea* was like that sometimes, and this was one of the things that gave Dracon interactions their spice – possibly a blessing in disguise, when too often the rest of the time you knew exactly what the other was likely to say. She shut her jaws; what smiling had been in her to start with was ebbing away.

'Hiriedh,' Segnbora sang, letting the growing complexity of the note make it plain that finding a Dracon voice was not a problem for her, 'I see time and the world well enough. I see what is coming, though dimly just now; maybe my humanity causes that dimness. Whether it'll last, who can say? But I do well enough to have *mnekh'eiea* of you, for example. I see us sitting by some riverbank, and Hasai is there, and you are telling me—'

'No!' Hiriedh cried, and Segnbora fell silent in shock. No Dragon had ever interrupted her before, not even the *mdeihei*; it was one of those things that wasn't done. Hiriedh's wing-claws came right about to point at Segnbora, as pace by pace she stalked towards her. For the first time, then, Segnbora wondered: *Just how tough is this hide? Will the Fire give me any advantage? What a time to have to find out* . . . But another thought occurred. *This is the fear – the same odd reaction as all the other Dragons have had, that they tried to hide. But Hiriedh has no need to hide it. Or has some other reason for not hiding it.*

Perhaps is unable *to hide it—*

The *mdeihei* were roaring inside her in anger. Segnbora had rarely heard them in such an uproar. 'You cannot!' Hiriedh hissed, pacing towards Segnbora. 'All you have is the memories of your *mdeihei*. Not one of them is yours! You can remember nothing without help! You are *not* Dracon—'

As Hiriedh came at her, Segnbora had been keeping up her circling, slow as a sorcerer setting the wards, trying desperately to keep her *ehhath* cool and proper. But now something snapped. Now she flung her wings up, and cocked their barbs forward at Hiriedh. 'In all the Immanence's Names,' Segnbora roared, 'what must I be to please you? *Here* is what I remember—!'

She lifted the blue-flaming shadow-talon that was Skádhwë, in this shape, and called on the Fire. It was the least kind of Firework to gather their minds in, Hiriedh's, and Aivuh's, yes, and Lhhaess's and Sd'hirrin's too – let there be no doubts about what Hiriedh would be seeing. And Hasai's – but he was there already, for the moment just one more voice of the *mdeihei* again.

Here is what I remember! she said.

Hiriedh was struggling, but it didn't matter; she was held hard. Segnbora gripped her in mind, with talons and tail and pierced through with Skádhwë's power, her Power. And she remembered. The world fell away, replaced by another; red stone, a dusky red sky darkening to black. Behind it sank an old pinkish sun; over it rose a great whirlpool of stars. But all the splendour of the light was a deception, for the world was dying, shaken by terrible tremors that threatened to rip it apart. Faintly lit by the light of the great pool of stars in the distance, thousands of small shapes went streaming away from the world that had given them birth, out

119

into the dark, mourning their old home, hunting a new one.

Behind them, the old pink star glowed pinker, and whiter, and white, too white to look at. It swelled, and burst, and reached out with its fires, and ate the Homeworld. All Dragonkind were orphaned in a day.

But there was one of them who had *mnekh'eiea*, and knew the way that they should go: the youngest of them, Dahiric. He remembered-ahead the small green planet with its golden sun. Some of the Dragons looked at his own livery, green scales, golden underside, and wondered to themselves. Dahiric never cared. He led them out into the dark between the stars.

There was no knowing how long they travelled that road. The oldest Dragons went *mdahaih* during it, and some of the second-eldest. But Dahiric never faltered; Something had told him the way. And finally they found the little yellow star—

—and found that something else lived on its third planet, and did not want them there.

Hiriedh was struggling still, and so was Aivuh, but it availed them nothing. Segnbora held them all in the past as if in amber, and inflicted memory on them, as dark as Skádhwë, and as sharp. *This I remember too*, she said, as they watched the formless blackness, like a horrible cloud, come boiling up off the planet to bar their way; intelligent, hating, murderous. Dahiric never hesitated, even at the sight of something so awful; he flew at it flaming and vanished into its bulk. And his body came floating out not long after, his Dragonfire all quenched, the life all gone out of him, not even *mdahaih* but *rdahaih*, lost to them for ever—

And this, she said, as the battle began, and went on and on, hopeless; as the space around the small green world began to fill with the corpses of Dragons gone *rdahaih*, all their Dragonflame spent in desperation, and wasted. Hope died, for there was nowhere else to go. The Dragons' strength had been sapped by their long journey; they needed sunfire to live, but the Dark was driving them out into the darkness again, and they would die slowly there—

The *mdeihei* sang dirges, and Hiriedh was frozen still with horror now, but Segnbora was past caring. *And this,* she sang, *this I remember too*—

—as the last moment came, the Dark spreading so wide that it hid the planet completely from their view, so close that it would engulf the last thousand or so of them. The DragonChief and the Eldest, those of them who still lived, did the only thing that they could; they gave up their lives to the Immanence, willingly, and convened Assemblage, speaking the Draconid Name in hopes of their people's salvation—

And light came. Right through them She plunged, a Dragon whose every scale was a point of light that burnt like a sun, and the webs of whose wings flamed searing white instead of black. The Dragons scattered, blinded and dazed, as the burning shape flew at the Dark, which reached up to swallow Her. She flamed, a blast like a star breathing out. The scream the Dark made echoed in every mind, as the Messenger closed with it, grappled with it, dragged it away howling from the blue world, out into the long night, Her light dwindling like a travelling star. The more keen-eyed who watched showed the others how that tiny point of light dragged the blackness into the yellow sun, and vanished with it.

Is that enough to remember? Segnbora said to the silent minds trapped inside her own. *Or how much further must I go back, how much of our history must I remember for you, and how much more of the Goddess's precious time must I waste on your unbelief?*

She let them go then. They reeled; so did she. The combination of the blue Fire of a trained adept in breakthrough, and Dracon memory, was more potent than Segnbora had suspected.

'Now,' she said to the crouching, scared Hiriedh, and the stunned Aivuh, 'I have had enough of your questioning.' Her tail was lashing, and her eyes were narrowed, and every fang was bared. The fire was broiling blue in her throat, and she didn't care if they saw it. 'You and all the others who have come to stare and consider everything so coolly, with all your *ehhath* in place. No more of it! The Messenger was sent you to bring you safe to this place, and all you did was dig snug caves in the world the Immanence has given you, and refuse to come out in the air and the light. Then the Advocate is sent you, in human form and Dracon, not once but many times, and you will not hear the message – to live here, and be part of the world, and involved with it. Well, I tell you, you *shall* hear this time: the Howe will ring with the choice to live, or to do nothing! And your wings will darken the sky – or something else will, and there will be no dawn after that darkness, and no way to fly above it and out into the starlight. The sky will be stone, and you in your graves, like Dahiric; and the Immanence will speak the Draconid Name, and no-one, not one of you, will answer!'

They stared at her, speechless.

And then Segnbora crouched down, swallowing her fire, suddenly both tired and embarrassed. The merely spoken mode of *mnekh'eiea* did not come upon a Dragon often, and Segnbora thought this was probably just as well. When speaking in that mode, one couldn't lie – but mere speech was not usually as revealing as image when it came to describing what was going to happen.

They stared at her still. Segnbora folded her wings down, and then threw the Dracon shape away and just sat there on the stone in her own body again, with her knees drawn up, and put her head down on her knees.

Hasai's shadow was over her, and his head bent down till she could feel the heat of the fire in his throat, burning through the hide. He was gazing at Hiriedh and Aivuh with poorly concealed rage. All their *mdeihei* were singing with a combination of shock and threat, an awful dissonance of anger. 'Go back to the Howe,' Hasai said, 'and say to the Dweller that we require her audience.'

122

'We were sent to bid you there,' Aivuh said, sounding subdued.

'So rudely?' Hasai said. 'No matter – we'll take that up with her. Go and tell Dithra that you've delivered her errand.' Hasai flattened his spines down and glared at them. 'We will come to the Howe when we're ready.'

Lhhaess and Sd'hirrin looked at one another in shock. When the DragonChief called a Dragon, that Dragon answered immediately. But both Aivuh and Hiriedh wore the wing- and limb-stances of Dragons who had been severely disconcerted, and were in no mood to try to assert any authority at all. Segnbora had been looking partly through Hasai's eyes, for the few moments she needed to gather her wits again. Now she looked up herself, and saw not just in Hiriedh's manner, but in Aivuh's too, the same odd combination of fear and yearning that she had seen in other Dragons who had come to see them in previous days. *What is it?* she thought, still shaken. *Why do they fear us? What is it we're going to do?*

Hasai had put a talon down beside her. Segnbora braced herself on it, pulled herself to her feet, and did her best to stand straight, for she was tired. '*Sehé'rae, lhhw'i'rae,*' Segnbora said to them, and bowed slightly.

They bowed back, the full bow with upraised wings that they had not vouchsafed her before. '*Sehé'rae, raihiw'sheh,*' Hiriedh said. And they raised wings, and flew upwards and northwards, and were gone.

Lhhaess and Sd'hirrin were looking at Segnbora and Hasai in concern. Hasai, though, was looking down at her with one great eye, a glint of humour and fear in it. '*Au sdaha,*' he sang, slow and amused, 'you hear what she called you.'

The Advocate is sent you, Segnbora heard herself singing, *and you will not listen . . .* She shook her head. 'We're really in trouble now, *mdaha,*' she said. 'The argument has started in earnest.'

'Your first *nn's'raihle,*' said Hasai. 'May its ending not end us as well.'

6

They tell the tale of the woman who went hunting the Goddess. She sought Her in waste places and the sides of mountains, in deserts and on the high fells, in the empty fields and by the shore of every Sea, and in every grand and terrible and lonely place; and she found Her not. And that woman returned in sorrow to her home, that was in Darthis city, and there was no food in the larder, and sorrowful still she went to market. In the market she stopped at a shrimp-seller's, and was picking over the shrimp, when she looked up and saw beside her a Woman wearing that Cloak which is the night sky, and with a basket over her arm, and bread in it and wine. And the woman looked at the Goddess in amazement, and the Goddess sighed and smiled, and said to her, 'It's such a nuisance, but sometimes you just have to go into town.' And She kissed the woman, and was gone . . .

Asteismics, 6

That night Herewiss dreamed, and oddly. This he was becoming used to, since the conduct of the world is not a simple matter, and the Goddess's messages about the business to human beings tend to reflect that complexity. Dreams are the quickest way for Her, better even than plain speaking, since in dream Her senses of eternal time and urgency are most closely matched by the dreamer's.

But perplexity came with the dreams regardless.

He was walking up a road that climbed along the shoulder of a hill. It was a narrow road, with old over-grown stone walls on either side of it, and hedge-bushes planted atop the walls to keep the cows and goats in. The thorny hedge was half again as tall as Herewiss was, so that he couldn't see past it, except for the occasional gap made in the hedging by some fox or hare. Bindweed and honey-suckle tangled in and out of the hedging, and the air was sweet with the smell of them; but strange sounds were coming from beyond the hedge, and he couldn't see what was making them. This made him nervous. Herewiss paused and turned to see if anyone was following him, but there was nothing in sight but the rutted dirt road. He turned again, and went on walking up the hill.

Towards the spot where the road crested, the hedging on either side gave way as the wall began to fall into ruin. He felt vague concern over the state of the wall: weren't the cattle going to get out? Wouldn't the goats be into the neighbour's garden? But there was no sign of cattle or goats, or gardens for that matter. He walked on past where the walls crumbled, and came to the shoulder of the hill.

There was a little house built there, fieldstone like the walls, with a slate roof; and off to one side, a small three-sided porch or shed. The smell of hot metal came from it, and the sound of blows. There was a man there, forging something.

Herewiss knew something of that work. He ambled over to the smithy to watch, and found the smith beating out something with a long thin blade, a scythe or reaping-hook. He was having a hard time of it: something wrong with the pincers, Herewiss thought, but at any rate the blade on the anvil kept slipping, and the smith's ham-merblows kept falling awry.

'Here, let me help,' Herewiss said, and went into the smithy. The smith, a big, broad-shouldered, grim-looking man, nodded and handed Herewiss the pincers. Herewiss took them two-handed and held the sickle hard and fair in the middle of the anvil, and the smith took his hammer two-handed and began making a fairer job of his forging.

They were at that work for some while, Herewiss relearning the shudder and jump of one's muscles when bracing against such heavy work, and the way you braced against them in turn to keep the twitching from ruining the work; and the way you had to pause, every now and then, to let the muscles rest. It came to Herewiss as he looked at the smith during one of these pauses that this was in fact the Goddess in disguise. Well, there was no particular surprise in that: She was disguised so in every human being – the problem being to keep reminding yourself of it.

The smith, of course, did not react to this discovery of Herewiss's, but went back to work. 'Here,' he said, 'turn it over.' Herewiss turned the blade and braced it again, and the smith began to beat out the blind edge.

'Harvest is coming on,' Herewiss said, by way of making conversation.

'So it is,' said the smith. He sounded regretful.

'A lot of work for you, then.'

'More than I want,' said the smith. 'It always is.' He stopped to look at the edge. 'Just a bit more. Then we'll have it in the fire again.'

Herewiss nodded and braced himself. All his muscles were beginning to complain now, but he kept them still as the smith worked his way down the scythe-blade to the socket end. It was a graceful sweep of metal now, not much like the lumpy thing it had been before he came along, and the much-beaten metal was beginning to shine. 'There,' said the smith. 'That should do.' He gestured with his head at the firepit.

Herewiss lifted the blade carefully with the pincers and turned to the pit. He noticed for the first time, now, that the fire in it was blue; but this seemed no surprise either. The smith was scuffling the coals about to make room to bury the scythe-blade in. Herewiss waited until he had a proper spot dug out, then laid the blade where it was wanted. The smith covered the blade over and began pumping at the bellows.

'You know,' he said between gasps of exertion – it was a large bellows, 'how we temper these.'

'Yes,' Herewiss said. 'Through the body, as a rule.'

'The heart works better,' said the smith, sounding sorrowful again. 'The blood leaps harder. And besides, make two of a heart, and strange things happen.' There was just a touch of mirth as he said it.

The smith worked the bellows until he was right out of breath, and Herewiss took a turn then, spacing his pushes against the lever as he had done in the old days, timing them with his breathing for the maximum effort. Finally, 'That's enough,' said the smith. He was feeling about in the coals with the pincers. 'Are you ready?'

'Yes,' Herewiss said, and a wash of awful fear went right through him from back to front as he saw that curve of metal come out of the coals, burning white. He braced himself against the frame of the forge as the smith reared back with it; and the smith's aim was good. Fire like the intensest cold went straight through his heart, so that Herewiss screamed and sagged, but somehow did not fall. The stink of burning flesh and cloth and leather was everywhere, and Herewiss looked down to see the socket-end of the scythe resting cherry-red and dulling above his heart. And then the smith pulled it out. That was worse.

But when it came out, the pain was all gone. Herewiss looked at the scythe with an obscure satisfaction. There was blood all down its ashy length, but underneath it, the blade was bright, bright. 'Am I two of heart now?' he said, feeling shaky but slightly amused.

The smith shrugged. He turned and went to the back of the smithy and began rummaging around among the staves racked against the wall there. Finally he found one to his liking, and came back and gave Herewiss the scythe, socketed. 'Just mind where you reap what you've sowed,' he said.

Herewiss took the scythe, thanked the smith, and went

127

out, back to the road. He looked down the far side of it, down the other shoulder of the hill. No more walls were to be seen; only a long expanse of poor stony ground, and some ways ahead, forest country. Nor could he see anything that he would be able to reap.

He turned to wave goodbye to the smith . . . and saw no house there, no smithy; only the hill, silent.

The dream passed into others that he didn't remember, and then into the sound of someone banging on a pan. Reluctantly, Herewiss opened his eyes.

It was an inn room – a pleasant change, that, for this was only the second or third room he had slept in for some days. He and Moris had ridden and camped their way right across northern Darthen, passing through hamlets too small to put up even just two passing strangers; or slightly larger places who might have room for the Ambassador Plenipotentiary to Arlen in the stable, or out in one of the barns with the midseason hay. Only in the last couple of days had they come to towns that might be large enough to have inns . . . only, that is, when they had come to the Kings' Road.

Herewiss turned over on the straw-stuffed pillow and sighed to himself. He had been avoiding the Road, even though it would have made his trip and Moris's that much swifter. This (he had told himself until now) was to give himself time to think, for he was uncertain what he was going to find in Arlen. But all his thinking seemed to have been little use. Even his dreams had been much less guidance than usual, having more to do with his own anxieties than with the problem at hand.

But perhaps my own anxieties are the problem, he thought then, and sighed again. Plain and simple, he was afraid. The world was shifting around him into patterns not unfamiliar by any means, but most uncomfortable nonetheless. Freelorn was no longer on the run, but moving to take back what was his own. Their roles were changing, had changed. Until now, he had been managing matters, taking care of the less experienced of them, the one who needed the help. But now Lorn was out there starting to manage his own matters, and Herewiss was left to wonder whether *he* was the one who needed the management.

Herewiss got up. The room was not a big one; on the sill, chewing idly on one of the shutters, sat a bright bird with feathers like fire. Smoke rose from where it chewed.

'Stop that,' Herewiss said, more or less automatically.

'Why?' Sunspark said, even though it stopped. 'It's been days since I burned anything decent. I'm getting hungry.'

'I noticed. This is a bad time for it, that's all. People are haying – you can't just burn up anything you like the look of. Especially houses. Now stop that!' For Sunspark had started again.

It stopped, looking slightly abashed. 'I wasn't even thinking about it that time.'

'I see that.' Herewiss sat down on the bed and started pulling his hose on, wrinkling his nose. He only had a few pair, and this was his last clean one; all the others were foul. 'Never mind. Look, somewhere south of here they're bound to be burning off the bracken, to make another crop of it for the sheep. When we get to Prydon, and there's no more need for riding, you go down there and have yourself a good feed. Is Moris up yet?'

For answer there came a knock on the door: Moris's usual three-taps-and-two.

'Come on in,' Herewiss said. Moris entered, yawning, in untucked shirt and breeches and boots. His normally long face was longer than usual this morning, and he was scratching. Herewiss looked at him sympathetically. 'Bugs?' he said.

Moris ran his hands through his dark hair, grimaced, and scratched there too. 'This place isn't as good as it used to be,' he said.

'Seven years since we were out this way,' Herewiss said. 'Bound to be some changes.'

'For the worse, it looks like.'

'Oh, come sit down for a moment,' Herewiss said, for Moris's scratching was making him itch too. Moris sat down on one of the room's two straw-covered stools, and Herewiss reached over for Khávrinen. He pushed Fire down into the sword and thought hard about making Moris unappetizing to the various forms of wildlife that were biting him. There was a second's pause, and then Herewiss wasn't quite sure that he didn't hear a chorus of tiny shrieks of distaste and annoyance. There was that problem with working with the Fire, Herewiss had found: one kept running into consciousness in aspects of the world that were supposed to be devoid of it. At any rate, a moment later Moris looked suddenly relieved. 'Where'd they go?' he said.

Herewiss was looking at the floor for signs of this himself. 'I think I hear them heading for the window,' he said. 'Never mind that.'

He turned and picked up the pitcher of water by the bed, poured some out into the lumpy stoneware cup next to it, and drank hurriedly to hide the other reaction to doing even so small a wreaking. He was shaking. It was a shame to him, and something he was going to have to learn to manage one of these days . . . if he lived that long.

For that was the other problem with the Fire. All power was paid for, of course. Herewiss had always known that, from the first time he had started working with sorcery. A sorcerer, doing worldly magics fuelled by the strength of the body and mind, paid for his or her work in physical and mental exhaustion. But the Fire came of a nobler source. It was the stuff of life itself; and life itself was the coin in which the price was paid. Body and mind might be tired after a particularly long and complex sorcery, but one who worked with the Fire could instantly feel the other price that was paid – time off the span of his own life. One less second, or minute, or hour, to live. In the first flush of his Power, when he was in the earliest stages of break-through, Herewiss had usually been too elated, and too busy, to recognize the feeling for what it was, or if he did, to think about it much. But now he had begun to notice it, and to think. When you didn't know how much time was allotted you to begin with, the feeling of that little span of time suddenly gone for ever was horrible. It also started you trying to put a price to a given wreaking. *How much life lost*, he wondered as he finished the last of the water, *for curing a case of lice? An hour? A day?* After a lifetime of searching for the Fire, longing for it more than for anything else, Herewiss was coming to understand how some Rodmistresses begged to have it taken from them.

He put the cup down. 'We ought to get going fairly soon,' he said to Moris. 'Have you eaten yet?'

'I didn't have the appetite for it. I have some chicken left over from dinner last night; I'd sooner have that when we go out on the road.'

'Right enough. Let's settle up and go.'

The inn was in a town called Iriv, and was one of the larger ones Herewiss had ever stayed in, since it was a major staging-point for Prydon, only a day's ride away, and on the Road. Or rather, as Moris said, it had been an important place once, before money started getting scarce and the relationship between Darthen and Arlen had begun to deteriorate, decreasing the number of travellers who passed that way. At any rate, the inn was big enough that none of the people who ran it were anywhere to be found when you wanted one . . . though it might seem that the rest of the neighbourhood was in the common room, drinking in a silence that indicated they knew one another entirely too well. Herewiss and Moris stood at the bottom of the creaky stairs, looking around slightly helplessly at the muttering locals. There was not a friendly look among them. This was another of the things Herewiss was having trouble getting used to. They had seen the Fire flowing about Khávrinen when he came in last night. He had expected astonishment, pleasure, welcome: not this suspicious hostility. *It's possible*, he had begun thinking, and thought again now, *that they see me not as a solution, but as another problem* . . . He wasn't sure he liked the feeling.

There was no sign of the innkeeper, a tall thin greying man with a stoop. The only one in the room who paid any attention to them at all was the cat on the courtyard windowsill, a big black creature with white markings like a herald's tabard, and surprised-looking white patches over its eyes.

Herewiss sighed and went over to it to try his luck. 'Sir,' he said, ignoring the suspicious or amused looks of the people who were sitting around drinking, 'have you seen the master of the house?'

The cat looked sidelong at Herewiss and tucked its paws up, so that it made a black-and-white loaf shape. It said nothing, and Herewiss was turning away when the small raspy voice said, 'He was out berating himself for not having stolen your saddle last night.'

Herewiss turned back, smiling slightly. 'Back soon, do you think?'

The cat flicked one ear, a sort of shrug, and looked away.

Herewiss reached into his pouch and came up with a four-penny bit. 'This should take care of what we owe,' he said, and slipped it deftly underneath the cat.

It looked at him and let its eyes half-close in amusement, for it knew as well as he did the proverb about the man who pays the cat, and what he gets for his money. It smiled slightly. 'Go well, prince,' it said. 'It's a wicked place you're going to.'

'It's not wicked here, with saddle thieves and all?' Herewiss said. But he smiled too.

'Go with Her,' the cat said, and closed its eyes, apparently intent on going to sleep.

'And you,' Herewiss said, and headed out of the door. Moris had gone ahead of him, making for the stable, and was busy getting the horses. Herewiss looked around at the scorchmarks on the walls of Sunspark's stable, and the ashes mixed with the straw on the floor. Sunspark was

132

standing there looking innocent: as innocent, anyway, as something that will counterfeit being the Phoenix when it's not being a horse, or one of a hundred other things. 'I didn't burn right *through* . . .'

'Let's be away,' Herewiss said, swinging his saddle up on to Sunspark's back. 'We'll be in Prydon tonight . . .'

'Coming and going . . .' Herewiss said to Moris, that afternoon, as they rode into the declining light streaming through broken clouds in the west. 'I thought I would be coming back here, all right, but not like this.'

Moris shook his head. 'Last time I was glad enough to be going,' he said. 'The whole place looked nasty to me. Everybody chasing after Lorn and all . . .' He chewed his lip and looked around at the townslands with an expression of profound distrust. 'And I doubt it'll change.'

'It'll change,' Herewiss said. 'Soon enough.' He let the reins slacken. 'Spark,' he said, 'see that hill there? Just the other side.'

Sunspark laughed softly. 'Which set of walls?' it said.

'Pardon?'

'How many walls will they have gone through?' said Sunspark. 'When I was here last, there were only two. The inside one, where the keep was, and the outer one, around the hall and the new palace they were building.'

Moris stared. Herewiss swallowed. Twelve hundred years and more it had been since Lionhall and Kynall Castle were built by Héalhra's descendants, to supplement the old inner keep. 'You hadn't mentioned you'd been through here,' Herewiss said, as calmly as he could.

'You didn't ask.' Sunspark ambled along, switching its tail at flies, incinerating them with an unsettling fizzing noise when one or another fire-golden hair made contact. 'Enough of us who walk the worlds were around,' he said. 'Power draws power. There was power here then, fresh and new. Some of us thought we would come test it. Some did.'

It got silent. 'And?' Herewiss said.

Sunspark flicked its tail again, left scorchmarks on Herewiss's boot. 'Some of us were bound,' it said. 'Some got away. Some just watched, and went elsewhere afterwards.'

Moris was looking at Sunspark more strangely than usual. '"Elsewhere"—'

'It must be odd for you,' Sunspark said, ambling along, musing. 'Living under just one sky, on just one earth. Don't the walls close in, sometimes . . . ?'

Herewiss shook his head as Sunspark fell silent. Moris was still staring. 'Its people move through worlds that way,' Herewiss told him, disquieted himself, 'the way we move from one room, one house, to another . . . Not all moves are possible, all the time. There's a Pattern, and it shifts, making some rooms accessible, others not. But beings travel through it – they spend all their lives travelling, some of them. They pass through hundreds of worlds, thousands . . . and sometimes stop in some backwater to look around and see the sights . . .'

'And are bound,' Sunspark said. Its voice was noncommittal.

Herewiss sat silent as he rode. Hearing Sunspark speak this way reminded him of his own desires – to walk the worlds, to see the things on the other side of the sky: to burn himself out in glory, if he had to be burnt. And he did. These days, Firebearers had little choice in the matter. Since the Catastrophe, human flesh had forgotten what it was like to coexist for a long lifetime with full-blown Fire: that was why using it now cost its users hours and days of life. Herewiss was meant to be about the business of changing that, he knew. But he also wanted some time to himself, to pass through the doors to those other places. And here he was, tied to a dusty road and an uncompleted errand – in the full of his Power, after all these years, but unable to indulge himself—

Moris was still bemused. 'But what kind of creatures are these?' he said. 'Or "people"?'

Sunspark laughed, a slightly sarcastic sound. 'Make no

doubt of their intelligence,' it said. 'But little worlds like this, all tight and snug, do strange things to minds used to larger places. One of them—' It sounded slightly disturbed itself, now. 'One of them went to ground not too far from here. In a river.' Sunspark laughed, the unease in its voice scraping around the joke. 'A creature that had frozen the hearts of stars in its time, and knew about waiting, and cold, more than any other creature alive: it went all to scales and icicles, and froze the river, and took a spear in its heart, and died because it believed it ought to. From such a pinprick.'

'The Coldwyrm,' Moris said.

Herewiss nodded. Anmod, King of Arlen had killed the Wyrm, about a thousand years ago now. 'An ice-elemental,' Herewiss said.

Sunspark laughed again, more sadly. 'As I'm one of fire, yes,' it said. 'And as much colder than the ice you know as I'm hotter than any fire this poor place can support. Do you know how long it's been since I was *warm*? Or dared try to be?'

Herewiss thought about that as they came over the crest of the hill, and paused there.

The roadbuilders had no doubt counted on this sort of thing happening, for there were pausing-places built on both sides of the Road. Otherwise the usual hexagonal basalt blocks ran side-to-side down the hill in easy curves, not to make life difficult for wain-drivers or others with heavy or carefully balanced loads. Down there before them, on the far side of the Arlid valley and across the old Bridge, lay Prydon among its townlands. Houses with roofs of tile or thatch lay clustered about the city walls, spreading far out into what had been the fields, and right across the bridge to the eastern side. All these years of peace had made the need to huddle inside walls seem remote. Now, though, Herewiss thought with some pain, a lot of those snug-looking houses with their market gardens were going to have their roofs burnt off them. Unless some other solution could be found—

He put the thought aside for the moment and nudged Sunspark. They started down the hill.

Prydon had four sets of walls. The inner, the oldest, had long since been torn down, but its outlines were still visible in the way the streets lay around the old town and the area where the old keep had been. The second, the one against which Lionhall on one side of the circle and Kynall on the other were built, had been cut through in numerous places, as had the third wall, built nearly as wide again as the diameter of the second. And then there was the fourth wall, latest built, in good condition – a more than adequate defence, easily two miles around, which could nonetheless be held by no more than a few hundred men.

Herewiss, examining that wall for the first time with an invader's eye, swore inwardly at Freolger who had built it. Mad that king might have been, but paranoia had its uses. The river ran close to it, but not close enough to be of use for attack: stone buffers ran up from the banks there, the stones of them leaning and making climbing the riverward slope impossible. And the wall itself was too damned thick, and too tall. Siege engines would make fairly short work of them, although all but the heaviest catapult-shot would be wasted on the rest of the wall. After that, towers and ladders—

He swore again. Siege engines were not normally the kind of thing Herewiss thought about. *I will not bring Lorn home to a ruin*, he told himself. But at the same time, if they couldn't achieve a substantive victory out on the open ground, it might well come to that . . .

They made their way down the hillside and on to the almost-level ground near the bridge. Even here the valley had not quite bottomed out; there was a long, straight, impressive sweep of black road to the bridge, and across it, to the gates in the white walls. The gates were blackstave wood bound with iron, each leaf thirty feet wide, each counterpoised to drop shut quickly if there was need. *Damn you, Freolger*, Herewiss thought again; then breathed out and stopped damning the poor crazy dead.

There were other ways into Prydon, and other ways out. He knew where they were, and would make new ones if he had to.

Houses began to crowd close to the Road as they rode nearer to the city. Young men and old women looked out through open windows, into the summer morning, bored by the sight of yet another pair of dusty travellers on their horses. Very nice horses, though, especially that big blood roan, look at the mane on him, you'd think it was on fire—

Herewiss smiled dryly at the comments, spoken and unspoken, of the people leaning on their windowsills. He reached over his shoulder and drew Khávrinen, laying it across his lap as he rode. Moris edged away, eyeing the point of the sword. Khávrinen was burning blue as usual, but rather more emphatically than was normal.

The faces looking out the windows got surprised, and mouths opened and closed and opened, and eyes got wide.

Herewiss schooled his smile to stay small. There was no question that he found this enjoyable – the astonishment, even the discomfort, that other people felt on sight of him. But enjoying it too much was a danger. He knew quite well that pride was the great downfall of many a Rodmistress: and no surprise, since the Goddess's intention was for Her whole world to recover the Power it had lost, and distraction from that cause – or attempts to keep the Power exclusive to a few – led inevitably straight to the Shadow and Its works.

There was a straggly crowd stringing out behind them now, people from the townland-houses standing in the road and staring, or following, slowly, as they crossed the bridge. A few minutes' more riding brought them to the gates. Herewiss glanced at Moris as they came to them, and paused.

There were guards there, of course; but Herewiss could never remember there having been so many. They were wearing the black and white of Arlene regulars, the White Lion badge embroidered small on their jerkins. Some of them were looking bored, and some looked panicked, and some just quietly wary. Herewiss nodded to the closest of them, and said, 'Gentlemen, perhaps you would direct me and my friend to the Darthene Embassy. We're expected.'

Naturally he knew perfectly well where the Embassy was, but it seemed polite to ask, to acknowledge their presence and give them something to do. One of them, one of the men with a bored face, edged out of a group and walked towards Herewiss.

'And what's your business there?' he said. His voice was bored too, but the swagger in his gait said that, Fire or no Fire, he wasn't impressed by this pampered-looking city boy. It was insolence, of course, and frightened insolence at that, in the face of the WhiteCloak. He reached up as he spoke to take Sunspark by the headstall.

A second later he snatched back a burnt hand, and just as well; Sunspark's head lashed out, its teeth snapped and missed – just. 'Gently,' Herewiss said. 'Sir, my name is Herewiss s'Hearn. The Queen of Darthen has sent me. That would be business enough, I would think. Considering that you see my token.'

'Darthen—' the guard said, and looked like he was trying to work up enough spit to make a more emphatic comment. But his eyes, fixed on Khávrinen, betrayed him. Even if they had not, with Khávrinen in his hands and the Fire flowing, Herewiss could hear the man's heart hammering as if it was his own, and could just catch the thought: *Damn, it's true, the rumour's true!*

'Of course it is,' Sunspark said, and the guard jumped in surprise. 'So show us our way, manling, or get out of it!'

The guard chose the latter option, rather hurriedly. 'Gentlemen,' Herewiss said again, nodding to them, and nudged Sunspark. With Moris behind, they ambled through the gates. Moris's horse shied and started picking its way with care around places where Sunspark's hooves had fallen, and the paving-stones were smoking, or molten.

Now that was unnecessary, Herewiss said.

You are too gentle with these people, Sunspark replied.

They mean you ill, and Freelorn through you. Why don't you make it plain to them what will happen if they try anything? It snorted. *And if you won't, I will.*

Herewiss made no answer to that for the moment. He was looking around him at the old familiar buildings along the main road that led into the city from the east gate. Everything was in its right place: the streets that opened off this one, the tall stone-faced buildings lining the way. This had been a merchants' quarter once, full of the houses of former greengrocers and silkmongers. But the houses, which had been stately once, now had a grim, defensive look about them. *Shutters,* Herewiss thought, looking around, *when did they ever have such a thing?* And the people in the streets— They were not the usual mixture of cheerful and annoyed and bland faces. There was a lot more annoyance, and also a look on all sorts of faces that Herewiss saw, an expression as shuttered as the windows: not so much bland but blank, as if the wearers were nervous about letting out any genuine look that might indicate some kind of opinion. People glanced at Herewiss and then hurriedly away, as if he was something that might get them in trouble.

Moris had come up next to him, looking uneasy. 'This place looks terrible,' he said.

Herewiss nodded. 'I agree. How do you see it, though?'

Moris looked over at one of the mansion houses they were passing. Its cobbled yard was full of wind-tossed trash, and the windows were all shuttered blind. 'That,' he said. 'Too many houses here look like that. Where is everybody? And where are all the people?' Moris gestured with his chin at the street. 'This time of day, these streets should be full. Especially this far over by the market. Dinnertime—' He paused to watch in mild confusion as a child staring at them from a side street was hurriedly pulled back into the shadows and hustled away. Moris's face set itself in lines of dismay. 'It feels all wrong,' he said softly. 'I don't like this. This was home, once. But not any more—'

139

Herewiss nodded again in sombre agreement. 'Something's missing,' he said. 'You know what.'

Moris breathed out, not saying anything.

They passed another street corner, and just around it saw the mounted guards, watching them go by. Herewiss nodded cordially enough to them in passing. One of them wheeled his horse and was off in a hurry, up a back street that Herewiss knew led in the general direction of Kynall.

Herewiss leaned back casually in the saddle. 'Checking out a wild story from the gates,' he said. 'Now they know it's true.' He sighed and reached up to sheathe Khávrinen again, and his heart turned over in him at the thought of what Lorn was going to feel when he came home to this at last. *Even if he only returns to the city after we've freed it, it's still going to be crippled. This healing is going to take a long time.*

Wordlessly he turned Sunspark off the road into the city's heart, heading for the north-eastern side of the second wall, against which Kynall was built. Lionhall was diametrically across the city from it, against the south-western side, around the curve of the wall. Along that wall's curve were Prydon's official buildings, the Arlene ministries, and the various embassies and guildhalls. The Darthene Embassy was quite close to Kynall, as befitted its status as Arlen's major ally. *Well,* former *major ally,* Herewiss thought, and found himself looking up the curve at Kynall's towers and thinking they were too close for comfort. They had never been so when he and his father were guests here when he was young, and Kynall was just Freelorn's house.

And here were the white marble pillars he remembered, marking the entrance to the Darthene Embassy's courtyard. They had been smooth and round once, but now there were cracks in them, as if they had been hit with things; and there were dull greyish spots on them and the walls stretching from either side of them, as if pillars and walls had been scrawled on, and only ineffectively cleaned. Herewiss shook his head and rode into the courtyard, looking up at the shuttered windows with foreboding.

Under the shadow of the great pillared portico, the central door opened and a woman came out, dressed in a long tabard of midnight blue over a finely pleated white shift. In a clatter of hooves, Moris rode past Herewiss laughing. 'Dati!' he said, almost in a shout: the first happy sound Herewiss thought he had heard all that afternoon. He watched as Moris ran across the worn white paving to hug the woman on the stairway. Andaethen d'Telha tai-Palaiher was the Ambassador; a tall, heavy-boned woman, with shaggy curly hair framing a broad face, and green eyes with a slight slant to them, like a cat's. She was also Moris's second cousin, and his foster-sister – it was his family that she had been sent to live with, as children of noble houses in both countries often were, to make sure that city people become no more citified than necessary, and country people no more countrified.

At the moment, the precaution seemed superfluous. 'Look at you,' Andaethen was scolding, but with laughter in her voice, 'you're a wraith! You're a wreck! What have they been feeding you?'

'Dati,' Moris said, half-strangling on his own laughter, 'I needed to lose some weight! Leave it alone!'

'This is all *your* fault,' said Andaethen to Herewiss as he joined them. 'You with your skulking about in the open countryside like a felon, afraid to set foot on the Road where my poor coz could have got a decent cooked meal once in a while—'

Herewiss was slightly surprised that she knew anything about their route . . . but then the Darthene Ambassador might be expected to have her own sources of information. 'Madam,' he said, smiling slightly, 'I did no better than he did in that regard. And I wasn't even *trying* to lose weight.'

'Don't think I don't remember your methods, Hearn's son,' she said, mock-scolding as she let go of Moris at last. 'Like father, like son, and bottomless pits, the both of you. You'll have your dinner soon enough. Come you in

141

and shift your clothing first; you both look like you've been rolling in the muckheap.'

Grooms came out and led Moris's horse and Sunspark away. Herewiss and Moris followed Andaethen in through the great brass door. The downstairs entry hall was much as Herewiss remembered it; a high, cool, empty space, walled in the pale Darthene marble, with tall glass-paned windows. Herewiss looked up as they passed through, heading for the central staircase, and saw that one pane high up in the right-hand window was missing, replaced with oiled paper.

Andaethen saw his look. 'Ah yes,' she said, 'we had a stone through that last week. Not exactly affectionate times in Prydon, these.'

Herewiss pulled a wry look. 'Unfortunately—'

'Save it for after dinner,' Andaethen said. And was that a warning look in her eye? 'It's dull work, talking before food.'

Moris glanced at Herewiss and smiled slightly. Andaethen's reputation as Ambassador to Arlen was a sound one; she was known as a careful representative of her land's interests, smooth-tongued and detached. She also had a reputation for employing the best cooks in town and setting a good table – and not slighting it herself once it was set.

'Here,' said Andaethen, and led them up the stairs, turning right into a long high-ceilinged corridor. 'Will a suite do for you?' she asked Herewiss and Moris. 'Two bedrooms with a connecting room. Baths are down at the end of the hall.'

Herewiss glanced at Moris, saw his nod. 'That'll do well,' he said. 'You'll have us fetched for dinner, then?'

'Nothing so formal,' Andaethen said, 'not tonight, anyway. Later this tenday, we'll have one after your kissing-of-hands.' Her expression as she opened the door of a room on the garden side was neutral. For the moment, Herewiss held his so as well. It was a king's hand one kissed on presenting diplomatic credentials, but there was

142

no king in Arlen – and Herewiss was unsure whether even the necessities of diplomacy could make him kiss Cillmod's hand.

'Your things will be brought up shortly,' Andaethen said cheerfully. 'Once you're bathed and rested, just come down when you feel ready. We keep a collation ready all the time, this time of year. Traditions, after all.' She looked sour at that, as if there was something she wanted to add. But, 'Later, gentlemen,' Andaethen said, and was off again.

This time of year, Herewiss thought as they went into the suite's shared room. It was getting on towards the beginnings of harvest, now, and in the Two Lands that meant that country households kept a feasting table ready all the time to thank the Goddess, through their visitors, for the year's bounty. But this year the bounty was going to be much less than usual, even in Darthen, and he suspected that was much on Andaethen's mind.

'This is lovely,' Moris said, going over to the window and looking out. There was an iron-railed terrace outside it that looked down on the garden. Herewiss joined Moris there and gazed down. There were paths laid out below, and flowerbeds. Cluttered, dense, friendly, it was a cottage garden smuggled into the city; there were even fruit trees over by the old wall, a little forest of them, some of them seventy or a hundred years old from the looks of them.

Herewiss sighed, feeling abruptly at rest, and strange to be so after so much travelling. 'Do you need to sleep a while?' he said.

'I need food,' Moris said. 'But a bath first.'

'That's for me as well,' Herewiss said, and looked into the other room. 'Dear Goddess,' he said, 'look at the size of that bed.' And he made a small wry face as he thought, *Though the one who would appreciate it most isn't here. Ah, Lorn . . .*

'Mine too,' said Moris from the second bedroom. 'It's not a bed, it's a county. But later for that. Let's go see about the bath.'

About an hour later they made their way downstairs to the banqueting hall. It was easily a hundred yards long and twenty wide, the marble the white 'spark' marble of the Highpeaks. The rows of braziers of iron and gold that lined the room were all empty and cold, and only the soft indefinite light of dusk came in the thirteen doors on each side that led out on to the garden terraces. Andaethen sat beneath an iron torchère near the table's head, papers piled all about her and another candlestick hard by. She was frowning, and scribbling on one curling parchment. Beside her sat a half-empty glass of wine and the remains of a roast chicken.

The Ambassador looked up with relief as they came in, and put the quill aside as they made their way down to her.

'Do have something,' said Andaethen. 'That's lamb there, on the big salver, in sour blackberry sauce: and roast chickens. And the spiced venison is good too. And pickled beetroot, and pickled onions, and sour bread, and—' She waved at the dishes marshalled far down the table. 'Whatever. Don't miss that big decanter, that's the Brightwood white.' She scowled meaningfully at Herewiss. 'Almost the last of my supply.'

Herewiss smiled and picked up a serving plate. Moris had already begun working on the spiced meat. After choosing his food, Herewiss filled a plain silver cup with the Brightwood wine. He raised the cup to the rose-tinged dusk coming in through the right-hand windows, saluting first the Goddess, and then thinking, *Lorn . . .* He drank.

The same flavour as always, of green leaves, cool wind; but slightly brassy around the edges. 'It never did travel all that well,' Herewiss said to Andaethen, as he carried cup and plate around and down to her end of the table.

'I know,' she said, 'but nowadays it's not travelling at all. Well, I understand your father's reasons.'

Moris joined them, sitting across from Herewiss. 'The advantage of this room at this time of day,' Andaethen said, 'is that with the doors closed, no-one can get close enough to overhear anything – unless the power being used to overhear has nothing to do with ears.'

'Why,' Moris said, 'don't you trust your staff?'

She laughed at him, though softly. 'Of course not. Half of them are Arlenes, and a quarter of those are in Cillmod's pay. When I put temptation in their way, it's because I want to. I'm not above misleading eavesdroppers. Or frightening them.' She grinned. 'But you in particular,' Andaethen said to Herewiss, 'have set everything upsy-versy, as I daresay you and my mistress expected. All the city, and Kynall Castle in particular, had heard wild rumours about you, and all with some substantiation. Mountains moving, battlefields cleared of enemies . . . all most disquieting. And then, la, the truth of the rumours walks in at the West Gate and asks for directions. Very droll,' she said, looking sidewise at Herewiss and taking a drink of wine. 'And bearing what you bore in your packs, too . . . which the Castle has rumours of, but no truth yet. I have it, by the way.'

'And what did you think of it?' said Moris.

She laughed at him again. 'Mori poppet, who says I get to think? I am my mistress's mouth. What *she* thinks, that I speak. Your hand-kissing is going to be interesting,' Andaethen said to Herewiss, 'since that's where the declaration of war will have to be acknowledged. We, of course, are safe – if safe is the word here, any more. The army groups billeted in town are encouraged to misbehave sometimes, make life difficult for foreigners – know what I mean? Or even sometimes for the locals. A little violence in the back alleys, the merchants' families threatened . . . Nothing serious, nothing that anyone *here* is willing to complain about, lest they draw more attention to themselves. But as for you,' Andaethen said, drinking her wine again, 'you will shortly be the man in Arlen that the most people desire to kill. The bearer of bad news – and more than that: the bad news incarnate. The end of the old powers, both secular and spiritual, and the uprising of new. I wouldn't be in your skin for any amount of Fire, my lad.'

'But here I am in it,' said Herewiss, 'so I'd best make the best of it that I can. For I do have more than one Mistress.'

'Yes,' said Andaethen, and looked at him with an expression uncomfortably like that of someone suppressing awe. 'Where will that work lead you, do you think?'

'It's hard to say. But I have business with Rian.'

Andaethen nodded. 'Well, he'll be at your kissing-of-hands, and the dinner after. There may be some delay about that – Darthen giving a dinner for the Arlene court on the same day as they declare war on it would go down oddly.'

'But the next tenday or so,' Andaethen said, 'that'll be fine.' She grinned at Moris's shocked look. 'Business goes on, coz. It's when I pack my bags and leave here that you should start to worry. And meanwhile,' she said to Herewiss, 'I can at least advise you on who's most likely to try to kill you first. It's a nice mare's-nest of plottings and subtleties that you've fallen into – half the Four Hundred plotting against the other half, alliances formed one hour and shifted the next, any wild rumour throwing everyone into a panic—'

'The truth is,' Herewiss said, 'they're all afraid to starve. And starvation is, well, not quite looking the Four Hundred in the face yet . . . but peering around the corner. They would like to evade it, for lords who can't keep their people in food get killed and ploughed in – as do kings who can't do the trick.'

'That's true,' said Andaethen. 'But here's Cillmod, who is patently of the royal blood – having been in Lionhall and out again. "Support me," says our Cillmod to the Four Hundred. "This famine is not my fault: it's the fault of the one who fled. I have been working hard to recreate the royal sorceries and bring back the rain and the food. Isn't the harvest already better than it was last year? This comes of the great sorcerer who's helping me. Support me now and everything will soon be well. But if you fall in with the pretender, then after I restore the kingship I will

146

not fail to remember who my friends were, and who my betrayers—"'

Herewiss found that the fist of his sword-hand was clenching on the table. He unclenched it and picked up a pickled onion to nibble. 'And there *are* potential "betrayers", then.'

'Oh, yes indeed! You'll meet more than enough of those. There arc plenty of people who would prefer Freelorn to Cillmod . . . if only because they feel they've been dealt with unfairly at Cillmod's hands, and they prefer the Shadow they don't know to the one they do. Others look more deeply into the situation, or less so, but support Lorn regardless. And others are dead set against him, for good reasons or bad. At least, that's how it all is today. Tomorrow or the next day, when you kiss hands, and I read out that piece of parchment – la!' Andaethen drank off what remained of her cup of wine and set it aside. 'All this flies apart and reassembles itself into some new and odder shape, the alliances change and change again . . . and you find entirely *different* people trying to kill you.' She shook her head, smiling wearily. 'Anyway, there's nothing you need do until the time for your hand-kissing is set. Day after tomorrow, I think.'

'Two more days for the Queen to work on her muster,' said Moris.

'If it matters,' said Andaethen. 'I think they suspect what you're here for, up in Kynall, and have started their own muster already. But no need to rush things . . . the proprieties should be observed.'

'Yes,' Herewiss said. 'I have a visit to make myself, in that regard. If it's all right.'

Andaethen looked at him curiously for a moment and, when he said nothing further, nodded. 'Indeed it is. Your duties are what you say they are – that much is plain in my mistress's brief to me. And anything I can do for you, only say the word. Meanwhile I can occupy myself with feeding up this poor starveling here—'

'Dati!' Moris said, more a groan than a name.

Andaethen chuckled and ruffled his hair.

Herewiss smiled and had another pickled onion.

It was some time after midnight when Herewiss finally slipped out of the Embassy. He stopped into the stables, looking for Sunspark, and found only one of two horses – Moris's. However, in the tack room, he also found a red-headed, amber-eyed young man in russet jerkin and trews, playing at dice with one of the grooms, and winning. Herewiss smiled in that door, waved, said nothing.

As he headed for the street, the voice in his head said, *Am I needed, loved?*

Always, Herewiss said. *But not for this. I'll be back in a while.*

As you say.

And when you're done, Herewiss said, *you should see the bed in my room—*

I shall give it full attention. It's almost certainly better than straw . . .

He slipped out the postern door in the larger gates, now shut. Earlier in the evening he had heard sounds of trouble in the street. He had Khávrinen slung over his shoulder, though, and a few bravos were the least of his worries tonight. He had more important business – and was intent on bigger game, if it would be drawn.

He had left the WhiteCloak behind, putting on a plain dark shirt and breeches; the night was warm and there was no need for anything else. He made his way back along the circle-road that paralleled the second wall, listening to the night-sounds as he went. Shouting, yes, but not like the kind he remembered from his youth, the friendly noises of night – the sound of taverns chucking out their patrons, of people chaffing one another on the way home, a homey, reassuring susurrus, the sound of the city breathing quietly before it turned over and went to sleep. There was a more threatening sense to this sound; sleep was not on its mind, and you would prefer not to meet its source face to face.

Herewiss shook his head and went on, following the buildings that hugged the old wall. There was little moon tonight, hardly visible through the thin cloud that was coming in – that old mist that always came up the Arlid after a warm day. Few lanterns hung in this street any more, and the feeble light did little to show the way along the uneven cobbles.

He stopped where the Street of the Second Wall crossed the Arlid's Way, and breathed in, breathed out. The old stink, at least, had not changed, nor the purpose that had given the street its name: open sewerage flowed down it and out an old cloaca burrowed beneath the walls, to the river. He looked up the street for the glint of lanterns, saw only a few – and a small hand lantern, swinging idly as someone, the watch perhaps, went about their business.

Herewiss crossed the Arlid's Way, being careful of where he put his feet, and went on along the curving street in the dark. After a couple of hundred cubits the paving changed, becoming large flat slabs instead of cobbles: and light or the lack of it no longer mattered, for he knew where he was. The street widened out, becoming a plaza; the buildings on the left-hand side of the street suddenly stopped, giving way to more paving, right up to the old wall.

Ahead of him in the dimness was a building, three storeys high, done in the old, simple way of Arlene architecture. The building was a cube, with a high dome atop it. The windows on the front half of the sides of it were not glazed, merely cut into the sides of the building, twenty feet up, straight through the six-foot-thick marble walls. There was no portico at the front, nothing but a great empty yawning entrance, without gate or door. Within the building, the darkness was complete.

Herewiss walked across the plaza, making little sound. Always before, there had been a lamp lit inside the outer precinct of the building, – but circumstances being what they were, this darkness did not particularly surprise him. He came to stand in the doorway, and paused there.

He waited some moments, letting his eyes grow used to this still deeper darkness, until he could just see the great dim form on the pedestal within. He let that silence sink deep into him, let that darkness make its point. Then he drew Khávrinen and walked into the outer court of Lionhall.

The statue was exactly as it had been seven years ago. Herewiss went softly forward into the silence and the darkness, with only Khávrinen to light his way – and that light a faint one, meant not to disturb the sanctity of the place. In the shadows behind the pedestal, he could just make out the bronze doors, shut, that led into the back of the building: the part of Lionhall that had no windows, and no other exit.

He came to the pedestal and stopped, grounding Khávrinen point down on the plain paving. Laven d'Hwuin tai-Héalhrästi, that had been the sculptor's name: it was graven on the pedestal, near the floor. Nothing more was known about her for certain, except that she was not directly of Héalhra's line, but a cadet branch. A millennium and more ago she had made this statue, in that clean, spare style of the day. Couchant in his majesty, one forepaw curled under, the other lazily pendant over the pedestal's edge, the White Lion lay and looked out through calm, half-closed cat-eyes, through the huge portal and out at the city and land He died for. The luxuriant mane and the longer tail were plain in the dimness, typical of the Arlene white lions, which are a third bigger than their Darthene cousins, the tan lions that run in prides. *Elefrua*, the Arlene word called them: 'mere-lions', as opposed to the 'great lions', *airua*.

But this one was more than merely 'great'. This one had been a man, and had been called by his Creatress to become more: and he had accepted the call. His humanity had been burned away in blue Fire – he, with Éarn, becoming one of the only two men since the Catastrophe to wield it – and he had taken this form on the battlefield, to the confusion of his enemies, the thinking Fyrd and other monsters that the Shadow had sent down from the mountains to destroy the human beings trying to establish themselves once again in the Kingdoms. Terrible power he had wielded; and the look of that power lay in Laven's sculpture, the death dealt out, the rage. But all restrained now, all past. This was the White Lion at peace, his battles done. He looked out with forbearance and calm, the power and the majesty no whit lessened, but at rest. He seemed to look out of the doorway but, for one standing at his feet, it was difficult to tell whether those eyes did not in fact look down, under the heavy, lazy lids, and examine the watcher.

If it was the artist's skill, and an illusion, it was one that Herewiss didn't mind. He sank to one knee there, and bowed his head, directing his reverence to the one who had accepted Her call when it came, and let Himself go to become more than a man. *We are all under Her together*, Herewiss thought, *tools to a purpose. May I take my toolhood as well as You did, Lionfather; and as Éarn my own line-father did. Help Your own son, as far as You may; bear him, at least, in mind, as he does You . . .*

Herewiss knelt there in quiet for a while, having no further requests in him. He thought of when he had last seen the Lion, in dream. Lorn had been there with him, and together they had looked up at a Being Who for the joke's sake was pretending to be His own statue, lying easy on a pedestal as the statue did. There was no question about the attention of the eyes that time, though, or the old power and wisdom in them, or the amusement. That by itself had been a great delight—

The clicking noise behind him brought Herewiss's head up. He didn't turn, but threw himself sideways and rolled. Only that saved his life, as the razory claws came down on the marble, one of them snapping with the force. He heard the crack of it right by his ear.

Herewiss was up, and Khávrinen was flaming like a torch, showing him what he had expected, and worse. *Fyrd*, had been his first thought as he rolled. Now he looked up at the keplian as it reared, seeing the wicked glitter of hating intelligence in its eyes. *Thinking Fyrd*, he corrected himself, as he feinted with Khávrinen. There was nothing unusual about keplian as such. They were a standard enough type of Fyrd, yet another of the beasts the Shadow had ruined during the time of the Catastrophe. They had been horses once. But keplian had been twisted into carnivores, with carnivores' teeth, and instead of hooves there was one great claw on each foot, and two lesser ones on each side of it. The body was lean and starveling, the eyes like cats' eyes, placed forward instead of at the sides of the head. They were hunters, plagues of the herd country. And this one was one of the Shadow's own breed, almost as intelligent as humans, and hating humans like nothing else – one of the kind of Fyrd Héalhra and Éarn had given their lives to wipe out. They had been wiped out indeed, until now: until a man had the Fire again, and old challenges were renewed. These thinking Fyrd were a message intended by the Shadow for the Goddess . . . but addressed to Herewiss.

And what is it doing in a city? he thought, as the keplian lunged at him again, and he struck it with Khávrinen, and it shied back screaming hatred and pain. Though he knew perfectly well. Rian had sent it. Rian had some connection with these things; Herewiss and Lorn and the others had seen that clearly enough at Bluepeak just now, where the field had been full of them. Amusing to find that he was being so closely watched. The image of that rider wheeling off and carrying word up to Kynall was in Herewiss's mind now. *Wasting no time, are we*, he thought. *Striking the first blow. Always an advantage.*

Well, we shall see about that.

They were circling one another now, the keplian's horrible half-horse, half-bear mask wrinkling in a mixture of anger and fear. It should have killed him with that first stroke. It now saw no chance of doing so, for Herewiss had the Fire, and there was no Fyrd alive that did not go in deadly fear of the blue Flame of Power. This one knew

Herewiss would kill it if it couldn't kill him. He could feel its fear as if it were his own. Pity washed through him—

The keplian leapt again, and Herewiss dived and rolled and came up with Khávrinen pointing at the thing. Blue Fire lanced out, but not to kill. The keplian fell over sideways on the marble floor, struggling, then frozen entirely as the nerve-seize gripped every fibre of it. It lay there, rocking ever so slightly, like a dropped stone: then became still.

Herewiss stood there gasping. *Let it lie so*, he thought, anger and satisfaction beating in him with his heartbeat as he watched the raging eyes go wild, though they could not move; as the lungs struggled for air and could not find any. *A more merciful death than what it had in mind for me*—

The silence reasserted itself. 'And as for You—' he started to say.

And paused.

Paused.

They were horses once, he thought.

He drew a few breaths, and then dropped to his knees by the keplian. It stared through him, desperate, as it lay there slowly strangling. Herewiss tucked his heels under him, laid Khávrinen across his knees, and took the keplian's great ugly head between his hands.

He released the muscles of its lungs. Air sucked into them in a long anguished gasp, blew out, sucked in again. Fear, beat in the air like another pulse. Herewiss shut his eyes and gathered the Fire inside him, forced it to concentrate until he could see nothing of his own inner workings in his mind's eye but that searing blue. He looked at the keplian then, and at its own inner being: not the cruelly twisted mind and heart of it, but the bone and brawn, the sinews and nerves and blood and muscle. Taken together they seemed all quite different, but far down in all their structures, buried, he could sense and see the tiny, tight, coiled pattern on which and with which all the greater structures were built – the Goddess's own plan, writ small in every drop of blood and every hair. Someone

153

had been at that plan, had rewritten parts of it with horrible malicious cunning, so that what should have been a horse now grew fangs, craved blood, tore and was torn.

But what had been written could be rewritten.

What use in doing it once? Herewiss thought, in a moment's despair. *Change one Fyrd, what difference does it make?*

Still better than killing. Killing serves no purpose but that One's satisfaction.

And he paused again. Death was no use. Change was no use either.

But rebirth, he thought. *It might – it just might—*

He looked closely at one of those tiny coiled messages, the keplian body's own reminder to itself of how it was built and should keep being built. *If one were to change this, and this,* Herewiss thought, *and this here – so that the next time this creature mates, the foals are keplian no longer – Fyrd no longer. And to make sure the foals carry the shift too, so that when they mate with other keplian, or even with horses, or each other, the shift back towards horseness will still continue—*

There were many, many changes to be made. But Herewiss was outside of time at the moment; nothing mattered but the blue blaze of Power within him. He slipped himself down and down into that tight-coiled ballad of blood and bone, made a change here, shifted a verse there; eyed his work, corrected it, made another change, and another. Then after an endless time, when everything seemed in order, he bound it all together and made it work—

He drew within himself again, let the Fire ebb a bit, opened his eyes, blinked. He could feel the change spreading inside the keplian, one version of that song overwriting another, the whole creature turning to one chorus of change. He waited until the uproar died down, listened one last time to be sure of his handiwork – then let the creature go.

It gasped, and blinked hard, then lurched and stumbled

to its feet, unsteady as a new foal. Herewiss got up too, rather hurriedly, with Khávrinen ready in case there should be need.

The keplian stared at him . . . and shifted oddly from foot to foot, as if its claws suddenly felt peculiar to it.

Herewiss breathed out, feeling something strange: jubilation. Triumph. 'Go free,' he said, looking back in mind to a stretch of empty country that he and Moris had ridden through that morning. 'And Her blessing on you and yours, mad and sane together. Go.'

The keplian snorted. Blue Fire flickered around it; it was gone.

Herewiss breathed out, then, and felt like sagging. *How many hours of life, for that?* he thought. *How many months?* But there would be time to worry about that later. He turned to Héalhra's statue, sketched it a bow, and turned again and walked out the doorway.

There he paused and took stance, resting Khávrinen's point on the stone, resting his hands on its hilts. Slowly the Fire wreathed up about it, and him, until Herewiss stood in a bonfire of it three times his height. The light of the blue Flame blazed up so that the whole square was alight with it, as if a star had fallen on to the paving. In his exultation and anger, Herewiss neither knew nor cared who might be seeing the light. The light itself was what mattered.

'Go and tell your Master,' he said into the night, 'that better than such poor blunt tactics are needed for *me*. I have come to mend what was marred. My weapon is in my hand now, and though it break on what it touch, yet what it touches will be made whole in its destruction. Go you and tell Him that: and also that he has nothing so simple and straightforward as mere defeat to look forward to – no more than do His slaves, who will be freed – one way or another. Go now and tell Him so!'

And then Herewiss let the breath go out of him, shocked by the power that had made its way into his voice. The naked exultation drained away as well, replaced by awe and unease. He had been the one who had started speaking. He was not at all sure that he was the one who had finished.

Echoing his mood, Khávrinen's Fire burned down, burned low. Slowly and thoughtfully Herewiss sheathed it, turned, and began walking back to the Darthene Embassy. He could hear Freelorn saying to him, not so long ago, *I don't want to be a god* . . .

And do I? Herewiss thought. *Do* I . . . ?

7

The Goddess folded Her arms and looked at the atheist with bemusement tinged with annoyance. 'This is getting us nowhere,' She said. 'I do godly things right here in front of you, one after another, and you say they're mere sorcerer's work, hedge-magic. What work is going to be big enough to convince you?'

The atheist looked dour. 'You could appear in your full glory,' he said.

'It would kill you,' the Goddess said.

'Hah,' said the atheist. 'All that means is you can't do it.'

'Won't,' the Goddess said. 'I've heard that line before, and I know What put it into your head. It's the Shadow's counsel. Do you think I started being self-existent yesterday? What good are you to Me, blasted out of existence? Glory has its uses, and that's not one of them. No, you're just going to have to accept Me as I am . . . as you do your fellow human beings.'

'As you are,' the atheist said, looking Her up and down, 'I don't believe you. Nor believe *in* you.'

'Or in them either,' the Goddess said, smiling a crooked smile. 'And I think I know how they feel.'

The Goddess and the Atheist, 5

Freelorn had heard it said often enough that, eventually, a criminal will return to the scene of his crime. Not considering himself a criminal, he had to laugh when it happened to him.

He spent some days working his way up out of the empty country near the mountains, considering his options. He took his time riding along; there was a lot of time for thought as he watched the mountains slide away behind him at last, slipping below the horizon. And the countryside itself disposed him to take things slowly. It was often rocky, with sudden pits opening, and the ground boggy or full of molehills and sinkholes. He let Blackie pick his way, and didn't rush him.

Lorn tried hard not to think. He had been doing so much of that lately. He tried just to be one with the landscape, the wind, the sky, the rivers he crossed. Those rivers were the first sign that he was coming into country where people lived. Down this far south, for the first couple of days of riding, the land he traversed was mostly good only for sheep; the pasture was too sparse for cows, all heather and bracken. But the stoniness began to fade out of it, and he started to cross the little streams that fed the Arlid from the west, and the land became greener, lusher.

He stopped near the ruins of one old farm building and looked around it, half-afraid he would find the black scars of fires on the stones, sure sign that the Reavers had been here. But there were no such marks. Mere abandonment had ruined these buildings; small sapling trees were growing through the tumble of stones and slates where the roof had been. Someone had found that they just couldn't make a go of it this far south. Lorn shook his head, and rode on north.

It would be nice if we could settle some people down here. Help them with money, for a while, until they got their crops in. It would be good land for cattle, once you got some decent grass on it . . . He remembered his father talking that way on many a ride out of Prydon. Half the time talking to his father had been like talking to a farmer; an agricultural expert full of tips on how to keep the clubroot out of your turnips. *Rather like Eftgan*, he thought. But then that was what kings did – put food in people's mouths. It was a business Lorn was going to have to learn.

The country continued to soften around him, his third and fourth days after leaving Eftgan at the borders. By his reckoning he was about ten leagues south of Egen, the nearest biggish town on the Arlid. He thought he would stop there for a while on his way north, get his bearings and some news.

When he came to his first real hamlet, he rode down into it, towards the rutted strip between fields that seemed to be the main street. Pebble's pots clanked softly as they made their way down the hill. Shuttered windows stood open to the warm summer air, and he saw a face look out of one and see him coming. The expression the woman wore was wary at first; then it relaxed when she saw the second horse, with the pots.

By the time Lorn made it down into the dusty track between the houses, they were all waiting for him, everyone who wasn't out in the fields: cautious-looking women, peering out of their doorways; wide-eyed children, staring at the stranger. Lorn remembered how he and his foster-sisters had stared at any new arrival in Elefrua, and smiled; but he wasn't entirely at ease. There was a nervous look about some of the children, and it troubled him.

'The Goddess's greeting to you this fine afternoon,' Lorn said as he reined Blackie in, 'and my own with it. I have pots, and I mend them: and I come looking for trade, or hospitality, or both if you have them.'

'Where have you been?' said the woman closest.

Lorn swung down out of the saddle, narrowly missing a chicken which had been strolling among Blackmane's legs. 'Darthen, madam,' he said, 'and eastward to the Stel.' All true enough, as far as it went, but he was not likely to mention how much farther east he had gone. The Waste was unlucky to talk about, even here.

'Do you have the news?'

'A fair amount of it,' Lorn said, and smiled. 'There's been battle at Bluepeak, and the young king's coming back. But there's plenty of time to tell you all that. Perhaps one of you have a stable I might sleep in with my horses tonight?'

There was an immediate embarrassed outcry, the aggressive courtesy of country people in this part of the world, at the idea that even a tinker should sleep in the straw; there was a bed at Lasif's house going spare, with a room to itself, and a door that shut, and come this way, sir, and what do we call you? For here as elsewhere, real names were not lightly enquired after.

'They call me Arelef,' Lorn said, lifting his saddleroll and pack off Blackmane. It was a common enough nickname for a traveller, meaning 'footloose' in the vernacular; though in the more ancient dialects of Arlene it meant the young 'unprided' lion who was still wandering around in his growing time, gathering experience and strength. Very few people would know that these days, and Lorn felt secure enough to allow himself the joke.

He allowed himself to be drawn into one of the nearby houses. Lorn touched the doorsill in blessing as he went through, and caught an approving look or two from the men and women who accompanied him; the gesture spoke of a country upbringing to them, of someone who knew how to behave. They brought him into the kitchen of the house – it was a sign of the success, or tenacity, of the people who lived here, that the house even had separate rooms. This room was airy and wide-windowed, with bunches of herbs hanging in the light and air by hand-twined hempen strings; and iron pots and a copper one, polished to a high shine, hung from hooks by the fireplace. There was an iron crane in the fireplace, well made, and the flags of the floor, polished from who knew how many decades of use, looked newly scrubbed. The people sat him down at the big scrubbed table in the middle of the kitchen, and gave him bread and oatcakes, and buttermilk from that morning's churning.

He broke off a bit of oatcake and dunked it in the buttermilk, and set it aside for the Goddess; then fell to with great pleasure, for he had been living on dry journeycake and water the past few days. Around him the farm people sat, and watched him intently. It was considered bad manners to ask a guest for news before feeding him but, at the same time, being stared at while eating made him feel both uncomfortable and amused. 'Please,' he said to them, 'you're kind to a hungry traveller, but you needn't wait. Who are you all, and what do you call your town?'

'Imisna,' said one of them, and Lorn nodded: it was Arlene for 'flint', and he had noticed when they first sat him down that the big stone lumps in the walls were whole flints, some chipped in half to show the beautiful brown and cream striping inside.

Introductions were made. The housewife was Lasif; her husbands Gare and Eglian, and her sister-wife Meo; their daughters Arine and Cylin, their son Orrest: and their neighbours were their cousin Paell and her wife Gierne. They were all tall, big-boned people. The family resemblance was strong among the fathers, the children, and the cousin – dark or dark-fair hair, light eyes, and prominent chins and cheekbones that reminded Lorn of the facial cast of some of the people in the Brightwood. Lasif's was the face that stood out among them, though; fair-haired, with eyes so light blue as to be almost colourless, and an intent, intense expression that sat oddly on a farming lady in a remote kitchen. Looking at her, Lorn knew the mistress of this family – their spokesman, and the one who made choices after options were discussed.

'What shall I tell you first?' he said.

'You said there was a battle,' Lasif said. 'At Bluepeak.'

'There was,' Lorn said. 'And the Queen of Darthen has set aside the Oath, since Cillmod attacked her there and at Barachael, with Reavers as his allies—'

161

Some of the family muttered at this. 'Broken oaths,' Lasif said, 'a bad business, always . . . But Reavers on Cillmod's side? That's worse yet. When did they ever come into our country except to do us harm?'

Lorn thought of the Reaver chieftain down south, and the man's frightened, resolute face.

'What happened to the Reavers?' said one of the smallest of the children. 'Did they all get burnt up and chopped and killed in pieces?'

Freelorn had to chuckle. 'No,' he said. And then he lost the laughter in the memory of that cold night up on the slopes of Lionheugh, the cold of the knife-edge on his wrist, of the arrow in his chest, and the echo of the feeling of a sword in someone else's heart. Slowly, hunting words, he tried to tell them what that night had looked like, and also tried not to make it sound as if he had been there himself. It was hard to dry it out to mere facts – an army routed, thousands of Reavers and mercenaries suddenly removed by Flame to their points of origin – when you had before the mind's eyes the reality of it: the huge black Dragon-shadow tearing itself away from the hillside, suddenly becoming real, the blaze of blue Fire running down the hill, the huge doors that opened awfully on to places thousands of miles away, the cries of the terrified souls falling through them—

Freelorn looked up to find Lasif's thoughtful gaze resting on him.

'You were near to the battlefield,' Lasif said.

'Too near by far.' Lorn reached for another oatcake. 'The people coming away from there . . . had quite some stories to tell.'

The people around the table looked at one another. 'And what happened then?' Lasif said.

Of that, Lorn had not much more than 'rumour' to tell them. Armies were moving, certainly, but Lorn was purposely vague about locations.

'And is it true the young king's coming back?'

'That's what we hear.'

This produced a storm of opinion. Some of the children scowled: one burst into tears and put her face into Lasif's apron to be comforted. Paell and Gierne looked at one another and nodded, with slight smiles. Gare looked concerned, and Eglian said, 'That one! He ran away until he saw his chance – the country half starved and ready to take off their belts for any ruler that's not the Uncraeft. A real king would have taken his chances right away, not left us to starve slowly and the land to rot, just to suit his purposes. He wants killing.'

'Cillmod will have his chance,' Lorn said, trying to hold on to his composure. 'There will be a great battle, this autumn.'

'And how many of us will die in it?' Orrest said, sombre. 'Or of it? No matter who wins. The winning side will punish the losers – and even winners are forgetful about the people who helped them, the country people, when the battle's done. There's nothing in all this for us.'

'But a moment,' Lasif said, and the room got quiet. 'There is something about this that matters more than mere battles. If the young king now knows he was wrong, and has come back to live or die, that's worth knowing. And more than that, even; is this true, what they say? About the man, the man with the Fire?'

'I saw him at Bluepeak,' Lorn said. 'It's true.'

'And is it true what we heard, that he found his Fire because of the king? For love of him?'

Lorn swallowed. 'That's what I've heard too.'

Lasif nodded for a moment, and drank. 'Then,' she said, 'the young king is an instrument of the Goddess, a tool of Hers, and perhaps had less chance in what he did than we might think. Such a one's to be pitied, poor thing.'

Lorn sat still, desperately hoping that nothing showed in his face of the hot wave of shame that ran right through him at her words. For he knew perfectly well that this was *not* the case, that it was his own cowardice, and occasional downright stupidity, that had dragged Herewiss into the situations resulting in the breakthrough of his Fire. No Goddess Who was good would force one of Her creatures into such idiocies, such thoughtlessness, just to produce a miracle in someone else, no matter how great.

. . . *would She?*

'But it's the Fire that's important,' Lasif was saying now. 'If one man can have it, so can others. *That's* the wonder of all this! And the danger too,' she added, more quietly. 'For the gift was lost once before, the stories say. By misuse. It could happen again . . .' She shook her head, and there was silence. Then Lorn turned the conversation to his supposed purpose, and so they adjourned to the stable, where his packs were disassembled and minutely scrutinized. Everything from his smallest hook and needle to his biggest pot was passed from hand to hand; offers were made and rejected; there were complaints about rising prices and declining values, and once or twice (for the sake of form) Lorn invoked the Goddess and declared that they were all out to ruin him. It was basic market-place stuff, but the pleasure of it was sharpened by the evening light, growing more golden by the moment; by the friendly stoup of wine being passed from hand to hand, and by the sheer delight that these people took in having someone new to talk to.

My people, Lorn thought. It was too easy to think of Arlen as mostly Prydon – as the city, all astir, with its high handsome houses and streets, and Kynall Castle off behind its ancient walls. But many fewer Arlenes lived in Prydon, in the houses, than lived like this . . . scattered through the empty fields, chaffering over bits of metal as if they made the difference between life and death . . . because they did. The Lion's throne might be in Prydon, but this was its foundation – the flagstones of this household's hearth, and all the others like it. Héalhra had been a farmer, had worked a holding like this once, had mucked out a stable like the one outside. And then the Goddess had spoken to him . . .

The family settled finally for a new pot, and Lorn added

four needles to this, a goodwill gift of the kind any tradesman might add on his first visit to a given customer. After that, nothing would do but that Lorn be shown the room with the bed and the door that shut – Lasif's room, he thought, that she shared with her husbands. And then Lorn was told to rest himself for a while, and the household went into a flurry of activity, as the oldest laying chicken was asked for pardon, and had its neck wrung. Parsnips were put on to roast, and more ivy wine was brought out, and the end of a side of bacon was fished out of the chimney with the smoking-hook. More butter was brought from the cold store, and milk from the afternoon milking, and buttermilk, and half a hard cheese, and half a soft one. Lorn, infected by the excitement, got no more than half an hour's nap before giving up and going to help out in the kitchen.

They gave him the best they had, and there was no way he could have talked them out of it: indeed, the talking went on and on. About midnight, Lorn toasted them all in the last cup of wine, and made his way to bed. Sleep, much longed-for, leapt out of the early-morning dimness and pulled him gratefully down as soon as his head touched the straw-stuffed pillow.

He awoke suddenly, in the dark. Something nearby had spoken his name. He could hear the shape and sound of the word in the silence that surrounded him now.

Lorn sat up and listened. No sound: not even that of someone breathing, waiting to see what he did. *No-one here after all. Just a dream.* The window was open, and moonlight fell through it as a silvery square on the flag-stoned floor. A soft rustling came from outside; one of the cattle, moving restlessly in its byre, the next building over.

Lorn realized suddenly that the last several cups of wine he had drunk were now clamouring to get out of him. He slipped out of the bed, felt around for his breeks, tugged them on, and then climbed out the window. Outside was the cowyard, all dirt and straw. Lorn made his way across it, found a handy drainage ditch up against the fence that divided the yard from the pasture, and eased himself.

About five minutes later, it seemed, he was finished. He sighed, and leaned on the fence, looking out over the fields. The cattle had stopped their shifting; he could hear the quiet breathing of them behind him. The moon was westering, sliding down the sky. Some distance away, across the pasture, Lorn heard a yowl: a cat challenging another night-rover perhaps. The yowl rose to a frightened shriek – then silence again. Lorn stood there a moment more, looking up at the paling moonlight, the brightening sky.

And froze, realizing where the moon was, and where the growing light was. *Dawn doesn't come up in the west!* But this wasn't a morning colour. Dark, lowering, long streaks of dark red—

Footsteps behind him, soft and heavy. The sweat broke out on Freelorn as he realized what the cat had been challenging. He turned. The moonlight that was fading in the face of that awful light in the west, somehow still fell full and cold on the white shape that loomed up behind him. Its breathing was soft and thick, a cold white fetid steam that jetted out in the icy air and blew in a sickening caress against his face. Claws reached, and the red on them was dried-on and flaking—

Freelorn leapt over the fence and ran. It was no use, as usual; that breathing, heavy, amused, was close behind him, getting closer second by second, toying with him. He splashed through a brook – some things of the Dark couldn't cross water. This one had no problem; it splashed through behind him, the spray of its passage hitting him in the back, ice-hot as molten metal, as he ran. He turned and fled north over the pasture, but it was no use; that disastrous sunset was reaching around into even that air now, so the whole sky was alight with it. And then Lorn felt the claws in his back, catching, pushing him down. He shouted in pain—

And was staring at the flint walls, and Lasif, with a

rushlight in her hand, who stood there looking at him in shock from the bedroom's open door.

He was breathing as hard as a man who's been running a race. It took him a moment to get enough breath to say, 'A dream.'

'So I thought,' she said, her eyes shadowed in the dim light. 'You were quite close to that battlefield, weren't you?'

'I think I still am,' he said, still shaking.

She nodded, and turned, and went away.

Lorn lay down again. His back smarted, and he knew he had much worse coming.

All but Lasif, who had to get up and milk the cow, slept late. She was working at the churn when Freelorn came in; the children were eating bread and butter, and Lorn was glad enough to sit down among them and do the same.

'Going north?' Lasif said.

Lorn nodded and munched his bread. 'Most of the business seems to be there these days.'

'As far north as Prydon, perhaps?'

'That far,' Lorn said, 'probably.'

Lasif pried up the churn-top, peered in, replaced it and started churning again. 'Just be careful,' she said. 'All these soldiers running around—' She shook her head. 'They get ideas.'

He thanked her, and went out to pack the horses.

. They all came out into their street to see him off. Lorn bade them goodbye, and could not get rid of the feeling of Lasif's eyes resting on him, thoughtful but oblique. Blackie was dancing, eager to be gone, and Lorn saw Lasif glance at him as well – thoughtful, noticing a horse better than a tinker needed, no matter how prosaic his packhorse might look.

He swung up on to Blackie, and nodded at Lasif. 'My blessing on all of you,' he said, 'and Hers.' And he rode away.

* * *

167

He made the best speed north that he could, without attracting attention to himself. Lorn was not a fool, to ignore his dreams. He knew which way he had been running, in the dream, and he was ready for the pain that would follow. So he kept telling himself.

The countryside warmed and gentled around him. Even high summer was cool, down south; but he was coming into the midlands now, no more than ten leagues or so from Hasmë; and the summer crops were standing high.

He passed his days much as he had in Imisna – arguing, bargaining, taking hospitality as he found it; a barn here, a bed there. He lost some of his newer pots, and gained some old, holed ones. His mind was less than completely on his 'work', though, for all around him was the constant distraction of country he knew much better than the high south. He had not been this way since his mother had taken him to be fostered out.

It was one of the few times she had ridden any distance with him – one of few memories he had of her, and one of the clearest. She had always been delicate. At least, that was the word they had always used. Whenever people in Kynall mentioned his mother, it was always as 'the good Queen'. But always the voices went hushed, as if there was something wrong, as if someone of ill intent, some *thing*, might hear what they were saying. Even then, when he was young, it seemed that people knew she was not going to be with them for long.

He had been told that his was a hard birth. There was an intimation, though no-one ever said it to Freelorn's face, that somehow his bearing *did* something to her, was the cause of the delicacy, the long wasting.

She had not seemed particularly delicate on that ride, when she took him out to foster. He hadn't wanted to leave Prydon. He was seven, with a castle for his playhouse and a city to run amok in. But his mother had insisted that he be fostered like anybody else of good house. She and his father had ridden with him down to

Hasmë, where they stayed in an inn that fell far short of Freelorn's princely expectations. He remembered being shocked when his mother remarked on how nice it was for a place so far out in the country.

But all during that ride, she had seemed unusually robust. Lorn had been used, all during his childhood, to seeing her tire easily, but on this ride it seemed impossible to pry her out of the saddle. She rode like the crazed youngsters Lorn had seen and envied: like a farm girl. She took mad jumps over brooks, and galloped, leaving Lorn and the rest of the entourage far behind.

'I grew up here,' she had said. He had known that – but the way she said it suddenly made him listen. It was the same tone of voice she used when she told him she loved him. It came as a slight shock to him that there might be something *else* she loved as much. He was unnerved. 'This is a wonderful place, Lorn . . . you're going to like it here. The fields, the sky . . . the way it is in the summer.' He had his doubts. But he worshipped his mother; he was willing to believe anything she told him.

They passed through Hasmë, and, after another day's ride, reached a tiny village. It had five houses and six farms, and a tiny market square: not much else. 'You're going to love it here,' his mother said. Lorn looked at the dirt street, and had his doubts.

He had missed her bitterly when she left. But what ashamed him to this day was that he hadn't missed her *more*. Belatedly, the excitement of being in a new place took hold of him. That excitement, the old bite of that shame, both came back now, and fastened on him hard, as he sat ahorse outside Elefrua. He was as afraid to go in now as he had been all those years ago. More so because it was mostly unchanged. The trees were taller, there were a few more houses, but everything else was the same. The way that light fell was the same. And his first love—

She wouldn't know him, of course, because of the disguise. Was she even here? Slowly he rode in.

It was market day here, as he had known it would be.

Small point in stopping in Elefrua otherwise. He was rather late – the market had been going on since dawn, and the choicest goods had already been snapped up. Most people had already spent whatever they intended to, and would be waiting for the house that doubled as Elefrua's brewery, tavern and cookshop to open up for business.

He rode down into town, looking at the fieldstone walls. There was the one he hid behind when he helped Mirik and Lal steal the neighbour's cow. The road curved, leading into the market square. They had cobbled it since he had been here last. *Eight years,* he thought. He swung down from Blackmane's back and looked around at the stalls for a place to stand.

'Are you selling this morning, friend?' said a voice at his elbow. The hair stood up all over Lorn as he turned to see Orl standing there, the neighbour whose cow he had stolen. Lorn went hot with embarrassment, then remembered that Orl would not recognize him. It was time as much as Eftgan's disguise that made this so, for Lorn saw to his shock that Orl was *old*. One of his eyes was grey with cataract, and his back was bent with the onset of bone trouble. *But what did I think? Was time to have stood still while I was gone?*

'Uh, yes,' Lorn said, trying not to stare. 'Usual fee, then,' Orl said. 'Three pennies, and a tenth of your take in goods or silver.'

'Three?' Lorn said, in good-humoured scorn, for he knew perfectly well it had always been two. 'Listen, friend—'

Orl glanced ever so slightly off to his left and behind him. Lorn followed the glance, then looked away quickly. Against the wall of Marbhan's house, the cookshop, three men were lounging. Their cloaks were shabby, but under them were black tunics that Lorn recognized. The White Lion badge was embroidered on the breasts of them. The men were all armed, two with swords, a third with an axe. Their expressions were bored, and Lorn thought it best that they should stay that way.

170

'I see,' he said. 'Three it is . . . How long has this been going on?'

'Just this last year. Used to be they just passed through. Now they live here. A lot more of them in Hasmë.'

His tone of voice, restrained and resigned, said a great deal to Lorn. Someone's beds were being taken up by these men, and someone's food being eaten without payment: with this unofficial wage, or protection payment, on top of it all. Lorn worked to keep what he thought from his face. 'Where do you want me?' he said.

Orl looked around. 'Over there by the shambles, if you like.'

Lorn wasn't wild about the flies that would come of being put by the butcher, but at least he was in the shade of the wall that surrounded the tavern's garden. He led Blackie and Pebble over there, past the three soldiers, and itched at the feel of their eyes on him. Lorn hobbled the horses, and started unloading them, spreading out his wares.

To his great relief, the soldiers showed no further interest. They had the look of men waiting for drink, and as soon as Marbhan's place opened its front door, in they went. Lorn began calling his wares, and one by one people began drifting over to see what he had.

There was Marbhan, in his big grey-stained, yeast-smelling apron, utterly unchanged after eight years. There was big fat Ulaidth, easily the jolliest woman Lorn had ever known, her hair gone streaky silver; and Curc, with the gap between his teeth and his soft way of speaking; and Bim, and Darrih, and many another.

He was praising a pot to Arvel at one point, and half thought he had a sale, when he looked up, and saw Lalen there.

She was changed, yes, but not as much as some. The red hair and brown, wide-set eyes were what he noticed about her first, twenty years ago, when they were both young . . . those thoughtful eyes, and the blazing hair, now streaked ever so slightly with silver. Otherwise she

171

was as she had been: petite, sturdy, solid. She glanced at him, a calm, impersonal look. Lorn swallowed, nodded at her.

She reached past Arv, and stroked a small iron pot. 'How much, sir?' she said.

'Three in silver.'

She snorted at him, and Freelorn almost burst out laughing. That sound had been the first thing he had learned to love about her – she refused to take him seriously, no matter what he did. Princes of Arlen had cut no cheese with *her*. Nor did his prices now, apparently. 'Too damned much,' she said.

'Don't buy it, then,' Lorn said, and turned back to Arv. She stared at him in mild surprise, and Lorn restrained his smile. He had long since learned that rising to Lalen's bait was useless – the best tactic was to refuse to play. She could never resist that.

'Why shouldn't I buy it? What's wrong with it?' she said.

Arvel made an amused face as Lalen shouldered in beside him. 'Everything,' Lorn said. 'Look at the rust on it. And it's obviously much too big for a lady like you, who eats like a bird. Here now, sir, look at this one—'

There were chuckles coming from the people gathered behind Lalen. It was unfair of him, actually, for he knew Lalen's appetite, having cooked for her in the past. If she ate like a bird, then the bird in question was the Darthene dragon-eagle, the kind that carries off whole deer when the mood strikes it. Lalen was amused, in the wry sort of way that came of being the butt of the joke.

'I might give you two for it,' she said.

Lorn looked skyward in comment. 'Madam, no-one's buying today,' he said. 'I'm not even going to be able to cover my expenses, at this rate.' Just a flick of glance, here, at the doorway where part of the 'expenses' lounged. 'And you're asking me for discounts.' He sighed. 'Two and three quarters.'

'Do I look like I'm made of money?'

172

'Poor tradesmen like me can only live in hope.'

She laughed at him. 'Two and one, and not a brass scraping more.'

They argued back and forth, and finally settled on two and one-and-a-half. The small crowd muttered approval at Lalen for having gotten the best of the deal, and then began to drift away at the sound of the iron bell ringing at Marbhan's for the beginning of the nunch-meal.

Lorn watched Lalen go off down the street to the house that had been her parents'. *Are they even alive, I wonder?* he thought, suddenly feeling tender and sad. *Is she alone? Or has she found someone? No way to ask, of course . . .*
Lorn repacked his wares, but didn't sling them on the horses, merely hobbled Blackie and Pebble to them and put on the nosebags. Then he went to see about his own feed.

Marbhan's was just as it had always been; the main room low-ceilinged, smoky with the hearthfire and the cookfire, the flagged floor covered with the same ancient oaken tables.

Lorn found a spot near one of the windows and waited to be noticed. Eventually Marbhan wound his way over. 'What's your pleasure?' he said.

'A cup of wine, please. And is there bacon today?'

'Pig trotters and roast turnip,' Marbhan said.

'Please!' Lorn said, his mouth watering with the taste of old memories. As Marbhan moved off with his order, Lorn saw Lalen standing in the doorway. She looked around the room with the expression of someone trying to work out the least objectionable place to sit. One of the Arlenes looked up at her and was about to say something when Lalen spotted Lorn and began moving towards him.

'Any new face,' she said in a low voice as she sat down, 'is Goddess-sent around here. May I?'

'Do,' said Lorn. He did not look in the soldier's direction as he said, 'A problem?'

'For the last few months, yes. Used to be we didn't have to bother with people from Prydon but once a year.

Now—' She shook her head, and regarded him curiously. 'Do I know you from somewhere?' she said.

Lorn's throat went dry. 'I used to pass through here every now and then,' he said. 'You didn't mention your name?'

'Lalen d'Ramien,' she said. 'And you're—'

'Arelef, they call me.'

'What did you order?'

That was Lalen all over: managing the lives of the people around her, even if she'd only met them a minute before. 'The trotters.'

'That's all right then,' Lalen said. 'Marbhan leaves the beef dishes too long sometimes, he's a pork cook really . . .'

She chattered on in the pleasant and inconsequential way that Lorn remembered, until their wine came: then she pledged him amiably enough, and said, 'Welcome here.'

'Thank you,' he said, and drank, and stole a glance towards the Arlene soldiers.

She caught it. 'They're manageable enough,' she said. 'There are a lot more of us than there are of them, and they don't want to risk being staked out on a hillside for the crows. But at the same time, we don't bait them. Some nasty stories have been coming down from Hasmë.'

Lorn nodded. 'Things are moving out east,' he said. 'I suppose they've been getting nervous in Prydon.'

Lalen looked out at him from under her brows, a resigned expression. 'Makes you wish for the old days, when things were settled. Ah well: a long time ago now, and no sign of it changing, really. Not for us, wars or no, since . . . since some time back.'

The food arrived, and Lorn pulled the first trotter apart as delicately as he could, but there was really no way to eat this food delicately, with the presence of many small bones to be gnawed clean of succulent, herb-scented, beautifully greasy meat. Lalen reached out as Marbhan went by, and yanked a clean linen towel out of his belt, putting it down next to Lorn's plate. 'He always forgets. Now then,' she said, turning to the little dark-haired girl who appeared at her side. 'How long did he say?'

'Till two hours before sunset,' the child replied.

'Why so long?' Lalen asked.

'He says it's the beans,' the little girl said. 'You didn't boil them long enough.'

'He's crazed,' Lalen said. 'We're going to wind up with mush again.' She drank her wine, resigned, then turned to Lorn. 'Marbhan cooks our dinner in his bread oven, for the price of the fuel,' she said.

Lorn put down one well-cleaned pork bone, picked up a fresh one. 'Your sister?' he said. 'Cousin?'

'No, my daughter. Nia.'

Lorn nodded at her. The little girl flashed a brilliant smile at Lorn. 'I know,' she said cheerfully. 'You're the damned cheat who sold Mam the pot.'

'Nia!!' Lalen flushed scarlet.

Freelorn laughed. 'Never mind,' he said. 'It's all part of business. And how old are you, young woman?'

'I'm nine years old,' she said grandly. And then screwed up her face in an annoyed grimace as her mother looked at her. 'All right, *eight* still. I get to be nine the night before Opening Night.'

Lorn found himself staring at Nia. *Eight years . . .*

The world tilted. This little girl was not just Lal's daughter, but his as well. *Not dead! Not dead after all! My daughter . . . !* And not just his daughter, but a princess of Arlen, the Throne Princess in fact, eight years senior to the daughter Segnbora was carrying.

But Lal told Herewiss she was dead . . . ! Why did she—

The Throne Princess's nose was running, and she had become absorbed in trying to peel a scab off one dusty knee. 'The father?' Lorn said, trying desperately to sound casual.

Lalen shrugged. 'Off east somewhere. He wasn't my loved, it doesn't matter.'

Lorn swallowed and felt the pain from his dream, but not in the back: in the heart, and no claw could have been sharper. He turned his attention away from them, with difficulty, and back to the pig's trotters.

Lalen chatted on, and Lorn made what he hoped were sensible noises every now and then. After a while, Lalen said to Lorn, 'Are you staying the night?'

'I may do, if the innkeeper has a room.'

'Well then, if we don't see you again today – this time next year?'

Lorn smiled at her. 'It might be sooner.'

Lalen got up. 'Come on then, Nia.'

They went out: the mother looking slightly weary: the child, wandering after her, bored with the adult world of the inn, looking bright-eyed around her for something more interesting. Lorn watched her go, and felt that claw in the heart again.

He knew that Marbhan had rooms. He resolved not to take one. *I want to be out of here this afternoon. The evening's ride will get me to Gierhun – I can put up there.*

He finished his meal, cleaned himself off as best he could with the linen, then paid his reckoning and stepped out into the sunshine. Lorn washed briefly at the well outside in the market square, and after drawing a bucket of water for Blackie and Pebble, he stood for a few minutes in the market square, at a loss, looking around him. There was the old road that ran north out of the square, past Orl's and Sas's farms, and Dak's place beyond them. *Is Dak even alive still?*

He began to wander up that way, scuffing up the white dust of the road. The afternoon light shifted, now bold blue and golden, now peach-coloured, once greenish when a shower threatened and half the sky began churning leaden-black. Lorn leaned on a wall and watched the storm go by, listened to the wind hissing, suddenly cold, in the branches of the pine trees planted in the middle of the wall. There came a low rumble of thunder, un-threatening, almost thoughtful.

The wind suddenly started to die off, and Lorn leaned there, listening. There was no sound now; just his heartbeat, slower than usual, and seemingly louder. It might have been the land's heartbeat, almost. But then his father would have said that it *was*.

It's all we're for. The words had been spoken, not leaning on this wall, but one like it, somewhere north-east of Prydon. They had been watching the weather, but it had been some hot still day with a sky burning blue, everything blazing under a pitiless sun, everything seeming straightforward and obvious: nothing like this equivocal weather. *There's no point at all in having kings if the land doesn't bear. The land has to be re-quickened, reborn, every year: just as the seed does. Blood does it, because it runs in us the way rain does in the ground; and the royal marriage, or even just lovemaking, does it, because male or female, you quicken the spirit in your loved, and they in you. And a family with experience in the art of making the land bear can pass the experience down . . . train its children and make sure the art isn't lost.* He had looked over at Lorn. *Don't you forget about that, when it's your turn.*

Lorn breathed out, once and sharply: a laugh, or a gasp of pain. *Train your children,* he thought. But until now, this hadn't been an issue, he having had only one daughter that he knew about, and she still in Segnbora's womb.

But Nia—

He sighed. It mattered little enough, for he had no idea what to train any child *in*. Oh, he knew the use of the Regalia, and the words and rites of the various royal magics, and a great deal about the mechanics of getting the crops in, managing the land. What he did not have, had never had, was that essential feeling that he *was* the land, and was also its father. He was sure his own father had it; he had seen him gazing out over the walls of Kynall, or leaning on a country wall like this one, all moss and ants, his face gentle with something Lorn wanted to share, but didn't, and didn't know how to ask for. The sense that your fleshly body and that earthy body were the same, and that earthy body and the Goddess's were the same: that you were Her lover, becoming fruitful, in the mystery, from your union with Her: and the land's lover too, so that you, the quickener, paradoxically were quickened yourself by the ancientness and power of what you sought to enter and fructify— In the dusty scrolls and tomes of the Archive, he had read about this, the most obscure and important part of royalty, until his eyes had smarted from rushlight and frustration. It had been no help. No feeling had come.

It's a shame that you can't manage this part of rule without *feeling it. I could be a king with the best of them, then.* He put his head down on his folded arms, watching the wind slide gently through the wheat.

. . . Unless you don't have *to feel it. Unless . . . it just is, and you take it as such. And feeling that way, or not, doesn't matter.*

And if that were the case . . . then his father was right: then the heartbeat he felt *was* the world's: or at least, his part of the world's. That his blood running, *was* the rain falling, that his quickening, the fertility or sterility of his life, *was* the land's.

But all this being so . . . if it is *so . . . then I can't be father to my country just by enacting the Royal Magics, or by using the Regalia. Not even by just giving my life for it. Something else is needed.*

Then he straightened up and breathed out a heavy, unhappy breath.

How the Dark can I be father to my country if I can't even be father to my own daughter?

The wind was rising again, taking the storm off eastwards with it. Lorn brushed the moss off himself. It was time he got started.

If I leave now I can be in Gierhun by twilight.

When he got to the market square, there were a few men and women lounging around the door at Marbhan's – done with the day's chores, drinking wine, gossiping, and looking out at the evening, golden again after its fit of squalls. Off to one side, lounging on one of the benches there, was Lalen; she was looking over at Blackmane and Pebble. When she saw Lorn, she sketched him a small casual wave and said, 'We were beginning to wonder where you'd got to. Thought you were heading out.'

'Caught out in the weather,' Lorn said. 'I would have thought you'd have been eating dinner by now. Was he right about the beans?'

Lalen laughcd softly. 'So he was. Embarrassing. Listen,' she went on. 'You might as well have some.'

'Pardon?'

Lalen wrinkled her face up in the original of the expression he had seen on Nia earlier. 'The Goddess invented hospitality so that She could partake, after all,' she said. 'You've got a long way to go before wherever you're going tonight—'

'Gierhun.'

'Those cheapskates at Witling's, they'll put you to bed on an empty stomach if you turn up an hour after sunset. You come have some beans.'

He was inclined to refuse . . . but his resolve was melting in the memory of how well Lalen cooked. 'Madam,' he said, bowing slightly, 'the Goddess thanks you by me.'

Lalen's house was the same one Lorn remembered, a big one for the town, five rooms and a roof of slate rather than thatch. Her family had held their lands successfully for some years, growing wheat and mutton, and the house reflected their prosperity. There was a quiet feel about it now that was not entirely the fault of the evening stillness. 'Do you have sharers?' Lorn said.

Lalen shook her head as she pushed the door open and led the way into the kitchen. Lorn said nothing, realizing that this meant that Amien and Rab, her parents, were dead.

The kitchen smelled of spice, and bread, and mutton ham: the pot he had sold Lalen that morning was hanging on a crane over the kitchen fire. Nia was laying the table, and looked up at Lorn. 'There you are finally,' she said in a voice almost exactly that of her mother. 'We've been waiting *all night*.'

'Hush, dear,' Lalen said, and put the pot from Marbhan's down on the table. She lifted the lid, and a rich smell filled the air.

'Thanks to the good creatures who gave of themselves,' Lorn said, and meant it. 'Where do I sit?'

'Over there. Nia means to have you to herself, I fear. Any new face . . .'

They sat down, put aside the Goddess's portion, then Lalen dished out and they all fell to. It was a quieter meal than nunch had been, at least on Lalen's side; she ate silently, and tensely, as if uneasy under her own roof. Lorn became determined to be out of there as quickly as he could. But Nia was fascinated with him, and wanted to know how he made nails, and where the pots came from, and a hundred other things. He told her, and told her, until Lalen finally looked over and chided her for making the guest let his food get cold.

Nia thought of complaining, then let it go. She curled up on the settle built into the wall by the kitchen fire, yawning. 'It's past her bedtime,' Lalen said, pouring out the wine, 'but when there's a guest . . .'

Lorn nodded absently, his gaze dwelling on Nia as she started to doze off. She looked entirely like his mother – the resemblance was shocking. He had tried hard not to see it at nunch, but in the intimacy of the firelight there was no mistaking it – the high cheekbones, the large soft eyes. *My daughter*, he thought. *What a beautiful little girl. This will be a good memory to take away with me, even if nothing ever comes of it . . .*

He turned to say something to Lalen, and then flinched back slightly from the suddenly suspicious, angry look in her eye. She was looking at him as if she suspected him of evil intentions towards Nia. What else was she to think, when a stranger looked at a child with such sudden tenderness?

He was going to have to explain himself.

But there was the problem of those soldiers, still sitting there in Marbhan's. And Goddess only knew how many more of them between here and Prydon . . .

The Dark with them.

He opened his mouth to start explaining, and Lalen suddenly sat back and shook her head. 'One thinks the strangest things, sometimes, out here in the country,' she said, looking suddenly contrite.

'I'm sorry,' Lorn said. 'She reminds me of one of my relatives, that's all. I hadn't noticed, earlier . . .'

He broke off. She was staring at him again.

'Sorry,' Lalen said abruptly. 'Sorry. You just—'

'Did I say something wrong?'

'No, you just sounded, your voice sounded—' She stopped, and laughed. 'Funny, it's been years. Amazing how something will make you think of someone that you haven't . . .'

'A friend?' Lorn said.

Lalen sighed and sat back in her chair. 'He was then,' she said. 'Quite a good friend.'

It was too much to bear. Lorn stood up.

'I've got to go,' he said. And something cold-voiced stood up in him and shouted: *Traitor!*

'No,' he said, 'wait. There's water in the kettle?'

Lalen looked at him as if suddenly concerned for his sanity. 'Yes—'

'A spare cup?' Lorn said, and got up from the table.

'Over on the sideboard—'

Lorn found it, an earthenware cup: hooked the lid off the kettle with the pothook, and dipped the cup into the water. 'Half a breath,' he said, and ducked out the back door, feeling Lalen staring at him.

Past the gravelled walk outside the door was the flower bed, as he remembered. Lorn reached down near the roots of a rosebush, scrabbled for a handful of dirt, poured it into the cup. Blood was no problem: he had thorned himself thoroughly in his digging. He wet his hands in the hot muddy water and scrubbed at his face. He stood up, dripping, and feeling foolish: he wished he had a mirror to judge the results by. Lorn wiped his face on his sleeves, and returned to the kitchen.

Lalen looked up at him with the beginnings of a smile. 'I've seen people be caught short be—' she started to say: and then her voice failed her. 'Who—' But she could see that the clothes were the same. Only the face had changed. And her voice left her again.

'Yes,' he said. He didn't want to say anything more.

Lalen stared.

'How dare you,' she said at last. 'How dare you come back, just like this! As if nothing had happened!'

Lorn looked at her in surprise. 'Plenty has happened—'

'Indeed it has! More than plenty! Well, what do you want?' Lalen said. 'What trouble are you going to make *this* time?'

He looked at her, openmouthed. 'What do you—'

'Doubtless you haven't a clue,' Lalen said. 'You never did think things through. When you robbed the treasury at Osta, a while back: what do you think happened? Who do you think paid four times the usual tax to make up for it? Well grown, Nia is, yes! No thanks to you! Who do you think went without food two days out of ten so that *she* wouldn't have to?' She paused. And even more angrily, but quietly, she said, 'And that isn't her real name. It's Fastrael.'

One of the old names of the royal line: a queen of Arlen four or five hundred years junior to the Lion. Lorn let that go, still flinching from Lalen's anger. 'Lal,' he said, 'I've come to start putting all this right.'

'It can't be put right! It's *done*! Do you think you can make eight years just vanish?' She glared at him.

'There is atonement,' he said, rather tightly, 'if nothing else. Whether you think it's worth anything or not, I *have* come back. And I mean to do right now, if I didn't do it earlier.'

She looked at him with scorn. 'And how long will *this*

182

phase last, do you think? A week? A month? Before you take yourself elsewhere, for yet another perfectly good reason?' Lal scowled at him. 'You were always somewhere else! What kind of king is it who's always somewhere else? A king needs to be *home*. Dead or alive.'

'The first chance,' he said, 'will happen sooner or later. And as for the second part, here I am.'

Lal's expression was still sceptical and cold. 'People always said you wouldn't be king,' she said. 'Not even right after your father died. You weren't Initiate then, and you aren't now. You've a way to go yet.'

There was a silence. 'Odd,' Lorn said, 'that feeling that way, you gave the little one that name.'

They both glanced over at Nia, momentarily guilty to be talking about the child as if she wasn't there. But she was sound asleep. 'No-one uses it around here,' Lalen said. 'Not with *them* around.'

'Why did you tell Herewiss she was dead?' he said.

Lal shrugged, a cool gesture. 'She wasn't your business any more,' she said. 'You were outlawed. What child needs an outlaw for a father? Had anyone known. So I protected her. I was the only one around to do it. But why should you care one way or another? I would have thought it would be one less thing for you to worry about.' The resigned scepticism in her voice was terrible.

'I'll be going tonight,' Lorn said. 'I don't want to take a chance of endangering her, or you. But I *would* like her to know. Not about the kingship . . . just about . . . me.'

Lalen stared at him, her face still. Then softly she moved to the settle by the fire and stroked Nia's, Fastrael's, hair. 'Sweet,' she said. 'Wake up: you have to go to bed. And say good night.'

The child yawned and smiled.

'But listen first. Remember I told you that some day your father might come back?'

'Uh huh.'

'Well, he has. It's a surprise. This is your father.'

The child looked at him, apparently unconcerned by his

change of face. Lorn had to fight to hold himself still. Her cool regard was so like Lal's that chills ran down him.

'Is that true?' Nia said.

Freelorn nodded. 'Yes.'

'That's nice,' she said. 'When will you go away again?'

His heart broke.

'Mam said,' said Nia, 'if you ever came back, you wouldn't be here for long.' There was no censure in the words: she was simply stating a fact.

'I don't know when I can come back,' he said. 'I have a lot to do.'

'All right,' she said. 'Good night . . .' And, yawning, she went through the door that led to the bedrooms.

Lalen said nothing for the moment, simply watched her go. Lorn felt the claws inside him catch and tear. *All the small betrayals*, he thought, *all the times I've run away; they come to this at last. When you finally come back, there's no-one left to come back to, and no-one who knows you, or cares. The price is fair.*

'You'll do what you like, of course,' Lal said at last. 'You always did. But if we don't see you again, we'll understand. It won't make her unhappy.'

Is there anything in life I can do that matters now, he thought in despair, *except die Initiate, and quickly, to bind the Shadow until someone more competent can be made king? Someone from one of the cadet lines. Perhaps even Cillmod?* And why not? It occurred to Lorn that everything that Herewiss had been working for, all his calm plans, were possibly simply *unjust* – because he was truly the wrong person for the job.

'I'll go,' Lorn said. He stepped outside, slipped on his cloak, then saddled the horses hurriedly. Lalen stood in the door, watching him.

Lorn swung on to Blackie's back, pulling the hood of the cloak up.

'Next year, about this time?' Lalen said.

He swallowed. 'Maybe sooner,' he said. 'The Goddess keep you. And the little one.'

Lalen turned away. 'And you,' she said, and the door shut.

Lorn rode on to the market square, not hurrying. There was a single torch in a bracket outside Marbhan's, its light a weak diffuse circle on the cobbles. One of the Arlenes was leaning against the doorpost, gazing out into the night. Lorn swallowed through a dry throat and said, 'Good night, now.'

''Night,' said the soldier. Lorn rode on past, sweating, not hurrying. He didn't start to hurry after he left the town – the sound would have carried: nor did he start hurrying when three hills over, for it would have made no difference. If anyone had realized who he was, the hunt would not be after him right this minute, but in a couple of days, and in more force.

He made it to Gierhun about an hour before midnight, and the kitchen fires had indeed all been put out. *Those cheapskates*, he heard Lalen's voice say: contentious, cheerfully scornful . . . loved.

For whatever good it did. Freelorn lay in the dark, his face bare again, now plain for anyone to see in this country where his head was worth the price of a year's harvest or a year's wage.

And the worst of it, he thought, *is that it all may have been for nothing. Nothing.*

Sleep came hard.

185

8

Ou'sta nnou'anv-Inrahaih thiemnh'sraihh staoiodh'rui.

Better the dark under the stone, than sunstorm unsuspected.

Dracon proverb

Looked on from above, the Eorlhowe was nothing special. Up here at the tip of the North Arlene peninsula, a chain of hills ran up to a north-pointing cape, tapering as they went. Then suddenly, at the cape's end, the great hill reared up. It had a look of melted stone about it – slumped and shouldery. The casual viewer could not see the tunnels, the cavern openings. It hardly mattered. There were no casual viewers of the Eorlhowe.

Segnbora looked down on it as they began their first descent. Even in a cloudy morning, with the mist not yet cleared off the water, the place looked forbidding to human eyes. To a Dragon— She could for one thing sense the heat in it, trapped in the heart of the mountain. There had been tunnelling in the Eorlhowe since it was first laid down over Dahiric, and some of that tunnelling had touched on old heats in the earth and brought them nearer the surface. There was another power there, too, one that spoke more clearly to the human in Segnbora than to the Dragon. Stirring there was something like Fire – a kind different from hers, perhaps, but still identifiable as the force of life, trapped and tamed to a purpose. She could hear the tremor of it, the slow beat of it, deep inside the hill. It was the Eorlhowe Gate. It was a door of the kind that Herewiss had opened in the old Hold – but one peculiar to the Dragonkind and their use. It had simply made itself apparent on the site after Dahiric's interment. The Eorlhowe Gate was not just a door into other places, Segnbora had heard, but a timegate as well. At least so the stories had run in the Silent Precincts – but how much truth there was to them, she had no idea.

But for a Dragon visiting the Howe— There were no comparatives for it in human experience. If there had been one king of the world, or queen – one ruler – who lived in a given place: if that ruler were king, not only of the living, but also of the dead and the yet unborn, able to call them, and bid them, and be obeyed: then that was what the Dweller in the Howe was. And if that ruler had lived in the same place since the dawn of one's presence in the world, if that place were haunted by the spirits of all the kings and queens who had gone before – then that was what the Eorlhowe was like. Segnbora's *mdeihei* were nervous about it. Some of them had been called there on one business or another, not in this Dweller's tenure, but earlier. They were hesitant to share those memories: especially the ahead-memories – something was going to happen there that frightened them . . .

She glanced over at Hasai. His *ehhath* was less certain than she had seen it for some time. He caught the look, and the feel of her concern.

'Well, *sdaha?*' she said, matching the bank. 'Will they have seen us enough now, do you think?'

'Enough for my taste,' he said. Since he had pitched Hiriedh and Aivuh out of Aired Marchward a few days back, Hasai had been out of temper, and less than pleased with Dragons that he would normally have respected highly and obeyed without question. She was seeing a different Hasai, one who was angrier, more assertive. Segnbora was not quite sure what to make of this change. She knew her *mdeihei* were upset about it. But then she suspected that was simply because *mdeihei* were not supposed to be *able* to change. The dead were, even among Dragons, dead.

187

She and Hasai landed near the chief of the cave entrances, at the base of the Howe. Hiriedh was waiting for them. The gold and green of her were pale in the cool silver light; the mist was not yet burned off, and everything around them looked indistinct. Greetings were exchanged, and Hiriedh led the way into the caves.

A long while, they walked into the mountain. Other Dragons passed them, though there were surprisingly few. They nodded courtesy here, paused for a word of recognition there. There were some whom Hasai had not seen for many years. They looked at him most strangely, as if they saw someone risen from the dead. The tunnels turned and twisted, and delved downwards; the air got hotter. The feeling of power, stifled, grew stronger as they went. Several tunnels came together, then; the one they were in became wide and high, and then abruptly opened out. They paused at the brink of it.

Segnbora looked around, and determined as she was not to be amazed, was amazed regardless. They had reached the centre of the mountain, the heart of the Howe – a cavern nearly half a mile across. The air was hot and still. At least two hundred Dragons were gathered around the edges. And in the centre, in shadow, lay the Dweller.

She was stretched at her ease. Segnbora immediately recognized the shadow about her. It was like that which came and went about *her* when the *mdeihei* were manifesting more clearly than usual. But the sight of it surprised her, for normal Dragons, living Dragons, did not manifest such. Here, though, the shadows lay thick, like the fog outside that would not burn off. But this was dark, and wings moved in it, and eyes; and eyes looked out at Segnbora. And the looks—

They yearn. They yearn towards us. But they hate, as well – and dear Goddess, the virulence of it! That she couldn't understand, for what harm had she and Hasai ever done them? Less still could Segnbora understand the greater darkness she now perceived behind the Dweller. Was there some trace of motion in that obscurity?

188

'Greetings, Hasai ehs'Pheress,' said the voice. Segnbora's attention was drawn back to the figure that lay in the midst of the shadows. She was not there the way a living Dragon would have been there. There was an uncertainty about her shape and colour: she was insubstantial, but not from a lack of substance; from a surplus of it. She could *be* any Dragon or any of its *mdeihei*. She *was* Dragonkind, in one form, one shape.

Hasai bent low and greeted the Dweller. 'And to you, Segnbora Welcaen's daughter,' the Dweller said, and paused, 'greeting.'

The phrasing, in Dracon, was rude, only one utterance-name being given. Nonetheless, Segnbora kept her *ehhath* quite proper, and bowed greeting to the Dweller, and said, 'Well met, Lady of the Dragons.' And if the Dweller's address to her had been a bit on the abrupt side, so was hers; the bare human phrase, and none of the long string of honorifics normally used by one who was meeting the Dweller for the first time.

They looked at one another, she and Hasai and the Dweller. It was a brief look on Dithra's side. Dithra's *mdeihei*, though, looked at Segnbora and Hasai out of the darkness, unswerving.

'Do you know why we bade you here?' the Dweller asked.

It was a 'royal' we, but with more cause for the plurality than usual, even among Dragons. Segnbora bowed again slightly, letting her *ehhath* speak irony for her. 'Perhaps the DragonChief will be so good to tell us. We thought that we had reasons of our own. Perhaps we will now find that they were *hers*?'

A soft rustling went through the gathered Dragons. They were not used to such insolence. 'You made your causes plain enough to Lhhaess and Sd'hirrin,' Dithra said, 'and to Hiriedh and Aivuh, who were sent to bid you here. Your *mdaha* has also made it plain.'

Segnbora glanced over at Hasai. He had lain down, and was gazing at the Dweller thoughtfully. 'Your motives and

189

your goals are unimportant to us. But what you *are* – that is of some interest.' Just once, Dithra herself gazed at Segnbora; only for a moment. Segnbora, *ehhath* forgotten for a moment, caught that look with her Fire and tried to feel what was at the bottom of it. Just a flash came strongly, as it had with Hiriedh; fear. But also that yearning, tangled about with an ahead-memory, vague even to the *lhhw'Hreiha*. That startled Segnbora. Dithra's precognition should have been clearer than anyone else's. But on this matter it was not.

'What we are,' Segnbora said, 'is *sdaha* and *mdaha*. Surely even by darklight the DragonChief can see that.'

'That's the seeming,' Dithra said. 'Your friend there, *dav'whnesshih*. And yourself – less so than usual, perhaps? For one who's egg-laden?'

Segnbora laughed. It was a backhanded sort of joke. *Mdeihei* could be pregnant only in the abstract sense; the business of clutching was left to the *sdahaih*. Dithra was implying that she was not spending enough time in her 'true' form. 'Maybe so,' she said. 'But the babe is well enough for the moment. Though your solicitousness is appreciated, DragonChief. However, my child is not the issue here. Your lives are, and your children's lives.'

Everything got quite still at that. *Ah dear*, Segnbora thought, *I've sat on the tail-spine now. Let's see if it was to any purpose.*

'*Your* solicitousness is appreciated,' the Dweller said dryly. 'Now let us move on to particulars. What is this matter of kingship about which you wish to consult us?'

'Dweller-in-the-Howe,' Hasai said, 'very well you know what kings and queens have ruled this peninsula, and the lands south of it, all this long while. We saw their fathers come down out of the mountains. We saw the battle they fought at Bluepeak, and what happened there. The power that rose up and moved there to save its own. Can the DragonChief deny that that power is worth cultivating, and supporting?'

'In matters of the welfare of this world,' Dithra said, 'we

190

have an interest. In its life, its death. But matters of . . . government . . .' She used the word as lightly as Segnbora might have mentioned housecleaning. 'We do not involve ourselves with such.'

'Madam,' Segnbora said, 'it is precisely the life or death of this world that we are discussing. You have seen many a ruler rise and fall, and so you think that their rise and fall is not necessarily associated with the wellbeing of humans as a whole. But the rules have changed around you, *lhhw'Hreiha*. You're in danger of being swept away by them.'

At this there was another rustle in the crowd of living Dragons, and many of the *mdeihei* stared at her. 'And you know it,' Segnbora said. 'That memory, *there* – the one you can't fully grasp, I am in it somehow, aren't I? And the man on whose behalf I've come to you – he's in it, too.'

Her voice was fierce. She had seen none of these things before, but she was seeing them now. Her Fire? She thought not. Segnbora glanced past the Dweller's *mdeihei*, catching some obscure motion there – and her attention fell again on that deeper darkness.

The Gate, she realized. *The Eorlhowe Gate—*

She slid a few steps closer to the DragonChief, and to the tantalizing darkness. It held something in it, a promise or potential. *But how to find out what?* 'You fear my coming,' she said, 'and Hasai's . . . for now you will find out what that memory is about. And you'll find it out the worst way: in reality . . . without having had any warning of its content.'

There was an uneasy rumbling. 'That ahead-memory,' Segnbora said, 'is a result of the change that's upon you. It is the Shadow reaching out its claw towards you. Your seeings are clouded, you have no certainty – and uncertainty is Its tool. It is carefully hiding from you what will happen if you do *not* become involved in this matter.'

'Who then is hiding knowledge of what will happen if we do?' the Dweller said. 'For we are no more certain of that.' She looked full at Segnbora and Hasai again, and

191

away, as if she could not bear the sight. And not from loathing: but from anticipation, and fear, and desire all rolled together. Segnbora, more bemused than ever, stretched her feelings out into that sense, pinned it to the stone with the black wing-barb of Skádhwë, tried to hold it. Nothing. Nothing.

And then a flash, and an obscure image – not inside Segnbora's mind, but there in the darkness of the Eorlhowe Gate. Afternoon, as if seen through mist; and the answering blaze of Dragonfire. But not Llunih dying, this time. Someone else's fangs in *her* throat – Dithra's. This time—

It was gone. The Dweller lay there, seeming unmoved. Segnbora knew better. Beside her, Hasai began slowly to rise. *Don't frighten her*, Segnbora said privately to him.

Her? She is the least of our worries.

Segnbora had no time to ask him what he meant. She began to pace, trying not to make it obvious that she was drawing closer to the Gate. 'As to that, I can't say. But quite soon, when all of us are dead, and the land is bare, and this world is a bare rock like yours was once; and the Shadow reaches out its intention to the little star that gives you all the food you have, and it flares up and dies one day – you will wish then that you'd helped us deal with what now threatens us.'

'You have no proof of this,' said the DragonChief. 'You have no ahead-memory of it.'

'No,' Segnbora said. 'I have what humans use instead. We call it reason . . . The Shadow wants this world dead. Wants *all* things in it dead, for Its own purposes. If you will let It destroy us and do nothing when good courses of action are laid out for you, then Dragons *lie* about their "protection" of us, and have lied ever since they first came here.'

The roar that went up from the walls around shook Segnbora where she stood. The Dweller sat upright, slowly, and spread her wings; and the barbs of them were cocked towards Segnbora and Hasai.

'Dragons do not lie,' the Dweller said, in the lowest rumble.

'We'll see about that,' Segnbora said, 'in a year, or ten, or a hundred; when there are no humans left, and there *are* Dragons. If we are wiped out, then all your denials will not make it less true. And you will wish you had died with us.'

It took a long while for the silence to settle down again. 'Here is your choice,' Hasai said. 'Be with us now, and be with us later. Otherwise—' He shrugged his wings. 'There is little help for any of us.'

'As for you, ehs'Pheress,' said the DragonChief, looking at him, 'you have already broken the ban. *Mdahaih* you were, and yet somehow you managed to rise up and go *dav'whnesshih*. That alone we would not have grudged you, strange though it seems. But then you interfered in the humans' battle at Bluepeak. What your Dragonflame wrought there, few of them will now forget. We thought you might ask pardon while you were here; but it seems not. How did you so far forget yourself, and our law? How many of them might you have killed?'

'What matters, Dweller, is how many he *did* kill, which is none: because we were one,' Segnbora said. Gently, gently, she had worked to within about a tail-length of Dithra. 'Killing was the last thing on our minds that night. He saved my life; should it be wrong for *mdaha* to save *sdaha*? How many of you have been saved by your own *mdeihei* from one folly or danger or another?'

'It does not matter,' said the Dweller. 'Hasai was outcast before, by his own choice. He is more so now than then, when he took a human for his *sdaha*.'

'I took what the Immanence sent me,' Hasai said, 'and have not been ill-served. In fact, there is a certain likeness between the way I am here, and the way *you* are.'

Silence fell again at that. Many eyes were turned to Hasai, noticing that even by darklight, Hasai's physicality had acquired a certain edge: a feeling that it too, like the Dweller's, might become abruptly more than it was. Segnbora welcomed the momentary distraction. The Gate was dark again, but she gazed into it, and called the Fire up inside her.

'Nevertheless,' said the DragonChief, 'we may give you no aid. Whatever your nature is, it is not in the Draconid Name. Dracon one of you may have been – but that nature has been perverted—'

'But our *mdeihei* are in you, DragonChief,' Hasai said, feeling Segnbora's struggle, taking up the thread as she would have. 'If they're not Dracon, then what are they doing there? And that being the case – I will have them back, thank you.'

He swept his wings out and gathered their *mdeihei* about them. For a moment, he was surrounded by shadow as the DragonChief was; and dim shapes filled it – twenty, thirty, a hundred, five hundred ancestors – eyes burning. Some of the threat went out of the Dweller's wings, and the barbs swung away. 'How can you . . . ?' she said.

'The same way I can remember what you cannot,' Segnbora said. 'The Gate no longer shows you its counsel clearly, does it? Nor on your command, as it used to do.' *More*, she willed, *tell me what I need*— '*Lhhw'Hreiha*, Dweller-at-the-Howe, I can feel the tragedy about to come upon us. You can avert much of it if you give us your people's help. Otherwise—'

She turned away from the Dweller, unable to bear the horror in her eyes and her *ehhath*, and looked at the Gate.

And *saw*—

The seeing struck her near senseless. It was not like seeing, but more like being *seen*, utterly known, by a million eyes and the minds behind them. In a thunder of Dracon voices and the wind of countless wings, she stood transfixed, struggling, blinded. Something poured into her, but Segnbora had no idea what it was. The pouring felt as it had to have Hasai's huge self poured into her small cramped soul . . . but this was worse, endlessly worse. It seemed to go on for ever.

When it stopped, Hasai was looking at her expectantly. Segnbora felt ready to slump down and die, but was astonished to find that somehow her Dracon body was still working.

'Otherwise?' said the Dweller, seeming to have noticed nothing.

Segnbora sought about for her thread of thought, and found it, though her head was reeling. 'Otherwise, with us, you will be swept away,' she said. 'And worse will come.'

'No more of this,' said the DragonChief, looking at Segnbora most peculiarly. 'Here is my rede. We will do you no harm. We will give you no aid. Go now.'

She returned slowly to Hasai's side. He looked at her, and she felt a gingerly touch from him on the borders of her mind. Used to his contact, she threw the gates open, let him in.

He flinched with his whole body, his eyes and all his *ehhath* full of consternation and astonishment. Then Hasai looked at the Dweller, and bowed his wings right down to the ground – a gesture of mourning.

'We will see you again, Dweller,' he said, 'once only. *Sdaha*, come.'

They made their way back up to the light of day. No Dragon went with them; none spoke to them as they left. Segnbora and Hasai raised wings, grasped force and flew.

When they were some miles away, Segnbora sang, barely louder than a whisper, '*Sithesssch* . . . what was *that?*'

Hasai looked at her in terror . . . but there was an edge of anticipation on it, like the sharpened edge of a sword. 'I am not sure,' he said. 'But I have an idea. We must have time to find out if I'm right.'

'Time is what we're shortest of, *sdaha*,' Segnbora said. She was too weary to think, too weary to try to figure out what Hasai's strange elation was about.

'Not as short as some others,' Hasai said, and actually dropped his jaw in a smile. 'To Aired, *sdaha*. Come.'

9

This tale they tell, of a Cat that went to
Courte, to see the King as was its ryght;
and half a tendaie later, itt came away
agayne in haste, saying, 'The cream is
very fine, but I am half deafn'd with the
compliments of mice, and well stick'd with
their knives.'

d'Kelic, A connceit

Herewiss had always had a fondness for getting dressed
up. His family had teased him about it since he was small –
since the day when they caught him, at the age of nine, in
his parents' bedchamber, wearing his father's oldest silk
surcoat, and the chain of Principality of the Brightwood. It
was rather too large for him, and he had been wearing it
around his waist, with a table knife stuck in it. Since then
they had given him no peace over his fondness for ornate
ceremony, and the clothes that accompanied it, silk and
brocade, good leather, and bright swords and jewels. *It's
not my fault*, he thought as he dressed. *It comes of all those
stories they told me when I was young* . . . His mother had
been a city Rodmistress before she married his father, and
had told him endless stories of the fine life in Darthis; he
had decided that some day *he* was going to be one of those
people who dressed in velvets and gilded mail, and had a
page to go before him to announce his name.

Now, of course, he had become one of those people . . .
and discovered that he didn't particularly care for it.

Though at least the dressing up is still enjoyable, he thought.

He had spent the past seven days settling into Prydon, doing nothing official as yet: until he was presented tonight, his status was still in question. He had met people that Andaethen felt he should see, members of the Four Hundred. Most of them greeted him kindly; the rest treated him with a reserve that suggested they were wary of entertaining a spy, or of entertaining a man whom the present government was likely to consider a traitor. For his own part, he had caged his mind around with Fire, to be wholly certain that no-one, either Rodmistress or sorcerer, could hear what he was thinking. He was beginning to feel as weary as if he was in the cage himself, for he dared not let the protection go, even when he slept.

Andaethen was sorry for his weariness, but she wanted Herewiss to be seen meeting these people. 'There's no point in being covert about it,' she said to him one morning over breakfast. 'People know you're here to feel out support for Freelorn. So why waste your time? Let Cillmod see you doing what he *thinks* you should be doing. If you sat quiet and seemed to do nothing, then he'd become suspicious. No,' she said, 'you do the expected thing, and go about and be vaguely treasonable . . . in the right company, of course. Your Fire will teach you readily enough who's reliable and who's not. Though I can give you some hints.' And she did. Some of the names surprised him.

The monarchy of Arlen, when it was functioning correctly, was not a monolithic one. The king ruled, and his word was final; but also taken into the reckoning were the Four Hundred. These were the great landowners of Arlen. The king saw to it that the royal magics were performed, to keep the land fertile and bearing. The Four Hundred, in return, submitted a certain amount of the incomes and produce of that land to the throne; saw the rest distributed among their people, and kept a proportion for themselves as organizers.

That was in theory, of course. Human nature being

what it was, the actuality was sometimes quite different. The Four Hundred tended to perceive any action of the Staveholder as dangerous if it seemed about to endanger their livelihoods, or the status quo, in any way. They were not above squabbling amongst one another for larger pieces of land – prevailing on the present ruler for increases in their own appanage at another's expense. They were also aware that if the fertility of their land failed, the people living on it would correctly surmise that their chances of being able to plough in the king or queen to rectify the problem were less than good – so that the tenants would be quite willing to sacrifice the local lord or lady, instead, as a possibly useful second-best measure. So a ruler who seemed to be failing at keeping the land bearing regularly would make the Four Hundred nervous indeed.

Cillmod was more or less in this position, since it was uncertain whether or not he had been able to do anything useful about the royal magics. The Four Hundred looked at him with only slightly less joy than they looked at the prospect of Freelorn seven years earlier. An untried, non-Initiate heir was a problem. Worse still was a ruler who came into his power without the usual forms being fulfilled – especially when they were not just mere forms, but vital religious necessity, deeply involved with the process of making the land bear fruit in the first place. There had been those first four shaky years of real hardship: then, slowly, the seeming recovery, as if things were getting better. Those members of the Four Hundred who had backed Cillmod on Ferrant's death were now perceived as the upholders of law and order. And those who had pushed for Freelorn's recall and enthronement, or at least a search for some other Initiate who could take the throne under more regular circumstances, were now seen as dangerous rebels, and possibly in need of being unseated from their properties.

Of course, even the most enthusiastic of their detractors were reluctant to actually suggest this openly. So nothing was being done yet. There were always rumours that, after

Cillmod's proper enthronement, many old scores against Freelorn's supporters might be redressed. It was these supporters that Herewiss visited in those first few days: some of them were muted and cautious, some of them openly scornful of Cillmod; some of them stayed quiet, feeling that their best chance was to lie low and see what happened.

'It's worked for a long while now,' one of them said. 'Anyone who spoke too loud during those bad years might be dead suddenly. Spies and counterspies were everywhere.'

Orfen laughed and shook his head. He was a small, dry man, sharp-eyed. His lands were some of the most extensive up north, near the North Arlene borders. Those lands were always assumed to be disaffected from the Arlene throne, through distance if not political needs.

Herewiss sat with him in the bay window of his house on one of the winding streets that led up to Prydon Castle. 'No, my boy,' Orfen said to Herewiss, 'we've all been studying to be quiet, or to say the right thing, in the past years.' He looked at Herewiss from under his brows, and twisted his arthritic hands together. 'There have been some people spoke out against Cillmod – or Rian—' He shot Herewiss another look. 'And it was odd how bad their weather went. All my part of Northern Arlen for a while, the crops rotting in the ground. That was after Lahain and Ruic began saying in the city that there should be a party for the old king's son, to bring him back. The people starved. Meleth, Lord Lahain, they ploughed him in. Ruic – he went up this street on his knees: I saw him go.' The old man's eyes gazed up the long hill of cobbles. 'He went on his knees to the palace, and asked pardon of the king—' He made the word sound like something vile. '—to take the curse off his land so that his people shouldn't die. He cared, you see. And true enough, the weather got better. A lot of us walked more quietly after that.'

'And Lahain?' Herewiss said. 'They ploughed him in, you say. Did it work?'

'Not until the new lady came in and swore fealty, a few months later,' the old lord said. 'The timing was noticeable.'

Herewiss had left from that meeting quite sobered. Control of the weather was possible, on a small scale, to someone working with the Fire, and on a *very* small scale, to someone using mere sorcery – though it tended to be fatal if overdone. But there was no way to produce a drought of a year or two. And mere sorcery should not be able to interfere in the bond between a lord and his land. *Rian*, he thought now, looking himself up and down in the mirror. *I'm going to have to make some quiet enquiries. Maybe tonight.*

Moris put his head in the door, saw Herewiss, and snorted. 'Still admiring yourself?'

'Still. I'll be ready in a moment.'

There was no denying it – he looked fine. He had a plain surcoat, white wool with gold wire picking out the Brightwood arms, quite restrained – but it was *too* restrained, he had thought last night, for this occasion. Especially since Brightwood people had a reputation in both Darthen and Arlen for being country cousins, dour, plainspoken and uncomplicated. Herewiss thought it wise that the courtiers here should realize who they were dealing with. So he had done a small Firework: had spoken to his father briefly, and then had reached out and pulled back in his hands his father's oldest surcoat, the one that he had slouched around in long ago. It fitted him much better now. It was a moment's work with the Fire to change the arms to the way he wore them now – the Phoenix rising from the flames, yes, but the flames blue against the silk gone ivory with age, and the ruby of the eye now glancing back sapphire instead. White silk trews – his own – to go with the surcoat, and the plain pale leather boots, cream to match the tunic: and over everything, Khávrinen.

He looked at himself again, with satisfaction.

'Dati says to stop admiring yourself and come on,' Moris said.

Herewiss glanced at Moris.

'Mori,' he said, 'keep your ears open tonight.'

'What should I be listening for?'

'Mmmm . . . Anything interesting, but principally . . . sounds of people who seem too friendly.'

Moris nodded. 'There have been a few of those this week, haven't there?'

'Yes. I'd like to see how many more. Andaethen's list of potential sellouts to Lorn – the bad ones, the ones she thinks will be unreliable – it's too short.'

'The trouble with you,' Moris said, 'is that you're a cynic.'

Herewiss laughed. 'I wish it were true. I'm worried that I'm not enough of one, in this place. Living in the country, moving around by ourselves the way we did for so long, you forget the nastiness that happens in court, in big cities.' He shook his head. 'And one misstep could mean that everything else we've worked for goes crumbling— Never mind. Let's go down.'

Andaethen was waiting at the bottom of the steps for them with their mounts. Herewiss patted Sunspark and swung up into the saddle, looking appreciatively at Andaethen. The tabard of a herald and Ambassador of Darthen in full state looked well on her, the cloth of it hardly to be seen for the gems. It was an old joke in the Darthene court that its heralds and ambassadors went in greater state than its kings and queens; and certainly Herewiss had never seen Eftgan wearing anything like *this*. 'Come along now, Andë,' Herewiss said, striking before she could, 'and stop posing there to be admired. Can't be late for my own party. Especially after I saw that note to you about the food! Are you renting the Castle your cooks?'

'My staff do work up at the castle sometimes,' Andaethen said demurely. 'And perhaps they drop the occasional overheard word in my ear? And perhaps I occasionally let them hear something I think it wise for Cillmod to hear? Besides, the pastry chef they have up there is terrible. It's merely self-preservation to lend them ours for a night.'

They rode to the castle. Kynall was not at the heart of its city, the way Darthis Castle was. The land near the river rose up in a bluff about three hundred feet high, steep and sheer on one side, kindlier on the other. The original castle was built atop that bluff, its wall encircling the bluff proper, and the former townlands, now the city, sweeping down from it and towards the river. Each successive wall around the built-up parts of the city came always back to that steep bluff. It was not as grand a seat as Darthis, but there was a feeling of great security in it.

As they rode up past the third and second walls, up the narrow, curving streets lined with walled houses and gardens, Herewiss looked up at the castle and thought how dreadful it would be to have to mount a siege of this place. He had played here as a child. He knew the cobbles and the walls all up and down these roads, the houses and the faces that used to look out of them. It was bad enough to come back to a place you knew as a child and find it all changed, and yourself too. It would be worse to come back, and destroy it, and know yourself responsible.

They came to the gate through the castle wall, and Herewiss looked at it, slightly shocked. There had been changes made. In Freelorn's father's day, it had been simply a gate; now, in addition to that old iron-bound door, twenty feet wide, there was also a portcullis on the inside, and one on the outside. And the guard presence around it was surprising. *Was this meant for me to see?* he wondered as they rode under the gateway. He glanced over at Andaethen; she rolled her eyes in response.

In the courtyard they dismounted. There too the armed presence was considerable; many men, drawn up in ranks, in the livery of Arlen. All were looking at the three of them, very thoughtful. Herewiss saw the groom come over to hold Sunspark's headstall, and said, *What do you think?*

I think I should like to see what's going on, Sunspark said, and vanished in a swirl of fire as the groom reached for its reins. And a Steldene hunting cat – some three times the size it ought to have been – was standing by Herewiss's side, blinking sleepily at the groom. The man stood there, staring, holding a bridle; the saddle had thumped to the cobbles beside him.

'Thank you,' Herewiss said, nodding graciously, as if this kind of thing happened all the time. Inwardly, he was having some difficulty maintaining his composure. He knew this courtyard, mostly from playing in it, tearing around after Lorn in a dirty tunic: or later, from staggering into it with Lorn, late at night, slightly sozzled and singing rude songs. The sight of all these armed men was surprisingly unsettling. He met their eyes, and watched their eyes drop, and felt a flush of satisfaction . . . and then shame at being satisfied. *I'm not here to make them afraid of me.*

If you're not, Sunspark said silently, *then we're wasting our time.*

The castle doors, with their brass facings showing the Lion, were opened for them. More liveried servants, armed and unarmed, lined the way in. Andaethen led; Herewiss went after her, with Sunspark padding along beside, and then Moris, with the rest of Andaethen's entourage.

He knew the way to the main presence well enough. Right out of the white marble front hall, then another right down a panelled corridor, and a third, down the long banner-hung hallway that led to the core of the castle. The doors to the hall were open, the light of candles and torchères gleaming off the polished wood. The sound of music came from inside, and laughter, and talk. The crowd, dressed in their splendour. This was the scene he had seen several times in his travels with his father. But as he made his way down towards the dais, one thing was wrong. It was the wrong person sitting in that plain old chair, not Lorn, and not the old King either. All wrong, and—

—he got close enough to get his first good look, and it smote him to the heart.

What's the matter? Sunspark said, hearing his stricken feeling.

Nothing, he thought. *Nothing I shouldn't have expected.* For the man in the throne looked much like Freelorn, more than Herewiss would have thought possible. He was only slightly taller, only slightly less muscular. *But why am I surprised? They have the same father* . . . The cheekbones were the same, and the nose – the set of the face somehow both cheerful and impertinent. But at the eyes, everything changed. Lorn's were soft and thoughtful. This man's were chillier. They rested on Herewiss with a tired expression as he faced a problem that had been lurking over the horizon for a long while, and had, finally, presented itself to be dealt with.

Herewiss reached for Cillmod's thought, more out of curiosity than anything else—

—and heard nothing.

Conversation had flagged as the Darthene party had entered, as people turned and eyes fastened on them. Now Herewiss came to stand before the throne, and looked at the people standing around Cillmod.

Ah, alas, Herewiss thought. *Father was right after all.* Looking into the cool eyes that watched him, he felt the rage and fear and simple annoyance of people who saw him, not as the return of justice, but as a disruption of their schedules, or as a potential source of poverty and loss—

It's not supposed to be like this . . .

'Andaethen,' said the man in the throne. 'You're welcome here.' And it was not Freelorn's voice, not quite; but very close.

'Sir,' Andaethen said, 'may I present my new assistant, Herewiss s'Hearn tai-Éarnësti, prince-elect of the Brightwood and kinsman to Eftgan the Queen's grace of Darthen. He comes to present his credentials.'

'He's welcome,' Cillmod said. His eyes rested on Herewiss, cool, and he put out his hand.

Herewiss drew Khávrinen and leaned on its hilt. He bowed slightly and said, 'I greet you, sir. But you will know that I come on the wings of the defiance and declaration of war from my good mistress and lady the Queen. Were there a king here, sir, I would kiss his hand. But the rightful king is elsewhere. Meanwhile, I do my duty to the throne of Arlen, at least.' And here he bowed again.

Cillmod leaned back a bit in the throne, looking not even slightly disturbed by Herewiss's formal courtesy and calculated insolence. 'Prince of the Brightwood, you're welcome nonetheless,' he said. 'And even though it seems that you've chosen the wrong side in this quarrel.'

'That the event will prove, sir,' Herewiss said.

'Doubtless it will,' Cillmod said, 'and doubtless the Goddess will adjudicate that decision as she did the previous one, which placed me here. Meanwhile, this is a social occasion. Allow me to introduce my ministers.'

One by one they came forward. Herewiss bowed to them, exactly as he had bowed to Cillmod, and noted names and faces.

'And Rian s'Heisarth,' Cillmod said. 'My consultant on the royal magics.'

Herewiss could have choked on that one. A king should need a consultant on the royal magics about as much as he should need one on breathing. He looked as casually as he could at Rian, and reached out to feel his thought.

And felt nothing, nothing: a void more complete than the cloak of darkness and confusion that had been thrown about Cillmod's thoughts. Here was the source. Herewiss looked at the man standing near the throne: a man of medium height, built broad across the shoulders, silver around his temples and scattered through the rest of the dark hair. Everything about him was businesslike and restrained, even to the cut and style of the clothes; he was a man you might pass by in any crowd of functionaries. Except that here was the source of all their trouble – this rugged face with its assured, kindly, middle-aged look. This was the heart of the evil. And it smiled at him. Not an innocent smile, but not a wicked one either. Thoughtless, unconcerned, settled, secure – utterly calm. This was not a man who saw his destruction coming.

And how could he not? Herewiss thought. *He* must *know that I know what he's been doing—*

Rian bowed to him and said, 'My lord Herewiss.'

Herewiss bowed, significantly less deeply than he had to the others, and said, 'Sir, I hope you are of use to your lord.'

'He's found me so in the past,' Rian said. It was a hearty voice, friendly and warm.

Herewiss was not to be charmed. *When you tried to kill me the other night, and failed,* Herewiss said to him in mind as clearly as he could, to see whether he was heard, *was I welcome then?*

No answer came back, not that he had been expecting one. Cillmod said, 'Leaving political abstractions aside, you bring us two great wonders. One is yourself and your Fire; the other—' He glanced at Sunspark. 'What manner of creature is that?'

Sunspark looked at Rian and said, 'His power constrains me to answer. I am Fire: he beat me in fair contest, and bound me. So I must be his slave.'

Herewiss kept his face straight, though the urge to laugh was strong. There was a soft sound of laughter in his mind.

'His power must be great indeed,' Cillmod said. 'Such power would enhance any ruler to which it became attached.'

'It will not enhance anyone,' Sunspark said, looking coolly from Cillmod to Herewiss. 'My servitude is involuntary, bound only by Power. Someday his will slip, and I will be free, though first I will kill him and his folk, and any other who seems to have been party to my binding. There is a great deal hereabouts—' And it smiled. '—that will burn.'

Herewiss lifted his eyebrows. *Loved,* he thought, *what are you saying to these people?!*

Bad enough that one person you love may shortly be within

their reach, Sunspark said quietly. *Would you have that one, the cold one there, think that he might have two? If they see me as an oppressed slave eager to be free, they will not try to use me against you . . .*

There was no arguing about that. But Sunspark's assertiveness on his behalf astonished him. *Spark—*

Later, dear heart.

'In the meantime, sir,' Cillmod said, 'your presence here and that of the sword you carry, and that which flows from it, are what we're here to celebrate. I appreciate your desire not to stand on compliment, but to say what's in your mind. I too will say it, so that we may start clean. This fight will doubtless go to the stronger. But I stood my ground, and worked, while the one you support ran, and stole. I'll say no more about it than that for now; we'll talk again in coming days. Meantime, pray partake of the entertainment.'

It actually only went on for several hours, though it seemed like much more. Herewiss had never been good at meeting large numbers of people all together, even though he now had the Fire to burn faces and names into his memory. And many of the minds felt alike – afraid, or intrigued, or angry, or wearing a barely-managed combination of all three. But Herewiss ate and drank, and chatted as politely as possible. The food was good, and the wine was very good indeed . . . but there was no Brightwood white.

He smiled slightly at that on his third trip to the table full of decanters, and looked up and down for something new to try. The courtier with whom he had been chatting pointed at one and said, 'That red from Lahain, that's very nice . . .'

Herewiss looked at it and wondered if the grapes tasted of their ploughed-in lord. But he said, 'Yes, thank you,' and held the cup out to be filled. It was a particularly dark, rich, toothsome-looking red; the resemblance to blood was certainly accidental. As he drank, the taste warmed him.

What came as rather more of a shock was the poison.

Ah, heaven, he thought, *it had to happen, didn't it? Well, now what?* For there were all kinds of reactions available to him, from the blatant to the subtle. At the moment, the state of his nerves inclined him to the blatant. Should the cup become a serpent and crawl away shouting accusations? Should the wine in it boil over? But it really was good-tasting wine, and it was a shame to waste. So Herewiss drank the rest of it, thoughtfully and with pleasure, while Sowan, the courtier, looked at it.

'Very nice,' Herewiss said to the poisoner. 'Another, please?'

Sowan filled the cup again, finishing the decanter. He had seemed a nervous man to begin with; now, as Herewiss stood and chatted with him about the crops up north, and various other small, inconsequential matters, Sowan watched him, and watched him, and developed a tic next to his right eye.

Herewiss meanwhile had some of his attention elsewhere. *At least no-one else will get any of that wine by accident. Now then—* It was slow poison, naturally. It would be impolitic to kill the new Darthene attaché actually *at* such a gathering. But two or three days later, a flux that turned to a gripe that turned to a shakiness and paralysis in the limbs, and finally the lungs and heart – that would be permissible. After all, everyone knew that there were numerous factions active against Lorn's cause. No-one would openly connect such a deed to Cillmod.

And who knows who poor Sowan here is acting for? I need more time to find out . . . But now he's afraid I might overdose, Herewiss thought, *and keel over too early. Poor man!* His main concern now was the manner in which he should handle the venom in the wine. Probably the best approach was to poison the poison itself. A moment with closed eyes, 'savouring' the bouquet of the cup, let him slip down into his Fire and go questing down through his gut and into the blood-vessels that were carrying the substance away through him. It was fortunately not one of those corrosive electuaries that ate one away from inside, which would have meant a lot of tedious repair work, but rather one of the poisons with an affinity for the nerves, that blocked their life-fire from running along them. Each tiniest particle of the poison had a sort of handle at the end of it, that was meant to push into the gaps at the ends of the nerves, and block them. With the Fire, Herewiss pulled off those handles from a few thousand particles, then turned them loose to subvert their fellows into dropping the rest. It was all done in a few seconds. He opened his eyes to see Sowan looking at him with growing horror.

There were more eyes on him than just one pair. He could feel it, that itch of the mind: someone noticing with annoyance, with ill intent, the use of Fire. He smiled politely at Sowan, and said, 'Dinner sometime perhaps, sir? We can discuss—' He smiled much more sweetly. '—politics.'

Sowan stammered, and hurriedly took himself and his tic away.

For another hour or so Herewiss wandered the gathering, and was back at the wine table when he became aware of a slight silence around him, a change in the way people nearby were talking. He looked up and around for the reason of it, and saw Cillmod next to him, eyeing the decanter Herewiss was holding. Cillmod offered his empty cup.

'Sir,' Herewiss said, surprised. 'This wine?'

'Of your courtesy.'

Herewiss filled his cup, raised his own – and stopped, looking at the cup, seeing and feeling the image-flash: night, the walls of Darthen, the shoulder touching his. He glanced at Cillmod.

'Your health, at least,' Cillmod said, with just a touch of irony.

'If nothing else,' Herewiss said, 'yours.' He drank.

They looked at each other. Cillmod glanced over to one side of the table, away from the people watching them.

Herewiss went with him as he stepped aside, out of the press.

'Sir,' he said, quietly, when they were private enough, 'again I'll presume on your hospitality and speak plain, as you say you prefer it. I wonder much that you desire to be seen being friendly to me.' He did not say, *You know I'm against you.* Though he was tempted to, and that temptation was born of nothing more certain than a slight, peculiar, sense of liking for the man. *And is it a true sense? – or am I being betrayed by his likeness to Lorn?*

'True,' Cillmod said, with the slightest shrug. He nodded towards the terrace doors on the east side of the room. 'Will you walk?'

'Certainly.'

They came out on to the terrace. It was as Herewiss remembered it from his youth, long and wide, with a marble balustrade on the east side; the view was towards the way the Great Road ran from the city gates, off towards the hills.

'They expect intrigue,' Cillmod said quietly, 'so we may as well give them the appearance of it. A fine mare's-nest of it you've fallen into. I wonder that you can bear it, after being out in the solitudes for such a long while, dealing with more important matters.' He looked sideways at Khávrinen.

Herewiss was taken aback by this annoyingly acute reading of what had been in his mind. 'It's not the business of a man with Power,' he said, 'to hide away. The business of Power is to be *in* the world, working in it, being of use. A man who can't do that—' He shrugged. '—should never have gone looking for it at all.'

'You say that so easily,' Cillmod said. They turned and started back down the terrace. '"A man with Power." All other things aside, does it not ride hard on you to be the only one?'

'If things go the way I intend, I won't be the only one for long. I have other business than kingmaking.'

Cillmod nodded slowly. 'To spread the Fire, then.'

'That's right.'

'But for the moment, kingmaking . . . is of a higher priority, I take it.'

'How should it be otherwise?' Herewiss said. 'Saving your honour.'

It was pointedly not the honorific one used with royalty. Cillmod smiled thinly and said, 'Don't think I don't hear that tone from my own. If you think to nettle me by it, you'll have to do better.' He shook his head and looked at Herewiss, and for a moment the look in his eyes was Freelorn's.

'How could it be otherwise for *me*?' Cillmod went on. 'Knowing I was who I was?'

'You'll say now,' Herewiss said, 'that they pressed the job on you. That you had no choice.'

'Indeed they pressed it!' Cillmod said, angry. 'Of course I had no choice. A half-king is at least better than none. And we had none when your *friend* refused to come back home after the old king died.'

'Quite a few of the Four Hundred wanted him dead,' Herewiss said.

'Some of them did,' said Cillmod. 'Others—' He shook his head. 'Even now I'm not sure. Those other lords were the first to jeer at my failures, though they did it secretly. The name, Uncraeft, that was their doing: do you think it didn't bite, reading it daubed on walls, while I thrashed around hunting for solutions, and watched the country people starve? Even now, when things are working better, I look at those lords and wonder if they truly support me. Something is behind their eyes: and you know it. That's why you're here.'

There was no dissembling with such directness. Herewiss said nothing.

'So off goes Freelorn, flying about the Kingdoms and making my job more difficult,' Cillmod said, in a tone more aggrieved than angry. 'If he shows his face here, it's only to steal my money—'

'*Your* money?'

'The money that I was supposed to be using to feed my people, and the army standing to protect them!'

That thought had already occurred to Herewiss – that Lorn's raid on the treasuries at Osta had itself triggered the Arlene mercenaries' raids on Darthene land. *It would seem to some a clever ploy to force Darthen to move against Cillmod,* Herewiss thought. *Not that it was, of course . . . But in any case, some people here at court were certainly glad enough to be given an excuse to attack the Darthenes at Bluepeak. It still takes two to make a fight . . .* 'Leaving armies out of it,' Herewiss said, 'it's not money that feeds people. It's the royal magics.'

'We have not been entirely unsuccessful at that.'

'*We*,' Herewiss said. 'The royal magics are no plural business . . . save when two rulers wed.'

'Once perhaps. But armies, once bought, have to be fed as well: and they have an annoying tendency to take what they like when they see it close to hand.'

'You're going to tell me now that the raid on the Darthene granaries was the army's doing, not yours. That you didn't order it. Or sanction it.'

Cillmod looked at Herewiss. 'I did not order it,' he said, 'but who would believe that? And I had no choice but to sanction it, afterwards, otherwise the army would have unseated me. And the army cares too little about anything but their own stomachs. Too many of them are from out of country, Steldenes and such, who hold the royal magics to be a myth, a legend outlived. Others—' He glanced at Herewiss with an odd expression. 'They would not have your friend, you know. He has an old name of cowardice among them, and they could never accept him. But there are rumours of another child of his blood, or Ferrant's, somewhere in the land, in hiding. One that could be brought here, and hand-raised by a regent to rule to order. *Their* order.'

Herewiss held himself utterly still, face and mind; and Khávrinen abruptly flamed searing blue, as something struck at it, and him, from outside. Not Cillmod, but

212

another mind, here in the palace, eavesdropping, and reaching out to strike with awful precision at the truth of something it wanted to know. The bolt was held away from him by the Fire caging Herewiss's thoughts, but only just.

Now then, he thought, and in his mind he swiftly reached out and grasped the weapon that had attacked him. It felt like a spear trying to punch through mail, so as a spear he treated it – grabbing it under the head with hands mailed in Fire, and moving sidewise out of its path, he yanked hard, pulling the one who wielded it off balance and towards him, close enough to see faces and come to grips. What he held twisted in his hands, like a spear made of lightning, burning and writhing and trying to get away. Herewiss hung on grimly, dragging the internal balance of the spell out of its worker's control and closer to ruin.

He recognized what he held – a spell meant to drag some one fact from his mind and then burn the fact away leaving no trace. *As if such a thing would work against the Fire—* But that was the problem. It *had* almost worked. There was horrible strength behind the thrust of the spell, anchoring it, trying to pull it out of Herewiss's grip before he could work his will on it.

Oh no you don't! Herewiss set his Fire deep into the structure of the spelling, the 'shaft' of the spear. Then, in one quick motion, he snapped it—

All the force bound into the spell rebounded like a snapped bowstring, into the mind of its worker. The silent, anguished scream that followed gave Herewiss just a breath's worth of time to be angrily satisfied: then he was too busy controlling the sick feeling in his own gut, the reaction to having been hit with the spellweapon in the first place.

Cillmod glanced in surprise from the sword, now beginning to dim down, to Herewiss's face. 'My lord Herewiss, are you not well?'

Herewiss smiled wanly and said, 'Someone tried to poison me earlier. Nothing serious.'

This had nothing to do with his present discomfort, of course, but it was the truth, if a misdirecting one. Cillmod looked shocked. *'Here?'* And then his face settled into chilly nonexpression that Herewiss knew, with a disturbing pang, from having seen Lorn wear it. Rage. 'Who would dare—'

'I shouldn't like to deprive you of the chance to find out for yourself,' Herewiss said, gently, but with angry irony of his own. 'The blow missed, sir. Poison is a poor tool to use on someone with the Fire.'

He said nothing of the other blow, busying himself for the moment with weaving the unseen mail of his Fire more tightly around him. *Rian was most interested in what I might be thinking. And possibly was hearing leakage: I must be careful. But why—* Surely he, and everyone else who might be interested, knew that Lorn's daughter was long dead. But—

Herewiss stopped that thought before it could progress any further. *I am going to have to guard myself most carefully. These attacks are going to continue until Rian is certain of where my strengths lie.* And that worried him. It would be pleasant to think he could misdirect those assessments. But he had had more than enough trouble just keeping this single attack from burning part of his mind away. *Where is he getting such power?!* Herewiss wondered.

He looked away from Cillmod for a moment, towards the terrace windows. He dearly wanted to get a glimpse of Rian – though surely he would have left the room before working a sorcery like that; no-one had the concentration to move about, talk, make sense, while dealing with such magic. *And the backlash alone would drop him like an axe in the skull*, Herewiss thought with grim satisfaction. *Not something that he would want the whole court to see.*

Cillmod followed his glance. 'They will be wondering what we're up to,' he said. 'I suppose we should go in. But my lord—'

'Herewiss will do,' he said, much to his own surprise.

'Herewiss, then. Your poisoner was none of my doing.'

'I believe you,' Herewiss said. *Though for what reason, the Goddess only knows: I have none. None but one that makes me distrust myself—*

Cillmod nodded and made his way back into the hall.

Herewiss followed at a respectable distance, and looked casually around the room. He got the shock that he had been half-expecting: Rian, unconcerned, laughing, in conversation with several Arlene courtiers. Herewiss caught a side view of him and saw the man's erect stance, his complexion not even slightly pale; flushed a bit, in fact, as if with wine.

He is immune to backlash.

Impossible!

Goddess help us all—

It was growing late, and he had too much to think about. Andaethen was making her way around the room, in the process of making her good nights. Herewiss went to join her, then paused a moment as he watched Cillmod head for the throne, and stop.

Sunspark was there, committing lazy and unconcerned treason. It lay draped over the throne, smoking gently, but (Herewiss noticed with relief) not singeing the cushions. Its chin was propped on the throne's arm, and its tail hung over the other one, twitching ever so gently as it gazed across the room at the courtiers who were staring at it.

Herewiss decided to play the part it had offered him. 'Sunspark,' he said, 'heel.'

That tail twitched once or twice more, thoughtfully, as the lazy, burning eyes slid sidewise to regard him. Then Sunspark stood up in the throne, and arched its back, stretching fore and aft like a cat by a hearth, and worked naughtily with its claws on the arm of the throne. The white-hot sickles scorched the wood, then hid themselves demurely in the huge paws again, while white threads of smoke went up into the still air. Sunspark stepped down from the throne and paced over to Herewiss, its tail lashing gently.

215

'Heel', indeed, it said. *I will get you for this, some day.*
You started it, loved.

As Andaethen joined him, Herewiss watched Cillmod take the throne again, and brush, rather bemused, at the ash on its arm. He looked over at Herewiss, and surprisingly, smiled – not a dissembling expression, not hostile: genuine amusement.

Ah, heaven, Herewiss thought regretfully. *Why can't things be simple?* He bowed to Cillmod, rather more deeply than he had at first. Then he turned, sparing no-one else a glance, and followed Andaethen out.

10

The rain is my blood, and the Earth
my flesh, and the stones my bones, and
the wind my breath: my thoughts are
my own, but let them turn to Her.

Regaliorum, 4

A tenday after Herewiss's hand-kissing, he sat in his room
at the Embassy trying to draw a map. 'Trying' was the
operative term: not all the Fire in the Goddess's world
could make a person a better draftsman than he had been
to start with. Herewiss looked at the blot he had just
made, right across the route of the Kings' Road about a
mile away from Prydon, and running up the slopes of
Vintners' Rise. He sighed and reached for the scraping-
knife.

From behind him came the sound of a throat being
cleared, and Andaethen put a hand on his shoulder. She
looked down at the map. 'Looks like chicken-scratchings,'
she said, 'but not much worse than the last one, I
suppose.'

'Thank you so much, madam. You fill me with
encouragement.'

She smiled and looked at what he had drawn. The map
showed the ground immediately around Prydon city and
for about five miles east, with special attention paid to the
various hills and rises that might interest an army heading
in that direction. There were a few small oblongs drawn on
it, meant to indicate the present positions of Arlene

troops; one north of the city, two south. 'He hasn't committed himself any more clearly than that, I'm afraid,' Herewiss said. 'Not yet, anyway.'

'Which "he" are we talking about? Cillmod? Rian?'

'No,' Herewiss said. 'Meveld, the Commander-General.' He was one of the many mercenaries who had been bought in, and it was Herewiss's unhappy opinion that Cillmod had really gotten good value when he bought him.

Andaethen scratched idly at a stray ink-spot. 'Why two groups to the south and only one to the north, I wonder?'

'Hard to say, this early on. Possibly that second group of troops will be moved somewhere else shortly. Seems likely, as it's mostly cavalry – they're no good over there among the hills and the wetlands.' Herewiss leaned back again. 'A lot of the mercenaries have been stabled out across the country, and have to be recalled . . . that's still going on. But by next tenday we should have a much better idea of their strength, and where to start putting our own. And the tenday after that, we're almost on top of the First of Autumn.'

Andaethen nodded. 'Will you be speaking to herself tonight?'

'In a while.'

'Read her this, if you would,' she said, 'and tell her I should have more news on that matter in five days or so.'

'Very well.'

'Then have a good night, after you've done your business. By the way, the night of your dinner for the court is set. Four days from now.'

She went out. Herewiss looked at his map for a moment, then pushed it aside and got up. He stretched, trying to get the crick out of his back: unsuccessfully, as usual. He had not been comfortable lately, either physically or spiritually. Increasingly, since his hand-kissing, he had the sense of Arlen, and of Prydon in particular, not as either a city or country, but as a web, with one huge, patient, smiling spider sitting at the heart of it, feeling every breath of wind that stirred the strands.

For his own part, Herewiss had taken to guarding his thoughts even more vigilantly than before. He was spending his strength, as well, extending the Fire's protection to Andaethen and several of her staff. It was wearing him out.

He went over to the door, shutting it gently. Moris was out in town somewhere this evening, having his own business to do for Andaethen; he would not try to come in this door when he saw it closed. But, just for safety's sake, Herewiss touched the lintel, and the door, leaving between them an unseen thread of the Flame that would hold like steel, but also reveal afterwards who had touched the door, and what their thought was at that moment.

That done, he pulled a chair to the middle of the room, near the writing table. Then he slowly walked around them both, describing a careful circle on the marble floor with Khávrinen's point. When he was done, he sat down in the chair, with the sword laid across his lap, and in his mind held a spark of intention to the circle, like a flame to the wick of a lamp.

Immediately, blue Fire sprang up along the path he had traced. He sat and waited for a moment, steadying his breathing and emptying his mind. Also, he listened, with all the senses now available to him. Since he had begun these sessions, he had felt something, not exactly pressing against the barrier of Fire, but leaning against it. Not an attack – merely an assessment, as if someone was trying to find out how strongly his barriers were held, and whether Herewiss perceived the 'leaning' presence at all. Herewiss made no response to these efforts.

This time, the feeling wasn't there. Herewiss shrugged, then closed his eyes and slipped down into the part of him where his Fire lived.

It was no longer, as it had been, a single forlorn spark buried at the core of him. Now his whole insides seemed lighted with it, like an open-windowed house full of sunshine. But he had made himself, as many adepts do, a place in which to work, something more congenial and less abstract than the sheer perception of light. Now Herewiss opened the door to it and stepped inside.

It looked like the old Hold in the far eastern Waste, with its many, many doors. He would walk among them, looking in each one either for the answer to the problem he was posing at the moment, or for the source of the repose he needed.

He wandered down the hallway, looking in the open doorways to see what he might see. Herewiss had long since learned that he generally found more interesting things when he wandered than when he went looking a-purpose.

He paused by one doorway that was dark, recognizing it for an aspect of one of his worst fears, some old threat sealed away, forgotten. No need for that. Herewiss passed by: passed a doorway on a wide, white sea, white beach, silver sky, one he hadn't seen before. He paused a moment, interested, then moved on. There was no use attempting to mark the positions of these worlds behind the many doors; they moved around at whim, or in response to motions in the great Pattern in which they coexisted.

Eventually he came to Segnbora's door, the gateway that led on to her own physical and mental realities. The doorway smelled to his othersenses of salt water, and also of hot stone, a faint scorched smell – the clean, mineral reek of Dragons.

He peered through the doorway into the gloom. There was a light like sunshine from a low doorway off to one side: not much else. All he could see was stone – stone floor, stone walls, the up-arching emptiness of a stone ceiling above. 'Anyone home?' he said, and heard his voice echo from the rock far above.

'Herewiss is here!' someone said: Segnbora's voice, sounding singular for a change. 'Come in, do,' she said.

He stepped in, making his way through the darkness towards that further doorway. It was a long walk – a

Dragon would fit through it with ease, and it was at least a quarter mile away. Herewiss went quietly across the stone, waving casually to the many eyes that gazed at him out of the darkness.

He came out on to a beach – the black sand of the western Darthene coast, in brilliant hot sunshine. Right in front of him was Hasai, lying flat on his back with his wings laid out on the sand at full extension. Lying all around were scraps and sheets of something black and glittering, twisted and stiff. Off to one side, Segnbora sat on the sand, half-naked for the heat, and leaned up against the huge wall of Hasai's neck while she worked at a sheet of the black stuff, picking at it delicately. 'Well met,' she said. 'It's been some days.'

'It has, that, but—' He stopped short, staring at her.

Segnbora was not entirely there: he could see Hasai through her, though dimly. He looked down at the sand, saw her shadow lying there, light black on dark: a human shadow again. He didn't know whether or not he should be alarmed by that. The tenuous look of her was alarming enough.

'Are you all right?' Herewiss said, to both of them. 'When did this happen?'

Segnbora's face fell a bit, watching his reaction. 'Well,' she said, 'it seems to have happened after we went to the Eorlhowe. And I may be wrong, but—' She held up a hand and turned it over, looking at it front and back. 'It seems to be getting more pronounced, the last day or two. If this goes on much longer—' She shrugged.

'If it goes on much longer, *what?*'

'I don't know!' said Segnbora. 'This has never happened to me before . . . But I'm all right otherwise.'

It was just like her to add something like that: as if any 'otherwise' could be enough to offset the fact that she was fading away. 'What brings you out this way, *rhhw* Herewiss?' Hasai said.

'Newsgathering. I'm going to talk to the Queen shortly; I thought I'd see what you had to say.'

'Well, we see that the Arlene mercenaries have been called in,' Segnbora said, turning over the sheet of black stuff and beginning to work on it again. Segnbora followed his glance and then laughed. 'Oh, this! Herewiss, even Dragons cast their skins.'

'But not after "the last time", I thought.'

'You remember that, do you,' she said. Far down the length of his neck, Hasai's eye shifted: he and Segnbora looked sidewise at one another. 'Usually,' she said, 'they don't. But he felt the urge come on him suddenly—'

'After you went to the Eorlhowe . . . ?'

Hasai gave his neck a half-turn so that his head came to rest right-side up, some feet from Herewiss. 'It is unusual,' he said. He glanced down the length of himself with mild satisfaction. 'It looks fine, I must say. A new hide always does. But I cannot say what it means.'

'And meanwhile, I think something can be made of this,' Segnbora said, shaking out the sheet of cast skin that she held. 'Once all the connective fibres are out of it, anyway. But the mercenaries. We've seen several groups from the west of the country, and two from the south, moving north and east and joining with others as they go. I would make it no more than three thousand at the moment. A better count would mean getting closer, and we've been at some pains to keep ourselves secret.'

'How about your other business?'

'With the DragonChief?' Segnbora laughed, a slightly bitter sound. 'We failed in that, I'm afraid. She'll give us no help, nor will the other Dragons. But—' She looked again at her half-transparent hand, let it drop and leaned against Hasai again. 'We were given something else – I just wish I knew what it was, and what to do with it.'

Herewiss looked from one to the other of them. 'We know what it was, *sdaha*,' Hasai said. 'It was the Draconid Name.'

'Well, so you say. I wouldn't know the Name if it came up and bit me.'

'And so it has,' Hasai said. 'See the result!'

Herewiss looked from one to the other of them. 'Who gave—'

'I don't know!' Segnbora said. 'I saw the Eorlhowe Gate. Or it saw us – and it passed me – this. This knowledge, this—' She shook her head. 'It's immense, it's—'

'It is difficult to describe,' Hasai said, with gentle irony. 'It is the inner Name of every Dragon ever born. And much else, I suspect.'

'You told me that only the DragonChief knows that Name,' Herewiss said.

'So she does, as a rule. But I am not sure that the Name she was told is the same one *we* were.'

'But what's it mean to us? And why should you be given it?' said Herewiss.

She shook her head. 'You know as well as I do that something like this never happens without a reason. It scares me. We're obviously meant to use it in some way – we could use it to compel the Dragons, some of them anyway, to our will. But that kind of force would be playing right into the Shadow's hands. So, I suppose we're meant to become something as a result of the Name. But what?' She looked at her hands, and laughed, a shaky laugh. 'Except perhaps more abstract than I've been previously . . .'

'If you get any idea of what this means, you'll let me know . . . Meanwhile, I should be glad if you were in the close neighbourhood of Prydon about a tenday from now. The Queen will have her people in place somewhere around the eighty-sixth of Summer: she won't want to leave it much longer than that. I'll give you more when I know more.'

'Right enough.' Segnbora looked at him. 'Have you heard any news of Lorn?'

Herewiss shook his head. 'No, and I don't dare go looking, even in mind. You or I or Eftgan can protect our end of a conversation, but he can't, and, at this range, I couldn't protect him either. And anyone who can find his mind can find him. He's just going to have to get along by himself.' And how the fear went through him, like a spear, when he said it.

'Well, if you should hear anything, tell him the child is well . . .'

Herewiss looked at her. 'I was going to mention. There are rumours in the court that they're looking for a child of Lorn's line. To make a regency for, they say.'

Segnbora snorted. 'As if any child would survive that.'

'No, but that's not my main concern at the moment. There's an unnatural level of interest in the subject. They want a royal child for something else . . . I don't know what. Keep an eye on your babe!'

Segnbora nodded. 'As for the other, we'll be where you need us, and when.'

'Just in case,' he said, 'if you find it comfortable to be in the city near the time, there's a house—' He showed it to her in mind. It was a private rooming-house near the outer wall, one that had a lot of Darthene travellers staying there in normal times. 'You shouldn't be noticed there.'

'If I can solidify myself a bit, I may do that,' she said. 'Living on light and air gets boring after a while: I want to get into the marketplace and taste bread and cheese again.'

'Ah now *sdaha*, what could be better than the good sun, like wine—'

'You haven't had enough wine to make a judgement,' she said, poking Hasai, 'and neither have I, of late!'

Herewiss raised a hand in farewell and made his way back, stepping out through the doorway into the cool stone dimness of the Hold in his mind.

He wandered a few doors further down, looking through as he passed them; strange landscapes filled with fiery mountains, barren places burnt by their suns, seas with no shore. At last he came to the doorway that looked into that quiet closet at the back of Eftgan's rooms in Blackcastle. He stepped through.

The Queen was sitting there in her nightshift, brushing her hair. She looked to Herewiss after glancing at his reflection in her mirror, and said, 'Take the seat there. What news?'

He gave her first the letter and message from Andaethen. 'Nothing I hadn't expected,' Eftgan said. 'How goes your work?'

'Slowly. There's a fair amount of support for Lorn among the Four Hundred, but most are afraid to speak.'

'Where will they be when the war starts?' said the Queen.

'You'll need a foreseeing for that. Most of them seem to be waiting to see which side is stronger . . . then that's the way they'll jump, quick as a cat into cream. Too few of them have the right of the situation at all on their minds.'

'Nothing new there,' Eftgan said, mild-voiced. 'Now, the troop movements.'

He told her what Hasai and Segnbora had given him, then showed her the map he'd made. She took it. 'There seems to be some interest in the southern ford.'

'Queen, it might be a trick to distract us from their real plans. Anyway, it's too soon to tell.'

'But you should at least have a guess,' she said.

Herewiss groaned softly. 'Most of my battle-experience is out of books. I thought you might have put Erein in this job: she seems to know which end of a battle is up.'

'So she does, as far as regards troop movements, matters of materiel and strategy and so forth. But *your* specialty is sorcery and Fire, which we have to take into consideration in these battles. Now tell me how you see it.'

He gathered his thoughts. 'There's a great ingathering of sorcerers,' Herewiss said. 'Almost two hundred of them, now. That means we'll have at least warfetter to worry about . . . especially since Rian isn't the kind to worry about the ethics of what he's doing.'

'That we can work to prevent: by killing the sorcerers, if necessary. I'm more interested in the troop movements. Cillmod's whole business is going to be to push as far into our territory as possible, to keep us from bringing the battle close to Prydon. Ours, of course, is to break through his people, and cross the river. But for the meantime, it would buy me time if something can be done about the border from their side.'

'Such as?'

The Queen shrugged at him. 'Keep them from crossing for as long as you can. You *are* still in breakthrough, aren't you?'

Herewiss thought about that. 'The Power is beginning to plateau out somewhat.' *Just as well*, he thought: *another month like the last one would leave me burnt to a cinder*. 'But I can still do some fairly large things.'

'How far in do you think they're meaning to push?'

'It's hard to tell. Certainly it's to their advantage to push you off the Kings' Road as soon as possible: just as it's to yours to stay on it for as long as you can.'

'Yes,' said the Queen. 'But when and where I leave it, *that* I'm at some pains to keep them from knowing. All we can try to do is hold them here, and here, west of Limisba, and you keep their main force from crossing! I chose the day of this battle, and that's the day I intend to have it.'

'And they, of course, will be leaning towards preventing that, Queen. And as for Rian—' He shook his head.

'No progress on that front?'

'None. I need to tempt him out into the open. I need to do something – blatant.'

'Goes against your grain, does it? Well, listen, my lad, you go off and be blatant . . . but be prudent about it. I will not have you tossed out of the city.'

'It seems unlikely that Cillmod would do it,' Herewiss said, rather ruefully. 'We appear to have some kind of understanding.'

'Oh?' But Herewiss did not amplify. He understood the matter poorly himself.

'Well,' Eftgan said, 'never mind that. But force the Rian issue any way you like. I do not want him in the battle.'

'You have a foreseeing, then.'

'I do. Disaster for all of us, if he's there. I am reluctant,' she said, 'to tell you to kill without giving defiance. But if

226

you must, to keep him out of that battle . . .'

'What have you seen?'

She shook her head. 'Death. Death everywhere. Just—'
She broke off. 'Undo him. One way or another, undo
him.' She sighed, and looked at Herewiss with an
expression of weariness and disgust. 'That's all for
tonight. More than enough, I'm afraid.'

Herewiss nodded. They made their farewells, and he
stepped back into the cool, dim hall of the Hold. For long
minutes he stood there, wishing that he dared go in search
of the door where Lorn could be found. But he didn't.

He sighed, and opened his eyes on his circle. The Fire
of it was burning low: he was tired. Just outside the circle,
tipped back in another chair, Sunspark sat and watched
him. It looked like the young russet-haired man he had
seen the other evening, except that this time it was a
woman.

Herewiss sighed and waved the Fire out, and stood,
staggering slightly. 'No, it's all right,' he said to Sunspark,
who was by him instantly.

'Bed for you,' Sunspark said. 'Now.'

Herewiss laughed weakly, but was in no mood to argue.
'Just another of your ploys. Do you ever think of anything
else?'

'You'd be surprised,' Sunspark said.

Much later Herewiss still lay awake in the dark. He kept
hearing Eftgan's voice, cool, certain, and seeing a man's
face, assured and smiling.

*He has a wife and a daughter. They don't know what he is.
They'll grieve him. They'll hate his killer.*

That was the clinch. He remembered how when his
mother died, for some months after, he had almost hated
the Goddess. *You took her from me! Why did You take her?!*
And it was the fire itself that had killed her. If you used it,
you burned out young. She had used it. And one day she
had quite simply leaned back and died. How he had railed
at the Fire, and its Maker: doubly bitter, for he knew then

that if he ever managed to achieve his Fire, that fate was waiting for him.

There's enough death about, Herewiss thought. *If I can spare him, make him harmless.*

'Loved,' Sunspark said.

Herewiss looked at it lying there, in woman's shape, the unpredictable mind showing clearly behind the eyes. 'Loved,' it said, 'what's on your mind?'

'I'm worried.'

'How can I help?'

He lay there gazing into the darkness. 'I'm worried about Lorn,' he said. 'And I dare not simply reach out to him now: if someone should "overhear" where he is—' He shook his head. 'I think you should go find him, and make sure he's all right.'

'And when I find him?'

'Bring him here,' Herewiss said, 'by any means that will keep him unnoticed.'

Sunspark gazed at him. 'I'll go. How soon?'

'Tomorrow will do.'

'Tonight,' it said. And it was gone.

Herewiss lay back and stared into the darkness again. He thought of the people standing around Cillmod's throne. He would be one of those, when Lorn came into his own. And there would be others: some from the old guard, some from the new. Moris would be there, and the rest of Freelorn's group: Eftgan in the background, making sure things ran smoothly. He would still have Lorn's ear, of course. But there would be a lot of other people competing for the same position.

What if he— The thought died half-formed, then sat up again. *No, we love each other, nothing's going to change that*—

Oh indeed, his thought answered. Kingship— He had seen the kind of work and commitment it required of a man. He had seen Lorn's father, wearing himself down in that work until his weary heart rebelled and killed him on his own throne. Nor had there been a queen competing for his attention. How would it be? – a ruler with a loved, but with something more important to pay attention to, a suffering, neglected country. Where would Herewiss be left then?

But this was what he had been working for, all this time. Lorn, in command, in kingship, on that throne, doing what he was meant to do. It had never occurred to Herewiss in all this while that achieving his goal at last would bring him worse pain than the company of Lorn unfulfilled.

Fool, he thought. *You didn't think it through.*

And if you had? the rest of him said, sterner. *Would you have done otherwise? Kingship is his by right. You want his rights for him. There's no wrong in that.*

And Cillmod, Herewiss thought. *What about him?* Easy, in the old days, to think about merely ordering him, in the words of the declaration, to be over mountain, over Arlid, over Sea, within so many days. But he was not going to be that easy to get rid of. And besides, the frank, open, amused, annoyed face – almost Lorn's face – came back to haunt him. Herewiss shook his head. To just kill him?

He sighed. *He's done right, by his lights, all this while . . .*

So has Rian, that sterner voice said. *What right he thinks he's doing, Goddess only knows. But his 'right' will kill the world . . . and for that reason, you see no problem with 'undoing' him. How is Cillmod any different?*

Herewiss groaned softly. *No more of this*, he thought. But sooner or later, he was going to find himself standing in front of Cillmod – or Rian, or both – with the Power in his hands. And he would have to use it, or not . . . and answer for the consequences.

Goddess and Queen, what am I to do . . . ?

Further south, a man who no longer had access to illusion, nonetheless now looked less like himself than he had in a long time.

Freelorn stayed out in the far countryside for nearly a tenday, cheering on the hurried growth of coarse beard that until now he had always sworn at. He cooked russetweed to dye it, and dyed his hair as well: he cut reeds, dried them with care, and slipped a short piece up each nostril. They hurt, but they changed the shape of his nose enough to make a difference.

Blackmane was a bigger problem. He was more difficult to disguise effectively – a thoroughbred can't be made to look like a sumpter-bred, no matter how you try. At least he was badly in need of a clipping, and he was fatter than usual from having been on grass so much. But more was needed. Lorn barbered Blackie's mane and tail ragged, and afterwards resorted to another weed, healwell, that old favourite of dishonest horsetraders everywhere. Shortly thereafter, Blackmane was black all over, stamping and snorting with the itch of the applied liquor. Lorn waited for the itch to go away, then got on the main road north, and rode straight into Hasmë early the next morning.

The place was astir. Hasmë was the main southern town for river traffic, home to many of the big broad-bottomed flatboats which are the only craft able to navigate the Arlid all the way north to the sea. As Lorn came clanking up the south road, he looked off towards the 'mooring roads', the extensive river-shallows just east of the river, and was astonished to see how many of the boats were there, riding light. Lorn suspected he knew why. Someone had ordered them held here for later use. As troop carriers? To bind together and make bridges of, when fords wouldn't serve?

The main gates of the town faced the river docks, and a paved causeway ran down from where the road met the gates, to the docks. That road was full of people in Arlene livery, loading the boats with predictable stir and confusion. *A lot of cavalry*, Lorn thought. *Not in as good shape as they might be, from the look of things. And how many of the others are first-timers, I wonder?* For no cavalry charge would work without a good number of front-line horses who had never done a charge before, and thus didn't have the sense to be frightened of it.

He turned his attention back to the gates. They were

guarded by more Arlene mercenaries, and Lorn glanced at them with what he hoped looked like utter boredom as he rode in.

Nothing easier than getting in, Lorn thought as he passed them. *I hope getting out is as simple.* He turned left and headed for the marketplace. There were a lot more people wearing the Arlene livery, mercenaries from Steldin, mostly, to judge by the darker skin and hair of the men and women he saw. *To them, this is just another fight; the question of royalty, of right and wrong sides, doesn't particularly matter . . .*

Lorn came into the marketplace and started looking around for a place to set up. He found himself an empty spot over by the south wall, and started undoing Pebble's packs.

He had hardly more than half his stock laid out when a voice behind him said, 'You have anything bigger than that one?'

Lorn turned, still half bent over, and so had a moment to compose himself at the sight of the black tunic, before he straightened up. The sergeant was a big blond man, and his tunic was regulation, the embroidery of the Lion on it old and well cared for. *A regular*, Lorn thought, and wiped his face as he straightened. 'Just one,' he said. 'It's second-hand, though.'

'Oh? Let's see the mend.'

Lorn reached around Pebble and unlatched the pot. The sergeant took it, upended the pot, looked thoughtful. 'Looks tight. I'll give you eight for the whole lot.'

Lorn put his eyebrows up. 'It's worth at least ten, piece by piece.'

They went back and forth over prices for a few minutes, and finally settled on nine and a quarter. They spat and struck hands on it, and Lorn wondered ironically when the next time might be that he would touch an Arlene regular, and how. He started unloading the rest of the pots from Pebble. 'Now then,' the sergeant said, 'about the horse—'

Freelorn straightened up. 'What about him?'

'How much for him?' The sergeant was indicating Pebble.

'Well—' Lorn started to say, relieved that it wasn't Blackie involved. *But why would a real trader sell him?* 'No, sorry,' Lorn said. 'I need him.'

'Had to ask,' the sergeant said, unconcerned: 'we can use every one we can get. Just leave those there, someone will be by to pick them up.' And he paid Lorn, and sauntered off to another stall.

Freelorn led Blackie and Pebble out of the market place and down towards the part of town where one might be expected to find a bed for the night. Lorn knew Hasmë fairly well: he had occasionally come up with his foster-parents from Elefrua for the big 'market fair' held once a month. He made his way to an old hostelry that he knew of, and saw to Blackmane's and Pebble's stabling. Then he went out into the city to do something he hadn't had the leisure or opportunity to do in a long time: wander.

He went up on the walls and leaned there with twenty or thirty other people, drinking wine from one of the wallside pubs, looking down at the mooring roads, and quietly counting the boats there. Some of the people outside the pub were teamsters on the boats, or independent shippers, and they were complaining about the inadequate compensation payments for the impounding of their boats. 'Troops,' one of the boatmen said to Lorn, an annoyed man who had come down with his boat loaded with wool, and had been ready to go out in grain, but now would be going nowhere at all. The man made a sour face and took a long swig of his barley wine. 'What's wrong with the fords then, if they have to have a war, can't they soldiers walk at all?'

Lorn heard more of this over the course of the day, as he made his way around the city. No-one paid him any attention, and he had no feeling of being followed. He had his nunch-meal at an eating house off one of the upper squares, a place specializing in Steldene food: hots and spices, mostly, with heavy reliance on pork and dairy goods, then took another cup of watered wine, and took it out into the sunshine to lean against the wall of the eating house, looking out at the square. A lot of other people were doing the same, for out in the midst of things was a band of country mummers, in town for market day, dancing and jingling to bring in customers for a play.

They started their first play, the short one, almost immediately. It was the Creation, one of the rude versions. The Goddess-actress – you could tell it was She by the dusty black cloak spangled with tarnished sequins – brought forth a hopeless pair of Lovers, one so preoccupied with metricated verse and Higher Matters that he didn't notice the other tying his sandal-laces together, the other a buffoon with a hilariously faulty memory and a tendency toward crude bump-and-grind lust. It was inevitable that the Lovers' terrible struggle over Her would go hopelessly farcical. 'Let Him come forward now, Him with Whom hands are Joined,' the verse had it: but the Joining of Hands between these two turned into an abortive arm-wrestling contest, with the Goddess passing among the cheering bystanders and dropping caustic comments on the Lovers' technique. And the Shadow that arose from Their spoiled love was a pathetic, ineffective thing, staggering around trying to Ruin the World, and whining, 'I'm only doing My job!' – while the Goddess chased It around and thwacked It with a broom, hollering backstreet abuse. The audience, including Lorn, laughed until it nearly wet itself. All this not withstanding, the tale ended soberly, as always – the reborn, now-mortal Lovers parted from the Goddess, and reunited and parted again: but, as the play has it, 'not forever, never forever: the Shore makes sure of that'. It was almost dark by the time they were done.

Lorn sighed and headed slowly back to his lodgings, looking at the lit lamps in the windows, as he went by outside in the cool and lonesome dark. He felt the melancholy settling into him, and didn't fight it. He missed Herewiss badly. That phrase, 'The One with whom Hands are Joined,' which had been meaningless to him in his young age, had suddenly come to mean a great deal when Herewiss had first become his loved. Freelorn had never until then understood the struggle that underlay even love, as two fight to become one, but still remain themselves, and the singularities of their natures, resisting this state, wrestle for dominance. *The lucky ones never achieve it, of course,* he thought. He wondered whether he was one of the lucky ones or not. There were times when Herewiss could be very—

'. . . definitely him. He's done some work on himself, but not nearly enough to hide the face.'

'. . . Surprised he would turn up at all. Give him credit, I wouldn't have thought he'd have the nerve. The stories and all.'

Lorn's contemplative state shattered at the words, and he became abruptly aware of his surroundings. He was in a long narrow street, barely more than an alleyway, about an eighth of a mile from his lodgings. A bad place to be alone, and to have to leave in a hurry: for the voice speaking those words was that of the sergeant from this morning, and someone else was with him.

Their footsteps became more audible as they approached, still talking. He had to get away, somehow or other, right now. But there was nowhere to run: nothing around him but sheer walls—

'Seven years . . . I guess it might put some backbone into you after all. Well, too bad, he's headed for the chop.'

'No he's not, you just lose that idea! He goes straight to Prydon and not a hair hurt on him. Why do you think they didn't just shoot him at the gates? They said see what he does, see where he leads us, don't frighten him off the nest!'

If they saw him now, they would know he had over-heard them. The plan they were now discussing would be useless: they would have to take him now. Lorn did the only thing he could. He put his back up against the stone, and drew his knife, and waited. It was still just possible to kill them silently and leave.

The stone behind him smelled of moss, and felt slightly warm, like that stone wall he had leant on outside Elefrua, cooling only slowly after an afternoon's sun.

But that stone *was* this stone, something insisted. Quarried from the same land. And this stone knew him. Knew its own. Could take care of its own—

They came into view around the curve, moving along at moderate speed, like men on business – the sergeant from this morning, and a companion also in the tunic and breeches of an Arlene regular. They looked right at him. Lorn gripped the knife, leaned against the warm wall, and waited.

They looked through him, and walked on towards him, and past him, as if they saw nothing but stone. 'No, there's something else that wants looking into, apparently.'

'Something else? What, then? Take the head off him, that's the answer to everything, I'd have thought.'

Lorn stopped being astonished at his sudden invisibility, and realized what they had said a few seconds earlier. 'Shoot him at the gates—'! So much for his 'excellent' disguise, so much for his cool handling of the sergeant. They had known all along. *How long have they been watching me? Since Elefrua? Before, possibly?* But it was at Elefrua that this strangeness had started to come to him, something to do with the land: the knowing of it. The *being* known by it: recognized, owned . . . He felt the stone of the wall against his shoulders and back, good Arlene granite, the bones of the earth hereabouts, and thanked it silently.

And did he hear it say something in return?

They were past him now, heading down the alleyway. 'Some business down south – they weren't too forthcoming, but I can guess. And they want to see who his friends are in Prydon, too. Use to be made of them.' There was a mutter of annoyance. 'All we have to do now is find him.'

'No problem there. What's he going to do, tunnel under the walls? He'll go out by the gate like everyone else. We'll put someone behind him the minute he moves.'

Their voices faded gradually. Much too gradually, Lorn realized. He had been hearing, not through his own ears, but someone else's. Did stone hear? Was a wall more than its component stones, but a kind of organism? It would take a while to come to terms with this . . .

He put his knife away and just leaned there against the wall for a moment, as much for companionship as to get his wits back after the fright. The stones, at least, knew who he was, or what. He thought with a twinge of fear of Lalen, and Nia. *Fastrael*, he corrected himself nervously. *Some business down south—* He swore softly. If his carelessness had endangered them— He could just hear Lalen's angry voice: 'What new trouble are you going to bring down on us?'

He scrubbed at his face for a moment, wiping the sweat away. *Nothing to do but get things moving as quickly as possible*, he thought. *Make certain people too busy with matters up north to worry much about the south. It's all I can do.*

He patted the wall as he stood away from it. The feeling was strange: did the hard stone curve like a cat against his hand for a moment . . . ?

Lorn headed back towards his lodgings, conjectures burning in his brain. Finally, feeling like a fool, he tested one of them. He found another small street, well-lit, and leaned against the wall of a house. The moss-smell, the feel of sun-warmed stone, was there as well, and a sense of bemused greeting. Lorn stood there and watched four or five people go by, and satisfied himself that they couldn't see him – by tripping one of them, finally: a drunken gentleman who fell down without hurting himself, and got up convinced that he had simply missed his step. More experimentation showed Lorn that he could get the cobblestones to recognize him as well, and could walk right through a crowd unseen, if he did it slowly. Sometimes the control slipped, and he became visible again. But Lorn learned to find his control again, more and more quickly, and he spent an hour or so practising – walking through city streets that smelled of rain and wheatfields instead of damp and dung, brushing past the city watch and many a late-night walker with no more trace of his passing than a slight breeze where he had been. *Now if I can lead horses while doing this*, he wondered . . .

He was sure he could.

He made his way back to his lodgings, checked Blackmane's and Pebble's fodder, and made sure that their tack was arranged so that he could find it quickly in the morning. Then he went up to bed and lay there awake for a long time.

Goddess among us, Lorn thought. *Who knows how soon this might have happened, if I had stayed here after Father died? Maybe all it needed was that I be past a certain age, a certain stage, for it to start happening. Or just had to be willing to be* known. He had to laugh slightly at that. Incessant seeker of action, lover of last stands and lost causes, of *doing* things, no surprise that it had taken him a long time to find out that what needed doing was to *stop* doing. *What if I had come back sooner, and stayed a tenday, a month?*

And maybe I would never have had it at all, without Herewiss, and whatever he's done to me.

And Herewiss, of course, had become what he now was because Lorn had *not* become king. The coil of it all ran back and forth in time, interwoven with other strands he couldn't even begin to understand, and Lorn knew Whose hand was on the shuttle. No matter. He had this piece of kingship, this power, *now*. The land recognized him, and was willing to help. All he had to do was make use of that help – get to Prydon without being noticed, get into the city, and go looking for what was his.

And perhaps find it . . . at which point a war might just become unnecessary.

Always assuming that he could find those things in time.

Hergótha, Lorn thought.

He turned over and went to sleep.

11

The Shadow was the first to have to claim
It was in the right: and ever since, the
claim has been suspect. For the Goddess
didn't need to claim – She *knew*.

d'Arien, *Charestics*

'I could not find him,' Sunspark said. Herewiss looked at it. It sat in the chair, leaning back indolently, in the shape of that young red-haired woman, and its glance went back and forth from Herewiss, to Moris, to Andaethen, with – was that a trace of unease?

'But surely you know the feel of his mind by now.'

'I know it,' Sunspark said. 'I'm telling you it wasn't *there*. Something—' It shook its head. 'There is another power interfering. Some other element, some other force . . . Every now and then I would get a flicker of his thought: then—' It waved a hand. 'Away again.'

Andaethen shrugged. 'We'll assume he's all right, then. Doing otherwise won't help us. Are you ready for this evening?'

Herewiss nodded. 'I'll be done with what I have to do by sunset,' he said. 'After that . . .' He smiled slightly. 'It should be an interesting party indeed.'

Keep them from crossing, Eftgan had said to him. *Just keep them on their side of the water for a few days more, until we're less than four days away. I'll manage the rest.*

It had been a pretty problem, despite the fact that there

239

were only two fords near the city, and the bridge. Some of Cillmod's forces were already on the Darthene side, but only about a thousand. The main levies were still coming up from the south, where they had been billeted on the smaller towns – partly to guarantee those towns' loyalty to Cillmod, and partly because Prydon and its environs simply couldn't support them all. They could spend little time near the city, and Herewiss made use of that fact.

At first, parties of fifty or a hundred had started crossing the Arlid by whichever ford was convenient. Herewiss had put a stop to that, several nights ago, by doing one of the things he had always wanted to do before he had the Fire: by becoming the river.

It was not a thing that one did suddenly. He had spent a long time in his circle of Fire, dissolving his physical self away in the sense and flow of Arlid's water; feeling the rocks of the river-bottom, every weed that grew and waved there, every fish and bug; and the water itself, endlessly malleable, but stubborn enough in its way to wear down rock. Herewiss let it wear him away until there was little left of his consciousness but that sense of flowing past the restraint of banks, himself shouldering himself aside in whirlpool and eddy, running shallow over Daharba ford; then running under the walls of Prydon, and dividing in turmoil around the piers of the great bridge before reuniting to run over the ford at Anish, and further north. Though gravity and the sea tugged at him, Herewiss confined his consciousness to that single stretch of water.

It took him half a day to become the river properly: and it became him, as a result, though not so completely. It found his complexities and commitments fascinating, being so different from its own – a river makes few promises, except to flow downhill – and took them on gladly for a short period, with what Herewiss found was a rather shocking enthusiasm. The result was that the first time a group of Arlene mercenaries tried to ford the river at Daharba, they and their escort of regulars were sucked down by a sudden whirlpool, and about half of them did not come up again, except several days later, bloated.

Their deaths were on his head, and Herewiss grieved over them; but a lesser number of deaths now could possibly prevent a great many more later, and he hardened his heart to what he and the river were doing. It was a strain to keep the Firework fuelled day and night, but the same thing happened again the next day, at Anish ford and Daharba both, and the next as well. It happened to fewer and fewer soldiers, though. Rumour had travelled fast, as Herewiss expected, and company after company arrived at Prydon on the western side, heard the news, and refused to cross. Short of moving the whole army down to Hasmë, there was nothing the commanders could do but march men up to the city and across the bridge. This made a fine bottleneck, and considering that the Arlenes would have about five thousand people to move within the next few days, this suited Herewiss well. Pressure from Prydon might insist that the troops should keep trying, and the fords might presently be proved safe. That didn't matter: Herewiss now had the bridge to deal with.

Nearly a tenday ago, now, he had strolled across the bridge with Sunspark, had leaned there on the broad handsome parapet and watched the water running under the graceful curve of the huge granite piers. It was twenty cubits wide and three hundred cubits long, of which two hundred fifty cubits was span, with five sets of arched pillars beneath on either side. All those arches were the circular and semi-elliptical kinds: besides being beautiful, they bore weight well, which was a problem for Herewiss. He was going to have to convince this bridge to fall down, and one so stubborn-built was going to be a problem.

A bridge's nature is to bear, he thought, gazing at the Fire as it leapt around him, *and to keep doing so despite whatever forces are being brought against it*. If it should decide to resist what Herewiss required of it – its suicide, essentially – he would have to 'kill' again.

He closed his eyes and composed himself. He had been having some difficulty with the ongoing discovery that almost everything seemed alive, at least to the Fire. He shrugged and went looking inside him for that long hallway inside the old Hold in the Waste.

There seemed to be a faint breeze blowing as he stood there for a moment, getting his bearings, then he started to walk, touching the stone briefly in greeting as he went, and didn't have to wander long before he found the doorway that led, in mind, to one end of the bridge. Herewiss walked through it and out on to the roadbed, looking down for a moment at the hexagonal paving-setts, and the ancient mortar holding them together. As usual, the mortar was even stronger than the stone; it wasn't nearly old enough, at a mere six centuries, to have started deteriorating significantly. *One more problem*, he thought, and strolled out into the middle of the bridge again, standing where he had stood the other day. The grace of the thing, the age of it, stirred his guilt anew at the thought of having to destroy something so beautiful and venerable. And he was going to have to pull it down in some way that would leave it wholly unusable, but otherwise mostly unhurt, so that it could be put up again later – no point in wasting the effort of hundreds of people in quarrying and shaping the stone.

He leaned on the bridge and let his selfness sink down into it, feeling the webwork of the mortar holding the huge blocks of stone together; and deeper still, feeling the way the stones pushed against one another, the transmission of stresses. He had done this with a mountain, not too long ago, but this was more difficult, possibly because the bridge was made by human beings, rather than grown by the Goddess: the scent of artifice clung about it. And so did that sense of consciousness. The bridge remembered the hands that chipped its stones out of a mountainside, that sank the cofferdams and set in its piers, that bound it with mortar and stained it with wine and blood when it was done – the builders' blood, still remembered, a hot hurting splash. The bridge was surprised to have been hurt. Until then it had not been aware of having *been—*

And not much else to do since then, Herewiss said. *But bear—*

The bridge considered this a moment. *What else is there?* For a moment it seemed to look back in time – there were moments of such strangeness or brightness that even a bridge would notice: a parade with banners and beaten drums, a garland left by a young boy over one of the bridge-posts as a present, and one afternoon when a young woman came and leaned over the other parapet of the bridge, looking north towards the sea, stroking the stone absently, smiling down at it once. Herewiss felt the darkness of her cloak, felt the light hidden in it, like the stars, and felt the bridge's awe. It knew Who had grown its stones, and Who loved them, like everything else She had made.

I am on Her business, Herewiss said.

Who isn't? What's needed?

The King is coming back, Herewiss said.

He felt the stones almost tremble. Certainly the stresses of the bridge shifted against one another, for a moment.

The King's enemies are coming as well, Herewiss said. *The enemies will be coming from the city: the King and his people, from over the river.*

This time the bridge really did tremble, and Herewiss hoped that tremor didn't transfer through into the 'real' world. So—

He took a breath. *I think you must lie down for a little while*, he said.

He was ready for the fear that would follow such a statement, the resistance. There was a long pause . . .

. . . and the stone began to shake again, in real earnest this time, mortar cracking and every stress-pattern twisting out of shape.

BUT NOT RIGHT NOW! Herewiss cried, clinging to its parapet, and the bridge lay quiet under him. He half-leaned, half-clung there a moment more, trying to sort out the terrible confusion of feelings running through it, of terror and acquiescence and sorrow for a long life suddenly

lost. *And we'll put you back together again afterwards,*
Herewiss said, stroking the stone. *For pity's sake, don't
think we'd ask, otherwise!*

They were quiet for a good while, together. Then
Herewiss set his Fire deep into the bridge, bound it into
the stone, and leaned on the parapet again. *That'll do it,
then,* he said, feeling sad and tired all of a sudden. *About
two hours after sunset.* He leaned there for a good while
before straightening up and making his way back down
the span, to the door into the Hold.

Tonight there was none of the dimness Herewiss remembered from his last visit to the banquet hall. All the
torchères were ablaze, eight of them on each side of the
room. The tables were set out along the sides of the room,
with great branched candlesticks on them, and the sunset
came in through the great windows flung open; cool air
and a breath from the rose gardens flowed in too, mingling
with the waft of aromatics from the braziers, and the
tangle of savours from the food. Herewiss walked around
once, while they were setting up, and had his hands
slapped once or twice by Andaethen's possessive cooks as
they laid out the roast ducks and the boned smoked beef.
He didn't dare do anything but stare at the centrepiece, a
huge game pie four feet high, in the shape of a sailing
galleon, with gilt pastry sails, and the Eagle banner, done
in sugar plate, flying from the foremast.

Andaethen was wandering around supervising languidly,
in a drift of smoke-coloured silk gauze over a tight-bodiced
dark grey gown. 'Going mate-catching tonight, are we?'
Herewiss said as he came up to her, admiring the view of
her bodice.

Andaethen laughed at him. 'It's as well sometimes to be
a distraction,' she said. 'Wouldn't you say?'

Herewiss merely smiled as she wandered off again.
Andaethen knew that he had something planned for later
that evening, but Herewiss had chosen not to give her
details. The Queen knew – that was enough. That

morning Andaethen had shown him her own map, rather better drawn than his, showing Eftgan's nearest levies, some six thousand men and women in all, leaving the Kings' Road just west of Awyn, and cutting north and south into the townlands of Adjaveyn and Lorbit. Any force trying to meet and engage them at this point would itself be divided and easier to deal with; because of Herewiss's work at the fords, there were no Arlene forces close enough to try it.

There were more levies coming still, from down south in Darthen: but Herewiss had looked with most interest at the first group. They had come the furthest, those thirty-five hundred in the northward-pushing group. They were the Brightwood levies, and his father led them. Others of his family, various aunts and cousins, marched or rode with them, along with many of his neighbours from the Woodward. But it was that lean, balding figure that he thought of most – not exactly the picture of chivalry, or of a great lord either, in his patched-together armour. But Hearn would let no-one else carry the Phoenix banner, and he was good at keeping hold of it . . .

The guests were starting to arrive. Herewiss went to the doors of the banqueting hall to greet them: prominent Darthenes living in the city, Arlenes of the Four Hundred with members of their families, and visiting merchants and traders. Herewiss had left the guest list to Andaethen, knowing she would have her own agenda for this dinner. His job was to smile and make conversation: he was an excuse, he knew, to allow Andaethen to assess the mental and political state of the Arlenes on the eve of war.

And when the Great Bridge fell down into the Arlid, Herewiss would be there conversing with the guests, obviously nowhere near the scene of the crime. It might fool no-one who knew anything about the Fire; but it might also give Cillmod pause, that a man could fuel such a wreaking and still sip his wine and chat with the guests unimpaired.

Cillmod arrived then, without any flourish of trumpets,

since this was not a state occasion. Various of his ministers were about him, with their families: and Herewiss particularly noted Rian at the back of the group, looking jovial and relaxed. *How does the man do it,* he thought in disgusted wonder, knowing perfectly well that that quiet presence had been dogging his every move, the past week, leaning against everything he did with the Fire to test the strength of it, the permanence of Herewiss's barriers. *Well, later for him.* But his heart was running harder than usual, and the feeling of excitement down in the pit of his stomach was getting more pronounced. *Not much later . . .*

'Sir,' Herewiss said, and bowed to Cillmod, just so low as to be polite, and no more.

'Prince,' Cillmod said, giving Herewiss his proper title, as Herewiss would not give *him* the one he claimed. 'Thank you for the invitation.'

The courtesy was rather hollow. Cillmod knew perfectly well why he was here, and would have been within his rights to refuse, or plead other business . . . like the marshalling of an army. But other minds and hands were managing that business: Herewiss noticed that Meveld, the Commander-General, was nowhere to be seen, nor were Daik and Ilwin, his deputy commanders. Herewiss's guess was that the three of them and their horses were either waist-deep in the Arlid, cursing their reluctant mercenary forces into crossing: or else already over on the far side, trying to get at least some of their troops far enough down the Kings' Road to keep the Darthenes from coming straight and unopposed to the Arlid.

Herewiss smiled back, knowing that all this was on Cillmod's mind as well. He looked drawn, like a man who has been having sleepless nights. Herewiss said, 'It seemed the only way to obtain your company, sir. Unfortunately, my duties here have kept me busy.'

'So I've heard,' Cillmod said. 'More of that later, I'm sure. Meanwhile let me go make my guest's duty to the lady Andaethen.'

Herewiss bowed again, that precise bow, and watched him go. The resemblance to Lorn was unnerving: as was his unwilling liking for the man; it got between Herewiss and his knowledge of what was going to have to happen to him after this war was over. Exile, at best.

'And this is Prince Herewiss,' said a kindly voice behind him. Herewiss turned to see Rian with a tall handsome woman on his arm, who smiled at Herewiss from under black brows: her hair was an astonishment, a sheer sleek fall of black a cubit and a half long over her deep blue gown, bound with a light filigree fillet of silver flowers. 'Prince, the lady Olaiste, my wife.'

'Madam,' Herewiss said, and bowed deep. She looked at him out of cheerful eyes, an expression of cool wonder filling them as she got a look at Khávrinen.

'Your highness,' she said. 'I heard the stories, but I didn't quite believe them. I do now. You've got a marvel there!'

'Not "highness" yet, madam,' Herewiss said. 'It'll be awhile yet, I hope, before I wear the prince-regnant's title. "Sir", if anything. But my name will do.'

'It's all burning,' said another voice from behind Herewiss, 'but it's not eating the scabbard or anything.'

'Paka, don't be rude,' Olaiste said, in a voice more loving than chiding: and Rian said, 'You little monster, come out in front of the host to be greeted properly!'

A child came slipping around Herewiss's left side, and peered up at him. She was about nine years old, and had her mother's hair, though in a curly cloud, and her father's unnervingly light eyes. She stared at Herewiss. 'Now Pakelnë,' Olaiste said, 'make your duty to the Prince like a good girl.'

'It looks like fire, all right,' she said, 'but I put my finger in it, and it wasn't hot.'

'I felt you do that, my lady,' Herewiss said. 'It generally doesn't burn unless I ask it, or else if I'm working hard at something and it gets hot accidentally.'

'Oh. And there's the kitty. Nice kitty,' Pakelnë said,

and calmly reached out to begin stroking Sunspark.

Herewiss's eyes widened, but he had no time to move before Sunspark, having appeared silently from behind him, pushed its huge hunting-cat's head under the small hand. It purred like a thunderstorm, but all the while its eyes were on Rian, and its eyes were fire: hungry, deadly, and impersonal. Rian had the good sense to look nervous.

'She has nothing to be afraid of,' Herewiss said, meaning it. 'Ladies, I hope you haven't eaten dinner. Or for that matter nunch, or breakfast. There's a fair amount of hospitality here to do justice to.'

'What would you recommend?' Olaiste said, looking away from Sunspark with difficulty.

'I want an ice,' said Pakelnë.

'What, before dinner?' Herewiss said, while her mother said, 'Paka, your manners!' and Rian said, '"I want an ice" *what?*'

They looked at one another, and Olaiste laughed out loud, and Rian raised his eyebrows, the expression of a doting father, helpless against his first child; and Herewiss smiled, though the smile felt a bit thin from inside it. *Goddess*, he said to Her, aggrieved, *why can't this be easier for me? Can You not afford the luxury to allow me a straightforward hate for my enemy? Must the picture be complicated by these innocents?*

But then, Hers was . . .

'"I want an ice", *Prince*,' Pakelnë said, with the air of someone much put-upon.

'Come on then, madam,' Herewiss said. 'Lady Olaiste, do you like fish, or fowl, or meat of the chase? It's all here . . .'

He played the host to Rian's wife and daughter for a while, then saw Andaethen beckoning him, and stepped away. Sunspark sat next to Pakelnë while she ate her fourth ice, washing its face as if bored with everything: but Herewiss noticed that it never quite left off looking at Rian.

I could save you a trouble, it said.

You behave yourself!
You are going to have to kill him.

Herewiss made no answer to that at the moment. He went over to Andaethen, who leaned over and whispered, 'Do you need rescuing from them?'

'Who? Rian's wife and child? Not them. They're charming.' He said it rather sourly.

Andaethen looked at him. 'Well, you know best.'

'I wonder,' Herewiss said, and sighed, and headed back into the crowd. His nerves were playing him up, though; the place seemed hot. Sunspark's eyes were on him.

Herewiss took a cup of iced wine, drank it off, found no relief. After a few minutes he went out on the terrace, half hoping to find Cillmod there.

Instead he found Rian, thoughtfully touching one of the white roses that grew in the great stone jars arranged down the length of the garden terrace. Herewiss, reluctant, would have gone inside again: but Rian looked up at him and said, 'It was kind of you to make my wife and daughter so welcome.'

'Why should they deserve otherwise?' Herewiss said.

Rian smiled to himself, turning his attention back to the rose. 'Indeed. But you certainly seemed to be enjoying yourself, showing off the food. For a man so fond of the pleasures of the table,' Rian said, 'you're lean.'

Herewiss smiled slightly. 'I burn it off,' he said. 'It's always been so.'

Rian smiled again, just a bit more broadly. 'Somehow I would not have thought you would have much in the way of a sense of humour,' he said. 'The first man to have the Fire – certainly a very determined man, very focused. Without much time for other interests, I would have thought.'

'Like other human beings?' Herewiss said. 'You could hardly be said to be human yourself, without at least that.'

'All the same . . . an exacting art, if what I hear is true. Demanding . . . leaving scant energy for other things. I would think sorcery would be much preferable. It's far more understandable, more manageable, doesn't kill the user . . .'

'Does it not?' Herewiss said gently. 'I remember one in the Square at Blackcastle, on Midsummer's Day, who found it fatal enough.'

Rian paled slightly. *He remembers the pain, at least,* Herewiss thought, with satisfaction. *Backlash may not touch him directly when he works through another sorcerer's enslaved soul, but the laws of sorcery can't be entirely flouted: the pain reaches him.* 'It is, though,' Rian said after a moment, 'altogether more amenable to the needs of man. Unlike the blue Flame of Power, as they call it, which everyone knows eats up the life . . .'

'Some people find it worth having, even so,' Herewiss said. 'It's not as if the gift can't be refused.'

'As you refused it,' said Rian, and laughed, a soft breath of a sound. 'Tell the truth. It drove you halfway across the world, for fear of its dying. It nearly killed you in achieving it. And now you use it, and fear it, and wonder why you ever sought it at all.'

Herewiss said nothing to this. Hearing his silence, Rian chuckled. 'Yes indeed: the bitch-Goddess leads another of the poor hounds howling on Her scent, and all for nothing. And you wonder why some people seek service elsewhere.'

Herewiss's eyes narrowed. 'How dare you name Her so . . . !'

'Why do you bother naming Her at all? She doesn't care. Call on Her, and She won't answer. While *my* Master,' he smiled again, 'is only too glad to do so. But as for Her, why fear Her anger, or anything else about Her? It isn't a very powerful force, surely, that creates uncounted souls only to get them to do its work for it. And bribes them with this children's story of reward, this feeble hope held out, of peace on a last Shore.' Rian shook his head in unbelief at the gullibility of human beings. 'What kind of reward for a virtuous life is an eternity of peace, of doing nothing? Living, striving, surely that would be a better reward. Not this timeless prison that we're told waits for us.' He laughed.

'There is rather more to it than that,' Herewiss said softly.

'Oh, I'm sure you *feel* you've been there.' Rian shrugged and smiled. 'Wishful thinking, at best: the mind's last desperate struggles as it perceives great danger or death approaching . . .'

Herewiss stood there, stunned at the man's cool debunking. He remembered the blessed silence of the Shore, the long curving waves of pure light that washed up there on the far side of existence, the Sea of purification and oblivion awaiting those ready to be reborn: and the sound of his brother Herelaf's voice in that silence, the grip of his hands, forgiving, and challenging, and *real*. He knew what *he* knew, regardless of Rian's ideas.

'I accept things as She has made them,' Herewiss said. 'Which seems wise, for one in Her service.'

'But what do you get for it?' Rian was saying. 'Service is supposed to be paid for in coin that you can spend. Even admitting . . . *that* place . . .' And he smiled tolerantly. 'What are you given that's of any worth? A life of difficult service, of self-denial and pain – and then you die young . . . for what? The sake of Her thin-blooded "good"? A world you'll never see again? A loved you'll never see grow old? What will have been the point of all your work, then, if *you* never get anything in return for it?'

'She has Her reasons,' Herewiss said, 'which will doubtless become clear, later on.'

Rian shook his head. 'A healthy man would look for a way to live, and change the world: not leave it early, not slink away like a coward, muttering about the unfathomable will of Divinity.'

Herewiss found himself getting angry, as if someone were insulting his mother. *And so he is*, he thought. But he pushed the reaction down. 'Rian,' he said, 'your "Master" has deluded you badly.'

'Me!' And Rian laughed at him, kindly. It was not an

attempt to infuriate: he genuinely thought that Herewiss was amusing, and pathetic. 'Me! How can you not see how *you're* being had?' Rian said. 'What kind of excuse is She for a god? Everything is ruined, from the beginnings on! The universe is broken, through Her negligence in letting the great Death into it, and there's nothing to be done about it, we're told, but wait for everything to run down. The next time, She'll get it right.' Rian laughed again. 'And what about the other excuse we hear – propagated by Her, of course? That our purpose in the world is to mend it?' He looked at Herewiss with amused outrage. 'To clean up *Her* mess? A poor sort of ruler for the Universe, She's made. A better one is available.' He smiled, and looked at Herewiss with subdued excitement. 'And some of us have begun working for Him. We will clean up Her mess, indeed. Let this Universe run down? Indeed not. Why spend so much pain, so many lives, for an uncertain ending? We'll end it *now*. And then rebuild, and do it properly. There will be no more pain, or sorrow, and no more death.' His face shone, transfigured with the vision.

Herewiss simply looked at him. 'And in the meantime,' Rian said, 'we will draw together the resources we need to hasten the change. Sorcery will not be enough, of course. Fire, eventually – some use will have to be made of that.' He looked at Herewiss with compunction. 'It's rather a poor tool, of course, the Flame. We'll turn Her weapon in Her hand, turn it against her: a sweet justice there. But after we get what use we can out of the Fire, it will be allowed to die out. No point in keeping around a tool that kills its wielders so young.'

'You know I will not permit any such thing to happen,' Herewiss said.

'I know you have to try to stop me,' Rian said. 'Poor dupe that you are: you would *have* to say that. The Fire She's kindled in you drives you to it – even makes you certain that you're right.' Rian looked at him with pity, and compassion. 'You're merely a weapon in Her hand, forged to Her purpose, which is to keep this poor ailing world in Her grip. That being the case, I fear I must break you, so that I can get on with the rest of my work. It's a shame, in a way. You're a man I would have liked to have on my side – but it does seem impossible. I had hoped you might see sense, if we had a chance to talk. However—' He shrugged.

This is it, then, Herewiss thought. The excitement began to rise in him. 'I can't let you live either,' he said. 'You've become the Shadow's tool willingly.' Herewiss was trembling with anger, and pity of his own. 'You've bought the Shadow's story of a world that needs recreating, but you can't see Its real intent, which is to recreate *nothing,* to destroy everything that is, to leave nothing but a void filled with Itself and bloated with Its hate and triumph.' He shook his head. 'The only question becomes: when shall we have it out?'

Right now will do, the voice said, abruptly, from inside his head; and the force came crashing down.

It came so suddenly that for a moment Herewiss stood paralysed, his tongue cleaving to the roof of his mouth, the breath stopped in his lungs. There was another power in his head with him, groping for control, feeling at his mind's connection to his Fire, and his Fire's connection to the Firework outside him, the distant but clearly perceived image of the Great Bridge, all its joints and mortar perfused with a webwork of blue Flame. The other power ran down the conduits of his Fire like some burning spirit down a resisting throat, scalding as it went.

Idiot, Herewiss thought, as he did his best to bear up against the invasion of himself. *Your courtesy will be the end of you. Sunspark was right—* He bore up, like a man bearing the whole huge weight of a mountain on his shoulders. That weight was familiar to Herewiss, and the burdens he had borne before were much more solidly set than what attacked him now – one man's mind, with a great weight of evil behind it, yes, but manageable, to someone who had shifted a whole massif at its roots not too long ago. Slowly he forced that tearing presence up out of his mind. Khávrinen flamed ferociously at his back, while Rian resisted being pushed out, and tore and ripped at Herewiss's connection to his Firework at the bridge. Once it was pried loose, Herewiss knew, the other would be able to set such sorceries there as would make even the Fire ineffective against the bridge for some days. *But not if I can help it—*

—the trouble was, it was slipping. He could breathe again, now, but that pressure on him was increasing. *Moving – mountains – may not have been enough practice*, he thought in utter shock. But this was only one man—

—one wholly and consciously given over to the Shadow, and used by It as Its tool. He caught Its bitter tang of hate, like the taste at the back of the throat after vomiting – a scalding rage, a crushing weight, determined to make Herewiss suffer before he died—

I told you. Your treacherous Mistress leaves you to your own devices. But my Master is glad to come when I call—

Herewiss stood there, frozen, oblivious to the outside world – seeing nothing but the bridge, and his link to it being torn loose from him by the hatred that was the Shadow, working through Rian. *No*, he thought, and ran Fire down his linkage to the wreaking, thinking desperately of lightning, Her spear: he fastened his Flame to that image, and struck at the bridge—

The image in his mind went up in Flame, hesitated for a long moment, and then, slowly, began to bend over the middle two piers. He could feel the groaning of the stones. And then, slow as a falling leaf, it seemed, the arch of the bridge buckled, and broke. The middle of the span slid in two pieces down toward the Arlid: Herewiss felt the spray go up, felt the almighty crash of tons of rock as the span went down in ruin. He could still hear the maimed scream of it as it finished breaking, as the last stones fell.

He opened his eyes. Rian was staring at him, and for all the Shadow's bitter hatred that was living inside him at the moment, the expression on his face was that of simple shock.

Herewiss pulled in a long gasp of air, like a man under water too long, and another. Inside, in the banqueting hall, the music and the dancing went on, and the eating and drinking and laughter. 'So,' he said.

Herewiss gripped Rian's mind. Rian struggled, and Herewiss let him. A moment, just a moment would be all it would take – and Rian gave it to him, a second in which he tried to compose the groundwork for a sorcery. Herewiss pulled, hard, and they fell together into his mind.

A moment they both stood in the black-stone halls of the old Hold down at the bottom of Herewiss's self: and the odd and terrible aura of that place, to which Herewiss was long accustomed, froze Rian where he stood. There was no guessing the shapes of its builders' bodies, or of their minds, and the feel of those minds, patient, unfathomable, and bizarre, still permeated the Hold. The place could throw awry any sorcery until you were used to it, as Herewiss well knew. That was his moment to move.

Shapechange in the body was one thing: you had the rules of matter in the real world to deal with, and if you bent them too far, they would kill you after the change was over. But here, in mind, shapechange was both more flexible and more dangerous . . . and Herewiss had become fluent in it. Fire swirled about him for a moment, his back bent, his face and arms and legs hurt briefly; but when the Flame died away, he was looking at Rian out of the body of a tan Darthene lion, smelling his enemy's fear with a lion's senses. Rian backed away, unable to do anything to help himself: they were in Herewiss's mind now, trapped there together, and no sorcery would avail him.

He turned and ran down the dark hall.

Herewiss loped after him, going easily. All the doors were dark: he would allow his enemy no passage out of here by that means. He would hunt him down these halls until he was exhausted. And when he caught Rian, he would burn out the man's mind and will, which would render him useless to the Shadow. A sorrow, about his wife and daughter: they would have a mute, immobile cripple to deal with for the rest of his life. But better a cripple than a corpse—

He paused at a meeting of two halls, looked around him. Scent led left: he padded after it. But then it faded. Herewiss stood still for a moment. *A little stronger to the right, and ahead*, he thought.

He turned, walked down that hallway. Turned—

And the dragon-eagle leapt at him, slashing, and buried its beak in his throat.

Shapechange! He can't have!

They rolled together over the smooth floor, tumbled down the staircase, still locked together. Herewiss kicked vainly for the dragon-eagle's guts: it buffeted him with its huge wings, half-blinding him, while one of those terrible talons closed its fist about his throat. Though they were inside his mind, Herewiss was not invulnerable: a fatal injury here would kill his outer body as well. The wall was nearby. Herewiss staggered to his feet, slamming the dragon-eagle that was Rian headfirst into the wall.

The eagle screamed, but didn't let go. *Will I die of this?* Herewiss thought. *Not just this fight – but this battle, this war: will it kill me? What use is it all when every wreaking strips months of life off me, when the whole purpose of all this was to be alive afterwards, to live long years with Lorn in peace—*

He caught himself, fury growing hot. That was not the purpose at all.

Leave my soul alone, damn you! he cried at Rian and the Shadow together, as they reeled back and forth about the black floor. The exertion didn't lessen Herewiss's horror. This was what the Shadow had done at Bluepeak, all those years ago. It had had a human accomplice then, and had accepted a bitter madwoman's sacrifice of herself to the Great Dark, and used her to become the Gnorn. Not even Éarn and Héalhra in their strength had been able to defeat It in that shape with anything less than the loss of their humanity, and then their lives. But this time the Shadow had found another willing host, one this time who was not mad, but in full possession of his reason – maybe too much of it. *But it won't be that way for ever. The Shadow will burn him out yet – reduce his will to just the right amount, so that It has access both to Its own full power, and to a human being's blindness. Against which there is no defence: from such, even the Goddess falls away defeated* . . .

Herewiss struggled, terrified even through his exertion. *He will be even more powerful than the Shadow by Itself was at Bluepeak*, Herewiss thought. *He almost is now.*

I am going to die here.

That awful dark strength was piling up against him again, and he bore up under it as best he could. But it was forcing him out of his mind. Their two souls were being forced out into the real world, the shapechange was beginning to impinge into it as well, and Rian was making no move to stop it. Lion and dragon-eagle, they rolled over and over together on the stone of the terrace, Herewiss getting the barest glimpse of the open doors of the banqueting hall, the lights, the sound of song and laughter. No-one had noticed them sliding out of Herewiss's mind into physical reality. And then something said to him, silently, eagerly, *Now?*

For a moment he had no idea what it was talking about – but he knew that mind. *YES!*

—and his next glance showed him fire bursting out everywhere. The rich hangings in the banqueting hall, the tables and the food on them, all burst into flame: doors slammed shut, and burned, the glass in them melting; decanters exploded with sudden heat, dancers screamed and beat at their clothes, sackbuts and olhorns fell to the ground, their wood afire, the metal melting off them. More screams pierced the air, and the stone of the outer Embassy walls itself began to burst into flame.

Herewiss felt Rian's mind, so certain and focused until now, suddenly teeter away from the dark and the certainty that held it. *Olaiste! Paka—*

Not quite inhuman yet, Herewiss thought, with bitter

257

satisfaction. *And you have no hope now. It would take your Master in the full of Its strength to deal with Sunspark quickly,* Herewiss told Rian, amused even through his rage and exhaustion.

The darkness was hammering on Rian to turn back to It, to finish Herewiss's destruction. But still he wavered. He cast a quick sharp sorcery, fierce and swift as an arrow, towards his wife and daughter—

Herewiss blocked it – that much he could do – and went back to struggling against the weight of dark.

Another arrow of words Rian cast, at Cillmod this time, inside the banqueting hall. Herewiss couldn't stop it: he was still recovering from the last blockage. Cillmod vanished away in a simple transport spell. *So he doesn't want to throw his own tools away—*

Their minds still bound together, Herewiss caught the answer, its tone amused – even *now* the man was not afraid of him! *Especially not one that's almost manned to the fist already,* Rian said, preparing another arrow, quicker, sharper, to take his wife and daughter the same way.

So you plan to keep a king around after the battle.

Well, not the present kind of king. Something better. And through Rian's distraction, while he used his connection with Herewiss's mind to undo his own shapechange, and prepared his third sorcery, Herewiss saw then what Rian and his Master had in mind. It was a kingship without will, without power except as authorized by another: a thing that would perform the royal magics, and then lie idle, like a run-down clockwork toy, until needed again. It was a black kingship: a king who was no spouse of the Goddess's, a king in isolation. Herewiss saw Rian's thought of Cillmod as a tool, and one that needed to be further ground down – one that had entirely too much will of its own, for Rian's tastes or needs. He would have preferred someone much younger. Better still, someone unborn—

Herewiss flinched away from the image. Rian, and the Shadow working through him, meant to take a babe or child of the royal blood, in which the potential for power descended, and make from it a thing in human shape that walked and spoke but had no mind, and no will. And best of all for this purpose were the unborn—

Herewiss carefully, carefully kept his mind away from any further thoughts on that subject—

So there is one! came the triumphant cry. Then came the thrust of power, piercing through the woven Fire that lay about Herewiss's inner mind, hunting for names, locations—

Herewiss smashed right back. For a long minute or two they simply struggled together in mind like two wrestlers. The pressure bore down on Herewiss from all sides, like iron bands, to squeeze the truth out of him. *No,* he thought. *Goddess, I'm on your business, but I must die before they find that out—*

The pain became excruciating, but not so much so that Herewiss couldn't see the bright line of Fire that bound his soul permanently into his body. The pressure increased. Before he lost the ability to do so, he reached out to that line, to snap it—

The next thing Herewiss knew, the world dissolved in fire. Only a faint wash of it hit Herewiss, but all his skin felt like he was roasting on a spit, and Rian screamed. The scream was more rage than pain, however, and that blazing figure somehow managed to totter to its feet, lurch around the garden, batting frenziedly at itself. The fire was fastened on it hard, ravening: the air stank of ozone, the pavement melted and bubbled: but Rian still stood, and screamed, and fought, while Sunspark wrapped itself around him as it had around the sorcerer at Eftgan's Hammering.

The sorcerer, though, had gone to dust in seconds. Rian did no such thing.

The screams from inside the banqueting hall wound together with his. One of them at least was a child's, too high-pitched to be any other: 'Da! DA!'

This, said the fierce voice that Herewiss knew well, *for her, for both of them, if you do not submit.*

The next moment there was a roar like thunder, and the fire went out. Exhausted, in desperate haste, Herewiss dived back down into himself, back into the black halls of the Hold, and made the change to his own soul-form: then burst up and out of himself and back into the real world.

He knelt gagging on the paving stones for a moment, fumbling over his shoulder for Khávrinen. He drew it, and looked for his enemy. No sign of him: but no sign of Sunspark either.

Khávrinen burned desperately dim. Much brighter were the burning tapestries in the banqueting hall, flickering through the smoke that billowed out of the broken, burnt doors. Herewiss could see no-one inside; the place was empty. No sign of Rian. But off on the paving, to one side, by one of the stone jars, lay a loose-limbed form, terribly still – an Arlene hunting cat, three times the normal size.

Herewiss staggered over to it, dropped to his knees, and pulled the great fanged head into his lap. 'Firechild,' he said. 'Sunspark!'

It was a long few moments before its eyes opened, squinting and wincing, and a low sound like a moan came from it.

'Are you hurt?'

Oh, I am. I could do nothing.

He cradled it.

Nothing, it said, sounding as if it wanted to weep. *That power that almost put me out before – stronger, now. It almost did it again, though I came at it with all my strength. And I couldn't even burn that silly form of flesh It wore.* Sunspark had lifted its head: now it let it drop back into Herewiss's lap again. *What will you do? It will be waiting for us, at the battle.*

Herewiss shook his head and stroked it. 'What kind of healing do you need?' he said.

Time. But that we don't have, I think.

'No,' Herewiss said, 'we don't.' He looked down at it,

trying to put on a brave face. 'All the same, you were clever to do what you did.'

You see, Sunspark said, sounding afraid, *that I have come to understand something about love. Enough, now, to use it as a weapon* . . . It coughed, and the sound struck terror into Herewiss.

He held it. All around him, the stink of burning, the sharp reports of cracking cooling stone, made a bitter counterpoint to his thoughts. *I was so sure I could solve this problem. Well, now we see the truth. My Power is far from being enough to 'do away with' this threat. It will need Segnbora, and Eftgan, and every Rodmistress in the Silent Precincts* . . . *if even all of them together will be enough to handle Rian.*

And what other help is there for us if they're not?

He scrubbed at his eyes. He was weary unto death . . . but not quite dead yet. And in two days, the Darthene levies would be within a day's ride of Arlen. A great deal could happen in two days.

It had better, Sunspark said.

12

The picture of the loved,
Long we hold in heart:
then come home to find
the two have grown apart:

Which to keep, and which to kill:
Should there be a doubt?
But how we clip the dead to us
and throw the living out . . .

from *Laeran's Song*,
anonymous, c. 2300 p.a.d.

West of Prydon, about half a mile beyond the outer wall,
there is a grove of trees known as Orsmernin. The trees
there are all pale-barked whitestaves. The one in the midst
is the tallest and broadest, and no wonder, it being now
almost seventeen hundred years old – Berlemetir Silverstock, the whitestave tree from which the Stave of the
rulers of Arlen comes. Ambyr, Héalhra's wife, planted it
in memory of him, the year that Kynall was built and
Prydon was founded. When Héalhra's son, King Frelic,
who built Kynall, died, his son, Fórlen, buried him near
the Silverstock, and planted another tree of the same kind
over his grave. Fórlen himself and Queen Tíla, his
daughter, and Hleon, her son, were buried there, with
trees over them; that finished the first circle, and another
was started outside it. One by one the rulers of Arlen came
to lie there, however they died. The trees rise up out of

their graves, giving their bodies back to the world.

Seventy-four trees, in eight circles, the outermost one with many places still left unfilled; they stand there by the little stream Nalash that waters the Orsmernin meadow on its way down to the Arlid. None of the trees have ever died, though some of them have gone green-rotten at the heart. Seventy-four trees: but there have been seventy-five rulers of Arlen.

There was a man standing under one of the outermost trees that morning. Nearby, his two horses were drinking leisurely from a pool of the Nalash stream, but the man's attention was turned away from them, inwards, towards the grove.

Freelorn looked at the slight mound in the grass before him. Off to his left was Fréol's tree. He remembered the day Ferrant had planted it, a handsome young whitestave sapling about three years old. Now it was well along in growth, some forty feet tall after twenty years. There was no tree on the slight rise of ground in front of Lorn, however. There had been no-one around, after they buried Ferrant, who was entitled to plant it.

There will be shortly, though, Freelorn thought, and looked toward the walls of Prydon.

At the gates of Prydon, the usual guard stood. The day had dawned bright and clear, hot already and promising to be hotter still. Such weather was common enough just before the harvest, but the oddity was that the town, for a change, was not full of country people having their last fling before getting the crops in. Things were quiet that morning.

One of the guards looked at the other as a horseman passed through, and a woman carrying a basket of eggs. 'You smell that?' he said.

'Smell what?'

'Smells like rain. It was cool.'

'Send it over here,' said the other guard, fanning himself and looking the other way. Then he looked back suddenly and said, 'I see what you mean . . .'

'Nice,' the first guard said, luxuriating in the breeze as it went by him and through the gates into the city, smelling of wheatfields under rain, and of cool stone with a cool wind over it . . .

Herewiss peered out the back window of the boarding house, carefully.

'Come on, you,' Segnbora said from behind him. 'Eat your breakfast, do. You'll ruin the rest of the day.'

Herewiss said nothing, since he held out no great hopes for the day as things stood at the moment. Sunspark had not completely destroyed the Darthene Embassy last night – most of the walls were still standing, and some of the upstairs rooms had been spared. The banquet hall, though, was a ruin, and Andaethen had suggested to him that he should make himself scarce. Herewiss, therefore, had taken himself off to the boarding-house near the second wall, with Sunspark in tow, and had found Segnbora already there.

Or rather, he had found her less there than he expected. When dealing with the annoyed old man who ran the house, or with his suspicious staff, she looked quite normal. 'It'd be a poor sort of day that I couldn't manage to keep an illusion in place,' she said to Herewiss with good-natured scorn. But for one who could see through such things, though Segnbora was there enough to support her clothes, her face and hands and anything else of flesh that showed were more like a pale thin stained glass than muscle and bone. One thing was new: she now wore a front-and-back tabard of the black dragonhide she had been working on when Herewiss saw her last. Herewiss almost coveted it, and Segnbora was pleased enough with it on her own part, for reasons that had nothing to do with the gemmy beauty of it. The dragonmail would turn any sword that hit it, and blunt anything else, arrow, dart or spear.

The rooms she had taken at the top of the boarding-house were large, for Segnbora had anticipated the possibility of guests: there were three bedrooms and a sitting room. But they weren't large enough to keep Herewiss from pacing, and looking worriedly at her, and out the window on to the back garden. All the roses were in bloom in a riot of gold and red, but Herewiss's attention was mostly for the view over the garden wall. The white dome of Lionhall was visible there, over many intervening roofs.

Herewiss eyed the hard, hot blue sky. 'Where's Hasai?' he said.

'Over on the coast,' Segnbora said, sitting down by the couch on which Sunspark was dozing in its young-woman shape. 'He keeps coming real suddenly, the past few days . . . he can't control it. When I came into town, I told him to keep himself nearby and out of sight. The first night I was here, he tried to sneak in, and almost wrecked the whole back wall.' Segnbora looked amused, but worried. 'His physicality is getting assertive . . .'

'And yours unassertive.'

Segnbora would not meet his eyes. She breathed out, looked over at Sunspark and carefully stroked a stray bit of that fiercely red hair out of the young woman's face. 'She's resting a lot, isn't she. He. It.'

Herewiss nodded. Hooves rang in the archway under the window: someone coming into the innyard.

'It wasn't this bad after Midsummer,' Segnbora said. 'Only a few hours, it took, before it was back to normal . . .'

Herewiss nodded, his eyes on the newcomer. Scragglylooking man, bearded – some kind of tradesman, just in from the countryside, from the look of him. The man glanced up at the courtyard windows in the sunlight, a cool, cautious look—

Herewiss froze.

My Goddess!!

Only the kind of discipline that adepts learn kept him still. ''Berend,' he said.

Her eyes widened as she caught his thought, even

through his heart-mail of Fire. *'Lorn?!'*

Herewiss was suffering such a rush of relief and terror and desire and confusion that his legs simply gave out on him, and he sat down hard on the wooden stool by the window. Segnbora looked abstracted for a moment, then got up and strolled over to the window, glanced out casually. 'He knows,' she said. 'Give him a while to sort out his room. After that, I can hold the protection for all our minds for a while.' She turned back to him and smiled. 'I think you could use a few hours off.'

It was a harder fifteen minutes, in many ways, than those Herewiss had spent duelling with Rian and the Shadow last night. When the door finally creaked softly open, he hardly knew what he did—

How long they held each other, he had no idea. He held Lorn away from him, and looked at him; but Lorn, after a moment of standing with his head scrunched down against Herewiss's shoulder, was looking around the room. That cautious expression again. 'Where's Segnbora?' he said.

Herewiss glanced around and saw that she had slipped into the next room. 'No-one else here?' Freelorn asked.

'Moris is still up with Andaethen,' Herewiss said. 'Dritt got here earlier: he has a room of his own downstairs. Harald is elsewhere in town – he'll be along tonight. The rest are with Eftgan's levies. Lorn, the Embassy—'

'I heard,' Freelorn said, looking with a tight, amused expression at the sleeping Sunspark. 'Neither sorcery nor Fire could have done a job quite *that* way.' He looked at Herewiss.

Herewiss was shocked. Freelorn was radiating certainty, and a sort of solid fierceness that Herewiss had never seen in him before. 'Oh, I missed you,' Freelorn said: but even that longing had an edge and a hunger to it that Herewiss hadn't ever heard. It was a joy to hear . . . and rather frightening.

'Lorn,' Herewiss said, holding him away, 'for Goddess's sake, how did you get in here? What happened to the seeming Eftgan put on you? *How did you just walk in?'*

'I have a lot to tell you,' Freelorn said. 'As for the walking in—' He smiled. 'I may have a trick or two to show you, once we've been in Lionhall.' His glance went out the window, to that high dome shining against the blue.

'But it can wait,' Freelorn said.

Very much later, Freelorn turned over and stretched, and said: 'What about Rian?'

Herewiss lay on the bed in a mixed state: satisfaction, and worry, and exhaustion – the sudden tiredness had hit him after the first flush of their lovemaking. 'I don't know,' he said. 'I haven't been able to feel any working of his mind since last night. Perhaps he feels the same way I do . . .'

'But it's not safe to assume that,' Freelorn said.

Herewiss nodded. 'I told you about his apparent immunity to backlash. His linkage to the Shadow seems almost to be a conscious thing, a being in its own right – all the backlash hits that and seems to be absorbed. Rian provides the Shadow with a connection to human calculation, and righteousness, and blindness . . .'

'And power.'

Herewiss nodded, though reluctantly. It still chafed him that he had not been able to do anything about Rian, even something so simple and unsubtle as killing him.

'Stop that,' Freelorn said, sounding gentle, but exasperated. 'We must work out what to do next.' Lorn sighed. 'A sorcerer whose backlash is being stored . . .'

'Bind enough energy in one place for long enough,' Herewiss said, 'and it'll start to "wake up" the matrix it's bound into. A pattern of energy will do. So would a sorcery, if it were complex enough, and strong enough to hold the energy in question . . .' He thought about that for a moment. 'The backlash of all Rian's sorceries . . . his weather magics, whatever else he's been doing . . . all directed into this "being", and stored for some use later. Against what?'

267

'You,' Lorn said. 'Eftgan. Me.'

'But why hasn't Rian used it already?' Herewiss said, sitting up, pulling the pillow out from behind him, and trying to punch it into a more comfortable shape. 'Why wait?'

Lorn looked at Herewiss. 'Because he's waiting for a particularly large infusion of backlash, to fuel a particularly effective manifestation . . . an appearance of the Shadow Itself, the way the Lion and Eagle were an appearance of the Goddess's other Lover.' Lorn raised his eyebrows. 'An infusion like that could come from the workings of a lot of other sorcerers.'

'Such as would be provided by the outbreak of a war,' Herewiss·said. 'By the first few battles . . .'

They looked at each other dubiously.

'Berend, Herewiss said. *Could we trouble you?*

Are you decent? she said.

'No,' Freelorn said, 'but come on in anyway!'

A moment later Segnbora opened the door and stepped in, carrying a plate and some napkins, and gnawing on a chicken bone. She put the plate down on the bed for them – the rest of the roasted chicken – and sat herself down on the window-seat.

There were a few minutes consisting of nothing but muffled exclamations at scorched fingers. Then Herewiss said, 'When's the last time Hasai was up on the wing?'

'A couple of hours ago.'

'What are the Arlenes doing?'

'Oh, they're moving,' Segnbora said, 'but not quickly. They still haven't been able to bridge Arlid near the city, and they're having to do all their crossings at Daharba and Anish. About two thousand mercenaries and a thousand regulars are on the east side of the river now, and so far about a thousand of them are moving down the Road. Supply trains haven't caught up with the others yet, and they're refusing to move until they do.'

Herewiss smiled at that. Those soldiers who had spent a hungry tenday sitting outside Prydon with only bread and water to sustain them were not willing to put up with such treatment just before a battle. 'Well enough,' he said. 'How fast are the forces on the east side moving?'

'Not very. There have been reports of Fyrd over there, quite a few of them.'

Herewiss looked alarmed at that. 'Attacking the Arlenes?'

'No. Just spotted by them. But the Arlenes are nervous about it, especially the mercenary troops. Apparently there are quite a few of the bigger Fyrd prowling around.'

'Rian's shock troops,' Freelorn said. 'I think we'd better force the pace.' He looked out the window at the dome of Lionhall, away across the roofs.

Segnbora followed his glance. 'It's guarded, you know,' she said. 'There are about a hundred soldiers around the place already, and there are sorcerers nearby. I think there'll be more of both as the time for the battle gets closer.'

'Best not to wait, then,' Lorn said. 'And I encourage witnesses . . . enough of them to spread the word, later, that I entered Lionhall and came out again afterwards. Once that happens, the whole tenor of this war changes. There may still be battles, but the question of who's in the right will have been sorted out for good and all.'

Herewiss swallowed, trying to put his feelings in order. 'Lorn,' he said, 'I want to have enough of our people handy to make sure we can get you in there. My Power—' He shook his head, and made the admission that had been galling him bitterly since last night: 'At the moment, and especially after last night, I'm about as powerful as any given Rodmistress. My breakthrough's over, and if you're looking for miracles, you're going to be disappointed. We're going to have to make do with strategy and precision rather than overwhelming force.'

Freelorn gazed at him. It was an odd, steady expression, and Herewiss wasn't sure what to make of it. 'Who else do you think we need?' he said. 'Besides yourself and Segnbora and Hasai. I assume we can count on Hasai for this—'

Segnbora laughed softly. 'We have at least one miracle on our hands,' she said: 'a Dragon who's itching to do something. I doubt we could keep him out of it.'

'Mori's with Andaethen. Dritt's here. Where's Harald?'

'He's in the city,' Segnbora said. 'I can send him word when you're ready, Lorn, and he can meet us.'

'It'll have to be tonight, then,' Lorn said. 'No point in letting Cillmod's people add more guards than necessary: no point in letting Rian have a breathing space, either.'

'Lorn—' Herewiss said. All his fears were standing up inside his head and shouting at him. 'Are you sure you're ready for this—'

Freelorn burst out laughing, and put his arms around Herewiss. 'Of course I'm not ready! But I have no choice. Neither do any of us. And this is what I came here for . . . what Eftgan is coming down the road with that army for. Cillmod may have gone into Lionhall and come out again, but he is *not* Initiate, and he wasn't able to make use of the Regalia. If he had been, I wouldn't have been able to invoke the Great Bindings at Lionheugh. They worked because I was next-best – because I knew the ceremony, and had the Regalia myself, and the Queen of Darthen working in partnership. But it's not enough any more. Time,' Lorn said, sounding grim, 'to resolve *this* part of the disagreement once and for all.'

Herewiss was in turmoil. He was realizing that though he loved this man, for the first time in many years he did not like him much: this abruptness, directness, was alienating. Herewiss felt the blade go deep, and found his heart made two. And Herewiss realized that part of his mind was screaming, *Don't trust him – he's messed it up before, he'll do it again!*

The voice inside him trailed off hurriedly as he looked for its source.

'Tonight, then,' Herewiss said. 'And then what?'

'We get out of the city and join Eftgan.'

Herewiss thought it might be more easily said than

done: but Lorn was right. He reached out to Khávrinen, lifted it into his lap, and stroked the edge thoughtfully. It needed sharpening . . . not a surprise, since it had only rarely been used as a sword.

Tonight it would have a chance.

The afternoon dawdled on, hot and still, until the light grew more and more golden, and the air started to cool. Westward the sunset began in long streaks of orange and gold and smoke grey. Now the rich light was gilding all the roofs of Prydon, turning thatch the colour of bronze, and slate to dark polished copper, from which the sunset glared in occasional intolerable brightness as the Sun declined. Lionhall's dome shone red-golden. But down in the alleys, everything was shadow: and that was much to Segnbora's taste.

She stood at the street-side window, gazing out as the sun went down and the darkness began to seep into the streets. 'Lorn,' she said.

He did not move from where he stood at the other window, gazing out westward. There was much less noise out in town than there would normally be, but that was not what Lorn was paying attention to, she knew.

'Not this one,' she said.

'What?' He finally turned to look at her.

'It's not the sunset you're thinking of,' Segnbora said. 'I've seen that one, briefly. It's not anything like.'

'You mean you've remembered it "ahead"—'

Segnbora nodded. It was beginning to be a curse, these last few days: for memories of things that might happen were crowding out those of things in the past. She glanced down at her hand on the windowsill; the sill was clearly visible through it, even more so than earlier in the day.

'How certain are these memories?' Lorn said quietly.

'*Ahiw mnek'hej*,' Segnbora said, and then laughed at herself, an uneasy sound. She had also been losing Darthene, the past few days. 'They're not utterly certain,

Lorn, and they're fragmentary. The sunset you're thinking of, I saw the afternoon we sat with Eftgan, after the
Hammering. But just a flash of it—'

There was an abrupt creaking sound. Segnbora looked
over to the bedroom door, to see if Herewiss was coming
out. But the door had not moved. She turned towards the
window again, and looked down in shock at the claw that
had come over the edge of the windowsill, just missing her
hand, and split the oak plank of it the long way.

The mate to that claw came up over the sill a moment
later. It hooked over the edge of it, and something on the
far end of the ugly coarse-furred limb began to pull itself
up. It was the closest thing to a living sickle that Segnbora
had ever seen, and her response to it was immediate. She
had drawn Skádhwë at the sight of the first one; now, as its
mate came over, she chopped them both off neatly at the
sill. The shadowblade went through the limbs, and the
wood, like butter. There was a hoarse grunting sound
from outside, and a thick crunching sound as something
hit the gravel down in the yard.

'Lorn,' she said. 'Look down!'

'What?' He looked out the window, gulped, stepped
back, and slammed the shutters closed, dropping the bolt.

'Here,' she said, kicking one of the disconnected limbs
towards him. 'What do you make of this?'

The inner door burst open, and Herewiss almost fell
into the room. 'What the—'

'I don't know,' Segnbora said. 'Some new kind of Fyrd,
perhaps? I haven't seen this one before. But look down.'
She glanced down out of her own window. 'One, two –
five—'

There was a thin scream from the horseyard out behind
the building: a human throat. 'How many out there,
would you say, Lorn?' Segnbora said.

'I saw six or seven – it was hard to tell—'

'Something bulky-bodied,' she said to Herewiss, as he
reached for Khávrinen. 'Four limbs, all like that. If there
was a head, I didn't see it.'

A scratching sound came from outside, rattling through the stone and mortar, muffled but ugly. 'Rian,' Herewiss said. 'So much for secrecy. He knows we're here.'

'But they're not coming in,' Segnbora said. 'They could, to judge by what that one did to the windowsill. Whatever those things are, they're just meant to keep us inside.'

The sound outside was getting louder. 'To keep *Lorn* inside, you mean,' Herewiss said, looking at Freelorn. 'The sun's going down. This would be his first chance at Lionhall.'

At that moment the door to the outer hall was flung open. All three of them whirled to face it, Herewiss and Segnbora with Khávrinen and Skádhwë at the ready, Lorn with the black knife he had been carrying since Súthan was broken. But it was only Dritt, with an armful of stuff, mostly weapons.

'Have you seen—' he gasped, out of breath from running up the stairs.

'Yes!'

'Goddess, it's cold in here,' Dritt said, looking around him in puzzlement.

Sunspark came padding out of the bedroom in hunting-cat shape, its eyes wide with alarm. 'There's something on the roof,' it said.

'Several somethings,' Dritt said, glancing upwards. The sound of grating claws on the slates was horrible.

'No, just one,' Sunspark said. 'I don't mean the things crawling up the walls. I just tried to burn one of them—' It shivered.

'"Tried"?' Herewiss said, glancing at it in concern.

The temperature was dropping fast: it might have been the other end of autumn, almost winter, from the feel of it. Outside, an uncomfortable silence had fallen, broken only by claw-scratchings on the walls and the roof.

'One way or another, we can't stay here,' Herewiss said. 'We've got to get to Lionhall. Segnbora, let Harald know we're on our way – tell him to get close enough to keep the

273

place in view, but not to be seen himself. And get Hasai.'

'On his way already,' Segnbora said. Her *mdaha* had felt her alarm, and was shouldering upwards through her mind; but he was finding it harder going than usual. This was another of the problems that had been besetting them – not only was Hasai having trouble 'going away' when he had been physical, but it was taking a lot of time for him to become physical in the first place. Segnbora found herself beginning to tremble. But the cause didn't feel like fear. Cold, possibly—

Herewiss rested Khávrinen's point on the ground, began to speak in Nhaired. Abruptly he stopped, glanced around him: started to speak again; then stopped and swore vilely.

'What's the matter?' Dritt said.

'Gating's blocked,' Herewiss said. 'We can't just vanish out of here. It's Rian's doing, and there's no telling how long he can hold it.'

'Until we freeze to death?' Dritt said, starting to stuff some of the weapons into a bag he had brought in with him. 'Is that part of the same sorcery?'

'No,' Herewiss said. 'Sunspark is right. Whatever's on the roof – that's the source.' He frowned. 'The trouble is, it feels like—'

'An elemental,' Sunspark said, sounding grim. 'Not someone I desire to meet, in my present condition. I told you: there are those who are to ice as I am to fire. Apparently Rian has decided to go out and get an elemental of his own from somewhere,' it said bitterly. 'My fault. I put the thought into his head by challenging him. And even if I were quite well, I doubt I could do much.'

Segnbora looked up. Rime was forming on the exposed beams of the ceiling. 'We can't deal with it from in here. And if we open the windows again, we're going to have more trouble with those knives-on-legs. We'd better get downstairs. At least that way we have two ways to break out if we must.'

'Right. Lorn—' Herewiss looked at him, standing there with nothing but the black knife of the Regalia. 'You need more than that. At least take a sword.'

'*No*,' Lorn said. 'No swords . . . it might confuse the issue. Dritt, don't you still have that bow you were so fond of?'

Dritt smiled, reached into the bag, and came out with the little Steldene horn-and-sinew recurve bow. It was no more than two feet long, and looked like a child's bow . . . until you tried to string it, or draw it. Freelorn strung it now, with a grunt, and took the arrows Dritt gave him, sticking them in his belt. 'Let's go.'

They pounded down the stairs: Herewiss first, Sunspark, Freelorn and Dritt, Segnbora last. The horses were screaming in the stable, probably terrified by the monster-scent from the things clambering about the walls of the rooming house. Segnbora clutched at the walls of the stairwell as they went down – she was shaking so hard that it was beginning to interfere with her balance. *Mdaha!*

Coming, he said, but he still sounded remote. Far behind his voice, she could hear the *mdeihei* singing a high frantic chorus of distress; she had never heard the like from them in all the weeks they had been in her mind. *But we've been in this kind of position before. They didn't sound like this at Barachael, or Lionheugh—*

The stairway ended in a middle hall: one door out to the front yard and the street, one out to the courtyard in the back. The cold was getting worse by the second. 'We can't stay in here more than a few minutes,' Herewiss said. 'We need help. *Where's Hasai?!*'

Au, mdaha, she heard the voice, from still too far away. *There is – a barrier—*

She was shaking all over now. Herewiss looked at her with astonishment. ''Berend—'

'No, it's all right,' she managed to gasp. Even speaking was hard. But what was shaking her didn't come just from inside: she was growing more able to understand it by the second. She was caught precisely between two forces. One was clearly the Shadow, for it tasted of self-preservation and blind terror. The other – she recognized the trying-to-happen feeling that had been teasing her at the Eorlhowe Gate: but many times stronger now. Something wanting to happen, needing to, almost pleading with her to *do it* and make it so.

But do what?

She gasped again, rubbed at her eyes, steadied herself against the wall – and saw her shadow, thrown against the wall by the dim light of the rushlight by the other doorway. The shadow was winged, and struggling.

Skádhwë was in her hand. She looked at the shadow. Far back in her mind the *mdeihei* keened, but Hasai was silent. Segnbora leaned there, as the cold grew around them, and icicles formed, and the air became like knives to breathe. And something was weighing down on her: a force – no, more than one – utterly silent, making no move to suggest or restrain.

That shadow. Not hers. Not *her.*

A hunch, she thought. *No more.*

There's nothing else to go on, anyway. Mdaha—

She felt about in her mind for him, and found that though he had been silent, his mind was no more still than hers was. He balanced too, against the updraft of her thought, hovering as perfectly as a Dragon could: afraid, but at the same time eager. The 'something' was trying to happen to him too.

Do it, sdaha, he said. *Do it!*

She turned to Herewiss, and frost sifted down off her. 'Light,' she said, all her attention turned inwards. 'I need light!'

'Which way?'

'Behind me. Out the back door. Dritt, pull it open when I say.'

Herewiss stepped behind her and lifted Khávrinen. The balance in the forces bearing down on her and Hasai shifted: the terror grew. Segnbora faced the door, and lifted Skádhwë, ready.

'Now, Dusty,' she said.

Behind her, Herewiss lifted Khávrinen, and the lightning broke loose inside the front hall, but lingering, terrible, a light too bright to see anything by. Her shadow leapt out utterly black against the door. *NO!* screamed the back of her mind.

'Now!' she said to Moris. He pulled the door open. Her shadow struck out through it to lie on the cobbles, long and razory, black as space against the oblong of searing light, and the wings spread from the shadow as it lay there, beating desperately. Segnbora took a great breath, a gasp of air like the last one before a dive, and struck down with Skádhwë, cutting the flagstones of the floor, but also her shadow.

The pain hit her, terrible and unfair-seeming, as always when you cut yourself. Her shadow fell away from her, and ripped itself free of the stones of the courtyard, and began to stand up whole: wings, tail, the gemmed length of body and neck, growing as they had at Bluepeak: but much more solid, much more real. Herewiss's Fire blazed rainbows from the black star-sapphires of Hasai's hide as he coiled the great mass of himself together, and the walls on the far side of the courtyard cracked and slumped outwards. The spear-long spine at the end of his tail lifted, and the wing-barbs cocked out, and Hasai lifted his head, and bared every diamond fang, and hissed thunder at something out of sight, up on the roof.

Segnbora had slumped to her knees as the screaming began in her head. The *mdeihei* sounded like they were dying, but she had no time to spare for them. She had done something, but she didn't know what. It was for *good*, that she was sure of. And *now* her trembling was genuinely from fear. *What have I turned loose on the world . . . ?*

'Come on,' Freelorn said, and helped her up. Together they lurched out of the door after the others. Segnbora looked around the courtyard and saw the black creatures clinging to the walls of the old house, and also saw what was on the roof.

It clutched the roofslates with claws of ice, and gazed down on them with milky eyes that seemed frozen blind: a lizard-thing, an ugly parody of a Dragon, wingless, all its blue-white scales knobbed with ice and frosted with rime. It smoked with cold in the warm summer-night's air, and it opened its pallid mouth and hissed threat at Hasai.

'*Au rhhu'h*,' he sang, scornful: *oh, indeed?* He reared himself up, the black wings spreading wide, and his jaw dropped.

Segnbora, who knew what was coming, had the sense to squint. The others staggered and almost fell, taken by surprise by what few humans had seen before: Dragonfire at full force – not the controlled sort used to merely melt stone, but *as'rien*, sunbreath, which they use on each other. It was like lightning that ran in a stream, like water, and thunder crashed around it as the violent heat of its passage destroyed the air between Hasai and its target. The ice-elemental screamed and writhed and struck out through the stream of Dragonfire that splashed over it. The front half of the boarding house simply vanished in that light, not even having time to catch fire, and some of the black four-limbed creatures went with it. The ice-elemental fell as the house did, and Hasai arched his head down, following its movement, destroying everything around it. It scrambled up out of the molten pit and, astonishingly, came on towards them, still hissing.

Segnbora suspected what would happen next, and wavered away from Lorn, raising Skádhwë. A wall of Fire, a dome of it, grew around her and Lorn and Dritt; Herewiss, off across the courtyard, had done something similar for himself and Sunspark. It was just as well, for Hasai paused, as if for breath. Abruptly, the air went like iron with the cold: all around them, the buildings sheeted over with ice, the very moisture in the air froze out of it and started sifting down as snow; stones in the walls and the gravel on the ground began to crack with the frost.

Hasai glanced at Sunspark. 'I mentioned that we would have a chance to compare technique,' he said. His eyes narrowed; Hasai drew himself up, and flamed again.

Everything went absolutely white. That violent light washed out everything but a faint greyish shape at the centre of it, which screamed and writhed, and rose up.

And suddenly was not there any more.

The light faded. The gravel around the circles that Segnbora and Herewiss had made had scorched away like sawdust. The five of them stood on two round pedestals of stone; everywhere else in what remained of the courtyard, the stone of the hill had burnt away. Some feet down, what was left of it bubbled uneasily. Sunspark was looking around it with an approving expression, its tail twitching thoughtfully.

Segnbora breathed out, and then froze – something was missing, something inside her. She glanced up and around. '*Mdaha?*'

He was nowhere to be seen.

'You're solid again,' Lorn said to her.

Segnbora glanced down at the hand holding Skádhwë. 'Yes,' she said. But somehow she wasn't relieved.

'Where did he go?'

She listened briefly to the back of her mind. 'He's not inside. The *mdeihei* are there, but they're not saying anything. Which is the first time *that's* happened,' Segnbora said, and smiled slightly, despite herself.

'It might be wise,' Herewiss said, 'to get out of here.'

'Can you gate?' Dritt said.

Herewiss shook his head.

'But the force that was oppressing *me* is gone,' Sunspark said. It lashed its tail, fire swirled about it; a moment later, it was standing in horse-form. 'I can take you where you need to go.'

'Good. Just don't stream fire all over the place. We need to be inconspicuous. 'Berend, let Harald know we're coming. Where is he?'

'North side of the square,' Segnbora said, 'about two streets up and one over to the right. You know, Lorn – the one with the fish stall next to the tavern.'

'Drover's Entry,' Lorn said to Herewiss. 'Spark, see it in my mind? Right. Let's go.'

Moments later they all stood in the alley, glancing around in concern that they weren't inconspicuous enough. *We might have saved our time*, Segnbora thought, tempted to laugh. *Everyone in this part of town heard the racket Hasai made, and no-one wants to come out for fear of finding out what it is* . . .

One sound was audible: someone pounding down the stairs in the tavern. A bolt was pushed back, thrown, and Harald came out of the door – which was then slammed behind him and hastily rebolted. 'You're late!' he said to Freelorn.

'Too damn nearly,' Lorn said. 'You ready?'

'For some years now,' said Harald.

They headed down the street. No-one was to be seen anywhere, not even at the windows, many of which were shuttered. Herewiss, pausing at the corner, looked around it and said, 'All right. I can't gate away the guards that will be around the place. I can hold some of them frozen in place, and so can Segnbora, but I doubt we can hold all of them. We're just going to have to kill any of them who resist. How did Hasai say the guards were dressed?' he said to Segnbora.

'They're regulars.'

'They would be. All right: shoot anything in Arlene livery that moves, until Lorn gets inside the hall proper. Or burn it,' Herewiss said to Sunspark, 'and don't let them suffer. All we have to do then is keep the Arlenes out of the place until Lorn's finished.'

'Then break out again, get out of the city, through the Arlene lines, and out to the Darthene army,' Dritt said. 'Nothing to it.'

There were rueful smiles all around. 'Lorn, how long are you planning to take?' Harald said.

Freelorn shook his head. 'No way to tell. The stories say

that some queens and kings have taken about an hour . . .
but some have taken all night.'

'I knew I should have eaten a bigger nunch,' Dritt
muttered.

Herewiss said nothing. He was leaning against the wall,
his eyes closed. Segnbora could feel him hunting about in
mind for the bodies of the Arlene regulars around
Lionhall. She slipped into communion with him. *Which
ones for me?* she said.

How many can you handle?

*I've still got about twice the reach I ought to have. Give me
those twenty there, the group strung around the east side.*

Herewiss agreed, marking the ones he would take.
*Those ten. Maybe a few more of the group around the back. I
want to make sure the archers are helpless.*

She nodded. That left mostly the soldiers around the
front of Lionhall, on the side facing the square. 'About
fifteen people in front,' she said to Lorn and Dritt and
Harald. 'Half of them are nearer the door: the others are
spread out towards the sides, a few out in the square. The
ones on the sides, we can hold. The ones at the back and
on the far side of the wall won't be a problem until we're
inside and more defensible.'

Herewiss opened his eyes. 'Sunspark,' he said, 'straight
into the front of the hall with you. Anyone in there, clean
them out. Be quick. Afterwards, when we're in, head out
again and burn any weapons you find.'

'Not the arrows!' Dritt said. 'Can you collect those?'

If you want them, certainly.

'Ready?' Herewiss said. 'Fine. Right around the corner,
next left, and you're out in the square.'

And he went around the corner, taking his time, while
he set up the wreaking that would freeze the soldiers he
had chosen in their tracks. The others followed, Segnbora
last, while she felt about in her own soldiers' minds and
made sure of her hold, though there was no avoiding
brushing past the people's thoughts in the process: *could
really use a drink . . . – old bugger, why doesn't he . . . – half*

an hour, then we can go off duty and . . . – eat something tonight, maybe . . . Segnbora swallowed in sympathy: one of the soldiers was pregnant, and suffering badly from morning sickness. She touched the child's tiny, slumbering mind in greeting, made sure her intervention would do it no harm, and had a word with the one nerve connection to the stomach that was frequently at fault in such cases.

Sunspark shot past her in a blaze of fire as she turned the corner. *Now,* she thought, and the people whose minds she held stood still or toppled. Herewiss had already gone around the corner ahead of her: Lorn and Dritt went after him. Harald slipped behind her to cover her back as she walked, for a person fuelling a wreaking was likely to be distracted. They were out in the square, now.

She concentrated on her walking. It was tricky, managing your own body while doing it for twenty-two other people as well, minding their breathing, having to deal with the screaming horror of their thoughts, and also trying to stay alert for the hiss of an arrow aimed at you. Across the square, inside the open front hall where the Lion's statue stood, a yellow blaze of fire painted all the window-edges with gold from inside. One scream went up, no more. Herewiss was striding ahead of her, Khávrinen flaming blue. *That* was when she felt it, like an unexpected thorn in the finger – the structure of the spell, all knives and edges, and almost built, wanting only a word or two. One of those words she heard, or rather felt, spoken. Segnbora knew the shape of the spell, and the rage that burst up in her almost ruined her control over the twenty-two. The managing mind of the sorcery was not close, though, and was not minding its own protection nearly as carefully as it should have. As the last word was pronounced, and the warfetter came loose of its spell-structure like a poisonous cloud and began to descend into the square, Segnbora found the sorcerer's mind, up in one of the neighbouring buildings. One of her soldiers came loose of her grip, and began to struggle to his feet: but the sorcerer, up in her room overlooking Lionhall from the other side of the square, fell over sideways. No sorcery works unless the sorcerer's immediate needs are fulfilled, and of them all, breath is the most immediate. The spell crashed in fragments, the warfetter dissipated. Segnbora kept walking.

It had grown quiet in the square. Herewiss was already into the front of Lionhall: Lorn followed, and Dritt. Sunspark plunged out past her, burning, radiating pleasure and anger. Segnbora concentrated on breathing, on walking, towards that great open door. The light shining through the door and windows now was blue, and a webwork of blue light filled every opening but the door, proof against arrows and other sorts of physical incursion. Next to her, Harald whirled, drew, let fly, fell against her. She just managed to grab him and pull him in through the door with her. The blue webwork filled it as she followed his weight down, controlling his fall and leaning him carefully against the corner of the pedestal of the Lion's statue. The arrow had taken him through the bottom of the left lung, possibly into the liver. That would be a problem. Segnbora struck one last bolt of annoyance down hard into all the minds she had been holding: they might get up again in a while, but not too soon, and their muscles would ache as if they'd all given birth the day before. Then she slipped into Harald's mind, fortunately already numb with shock, killed his consciousness and his muscular control, and began talking the arrow out the other side of the wound, and the wound closed.

Off at the back of the hall, behind the statue, she could just see Freelorn standing in front of the great bronze door. There was no lock on it: it needed none. Herewiss stood there too, facing Freelorn, and all the strain and fear he had been trying to conceal was showing in his face now. Khávrinen blazed like a firebrand with his fear. Lorn fumbled at his sleeve for a moment, then handed Herewiss the One Knife of the Regalia, his only weapon: and drew

Herewiss close, and held him. They stood that way for some breaths.

Shouting came from out in the square. Freelorn let go of Herewiss, and turned away to the door: pushed it open, and passed through into the darkness. Then it shut behind him, a deep hollow sound, like a knell.

Take care of him, she said to the Goddess, all she had time for at the moment. Herewiss knelt down beside her. Segnbora breathed out in relief as she felt the wound finish knitting itself closed, and the arrow vanished. 'He didn't lose too much blood,' she said, and sat back on her heels, looking over at Herewiss. His eyes were haunted, and there were tears on his face.

Her heart turned over with pity for him. 'I know,' she said. 'There's nothing we can do for him now. We must make this place more defensible, so that when he comes out Initiate, we can keep him alive long enough to see him King as well.'

Segnbora nudged Harald's mind towards consciousness. After a moment he opened his eyes. 'What the Dark—'

'You always miss the point,' Herewiss said, dropping the arrowhead into Harald's hand. 'Pity it doesn't miss you! Come on. I could use a lookout.'

Between them they got Harald to his feet again, and Herewiss headed off for the easterly-facing windows. Segnbora stood there a moment, looking up at the statue of the Lion. But the eyes of the image stayed shadowy and unrevealing as their gaze rested on her.

Bright eyes, not these dark ones, were on her mind. *Au bvh'Hasai, bhv-dei'sithesssch!* she called silently. But no answer came, any more than from this cool, unmoved stone; and the *mdeihei* were still silent.

Segnbora sighed, and went to see what she could do to help Herewiss.

13

No woman or man finds anything in Lionhall that
they themselves have not brought there. But
some do not bring enough: and their stories
are silence.

d'Kalien, *Asteismics*

It was utterly dark. Freelorn stood still, and just listened.

I should have brought a lamp, he thought; but at the same
time it occurred to him that it was probably forbidden. All
he had were guesses, though, as far as the inside of this
place was concerned. His father had never spoken about it
when he was alive.

Lorn took a hesitant step forward. As he moved, he felt
the power rising in him – and understood perfectly why
the rulers of Arlen performed the royal magics here by
preference. There was nowhere else where their royalty
was so strong: this was the heart of it, this place founded
on Héalhra's own power. The sensitivities that had been
building in Freelorn all the way across Arlen, and getting
stronger as he came closer to Prydon, were at their
strongest here. In fact they almost blotted out the inner
powersense.

But strength would not be the whole story of this place.
This was also where the Lion's children were at their most
vulnerable. Many of them had died here . . .

'Your father is dead,' someone said.

He whirled, for the voice was Herewiss's. But the door
was shut. 'Dusty?' he whispered.

285

'He just fell over sideways in the throne, they said,' the voice said. How many years ago, now? – for it sounded raw and frightened, a much younger Herewiss. And at the same time, very sorry for Freelorn.

The warm presence was beside him, the shoulder touching his: he could feel the look of the eyes dwelling on him, concerned, gentle, even though there was no light. The presence waited.

'I don't think I'd better go back just now,' Freelorn said, hesitantly, as he had said it then.

'Well,' Herewiss's voice said, 'I guess here's what we do, then . . .' There was no guessing about it. He had plainly seen this coming for a long time, had had his plans ready.

His plans.

How did he know what was going to happen?

How did he know how I was going to react?

Is it just me . . . or does he sound pleased?

About that last, there was no telling for sure . . . it was all too long ago. Herewiss spoke on, getting warmer and more solid beside him all the time: the hand found his, grasped it in reassurance. Freelorn thought, *He might have tried to talk me out of not coming back to Arlen after Father died. Certainly later on, when he lost control – how rarely! – he berated me for not standing up for myself. But what would have happened if I had . . . ?*

'—and then we'll get you back into Arlen somehow. We need Darthen on your side first, though: Cillmod wouldn't dare—'

He held the hand that held his, and was astonished by how his own shook, and how tightly it held Herewiss's. It was not affection in the fierceness of the grip, but anger. *Why does he automatically assume that he knows best? More, why don't I disabuse him of the idea?* The problem was that just about all of Herewiss's ideas had been good. Freelorn had not been blind to how he was letting himself be managed: for lack of better ideas on his own part, he had thought. And as a result, there had always been in the back of his mind a sort of realization that Herewiss *was*, for him, the One With Whom Hands Are Joined, and would be when Freelorn finally made his way into Lionhall – the focus and catalyst of this particular conflict. But the conflict between the Two, at least, was meant to have no winner. Lorn had not realized his own anger, had not realized that after seven years of being led around, he meant to beat Herewiss down once and for all in that conflict, run things *himself* from now on, be truly King and Lord: the master, in his strength, and not the pitied client.

And on top of it all came the resentment at being pushed through one's own reluctance and fear: even though the other was doing the right thing, the thing you wanted, even asked him to do. The feeling of aggrievement, anger, resentment, grew and flowered as it had had no leisure to for a long time. *It was supposed to happen at my own speed. Not frightened all the time, running everywhere, Herewiss running everything—*

But had it happened at my own speed, it would probably never have happened at all. Freelorn could clearly feel something bearing down on his mind, and not with kindly intent: it made these old familiar feelings rise to the surface more easily than they had for months. Suspecting what dark Source it came from, he resisted that pressure, though the path down into the old 'grievances' was easy. *I've been afraid of what he's been becoming for a long time.*

Yes – and what is *he becoming?* Suddenly Freelorn found himself seeing clearly what would happen when Herewiss found out what the Goddess really intended for the first man with the Fire. A long goodbye, like the long hellos: but inexorable. *You know how he gets when his mind is set on something.* And after that, nothing for Freelorn but the long days of rule – oh yes, work, a lot of it. But no joy. And nothing but empty nights at the end of those days: the arms that held you gone for ever. *All that comes when you achieve the kingship at last.* Surely, if you loved him, wanted him, it would be safer to simply sabotage the whole business, make sure it never happens – thus making certain that that final, horrible testing point, where he renounces you and goes off about the Goddess's business, is never reached. Better to fail than to succeed and see the whole purpose of one's life go riding away after a work that will never be ended—

No, indeed, Lorn thought. It was the tone of thought – piteous, inward-turned – that alerted him again to the real agenda here – that of the inimical force that worked behind these thoughts. Better to bind Herewiss to him, in failure and frustration, for the rest of his life. Better for the Shadow, certainly. Best of all, to have no king: nearly as good, to have a king on the throne embittered and made cruel by the pain of his loss: better yet, to have one locked in mortal combat with his 'loved', while around him, the land suffers, and the Shadow's other attempts go ignored. Much better indeed . . . for It loves best to sabotage human loves, as It destroyed Its own: so that the struggle with the One With Whom Hands Are Joined is no cleansing battle, but a clutching at one another's throats, for ever, while hearts wither and precious years are wasted, and the love itself dies . . .

Freelorn held the Other's hand, and found his hold much relaxed from the angry grip of earlier. There were other fears, of course, and he could feel the down-pressing Force move its attention to those. It was folly to be here at all, of course, for being here meant that there would never again be a single part of your life that was exclusively yours. Going into Lionhall, becoming king, meant that your life was now Hers: nothing of your own would be left; love itself would have to be put aside when She called, the Tyrant in Her starry cloak—

She made a lot of love, Lorn thought, *to ask Her creation to give it up, business or not* . . . He was struggling now, for there was no part of his relationship with Herewiss that meant more to him: the breaking down of the physical barriers, the Other who took you out of yourself again and again, made your gut turn with astonishment and joy that he should care about you at all. *Would you lose all that, for ever, no matter what She seems to be offering in return? And it's not much, really. She took your mother, and left your father bearing the burden, and gave him* nothing *in return but his own death, too soon. Even did Herewiss stay with you, as King you will have less and less time for him. Finally he will grow tired and fall away from you, finding another. Indeed, there's another already, and despite their protestations, you suspect the truth—*

He shook his head at that, but his traitor body had its own ideas, and already the tears were creeping down. Sorrow and self-pity washed through him. *But without Her, where would our love be? Where did it come from in the first place?* That sense of having been 'made' for another – was it, then, untrue? And if it was true, didn't She have first call on the lovers?

You do come first, he said to Her. *It seems hard. But the gift has to be returned, eventually . . .*

Something in Freelorn raged and screamed at the feeling of him giving in, and insisted that only weaklings let Her into their loves, or bothered remembering Her at all. It was Her fault to start with that love could not last forever, must die. Take what you can, and while you can: let Her wait!

Freelorn wiped his eyes, and slowly, with difficulty, put aside the hand that was holding his.

There was silence, and no change in the darkness around him. But Herewiss's voice was gone. *Lost!* screamed the guest he had been hearing in his own thoughts. Freelorn laughed once, just a breath of sound, and wiped his eyes again.

He breathed out and took a step or so forward. Still no sound, no light, and no reason to expect either. At least the floor was smooth. *How did Cillmod manage to find the Regalia in here?* he thought. *There has to be a place where they were kept. And if there's such, then perhaps Hergótha—*

—and he stopped stock-still as from behind he heard the breathing, the wet chesty sound of it. Freelorn knew what was there – the pale white shape that had been chasing him through his dreams for all these months. But it was here now, and no dream; and there was nowhere for him to run, except out the door – which would be his death. *Though if I—*

Outraged at himself, he discarded the half-formed thought, turned, and grabbed the thing right about its thick throat.

Instantly it seized on him and hugged him close with those awful, flabby-soft arms, pulling his face into the rough hair of its chest. The stink of it was terrible, and he could feel venom burning against his face. But Lorn thought to himself, *Let's see how you like this.* He pushed, and pushed, wondering if he might run it into a wall . . . though that seemed unlikely: Lionhall seemed half the city wide, once you were inside it. But he didn't need a wall. The stone under his feet was enough. *Not just the sense of it, this time,* he said to the stone. *The reality. Make it happen!*

Nothing happened. The arms around him were pressing him more tightly into that huge chest: it was getting hard to breathe.

Come on. Now or never—

Out of the darkness, it begain to rain. Softly at first: then harder, pattering on the floor, spattering so that he could feel it on his legs: and harder still, so that it came down hard, drumming on his head. The pressure did not let up. *More,* he thought, *come on, I need more than that—*

The rain backed down, as if the shower were pausing for breath. Then came the real downpour, one of those late-summer storms that beats the air down from around you, a storm that would look like steel rods coming down if it could be seen. There was no seeing it, but it beat on Lorn's head and body like whips, and the wind rose behind it, pushing the way he pushed. The pressure on his chest began to lessen slightly. He gasped for breath, and kept pushing. The thing's throat was too thick for him to choke it by hand, but from the wheezing noises it was making, he was succeeding by other means. *Harder*, he said to the land. *Just a bit more—*

—and though he staggered with the pain of the water coming down, he kept pushing. *Let's see how you like it now, you misery. All this while you've chased me. Now see what you've caught—* The grip on him was relaxing. He finally managed to push his head away from the thing's body, arched his back against it: the rain slammed down into his face, hammering on his eyeballs as he squeezed his eyes shut. *Now*, Lorn said. *Right in front of me. Don't miss.*

The lightning struck. He felt it through his own body first, as if it had to pass through him to get where it was going. Possibly it did. It held him in an awful searing rigour, then passed, leaving him staggering. But what it struck went flailing away in a great thrashing of limbs, and there was a flat wet sound as its huge head crashed into the stone floor.

Lorn swallowed, for by the lightning, for the first time, he saw it. White. Four legs: and a long tail. And a mane.

Darkness fell again. Freelorn stood there gasping in the rain, then said, *Let up, please—* It did, as suddenly as those summer thunderstorms will: a sort of sigh of wind, and then silence, and faint dripping noises.

The form that lay on the floor before him was becoming apparent. It was bigger than the thing that had held him: much bigger – ten times the size at least, towering over him. The shape grew more distinct as it got slowly to its feet and shook itself. Not to say it glowed: nothing so mundane – but it was bright as sun on snow, and it was *there*, the first thing that had truly been there since Freelorn came in. He stood there, panting and dripping, and gazed up at the White Lion.

'It was You, in the dreams,' he said softly. 'It was always You . . .'

The Lion gazed down at Freelorn with the original of the expression His statue wore: but this look was lively with additional meaning that the sculptor had not anticipated – amusement. 'I have wrestled with many a one of My children over the years,' He said, wry, 'but none of them ever made it rain indoors.'

'After things quiet down,' Lorn said, unable to look away from those eyes, 'I'll come back with a mop.'

The Lion smiled, showing His teeth. 'A long time I sought you,' He said. 'You have taken longer to come to grips with than most. Has it been worth it?'

'Ask me again in a week,' Lorn said. 'But meantime, You might have tried looking like something other than the personification of the plague!'

'I take no responsibility for your perceptions,' the Lion said. 'There are few images that fear won't distort, no matter how powerful the original.'

'But I'm not afraid of You—'

'Of Me? Probably not, My son. But of what I represent – the price to be paid . . . That's been your problem to deal with. It's not My affair.' The Lion stretched and flexed His claws. 'When we last spoke,' He said, 'you were asking for miracles. None this time?'

Freelorn wiped water out of his face, and shook his head hard, like a wet dog, to stop the dripping down the back of his neck. 'No, sir.'

'That's as well,' the Lion said. 'So tell Me: what have you come for?'

'My Initiation,' Freelorn said.

'Most of that you have, as you've guessed. You passed through much of it, or what comprises it in your particular case, on the way here. Most do. The rest of it lies in being willing to attempt the fatal unknown, and accept that uncertainty, and power, into your life. Lionhall is the end of Initiation, not the beginning. All the same, no-one ever comes here *just* for Initiation's sake.' The Lion finished his stretching and lay down on the floor, sprawling comfortably. 'There are always other issues.'

Freelorn considered that, while noticing that the Lion's head was still slightly above his own, even lying down. 'I had other matters to settle,' he said. 'Most of them—' He shrugged. 'They're broached, at least: they'll settle themselves later . . . if I survive the next few days. Besides that, I want nothing more than Hergótha.'

'And if it is not forthcoming?'

'I could make it rain again.' Freelorn smiled again. It was not a joyful smile, but not exactly a sad one, either. 'I know You're the fount of the power of this place. But it seems I have some share in that power myself. It took me a long time to find it, and since I'm in a bit of a hurry, I don't mind exerting it.'

The Lion looked at him, cool-eyed, and gave Lorn his own smile back. 'I am only a legend,' He said. 'What power I have these days lies in what I was given to work with. *She* gave Me much, of course; and what I was given, I pass on. Don't mistake Me for more than I am. But it seems you've got over that particular misapprehension.' And the expression was approving. 'It's just as well. Besides being a barrier to other achievements, well, She desires love rather than mere worship; and as Her Lover – or one of Them – Her desires are Mine.'

'Father,' Freelorn said, 'where is Hergótha?'

'In here,' said the Lion: and His voice abruptly sounded rather like Ferrant's. 'Where I left it.'

'But Cillmod was in here, some time ago, and didn't find it—'

The Lion blinked at him, a sombre look. 'He didn't make it rain on Me, either,' He said. 'I have little to say about his affairs, though. He was not Initiate. Was there anything else? For you said you were in a hurry.'

Freelorn thought of Herewiss, out there in the front, wondering whether he himself was alive or dead. 'Nothing else, Father,' he said, 'except possibly Your blessing.'

The solemn eyes gazed at him. 'What I have from Her,' He said, 'I pass to you. Go do the job to which She has called you. That was all I did.'

The Lion glanced over into the corner of the room. Lorn followed His glance, and saw a plain marble table there, with something long and slender lying on it: a scabbard. His heart leapt as he went over to the table, and reached out to the scabbard, lifted it up. It seemed smaller than he remembered. But there was the great golden hilt, with the mantichore sapphire in the pommel, though there was still no light to bring out the blood-red glint in it. Lorn hefted the scabbard in his hands, looked over his shoulder to speak to the Lion: but found all dark again, and the Lion gone.

'Hergótha,' he whispered. He gripped it in triumph, and turned to go.

He was halfway back to the door, he thought, when from behind him something hard whipped around in front of his neck and cut off his air. A stick of some kind, pulled back tight by two shaking hands.

'Who were you talking to?' came the voice from behind him – choked with rage and hopelessness, and old tears. 'Who do you think you were talking to?!'

'You know,' Freelorn said. There was only one person to whom that voice could belong. Choking again, he took hold of the stick one-handed, having had enough of this sort of thing for one day: found his balance, bent over forwards, and pitched Cillmod right over his head and across the room. The stick went clattering away.

'You know perfectly well,' Lorn said, standing there and breathing hard. 'My Father. Not yours. You couldn't even hear Him.'

The wash of pity hit him. How must it feel for this man? To have held a difficult sort of almost-kingship for seven years, and then to know he was about to lose even that? To know that the Force he most desired to recognize him was invisible, inaudible to him? But Lorn frowned and put the thought away. This was his old enemy—

A body caromed into him. Lorn kicked out, slammed Hergótha, still sheathed, into Cillmod as he passed. He heard the man crash to the floor. Then the sword was yanked downwards, hard, and Lorn went down with it rather than let it out of his hands. Other hands fastened on his, wrestled with Lorn for control of Hergótha. Freelorn pulled one of them off the sword, found the other, and forced Hergótha down again, hard, across the other's throat. There was a choking noise.

Now then, Freelorn thought, in bitter satisfaction. *Finish this disagreement between us once and for all.*

Beneath him, Cillmod gagged and struggled for air. Freelorn felt the straining hands joined with his, clutching, pushing, and found himself wondering just who he was strangling . . .

A poor way to start a kingship, he thought. *With a murder.* For this would be nothing else.

He would do the same for me, though. Look what he was trying!

The hands trying to push Hergótha away from Cillmod's throat were weakening, and Freelorn could feel their sweat, their trembling. A little more pressure would do the job. Save everyone time and trouble. Give the army an excuse to stop fighting right away – because what mercenary will bother fighting after the paymaster's been killed? Three quarters of the opposition's strength stripped away in one stroke.

Freelorn gulped. All the excuses sounded plausible. He thought of the Goddess's Lovers, Her sons, two brothers, into Whose love the great Death entered – at each other's throats, wrestling for dominance: and the Shadow that fell over the winner.

'Father,' he whispered, 'what do I do?'

No answer came back. But his own mind said to him, *You had better stop this, before someone wins.*

Freelorn grimaced, and let up, pulling Hergótha out of Cillmod's hands and standing up again. As he backed away a few steps, he put his foot on something round that rolled: the stick Cillmod had been using to choke him with. Freelorn bent and picked it up . . . and drew in breath as he recognized the feel of it in his hand, and the metal filigree – silver, he knew – all up and down the shaft.

'I don't think any ruler of Arlen has ever used the White

Stave as a weapon,' he said, his voice shaking, but still fairly conversational, 'and I don't plan to start. What you do, of course, is your own business. What were you doing here?'

There was a shuffling on the floor, and a choking noise. 'Seeking my Initiation,' said Cillmod.

'You will not find it,' Freelorn said. 'There is an Initiate.' And somewhat to Lorn's horror, the triumph that he felt at finally being able to say the words was alloyed with pity for the man.

'I thought,' Cillmod said, 'that if there were an Initiate, the armies wouldn't fight: there would be no reason. If this could be stopped—' He coughed. 'But now it can't. Initiate you may be, but they still won't accept you as king.'

Freelorn stood quiet in the dark for a moment. 'As regards that,' he said, 'we'll have to see. But in the meantime—' He guessed at direction, from that last cough, and threw the Stave gently towards where he thought Cillmod was. It clattered on the stone.

Then Hergótha scraped as he drew it from the scabbard. Freelorn heard Cillmod's gasp of fear, and was well satisfied with it, and was instantly ashamed of the satisfaction. 'You have nothing to fear from me,' he said, 'at least, not right this minute. But the battlefield is another matter. If you live through the battles, come see me when I'm king, and we'll resolve what to do with the Stave. If I haven't already taken it from you.'

He turned and headed for the door.

Herewiss sat with his back to the pedestal of the Lion's statue, trying to avoid listening to the cries outside. He leaned his head back against the stone. It was an hour past midnight: five hours, at least, since Freelorn went into Lionhall. All that time his heart had been hammering terror in his ears, and he had been trying to ignore it. Now, though, he had found the measure of his own bravery, and it was bitter to him. They had killed four of the sorcerers outside now, and Herewiss doubted that any more would be wasted: they would be wanted for the battle. He had been efficient in dealing with them, but there was no satisfaction in it, for they didn't really frighten him, didn't really matter. What mattered was that—

—*door*, he thought, stricken, as he saw it open.

Lorn came out. He was soaking wet, which was strange. But he had a sword in his hand, the hilt massy and golden, with its beautiful carving, and the blade with that familiar, bizarre mirror-polish gleam, a sword that had refused to scratch or wear since it first left the smith's hands at Bluepeak. The mantichore sapphire caught the Firelight and glanced back blinding purple; the blade caught the light, blinding too, as if on Fire itself. Herewiss's heart leapt in relief, and great joy: and strangely, terror.

Lorn paid almost no attention to Hergótha, or Herewiss, or anything else. He stopped, some steps out of the doorway, and his face went first blank, then alarmed. Then he glanced at Herewiss and Segnbora, and said to them both, 'Get us out of here. *Now.*'

All relief and reaction and question were driven out of Herewiss by the plain naked tone of command in Freelorn's voice. *Gating's still blocked*, he started to protest, but Segnbora had already lifted Skádhwë with the expression of a woman who had suddenly decided not to take no for an answer. 'What's breakthrough for, otherwise?' she said, and pushed Fire down into her focus.

Herewiss felt his mind gripped by her wreaking, and knew better than to resist. He felt, through her, the straining of her Fire with space and the webwork of forces, sorcerous and otherwise, that surrounded Lionhall. There was an undercurrent trembling in the stone underfoot that he hadn't felt before, but Segnbora was sensitive to it, and frightened by it. He felt her Power strive with the force that tried to make piercing the worldwalls impossible. It resisted, but Segnbora stood there with that stubborn look on her face, and Skádhwë clutched in her hands like a sliver of night set on Fire, and the light burned away the resistance she strove against. The whole place whited out. And then the thunderclap—

Herewiss shook his head. They were two streets away, around the corner from the square, half-deafened by the noise. Segnbora was leaning against the fieldstone wall, gasping for air, Skádhwë now dimmed to a blackness outlined in pallid blue. Another thunderclap came from behind them.

Herewiss made for the corner, with Lorn beside him and Sunspark just behind. As they ran, the screaming started, and they glanced at each other uncomfortably. Together they reached the corner, peered around it.

They were just in time to see the great crack that had stitched its way across the square yawn further open. Lionhall was sagging over to one side, its stones groaning uneasily.

Then the lightning struck for real; a huge bolt that came arcing down from the cloudy sky. The dome was struck full on and it fell in ruin: the two men saw the roof of the great foreporch fall in, and one huge slab of marble-faced granite crash down on the Lion's statue, and shatter it. Only a glimpse of that noble head, sliding down to crash on the steps of the pedestal – then the rest of the roof followed after.

Freelorn's gaze lingered on Lionhall for a moment: then he looked over at Herewiss and said, 'I think the battle's started in earnest. We'd better get out of the city.'

The others had caught up with them from behind: Harald was helping Segnbora, who could barely walk. '—be all right,' she gasped. 'Felt the earthquake coming, that was all. I think I ruined his calculations, just this once. Better get out!'

'How?' Harald said. 'All the gates are held. And you can't do that again.'

Segnbora protested weakly, but Freelorn frowned at her. 'You're off your head,' he said. 'Save yourself for later.' And he grinned at Herewiss. 'Besides, there are other ways.'

Herewiss looked at Freelorn blankly. Then he heard

what Lorn was thinking. 'Oh, Lorn,' he said. 'No!'

'Why not? We know the way in. And we know the private ways out. What else were they put there for?'

'Lorn,' Dritt said, and poked him in the back with his bow. 'What're you thinking of?'

'An easy way out of the city.'

'Easy!!' Herewiss protested.

'Kynall,' Freclorn said. 'There are "private" ways in that only the family knows. And ways out.'

'The place is going to be crawling with Cillmod's people!' Herewiss said. 'Possibly even Rian—'

'Good,' Harald said. 'A chance to put an arrow through him, then.'

Or light a fire under him when he's not prepared for it, Sunspark said, baring its teeth.

'It has the advantage of being unexpected,' Dritt said, pushing his hair back out of the way. 'Who would be crazy enough to do something like that?'

Herewiss opened his mouth, but Segnbora said, 'Have you got a better idea? No? Then we'd better move, because that square has about fifty Arlene regulars still alive in it, and if we don't get out of here before they recover themselves—'

'This way,' Lorn said, and began threading his way into the dimness of the surrounding streets.

Herewiss followed, shaking his head.

It has really started, hasn't it? Segnbora said to him, some minutes later. They were leaning against the darker wall of a tiny alley, while Harald silently worked his way along to where it intersected with another. Sunspark stalked behind him, all its fires damped down, its coat now black as a quenched coal.

There are sorcerers working in force out there, Segnbora said, watching Harald as he poked his head cautiously around the next corner. *I can feel their backlash even from here.* She paused: Harald had vanished from sight. *But it's not dissipating. It's being – absorbed.*

You've been feeling it too, then.

Harald's hand came back into view, waved them forward. *Like something trying to be born,* Segnbora said, as the group headed towards him. *Something dark.*

Herewiss nodded, came to the corner, looked around. This was a street he and Lorn had staggered down once or twice in their youth: but this time of night, before, it had always had other people in it, doing the same. No-one seemed to have had much heart for going out drinking tonight, or out of doors at all . . . No-one had lit any of the lamps, either, and the street was as dark as the inside of a cat. Even with good memory of the way the streets were laid out, a night like this ruined your sense of direction: the moon hidden above clouds, and no stars. Here and there a patch of light showed where some cloud thinned and hinted at the moon one day off her full, standing high now, but almost always hidden. *The weather-change,* Herewiss thought, *is his somehow. Of all times not to need rain, this is it.*

Dritt had taken point now and was waving them still again. Herewiss put his back in a handy doorway, leaned his head out just far enough to watch: Segnbora, behind him, found another across the narrow street, and watched the way they had come. He felt the alarm flare in her mind as she saw something move, back down the street: her Fire towered up inside her like a hastily-lit beacon, mind-blinding, and struck out. The shape at the intersection of streets crumpled down into darkness. *Dritt,* she said, broadening the thought out far enough so that the rest could hear it, *that was a regular behind us. There are about ten more coming: he was an advance. They'll be along in about three minutes.*

'Down there,' Freelorn whispered. 'Down that alley, then left.'

That's the direction our friends will be coming from, Lorn.

'Can't be helped,' Freelorn said softly. 'That's where the entrance is.'

Down the tiny street they went, a pause at the corner to

see that all was clear: then right, down the alley Lorn had indicated. There were no doors in it, or windows even; just blind walls. From up in front came an abrupt scrabbling noise, and what sounded like a loud sigh. Herewiss looked down with regret at the source as he passed it: a man in Arlene livery who had had, from the looks of him, a thin knife put into him just above where the heart-nerves meet and knot. To the othersenses, a thin cloud of radiance hovered about the body: undifferentiated soul, in shock, not knowing it was dead yet. In passing, Herewiss reached out in mind and snuffed out the sputtering glitter of nerve-fire in the brain, the true 'silver cord' that bound soul to body, and wished the man well on his way to the Shore.

'Here,' he heard Freelorn say to Dritt. They paused before a blank space of wall, and Herewiss and Segnbora caught up with Lorn and the others, and looked at it doubtfully.

'Are you sure, Lorn?' Herewiss said.

Freelorn ran his hands up the wall. A narrow section of it, one which had looked like a six-foot-high pillar of square-hewn stone, slid abruptly inward.

'Can I have a week to diet first?' said Dritt, eyeing it unhappily. The opening was no more than a foot wide. Freelorn turned sideways, and squeezed in: it took him a moment. 'Breathe out first,' he said, and his voice echoed slightly. 'Come on!'

Segnbora slipped in after him, and after her, Sunspark, flowing through effortlessly. 'All very well for *you*,' Harald muttered, but went after, grunting. Herewiss stood and watched the street, up and down: there was a sound of footsteps somewhere not too far off.

Dritt squeezed in, having trouble. Herewiss waited, forcing himself to calm, though all his mind was shouting, *Come on, come on*— And then the first of them came around the corner and saw him. Before the man could understand what he was seeing, and pass that information all unwitting to whatever mind looked through his,

Herewiss put a bolt of Fire straight into the soldier's brain. He was dead before he finished falling. And Herewiss did the same for the second, who was following close on the first man's heels, and then the third; behind them, in the next street, outcry broke out as their bodies fell. With a last gasp, Dritt made it through the gap, and Herewiss, swearing at having had to kill, went after him as the fourth man came around the corner. In anguish Herewiss killed him too, pushed through the opening, and staggered forward into a small shadowy space.

Behind him, the stone thumped into its former place. 'All right,' Lorn said, and light flared from Skádhwë, showing a narrow stair cut into the grey stone. He led the way down it. At the bottom was a long hallway.

'You never showed me this,' Herewiss said.

'I never had time. My father only showed it to me about half a year before he died.' Lorn looked thoughtful. 'That end goes to the north rivergate.'

'There've been regulars there in force for three days,' Dritt said.

'What's down the other way?'

'Come see,' Freelorn said, and headed along the tunnel.

They walked for some minutes, sometimes up small flights of steps, sometimes down, always heading more or less east. 'Thank the Goddess for my nervous ancestors,' Freelorn said softly. 'If they hadn't been so certain the Steldenes were going to invade, we wouldn't have had any of this.'

'It may not help,' Herewiss said. 'Lorn, I'm sure we were seen.'

'Even if we were, it'll take a while for the news to travel.'

'Don't bet on it,' Herewiss said. The whole city had a feeling over it of a chilly, watchful consciousness, dipping down into unprotected minds at its leisure and using their senses for its own purposes. It was a kind of casual mind-rape that horrified Herewiss, but would not bother the spider at the centre of the web even slightly: and Lorn's side might suffer because none of those with him were willing to use such tactics. *Or capable*, said one of the more ruthless parts of Herewiss's mind. *And what about that? What do we do when the battle starts in earnest, and Cillmod's sorcerers drop warfetter on half the Darthenes, not caring about the ethics of it, not even caring that they themselves will die of the backlash?* But there was no using such sorceries on the Goddess's business: that would be to play directly into the Shadow's hands. Lorn and Eftgan would just have to find a way to be cleverer, or at least faster . . .

They came to a steep narrow stairway. 'Here's the tricky part,' Freelorn said. 'Up at the top is where we come out. Put yourself up there and see what you "hear".'

'Where are we?'

'I told you, Kynall. Go on.'

Herewiss softfooted it up the stairs, put himself against the wall, closed his eyes, and listened.

Rian! was the first thing he heard: that particular bland-sharp taste of mind, unmistakably shadowed, the darkness hanging over it – but bizarrely unconcerned, as if a bird should nest in the snake's coils and sit there singing. Herewiss shuddered all over, but a gingerly touch here and there told him that the other's mind was preoccupied. Rian's mind was all business – purposeful, almost cheerful, untroubled by the turmoil in the city.

Herewiss felt about him, the Fire glancing off stone, wood, questing up and down and about, until in his mind he had made a shadowy diagram of walls and floors, and moving in it, the bright sparks of minds attached to bodies.

'No-one nearby on this level,' he said to Freelorn. 'About ten on the next floor above, and seventeen on the floor below. How long will we be exposed when we come out?'

'Just a couple of minutes. There's another doorway I have to find.'

Freelorn pushed past him. Herewiss touched him in passing: not so much in reassurance as to quietly attach a spark of Fire to him. It wove a quick webwork about Freelorn, disguising somewhat the specific and unmistakable signature of his mind, blurring it into an impression of vague excitement. It was the best Herewiss could do for him at the moment.

'Now?' Lorn said.

Herewiss nodded, and Lorn reached up, touched something on the black wall.

The panel slipped inwards. Herewiss damped down Khávrinen's light, and slipped through after Lorn, into blackness: but not total now. A faint square of moonlight glowed on the polished floor in the middle of the huge room, then faded again as the cloud covered the moon over.

They were off to one side of the Queens' Hall. Lorn spared the throne only a glance: then he was heading for the corridor that led away to the right. Sunspark bounded silently after him.

Herewiss followed them, moving silently: the others came after. *Now what is he—* he thought, as Lorn headed up the long stairway that led up to the old living quarters.

Up the stairs they went after him, a pause there to look around the corner, down the long hallway: Herewiss's othersenses were ahead of him, questing about for any life – but there was none, at least at the moment. The sense of Rian about his business hung over everything, though, and sweat broke out all over Herewiss as they made their way down the hall, past the old wooden presses and tapestries. And that door off to the right, one he knew well—

Freelorn paused, looked at Herewiss: Herewiss felt about ever so gingerly with the Fire, and nodded. Lorn pushed the door open. It opened slightly – if there was one technique Lorn had ever mastered, it was getting *that* door to open without a squeak. He vanished into the darkness of his old bedroom, and Herewiss followed him.

They slipped, one after another, into the room, and Lorn shut the door behind them, silently again. And to

Herewiss he whispered, 'Look at it all. Just *look*. Guess whose room this is now.'

Herewiss allowed the faintest possible trickle of Flame to run down Khávrinen's blade, for there was no other light. The old sword-hacked four-poster bed was gone. Big tables lined the walls, and on them— He frowned with distaste. Books, many of them from rr'Virendir, the Palace's archive – some of them he recognized, having consulted them himself. But some of them were obviously grimoires, with old mouldering bindings. Their looks were unpleasant enough, but the feel they made against the air, against the fabric of things, was more vile. The room had become a sorcerer's workshop.

Freelorn was off to one side, fumbling with the panelling over the stone. A faint grating noise—

The panel slipped back, revealing darkness. 'Come on,' Herewiss said, getting an itchy feeling that boded no good. 'Hurry!' He practically pushed Dritt through the opening ahead of him: Sunspark went after. Harald followed. Herewiss glanced around, and saw Segnbora moving around the room, peering into corners, lifting hangings aside. ''Berend!' he hissed.

'Patience,' Segnbora said. 'There's something here I have to—' She took in breath. '*Here* it is,' she said, reaching into a dark corner. She pushed a tapestry aside, and seized something. A long pole— Herewiss stared at her as she swung past him, smiling in the darkness.

'What—'

'Come *on*,' she said softly, and vanished through the secret doorway.

Herewiss went after her, and almost tripped on the first step, as he had always almost tripped on it. This tunnel he knew: it connected with several others under Kynall, but its main purpose was to lead outwards, with its exit on the far side of the river. He tapped the lever that sent the panel back on its tracks again, and followed the others down, pacing himself by Skádhwë's soft light ahead of him. Cast shadows bobbed all down the hallway – from Lorn leading

305

the way, from Sunspark, trotting along low and smooth, from Dritt and Harald following it, from the pole Segnbora carried. But not from Segnbora.

They came to that long, long flight of stairs Herewiss remembered: twenty steps down and a landing, another twenty and a landing, on and on and on. Then the tunnel bottomed out, and went ahead straight and level for a long way. The air grew cold; the walls were damp, and the silence was profound and oppressive. Herewiss had always thought, when they came down here, that you should be able to hear the river above you, running over its stones: but there was never anything but this silence. *If nothing else*, he thought, *at least that 'watched' feeling is less.* He tested, extending the Fire within him against the fabric of the world, in what would have been the first move towards attempting a gating. The world gave under the pressure most satisfactorily. It was as he thought – even Rian couldn't suppress gating for miles all around. Especially not if the battle had started, and he had other things to concentrate on . . .

The stairs began again, going up this time. Dritt looked at them and moaned out loud. 'Won't need that diet now, will you,' Harald said cheerfully, and started up the stairs, with Dritt behind him puffing to keep up.

They climbed and climbed for what seemed an hour. At the tenth landing, the second-to-last one, they paused. 'Can you hear Eftgan?' Herewiss asked Segnbora.

She nodded. 'Hard to make out distances, but I would say she's perhaps ten miles or so east of us. I don't get a sense of motion from her – whatever else may be happening, the force she's with is encamped.'

'Ten miles,' Freelorn said, looking over at Herewiss. 'That would make it somewhere around Memith.'

The scream from above brought every head up. Herewiss had only a confused image of motion, something leaping – and then a flash of fire, another screech, ash falling in air. The second shape that came arching towards them sprouted an arrow from Dritt's bow through its eye, and its corpse came crashing down on top of them, so that they had to huddle themselves against the sides of the narrow stair, and Lorn almost got knocked down a flight of stairs. Herewiss looked down at the shape, still struggling feebly – the long clawed legs, the horrible face, half horse, half bear. More came down, and one by one they killed them: but about the tenth corpse, Segnbora turned to Herewiss and shouted, 'We're just being held for something worse. Do that gating *now!*'

From a few landings up, Herewiss could hear a horrendous roaring noise.

He fixed in his mind the picture Segnbora had given him – a tent among many others, hills arranged around it *so*, and nearby – what was its name? – Valinye, the closest hill, with that strange flattened top. He felt for Lorn's mind, Segnbora's, Dritt's and Harald's and Sunspark's. Gripped them, whirled Fire about them, showed them how to be, not here, but *there*. With minds convinced, the bodies had no choice but to follow. The slam of air rushing into where they had been—

—and exploding out and away from them, shattering the quiet night. At least it was quiet here: off on the horizon an uneasy light flickered – burning thatch or sorcery, there was no way to tell which.

'Say your names,' a calm voice said from nearby, 'or be quickly dead.' Herewiss looked off to one side, and saw, against the shadow of a tent, a shadow with a Rod in its hand.

'Eftgan,' he said, and held Khávrinen out for her to see.

After a moment, stifled laughter came. '*Your* name, not mine, twit!' the Queen said. 'It's right what they say: you Brightwood people *are* thick as planks.'

'Now then, Queen,' said the low, drawly voice from behind her, 'you might at least wait till we're out of earshot.'

'Father!' Herewiss cried, and leapt at him. For some moments nothing else happened but hugging: Herewiss had not seen Hearn since the spring. His father finally pushed him back, gazing down thoughtfully at Khávrinen, and looked over at Eftgan.

'Changes,' he said.

'Indeed,' said the Queen. 'I see you brought my people back safe. Dritt, I swear, you need dieting again. Must you do your best work for me in cookshops? 'Berend.' The Queen's eye rested momentarily on the long pole Segnbora was carrying, then swung away. 'Lorn—'

She looked at him for a long moment, and then came the smile: slight, satisfied, and openly admiring. 'Sire,' she said. .

'Not yet, madam,' said Freelorn. 'There's a piece of woodwork I intend to have given back to me. But for the moment—' He drew Hergótha, and Herewiss's heart leapt again, in delight and fear, as the blade and the gem in the pommel flashed red fire in the light from the torches brought by Eftgan's people.

'And I saw myself finding this,' Segnbora said, 'so when we were passing through where it was to be found, I picked it up.' She was unwinding something wrapped around the far end of the pole. For a moment it looked like a piece of night unfurling itself – a great swallow-tailed width of black silk, with one figure done on it in white: a Lion, passant regardant, bearing in the dexter paw a great golden-hilted sword. The design was more intricate than the one on the present Arlene livery, the silk of the black field diapered with smooth-and-rough work, and the Lion's shape flamboyantly drawn, claws and tongue and teeth showing, all tinctured, the tail heraldically tufted, the mane a mass of tongues like flame. His eyes were cabochon ruby: the silver and gold of Hergótha were real, in tissue and wire embroidery.

Segnbora looked up at the standard, then over at Lorn, with mild amusement. 'Sticks, I think I said once: and stones. We had plenty of the one, tonight – so there was no escaping the other.'

Freelorn stared at the standard as it moved slightly in the wind. 'That's the oldest one surviving,' he said.

'Anmód carried it at Coldfields. Only my father knew where it was kept. How Rian should manage to lay hands on it—' He swallowed, fighting for control: then Herewiss saw his face change as a thought occurred to him. 'And so you earn your name,' he said: for in the Darthene, *segnbora* meant 'standard-bearer'.

Segnbora leaned on the standard-pole. 'I'll try to make it last me a while. Meanwhile—' She yawned. 'Eftgan, you know me. I could never sit up late. When are you planning to move?'

'Four hours or so,' the Queen said. 'Our forward force came up with the Arlene van just before sunset, but it was too late to engage, so we pitched camp. The sorcerers and my Rodmistresses are feeling one another out at the moment. Nothing major, and our position is the better: so we can afford the sleep. Tents for these people,' she said to the officers around her, 'and beds. Now.'

Herewiss looked over at Hearn. His father was regarding him with the usual lazy, sleepy regard, and with a look of simple pride that was almost worth more than any sleep. But, 'No,' his father said, 'it can all wait until the morning. We've another eight miles to march before things even start to get interesting. Go to bed, son.'

Freelorn took Herewiss by the hand and led him off: and, for once, Herewiss didn't mind.

14

Ohhaih wnh'ehhe'Thae,
'Thae-eilve sta'stihuw
hh-Aas'te're'sta thiehuw,
as'ahiie deha'thae es'dhsuuw
iw-khai Hreihhad vuidhuw
'ou rhai'stai'tdae nnou'annvuw:
stamnek'eia iwkhai mnekuw,
'ou dei-vehhyih hrihhuw:
khaiiw mda'i't'dae s'rai-luihuw,
sda'i't'dae'ou deiystihhei'uw.
He-steh hr'nn's'raihle es'dhsuuw
ouh'he haurh'thae rui'iuw
o'wh-taiush'sdau ou't'hhuduw
ou' taiush-rui'ihd rahhuw
as'hh'asryhn iwkhai eilvuw!

Its subtleties are many,
and Its end is not yet:
nor will be while sun shineth,
yet there comes the day of choices,
when the Chieftainhood lies in ruin,
and other wings shadow than ours:
when the forgotten is remembered,
and the irretrievable regained:
when the *sdahaih* rise and sing edicts,
and the *mdahaih* do as they're bid.
Then the Great Choice comes upon us,
in which shall hearts be known,
and the cast skin be put on again,
and all outworn certainty be buried
as the day ends in fire . . .

M'athwinn ehs'Dhariss,
c. 1100 p.a.d.
(tr. d'Welcaen)

Morning came up misty on the First of Autumn: not
surprising, since the Darthenes were camped so close to
the Arlid valley. All the hot days in summer and early
autumn were followed by cool nights and fog, which might
take half the morning to burn off completely in the lower-
lying vales. It was the Shadow's own weather to campaign
in, but there was no helping it.

There was no clarion cry of trumpets to get up by –
someone came by Herewiss and Freelorn about half an
hour before dawn, banging on a pot and shouting, 'Rise
up, all, trough's full!'

Four hours was not enough sleep for Freelorn, but he
sat up and shook Herewiss. 'Come on,' he said. 'Welcome

to the high art of noble war. "The trough's full."'

Herewiss just groaned and tried to hide his head under the pillow. Another head appeared, and rested itself on the end of Freelorn's camp bed: Sunspark, in hunting-cat form, blinking.

Lorn paused, going through his pack, and straightened. In his hands was the Lion surcoat.

'Dusty,' he said, shrugging into it, 'better get moving. You know who doesn't like to be kept waiting at breakfast.'

'Mmmnnhhhh,' Herewiss said, and turned over, covering his eyes. Then he sat up, rubbing his face, and reached down to Sunspark. 'How are you today?'

No worse, it said. *I could use about half of one of the local forests.*

Herewiss looked thoughtful. 'Maybe we can talk Eftgan into letting you burn a couple of the Arlene supply camps. Plenty of wood and canvas and so forth.'

If she can work me into her plans, Sunspark said, *I would be heartily grateful*. Its voice had an edge of humour to it: it was looking at Freelorn as he settled Hergótha's sheath around him and stepped back and forth.

'Keeps banging into my legs,' he said to Herewiss. 'I can't get it set right.'

Herewiss looked at him speculatively. 'Héalhra must have been taller than we thought. Here, wait a moment.' He climbed into his own clothes, then came over to Freelorn and started working at one of the side-buckles on Lorn's belt.

Freelorn looked at him sidewise. 'Do we have time for this?' he said softly.

Herewiss glanced up, and smiled: but the smile was sad. 'No, but I can think about it, can't I?' *Especially when there's no telling whether we'll ever have time to share again in this life.* 'Try this,' he said, changing the hang of one of the straps fastened to the scabbard.

Lorn kept his face still, hearing the thought. He took a few steps, walked back again. 'I think that's done it,' he said. 'But I think I may want to go over to a backscabbard like yours, in the long run.' He went back to his pack and stuffed a tunic back into it.

He felt Herewiss looking at him, thinking: *Goddess bless him, he still has no doubt that there'll be a 'long run'. May it only be so.*

From your mind to Her ears, Freelorn thought.

They joined Eftgan outside her tent, where she and her officers were busy eating: hot bread, and butter, and a roast of beef, and cold boiled bacon, along with hot wine and barley-water to wash it all down with. Segnbora was there ahead of them, sawing away at the roast, her attention on Eftgan.

The Queen was buttering bread and talking to Erian, her Commander-General: a tall, black-haired woman with the dark skin of someone born down by the Steldene border. 'Straight in, Queen,' Erian was saying: 'no point in delay. We have the advantage at the moment, even in this mist – Meveld's van is all swamped in it, and once it burns off even slightly, we'll be able to see where we're going with just eyes.'

'Where are the rest of the Arlenes?'

'About thirty-five hundred of them were arrayed close to the city last night,' Erian said. 'A thousand are holding the near side of Anish, and about five hundred are on the near side of Daharba.'

'They're more concerned about us trying to force a crossing in the south,' Eftgan said. 'I wonder why . . .'

Erian shrugged at her. 'No way to tell yet, but it's worth bearing in mind. Our people pinned down another thousand last night about two miles east of where the road goes between Elsbede Hill and the Bottoms. They'll try to move as soon as they can make out where we are, so I'd like to be off this high ground fairly quickly.'

'Order's been given for that,' Eftgan said. 'Half an hour and we move. Anything else?'

Erian looked thoughtful. 'There were reports of

movements in the night, north of Elsbede – the Rod-mistresses thought they heard minds up that way. But they were busy with about half a dozen of Cillmod's sorcerers at the time, so they're none too sure of their own accuracy.'

'Attention to our own right flank, then, as we move. How did those encounters go?' Eftgan looked over her shoulder at a white-haired woman sipping at a cup of hot wine.

Freelorn smiled slightly and glanced over at Herewiss, for the lady was Kerim d'Ourven, the Chief Wardress of the Brightwood, with whom Herewiss had had more than the occasional disagreement while he was still trying to focus his Fire. Herewiss, though, was absorbed in folding a slice of roast beef inside a thick slice of bread and slathering horseradish all over it.

'We killed ten of them, Queen,' Kerim said. 'There were some peculiarities about the business, though. Backlash that would normally have killed an average sorcerer doesn't seem to be doing so.'

'It won't for any of them,' Herewiss said, having just gulped down a bite of his bread and meat. 'Their minds are not their own, and the backlash is being siphoned off elsewhere. Most especially, backlash won't affect Rian, so warn your people, madam. But I suggest that they leave him strictly alone until the battle starts turning in our favour. That's when he'll show his hand.'

Kerim looked at Herewiss doubtfully. Freelorn knew that she had been uncertain about the propriety of a male having the Fire. He remembered Herewiss describing one of their discussions on the subject. 'Of course,' Herewiss had said, 'she knew how everyone had had the Flame in the old days, but now we have to be content to have things the way the Goddess has allowed us to . . .' Lorn remembered his ironic look. '"The old days". She said it as if she meant "the *bad* old days". I got the feeling she thought it was a good idea that men lost the Fire: great rough clumsy insensitive things, they might have done something, you know, *male* with it.' Herewiss had chuckled softly. 'Well,

Goddess protect her from the new days. She won't like them.'

'How many more sorcerers have they got?' Eftgan asked Kerim now.

'It's hard to tell, Queen. Minds in the approaching groups are guarded against casual touch. We think there are about two hundred, all told.'

'Tell your people,' Eftgan said, putting down her cup, 'that I want those sorcerers killed. That is to be their greatest priority. Find their minds and destroy them. We have no time for mercy today. They've chosen their side, and must take the consequences.'

Kerim bowed. 'What's our strength in the Fire today?' Eftgan said.

'Three hundred and forty-nine,' said Kerim, 'about half mounted. Of those, a hundred and ninety are independent – the rest are working in circles of varying size.'

'Very well,' the Queen said. 'Tell your people that if Herewiss asks them for any kind of assistance whatsoever, they are to give it to him instantly. Whatever he's engaged in at that moment may win us the battle. His authority is to be considered as equal to yours in this regard.'

Freelorn kept his face quite still while watching Kerim's reaction. She bowed, but to the Queen, not Herewiss; and the expression she wore was less than happy. Then she took herself away.

Eftgan sighed, and glanced over at Herewiss after a moment. 'I suppose that was unavoidable,' she said. 'Where will you be riding?'

'I was going to ask where you wanted me.'

'Wherever you think you need to be, is my first answer. But somewhere near the leading group's right flank, otherwise.' She picked up her cup again and took one last deep drink. 'I'll be with the left: Erian is minding the centre group, and the banner. The Brightwood levies are over on the right. Lorn?'

'Unwise to keep the two principals too close together,' he said. 'I'll go with Erian.'

'So will I, then,' Segnbora said. She was leaning on the Lion banner, where it was struck into the ground not too far from Eftgan's.

'Well enough,' Eftgan said. 'I intend to keep the rest of our forces rather strung out behind the first curve of assault, at least until I see how the battle begins to shape itself. We shouldn't meet the Arlenes before Ostelien Hill, no matter how hard they march: their main force is still too near Elsbede.' She wiped her hands with a napkin and loosened Fórlennh in its sheath, and looked around at them. 'To work then, all,' she said, 'and may She go with us.'

The sun was beginning to show peach-coloured through the mist as Freelorn watched Herewiss ride off towards the northward-flung wing of Eftgan's troops. All around them tents were being struck, carts packed with untidy bundles; here and there horses were being saddled.

They had kept the goodbye brief, according to custom between them. *Just as well,* Lorn thought to himself, watching Sunspark ambling away, and the Flame winding about Khávrinen's hilt where it jutted up behind Herewiss's shoulder. It was not his usual, leisurely flow of Fire, but a tense, quick wrapping and curling, hectically bright even in this morning sunlight.

He's terrified, Freelorn thought. *And I'm just numb. I could hardly feel anything when I let him go. But that was probably just as well. Would I really want him to know how scared I am? What if we never – what if I—*

He cut the thought off: it was a waste of his time, and anyway, the whole business was with the Goddess now: they would at least meet on the Shore, if nowhere else. He glanced over at Segnbora. She looked rather drawn.

'No sleep last night?'

'Uhh?' She glanced up at him. 'I slept well enough.'

'No word from Hasai, then.'

She sighed and leaned against Steelsheen. 'No. And there's been no sound from the *mdeihei,* either. Not absence: but complete silence. I did *something* when I cut my shadow off . . . but I don't know what. He's gone. I just hope he can come back . . .'

Someone was making her way towards them, leading a couple of horses. Lorn looked at her half-heartedly. Eftgan had told him in passing that she would find him a horse this morning, but what was the point, it wasn't *his* horse.

Lorn's jaw dropped. Next to the bigger of the two horses, a few steps behind the tall blonde girl who was leading him, Blackmane came strolling along on the long rein. The girl looked Lorn up and down as she approached with an expression of calm assessment that said plainly, *This is what we're fighting for? I'm not impressed.*

'This your horse?' she said.

'Yes, thank you. Where did you find him!' Freelorn said, taking the reins.

The young woman nodded over her shoulder. 'Fellow on a big blood roan back there,' she said, 'asked me to see that you got him.'

'Apparently no-one's bothering to prevent gating out of Prydon this morning,' Segnbora said, swinging up on to Steelsheen.

'Apparently . . .' Lorn looked up to find the blonde girl's very brown eyes waiting to catch his. 'If you're going back that way,' he said, 'please thank the fellow for me.'

'A command, sire?' the girl said, and mounted up on her own horse, her gaze dwelling on him insolently, but not without some friendliness.

'Hardly,' Freelorn said.

She raised her eyebrows. 'You're not forward,' she said, 'I'll give you that. You'd damned best be worth it all, though – that's all I can say. I left off putting in spring wheat because of you. Goddess knows what the Dark I'll be grinding meal from, this time next year.'

Freelorn mounted and looked over at her. 'Come see me in the spring,' he said, 'if there's a problem.'

She laughed at him, a cheerful sound of complete scorn: sketched a small salute, and was gone.

Freelorn patted Blackie, and watched Segnbora trying to get the standard properly settled. 'There,' she said finally, 'it'll have to do. Come on, Lorn, they're moving out.'

The horsemen were foregathering on and around the road. There were perhaps seven hundred of them in this group, lancers and the sword-armed, with another seven hundred foot in support, in varying armour. Further back, east down the road, Lorn could see another group coming, almost all pikes, perhaps fifteen hundred of them: the upraised tips, both metal and plain sharpened wood, shone like gold where the early sun caught them. Lorn put aside with difficulty the thought that they would be darker soon.

He touched Blackmane with his heels, slipped past Segnbora and out into the open on the road. Behind him came a huge dark repetitive sound, like hail on slates but deeper – thousands of hooves, starting to follow him slowly west. He rode along, oblivious for a while to everything but that sound, and the closer ones – the creak of leather, the twittering of larks high up, the chattering of swallows that swooped under the horses' very noses and inches above his head, hawking after the bugs that the hooves of the horses were stirring up on the road and on either side of it.

'Sir,' said a voice by him, 'the Queen says next time you should wait for the signal.'

Freelorn glanced over to his right and saw a young Rodmistress riding a dun gelding – a plump young woman with hair that colour halfway between blond and brown, braided back tight. She had a leather corselet that was a bit too large for her, and a leather helmet stitched with metal plaques.

'You're my liaison, I take it,' he said.

She nodded. 'Blanis,' she said.

'Well, Blanis, you tell the Queen that next time she

should get someone to me in time for me to *know* there was a signal.' He smiled slightly as she blushed. 'Does she want me to stop?'

'No,' Blanis said, 'just keep going. She'll tell you what she intends as soon as she knows.'

Freelorn laughed. 'Fine. I take it you're keyed to my upper thought, at least, so that if I think something she needs to hear but I can't say, she'll hear it anyway.'

Blanis nodded.

'Not much of a job for you, my dear,' Freelorn said. 'Tends to leave you open to attack, from one direction or another.'

At the look in her eyes, he immediately wished he hadn't reminded her. 'Someone has to do these things,' she said, 'and others may be busy.' She shot a look back at Segnbora.

'You do your job,' Lorn said, 'and I'll watch your back – after all, you're watching mine. Now then—' and he lifted a finger, for she was starting to protest. Blanis subsided.

'Good,' Freelorn said. 'Darthene Bay coast, is it? Over by Sionan, probably. That north-country delivery, all drawl and seawater—'

'Who are *you* accusing of drawling,' Blanis said, suddenly indignant. 'Listen to you, everything comes out as one word, no spaces between them—'

They rode.

They rode past Amnyssa, and the Old Dikes, and the Grange at Aranashown. In the old days, it would have been a pleasant morning's ride for a prince on holiday, after a night spent over the border in Darthen. He and Herewiss had done the ride often, in happier times. But the view of that countryside was different now. The scattered farmsteads were there, but their beasts were gone, and no smoke rose from the chimneys. There were no people at all. The only smoke that rose came from westward, and it was white, unlike hearthsmoke: burning thatch, or standing hay on fire. It was an hour before noon.

'The scouts have seen the back of the force holding down the Arlene van,' Blanis said. 'The Arlenes are trying to break through, but it won't help them – our people are right across the road from the western slope of Elsbede to the rise where the woodland comes down.'

The relish in Blanis's voice was surprising. 'You're enjoying this,' he said.

'No I am not,' she said, though cheerfully. 'The Queen is, though.'

'I'm delighted for her. What does she want us to do when we come up with the back of the holding force?'

'Their centre will fall away towards us. We go straight through. Our left and right coming up behind will replace theirs: they'll duck around behind. Then we push.'

'How hard?'

Blanis looked at first vague, then wry. 'Until we get to Prydon, the Queen says.'

Freelorn snorted. 'That's six miles' worth of push. Supposing we do it—'

'There they are,' Segnbora said from behind. She drew Skádhwë.

The road had just topped a rise. Down on the far side of it was a great dark muddle of people and horses, half-obscured by wisps of mist. The sun caught on the occasional uplifted pike or sword, golden: here and there Fire lanced out, curling and whiplike, or straight like a spear. No banner showed.

Freelorn reached down, unhooked his helmet and put it on, then looked over his shoulder. He couldn't see the Eagle banner anywhere. *Guess I've been given the honour of getting all this started*, he thought, and tugged Hergótha out of its sheath. He reined Blackmane in, looped the reins around the pommel so that he could work two-handed, and glanced behind him at Segnbora. She nodded.

'Right,' Freelorn said, his heart hammering. His hands were all a-tremble. He stood up in the stirrups, looked over his shoulder at the great crowd of people and horses behind him, lifted Hergótha so that the sun glanced off its blade for them all to see, and shouted, *'The Lioooon!'*

His voice cracked in the middle of it. He thumped back down into the saddle, and kicked Blackie, probably harder than necessary. The horse sprang forward as the cry *'The Lioooon!'* went up from behind him, and all his hair stood on end at the sound of it – at the excitement and anger in the voices of those who raised the shout. How long since that battlecry had been heard in these fields? Six hundred years, perhaps, when the Reavers struck north as far as Darthis 'but Lorn found it difficult to care about history, just now: found it difficult to do anything but try to keep his seat as Blackie swung from canter into gallop.

The thunder of hooves caught up with him as the Darthene cavalry caught up with him and surged past. Freelorn glanced over to left and right and could catch no sight of the Eagle banner: though Segnbora galloped past him on his right, her silvering hair flying, Skádhwë aflame and the Fire streaming from it. Ahead of them, the milling mass of fighting people was pulling aside to left and right as Blanis had said. Ahead of him now, the Lion banner streamed out, cracking in the wind, the sun flaming on the rubies of the Lion's eyes. *Hey now, wait for me*— Lorn thought, and galloped after it. A hundred yards, now: fifty: they passed the rear of the forward Darthene force—

—crash! and they were in among the Arlenes: a confusion of screaming horses, pikes jostling every which way, arrows whining through the air. The glitter of lances, swords hissing in the air, metal clashing on metal, Fire lashing out here and there. This was the point in previous battles when things always had stopped making sense to Freelorn, and they did so now. Blackmane, having been in this situation before, had slowed down somewhat when he saw the confusion starting in front of him, wisely having no intention of running headlong into anyone's pike or spearhead. But the Arlene force had lost any formation it might have had earlier in the day, and the pikes, rather than presenting a unified wall to the charge, were now

320

scattered all over. A smart horse could avoid them while still obeying his rider's knee-commands, and Blackmane was smart.

This was just as well, since Freelorn was busy. All the advice he had ever heard about watching people's eyes during a fight turned out to be useless, as always, because he hardly ever saw any eyes. Helmets, yes, and the nasals of them, and riders' legs, and arms and spears and swords, those he saw, and struck at.

For that first while, before he got tired, Lorn fought in a kind of bizarre resignation, certain that he would be killed shortly. Then, when the tiredness started to set in, and the heat and the thirst, the fear came awake, and worry for more than his own skin. Where was Herewiss? The press around him had drawn away; he looked back the way he had come, and saw, several hundred yards back, the Eagle banner and a great crowd of Darthenes around it, making their way towards him. Past them, up against the southern slope of Elsbede, a great flame of Fire went up. *I had to wonder*, he thought. Terror rose up in him as he saw the dark mass of men plunging down that steep hillside towards Herewiss: but at that moment the shouts off to his left grew fierce, another group of Arlenes ploughing into the Darthenes. That was where his business was, and he went to it.

Time passed quickly in the confusion of fighting. One of the Darthenes accidentally backhanded him with a mace. He hurriedly kneed Blackie aside, swept down with Hergótha to break the pike of a big Arlene who was trying to spear him, and caught her hard in the chest on the backstroke. She fell. Freelorn panted, desperately thirsty, then spun Blackie right around, practically on his haunches. No-one was around him but Darthenes now, all heading west down the road at a good rate. His banner was well in the fore, and so was the Eagle banner – Goddess knew how it had gone by him unnoticed.

'You're not too good at keeping up with the rest, are you?' Blanis said from off to one side, breathing hard.

'Always either too far in front, or too far behind. I had to come back for you.'

'You're pert, young madam,' he said. 'When I'm king, I shall decree your spanking.'

She snickered at him. 'Too big a job for you, eh?'

Freelorn swiped at her with Hergótha, being careful to miss. The sword had a tendency not to. He glanced up, and was shocked to see the sun standing nearly an hour past its nooning. 'Where now?' he said.

'Straight on, as I told you. It's going pretty well.'

'Oh? What was all that Fire I saw back there?'

Blanis grinned, an astonishingly feral look. 'The Queen's hunch paying off. The Arlenes had a few hundred horsemen hidden up on the north side of Elsbede, and several other companies over on the south side of Kelasta. They came down the hill after we passed and tried to split the main march of the army off from ours. Those Arlenes would have come up behind us and cut off our retreat, and the force behind the one our group hit would have come in in front of you—' She shrugged.

'But they didn't.'

Blanis shook her head. 'The ones who came down Kelasta got mired in the brook that runs by the bottom. They exposed a flank, and our horse broke them in the water-meadows. As for the others, Elsbede hill isn't quite the shape it used to be. There's a great big crevasse halfway down it, and about two and a half hundred Arlene horse in the crevasse.' Her smile got even more feral. 'I think I would like to meet your friend.'

Two hours later they had made three miles more progress, but at a cost. The Darthenes had pushed into the wide flat meadowlands on either side of the road, about two miles from Prydon. Some of the forces in front of the city had come out to meet them at about the three-mile point, and had engaged them: but most of the Arlene forces were still arranged in a long crescent, its left resting against the small steep hill called Vintner's Rise, and its right against the small wooded ridge leading up to the hill called Hetasb. There the main force stayed, four thousand foot, horsemen, and well-emplaced pikes: and nothing would budge them.

The Queen was staying with the Darthene forward right wing. Her own army was still about six thousand, about half horse and half foot, and her desire was to break through or past the Arlenes to one or another of the fords, cross the Arlid, and then come at Prydon from its undefended side. But she had to get past them first – and even if she took the city, there would still remain the army to be reduced afterwards.

'Better sooner than later,' she said to Herewiss. 'I would rather go through them than around, but I'm not going to attack into their strength.' She was standing near her horse, Rascal, looking down the long slope of ground that followed the path of the road to where it began to bottom out. Down near the eastern foot of the rise, a dark, shifting tangle of people and horses moved and worked from side to side. Beyond, about parallel with the other side of the rise, and a mile from the river, the main bulk of the Arlenes could be seen, drawn up in their ordered ranks, waiting patiently.

'Well, I've dragged the straw in front of them,' Eftgan said, 'but they won't play cat today, more's the pity. Damn Meveld.' She sighed. 'We're going to have to budge them somehow.'

Herewiss glanced over at Sunspark. *I've discomfited an army or so in my time*, it said. *I might be of help.*

'I'm not letting you go down there unassisted,' Herewiss said. 'Rian hasn't been heard from all day so far, and he's waiting for something. I suspect you're one thing he's waiting for – and he knows that where you are, I'll be somewhere nearby. No, not just yet.' Herewiss thought for a moment, leaning against Sunspark and gazing off to the left, where he could see the Lion banner resting in the middle of the Darthene centre. Far off into the left wing, he could just make out the Brightwood banner, and past it, the eastern-leaning slopes of Hetasb. Everything looked bizarrely peaceful in the hot sunshine, under blue sky and fat white clouds. More a day for getting the hay in than a battle, except that any hay there had been in this part of the world was now burnt or trampled.

He stood up straighter. 'That might do! . . .' he said to himself.

Sunspark's eyes rolled. *Oh no*, it said. *You leave me out of this!*

'What? Out of what? Herewiss?' the Queen said.

He was already unsheathing Khávrinen. Sunspark was sidling away from him with a slightly nervous look. 'You want them to move?' Herewiss said. 'Which way would you prefer?'

'Why, why I'd like them to break right and left, ideally. String them out around the Rise and Hetasb— What are you thinking of!'

You keep me dry, Sunspark said. *I'm not going to leave you, but if you get me wet—*

Herewiss gazed off westward. 'Look at those clouds,' Herewiss said. 'You can see what they're trying to do even from here. Look at that anvil on the one just past the city, there. We shouldn't be seeing midsummer weather this time of year. Someone's been helping it. Someone has plans for those clouds.' The smile got broader. 'I think I have a better idea.'

Eftgan's eyes widened, and she patted Sunspark. 'I'll keep you dry, my dear. I think we'd better leave him to his own devices.'

Herewiss's attention was on those clouds. He had been water, and the river Arlid: he had been the earth, and the fires under the earth: he had been fire itself. Air he had not yet attempted. It was the most unmanageable of the elements, the least predictable. But also the most easily disrupted – as Rian would shortly find . . .

Blue Fire ran around him in a circle, shutting other influences out. Herewiss closed his eyes. He took a deep breath, held it, considered it. In the image of himself in his mind, that lungful became all shot through with the Fire, became part of him, did not leave. When he breathed out, since something had to be exhaled, it was some of his own solidity that vanished invisibly. The Fire-and-air of his last breath spread to replace the solidity that was gone. He breathed in again, felt the air swirl in, felt the corporeal nature in him attenuate, flow out with his exhalation. Two breaths, three—

—and there was nothing solid of him left: only a movement all sparked through with Fire. Other forces were there, too. It was with those that his business lay. Currents of heat and cold flowed all about him, pushing one another aside. He was part of them. He felt the way the heat stored in the land bubbled out of it, stirred the lower airs, pushed them against the cooler, higher winds. The cooler winds, trying to sink, resisted, arched their backs up, curled and doubled on themselves. It was the lower airs in which Herewiss chiefly invested himself, feeling the mass and potential destructiveness of the water that they bore. He pushed them up into the clouds already there, shouldering more water into them. Already he could feel the tension there, as the currents in the clouds roiled and pushed against one another, trying to release their energy, preventing one another from doing so.

Good, he thought, and chose for his purposes one cloud over the river that was particularly heavy-laden, already hunched and growling, dim flickers of menace sparking in its roiling innards. Herewiss rose up under it, pushed more dissolved water up into it. The cloud's irritable tension grew worse, and the muttering grew to a growl. Herewiss felt the slight shift in energy that meant it was looking for somewhere to turn and attack.

Right there, he said, all helpfulness, and traced a path of least resistance to one particular place on the ground.

The lightning came down in the very middle of the Arlene centre-battle. Somewhere he could hear something like a shout of rage, but he paid no attention to it, and shifted the energy in a couple of more spots – then slid away to find another cloud, pressed water into it too.

In a matter of minutes the whole sky was full of irritable thunderheads, blundering into one another, roaring. Herewiss opened his eyes to a vista as horrifying as it was satisfying: the sky black with lowering cloud, lightning scourging the ground like whips, and the Arlenes running higgledy-piggledy north and south, but mostly east.

Eftgan, next to him, had her Rod out and was gripping Sunspark's saddle, to reassure the elemental or herself, Herewiss couldn't tell. 'Is that what you had in mind?' he said, gasping: odd how hard it was to breathe again, when you had just been nothing but air.

Eftgan opened her mouth to answer him – but that was when the screaming started all around them. It didn't last long: it was cut short, in every case, almost as soon as it started. It swept across the Darthene force in a great wave, and people fell to the ground, eyes open, blind, deaf, mouths working with screams that would no longer come out.

Warfetter! Eftgan cried to her Rodmistresses, and anyone else who could hear. *Find the sorcerer's mind!* But Herewiss knew what mind was fuelling this huge effort, and what sorcerer would not die of the backlash of it, no matter how many of his puppets had built the sorceries proper. Herewiss might have taken the other's waiting weapon away, but Rian had had another one ready. If the sorcery were not broken quickly, these people would die of the fear that comes of being trapped in one's own mind, separated from every sense and not even able to feel heartbeat or breath.

Amid the crash and stink of the lightnings, Herewiss lifted Khávrinen two-handed, and it blazed with his wrath. *Find him for me*, he said. *Bring us together. Let's finish it now.*

Only silent laughter answered.

Eftgan stared at him, horror in her eyes. 'Sunspark,' Herewiss said, and mounted up. It tossed its head. It was shivering, but it leaped into the air and was gone across the field like disaster's own self, trailing fire behind it.

Freelorn stood and watched the lightnings in astonishment. The danger of it horrified him. But Herewiss seemed to be in control—

He looked over at Segnbora, who was standing by Steelsheen, leaning on the Lion banner. She looked nervous. 'You feel it too?' he said.

'Not just that.' She gripped Skádhwë, and Freelorn saw that her hands were shaking. 'Something's going to happen.'

'Sorcery?'

'Yes, but that's not what I'm feeling!' Her expression was strange. The fear in Segnbora's face was getting worse, but at the same time, there was the beginning of a smile fighting with it. 'It's something else. Something of mine – my—' She paled, and stared at him, her face working with terror and delight. 'My Name—'

And she was gone, just that suddenly. The Lion banner fell over against Steelsheen, who squealed and shied away from it. Freelorn grabbed it before it fell.

And then the screaming started, and he had other things to think about, as the darkness came down on him and left him blind and deaf and dumb.

Herewiss!!

No answer: nothing but the silence, and the dark. They lasted for ever.

She had spent the whole day feeling that things were wrong inside and going rapidly more so. *I used to beg the* mdeihei *to shut up,* she thought, *and now that they have, I can't bear the stillness.*

But there was more to it, this sense of impending doom – doom in the old sense, of some prophecy coming true, some change long predicted. She rode distracted through the bright sun of the day, and though she fought in the battle near Elsbede, and killed in it, none of it seemed to matter. What mattered was still coming.

And then it came. She heard her Name called in

Dracon: and since calling the inner Name with authority gives power over the being who wears it, she had no choice but to answer. Her Fire leaped in her and burst away to find what had called, dragging her body along, irresistible. She vanished from the battlefield—

—a moment's whirling confusion, and then the blaze of blue light cleared; she looked around her. Rocks: and the smell of the sea was in the air. Sunlight—

—and Dragons – more Dragons than she had ever seen before. She stood on a stony slope that ran down a shoulder of the Eorlhowe to the sea: and clinging to the rocks, pouring among them, landing on them, lying on the beach, perching among the crags, were hundreds and hundreds of Dragons. Segnbora gazed around her and tried to count. *Possibly twenty-five hundred. Is that how many Dragons there are alive today . . . ?* It seemed likely. The DragonChief had called the Draconid Name, and they had all responded. So had she: and Segnbora smiled slightly, for if Dithra still maintained that she was not Dracon, it would be in the face of all evidence to the contrary.

She looked around, saw a flash of emerald and gold up near the entrance to the Howe. The livery was hardly exclusive to the *lhhw'Hreiha*, but Segnbora knew no other Dragons of quite that size. Slowly she made her way up the slope, greeting the Dragons she passed as she went.

Then she stopped. The big he-Dragon she had just spoken to, blood ruby scales and garnet eyes, bowed its wings to her, a gesture friendly if uncertain, and said, 'Rui'i-sta'ae, hr'sdaha?'

She stared at him. 'Rr'nojh!' she said. 'Of course I know you, but—'

But he was one of her *mdeihei*!

Segnbora looked around in astonishment. 'Who else is here?' she said. 'How did you get *out*?' *And what in the world is a* hr'sdaha? she thought. 'Hr—' was one of the augmentative prefixes: it could mean something greater in number than usual, or bigger, or simply different or new.

'There are a lot of us,' Rr'nojh said. 'All the lineal *mdaheih* you knew are here. But suddenly we seem to be *dav'whhesnih*. We were called, we came—'

'Come on,' Segnbora said. She started making her way up the slope again, and Rr'nojh went with her. Before too long they came across others from the chorus of shadows that had been inside Segnbora for all these months. Shadows no longer, they followed her, so that shortly Segnbora had the familiar rumbling chorus behind her again.

When she finally came to stand before Dithra, with Skádhwë in her hand, Segnbora saw exactly what she had expected to see in the DragonChief's *ehhath*: rage. The wing-barbs had been cocked towards her since she had been halfway up the hillside, and the tail-spine was coiled high and poised to strike. Dithra's mouth was open, and fire broiled at the back of it. Segnbora just bowed, and said, '*Lhhw'Hreiha*, I was called, and I'm here.'

The soft, restrained roar that came out of the Dragon-Chief was horrible to hear. It was the sound of wounded pride, and of a Dragon threatened past endurance. 'So I see. And so was I,' Dithra said, 'called. Like all these others.' Her claws scored the stone she lay on. 'Now you shall tell me who—'

'But surely you know,' said a voice from inside the Howe. All heads turned at that: and Segnbora laughed out loud for joy and relief.

'Hasai!' she said. And winged darkness came stalking out of the entrance to the Howe: the sun struck down on the old familiar livery, black star-sapphire above, pale diamond below. 'But you're bigger,' she said, slightly awed. He was at least a third again the size he had been: as big as Dithra.

'Am I so?' He looked at himself with mild surprise. 'I had not noticed. It may be the effect of what I bear.' Hasai gazed over at Dithra. Their *ehhath* was totally different – his all ease and calm, hers all spines and defiance: but it was easy to see where the power lay.

'The Draconid Name is *mine*,' Dithra hissed. 'It was given into my keeping: I guard it. And by its virtue, I am DragonChief – until one with a better reason than mine for holding it shall come to take the Name by force.'

'I make no claims as to "better",' Hasai said, 'but as for the other – as you wish.' He lifted his wings, and the shadow of them fell all over that side of the hill, and over Dithra, so that the emerald and topaz of her livery went cold, and the only thing about her that burned any more was her eyes.

'*Bvh'Ohaheia-haa*,' Hasai sang, all on one long sombre chord. 'This then is Assemblage: here shall there befall *hr'nn's'raihle*. All the *Lhhw'hei* are here, so that what Choice befalls here shall be the Great Choice, binding on all our folk, living and dead.'

'You have no right to convoke Assemblage!' Dithra roared. 'Nor to commit others to paying its price!'

'If I have no right of Convocation,' Hasai said, 'what is the whole of Dragonkind doing here? Dismiss them, if you can.'

Dithra lifted up her head. '*Tteid'i'rae-huw!*' she sang, one long angry note: *you shall all depart!* But it was untrue, and choked itself off; and the Dragons looked at one another, distressed.

'As for the other matter,' Hasai said, gazing calmly at Dithra, 'the issue we shall argue here, and decide, is greater than any other since the *hr'nn's'raihle* called when our people decided to leave the Homeworld. We had a choice then too, to live or die as a species. That is the issue again today. The Sign has come which M'athwinn spoke of, the day when the cast skin is put on again. Look at me!'

They looked. He was real. 'I was *mdahaih*. But that is over. The Draconid Name has passed to me; changed, as we have been changed, by the new world we live in. It was given me through my old *sdaha*. But she is my *sdaha* no longer.' A pang went right through Segnbora as he said it, but she held her peace: that feeling of trembling on the edge of something tremendous was with her again. 'And I have no *mdeihei* any longer. I have been freed: pushed past the point where one must cohabit with the dead to be alive.'

A rustling of uncertainty went through the Dragons. 'Have you forgotten the old songs so completely?' Hasai cried, singing almost in anguish. 'How they sang on the Homeworld of the times in the most ancient past when the living lived in their own minds, in freedom, and chose their own actions unadvised except by others of the living, and by *Mn'Stihw*?' Every neck bent, all wings bowed, at the Immanence's rarely-sung Name. 'But our world began to die untimely,' he said, 'and here, as in other times and places, the Immanence saw Its making marred by the Shadow. But It was not to be foiled so easily. It conceived a plan.'

The rustle of wings was getting louder. 'It saw our coming here,' Hasai said. 'It knew that many of us would die in the Crossing. And indeed that happened – but not as many died as might have. To spare that needless death, the Immanence invented *mda'had*. The dead began to pass in-mind to the living, and were sheltered there, safe from the cold of the night between worlds . . . so that when they had been led at last to the place appointed, they could be released.' His song was anguished, but joyful as well. *'This is the place appointed: this is the day of your release!* The imprisonment of the untimely dead is truly over at last. It had to wait till a human was one with us in mind, to remind us from inside what a single soul feels like. We have made many unwitting attempts, living and talking with our human MarchWarders over centuries, sensing obscurely that they had something we needed. But none of these attempts came to fruit, until a woman in the wrong place at the wrong time became *sdahaih* to a Dragon. Even that was not enough: it was still required that great need should force the bond apart, and love dissolve it willingly. But all conditions are now fulfilled.'

He looked over at Segnbora. 'I said I have no *sdaha*,' he said. 'I had one, but in her wisdom, or her Goddess's, she freed me. And now neither of us have *mdeihei*. But look what we have instead!' All eyes turned to the crowd gathered around Segnbora: some three hundred Dragons who had long since 'cast the last skin' and become physically unreal. They were real enough now.

Dithra was hissing with rage. 'How can you be so sure of yourself?' she sang. 'This world has its own creatures, and its own deity: have you asked *them* whether it approves these plans? And even were all this wild conjecture true, why should we change? Why give up what certainty we have for we know not what madness, an empty aloneness in one's mind, with no other presence to counsel it against foolhardiness?'

Segnbora laughed, then, and stepped out from among the former *mdeihei*, for this was the moment for which Hiriedh had named her *rahiw'sheh*, and her advocacy was upon her. 'The old argument!' she said. 'Listen now! Your coming freed our world from the Dark that lay over it, all those years ago. You're welcome guests. But you must *act* to accept the hospitality, or die out of the world, as you've already begun to do. Where are the Dragonets? You are so careful of this world, so nervous about it, that you haven't even managed to breed in it! One by one you'll slip away and go *mdahaih*, until there's no-one to go *mdahaih to* any more. You'll go *rdahaih*, the whole species of you together! The Immanence Itself will speak the Draconid Name, and there will be no answer . . .'

Wings unfolded and furled again all over the Howe, a mass Dracon shudder. 'Yes,' Segnbora said, 'and that's exactly what the Shadow wants. We the humans invite you now: come be with us, and of us: come fight on our side! For there's no other way we can save you from the fate awaiting you. Let us return the favour you did us, and even the balance!'

Dithra arched her neck at Segnbora in scorn. 'What right have *you* to speak for all humankind?'

Segnbora held out Skádhwë. Outside the core of its darkness, it blazed like a star with her certainty. 'Oh, I do more than just that. I speak for the Goddess, Who made this world, and Who speaks through me as through all humans, for She has no simpler way. Are you going to demand that She come Herself to make Her case? Why should She, when She *has* done? Wasn't the Messenger enough, to make it plain to you that this was to be your world? How can a people with such eyes be so blind?!'

'*Lhhw'IIreiha,*' Hasai said, in a long low chord, 'make your choice: and abide it.'

From under the shadow of his wings, Dithra looked up at Hasai. 'I will have things as they are,' she sang softly. 'With one exception.'

The Dragons began to clear hurriedly out of the way to give them room.

Segnbora moved back too, but not too far. Her eyes were on Hasai: she could feel his uncertainty. *Sithesssch*, she thought, *the price of Assemblage is always the Dragon-Chief's life.*

I know, he said, watching Dithra move down into the centre of the space left open for them, watching the way she moved: her *ehhath* was surprisingly calm, all of a sudden, the manner of a Dragon who knows she is superior in fight – or remembers-ahead that she has already won. *One of us is going to die. But your business,* sdaha, *is to make sure that you remember how you managed it last time.*

Segnbora stared at him, confused. But he had already turned away, moving down after Dithra.

She leapt at him, and a great dissonance of shock and distress went up from the Dragons who watched, as Dithra ignored the protocols of proper *nn's'raihle* – no dance, no statement in *ehhath* of her own case, just this bald, rude attack. But Hasai flung himself back, a quick back-raking of wings and a spring of the haunches, and Dithra missed and came down short. Hasai flowed swiftly off to one side, his jaw dropping in a smile, or in preparation of Dragonfire, it was hard to say which. '*Au uuzh'aave*', *ha-nnha'mdadahé, ou ylihhaih'errhuw,*' Hasai sang as he circled her in courteous reminder of the dance she had discarded: and one wing was raised over her as he closed in, to prevent her taking to the air. All his *ehhath* was tense and ready, but nonetheless full of cheer, the tail wreathed in amusement and excitement at something that was finally happening. *A bad beginning, Dweller; no matter, it will end well—*

Dithra flung herself at him again, but sidewise this time, fang-sheaths retracted, the great curve of her tail whipping around to pinion Hasai's tail harmless. They closed, and tangled. Hasai whipped his neck back out of the way of her fangs: but at the same time Segnbora saw the fire build abruptly behind Dithra's eyes, knew that a blast of Dragonfire was coming, and lifted Skádhwë.

NO, Hasai cried into her mind, *do not! Use it now and it will be useless for the most important part.* He lunged with his head like a striking snake, his jaws open, and clamped them down hard around Dithra's, so that she struggled, impotent to flame at him. From behind, what was left free of her tail came flailing around, the terrible spear-long spine ready to strike. Hasai's tail writhed itself free and twined with hers, straining against it. The two fell together, rolling over and over on the stones.

Hasai was just holding Dithra away from him: she was mostly kicking air, and her song was reduced to a choked hissing thunder of rage and fear. Hasai planted his hind legs hard in Dithra's gut and pushed her away, all the time holding on, holding like grim death to her jaws, still clamped in his own. *Now, sdaha,* he said in Segnbora's mind, *very shortly now—*

Segnbora still had no idea what he wanted from her, and was shocked by the tone of his mind, all merriment and anticipation. He had no time to answer, though. They rolled again, almost to her feet, and Segnbora backed up hurriedly.

Now, Hasai thought again; and then he lost his grip on Dithra's jaws. They opened, and Dragonfire burst out with awful force, real *as'rien* such as Hasai had used on the ice-elemental; the air exploded out of its path, thunder followed it. The stream of it went over Hasai's shoulder, moving as they still rolled, and Dragons scattered so as not to be caught in it.

Then Hasai caught Dithra's head again, with a coil of his tail, and began pulling it slowly back and back, away from him. Segnbora's breath went out of her in a rush as she saw the awful dead-white scorch where Dithra's Dragonfire had caught him under the breast and at the wing-root. Hasai's *ehhath* was pained now, but the cheer was still there, and his looped tail threw another loop around Dithra's neck and pulled her head down and down as if on a rope. Fire came raging out of her again and again, in that terrible destroying stream, but it hit nothing but air and stones, which both burned away to nothing.

Then Hasai snaked his head around behind Dithra's. A final flare of terror in the eyes, a final wild struggle, all her body writhing now, Dragonfire spewing out with desperate violence: but to no effect. Hasai's jaws clamped down with great accuracy, just behind the spine of her face-shield, and bit her in the brain.

Her body started to go limp: her thrashing began to slow. *Sdaha!* Hasai said.

Segnbora came forward slowly, looking at the twitching body, but mostly at the eyes, dimming now, the fire going out from behind them. She put Skádhwë away. Now she understood Hasai's fear, earlier. It was not himself he had been afraid for.

Segnbora remembered how it had been, that first time. The outrage, the violation of having a crowd of Dragons poured into one's head. She had got used to it. But could she get used to *this* – the whole species sharing soul-space with her? Could she bear it and not go mad? More – could she survive it?

She looked up at Hasai. He said nothing, just waited, while the light in Dithra's eyes pulsed feebly, dimmer with every pulse.

Well, rahiw'sheh, he said finally. He did not say the rest of it: *let us see how far your Advocacy goes.*

She nodded and reached down to touch Dithra, stroking the head-shield. 'DragonChief,' she said, 'you have no-one to go *mdahaih* to. No-one but me.'

Those eyes dwelt on her, fading. Rage was still in them, and now grief as well, and wounded pride. Dithra tried to open her mouth, but there was no song left in her.

You can be right, Segnbora said to her, stroking her still. *You can win. And kill all Dragonkind doing it. Or lose. Au, Dweller, for the Immanence's sake if not theirs!*

A long pause. The last twitches of the limbs became still. Dithra's eyes grew dark.

And the last thought came, faint.

For theirs, then.

The crack in Segnbora's mind opened, was shouldered wide. She knew the pain that would follow, and braced herself. It was useless. Compared to pains she had felt earlier, this one was like the pain the Goddess felt in giving birth to the worlds, though reversed: inexpressible masses of something living that came thrusting inward, not out. The pain was as much to be resisted or prepared for as one might resist an avalanche with one's bare hands. Minds and minds and minds came crowding into Segnbora's. Not merely Dithra's, not just those of her *mdeihei*, but also the minds of every Dragon alive – the concrete reality of which the Draconid Name itself was only an abbreviation. All the Dragons' lives, thoughts, emotions, desires, fears, and the business of all their bodies, hunger and weariness and age: all poured down into Segnbora's self, and she could not even scream for the pain of it. All she could do was make room for them inside her, and she did that, and did it, and did it, for ever and ever, it seemed . . .

Eventually the pouring stopped. Sight came back to her slowly. Hasai's head hung over her; she half-knelt, half-slumped against the body of a dead Dragon. The clamour in the back of her mind was frightening. She felt near dying herself: her Fire was going out, pressed down and away from her use by the presence and weight of so many other souls.

She knew she had little time. Even Dragons had died of having too many others become *mdahaih* to them too suddenly, when the Dark attacked them at the end of the Crossing. Segnbora reached up and clutched at Hasai's face for help in getting up. He pulled her carefully to her feet. All around them, Dragons looked on, frozen in fear and wonder.

Segnbora's shadow stretched out long and black from her in the late afternoon sunshine. She lifted an arm, and watched the dark shape of a Dragon's wing reach out across the stones in response. Her shadow was a Dragon's, now, and much bigger than it had been before.

'Yes,' she said. And she drew Skádhwë, and lifted it carefully, for her aim was wobbly, and she cut the shadow free.

Then she collapsed to her knees again, feeling the pressure within her suddenly ebb, and her Fire begin to spring up and recover. A great silence came, filled with nothing but the breathing of the sea against the shore; and a shadow came between Segnbora and the sun.

She looked up. It was not Hasai. It was Dithra, in her green and gold, unstained, younger, her *ehhath* astonished as she looked down on her old body – the 'cast skin' that suddenly she wore again. At the sight of her, the something in Segnbora that had been holding its breath all this while – that feeling of something tremendous about to happen if only, against all hope, things went right – let itself go at last, and the joy of it flooded her. She scrambled to her feet and looked down the mountainside.

Her old shadow was flowing down the slope like a live thing, and spreading, swallowing every Dragon's shadow up in itself: a carpet of darkness, but darkness with movement hidden in it, like the Eorlhowe Gate. Perhaps the same movement – for shapes began to rear up out of it, cloaked in the shadow's dimness, and then shook it off them like dark water in the low reddening light of the sun. They flung wings out that had not felt air since the Homeworld lost its own, reared up glittering in liveries that had not seen light since their wearers were lost two hundred centuries before, in the empty places between the stars. Hundreds of them reared up, thousands, shaking off the darkness, *mdahaih* no longer, but alive; the air filled and darkened with them, and the song of their speech went up in a mighty concord like all the horns and viols of a world gathered in one place.

Segnbora looked up at Hasai. He and Dithra were gazing at one another with an odd sort of understanding. 'So that is what *hr'sdahhad* is like,' Dithra said.

Hasai dropped his jaw in agreement. '*Au*, Dweller.'

She wreathed her tail in negation. 'I am not,' she said. 'That title has passed now to you – or you and your *hr'sdaha*, however you like – for to hold so many in-mind would kill me, and I am not suicidal. There must be five times as many of them as there were.'

'Six,' Segnbora said, 'at least.'

'We'll count later,' Hasai said. He stretched his head up, and emitted a sound that could be called a roar only by virtue of its volume. It sounded like a chorus of many trumpets blowing to the charge, and Segnbora had to cover her ears at the sound of it; rocks burst like holiday fireworks, startling even Dragons. The silence took a while falling, but succeeded at last.

'We are home,' Hasai said, the song coming down on the last note in a great chord of satisfaction. 'But we have one last bout of *nn's'raihle* to enact yet, with the One that gave us such trouble long ago. It killed our Homeworld, and drove us out: It killed many a one of you, as you know in your own flesh: It killed Dahiric—' Many heads turned at that. 'No,' Hasai said, 'he is not here as you are. I have no reasons for you now: maybe we will have some before the end. But that One walks the fields not too far from here, and our human kin – our hosts once, but we must learn to think differently – fight against It to keep It from

338

killing this world as well. I go to argue our case with It. Who comes with me?'

Segnbora prudently used the Fire to make herself deaf. It didn't work entirely: the song of defiance and eager challenge that went up could be felt through the ground, and in the air, on the skin and in the body. More rocks shattered.

'Well enough,' Hasai said. '*Sdaha*, you had better put your wings on: we must make speed.'

With the others, she rose and flew.

15

Even the Goddess cannot change the past. But human beings can: and to that purpose created She them.

Charestics, 190

'Is this close enough?' Sunspark said as they came down on the hilltop.

'It'll do,' Herewiss said, dismounting hurriedly. They stood together among the stones of Vintner's Rise, the hill just across the river from Prydon. Down at the bottom of the hill was the main Arlene army, three thousand strong, surging forward now to take the Darthenes while the warfetter still affected them. Herewiss drew Khávrinen and sat down on the stones, trying to compose himself. It was difficult: the part of him that could usually feel how things were with Lorn was frighteningly dark and silent. *Just warfetter*, he thought, trying to reassure himself. But that could be deadly even in short doses, if the mind resisting it was vulnerable.

He gulped and tried to calm his breathing. 'All I need to do is disturb him and break the sorcery,' Herewiss told Sunspark. 'If I'm not conscious within a few minutes, move me well back from here: he might have a grip on me, but distance will break his, too.'

Sunspark looked at Herewiss, its expression still. 'Go well,' it said.

I love you, too, Herewiss said to it, and closed his eyes, letting the Fire surround him.

* * *

It was dangerous, walking out of body with so little protection, but he was out of options, and out of time. Herewiss waited a moment to let the otherworld settle itself around him, and then looked around. To some extent, as usual, it mirrored the living world, but not entirely. A murky fog lay over everything, expressing a sorcery in action. And between Herewiss and the river, at the bottom of the dark fog, lay a long patch of forested country that was not there in the real world.

The road ran straight into it, vanishing in its shadows. There was a sense of enmity in the gloom, of old unexpressed angers. And there was a sense of being watched. He knew who the watcher was. Herewiss held Khávrinen ready, and walked under the eaves of the forest.

He found as he headed inward that the trees were encroaching on the road itself, shouldering the massive hexagonal paving-stones aside, cracking them with their roots. The surface grew humped and treacherous: the road grew narrower. Yards ahead of Herewiss it pinched down to three feet wide or so, barely a track, and further ahead yet it seemed to end altogether – or it might still go on through the dark, but the trees were crowding so closely together that there was no way to proceed but by squeezing between the trunks.

Some ways ahead of him there was a hint of paleness, where light came in: a clearing, possibly. Herewiss made for it, working his way slowly between the trunks of the huge, silent trees. It was hard going: the harsh bark scraped at him like teeth, his clothes caught on spines and snags, low branches whipped him in the face till his eyes smarted with it. He could see a lightening of the air, up there ahead of him, a light that came from within the clearing itself.

Herewiss worked his way through the trees. This was a symbol, he knew, of the sorcerous barriers that Rian had erected around his working: but there was nothing symbolic about the way the trees seemed to press more

341

closely together when he was stuck between two of them, pushing the air out of his lungs and trying to trap him there. The temptation was constant: *use the Fire on them, wither them where they stand!* But the impulse made him suspicious, and Herewiss restrained himself.

The clearing was close. He pushed between two last trees and tore himself free at last, panting for air. The calm figure sitting in a chair in the middle of the clearing opened its eyes and looked at him, with only mild surprise. Rian sat there in one of the old chairs Herewiss recognized from Freelorn's bedroom: and in his hands he held a cubit-long piece of white wood, filigreed in silver. He rolled it between his hands, idly, while he watched Herewiss.

'I thought you might try this,' Rian said, his voice almost admiring. 'It says much that you got this far: the other Rodmistresses who've tried have died of it.

'Nonetheless,' Rian said, and got not another word out, because Herewiss lifted Khávrinen and focused all his Fire through it, and put a bolt of it straight into the man's brain.

Rian froze expressionless as the Flame washed over him – then laughed at Herewiss, not unkindly. 'Come now,' he said, 'this is *my* mind we're in this time. I rule here, as you ruled in yours, however marginally—'

'This is *not* your mind,' Herewiss said, lowering Khávrinen. 'You know perfectly well that this is one of the overworlds—'

'But it's in my Master's mind now,' Rian said, 'and so in mine. We are very nearly one. Just a little more power is needed to bring about His rebirth in the physical world.' Rian looked thoughtfully at Herewiss. 'I wonder if that would do?'

He was looking at Khávrinen. Herewiss gripped it—

The sword was wrenched from him and went spinning off through the air, into Rian's hands. Herewiss fell to his knees with a cry of pain, discovering that having your focus taken from you against your will felt much like having your heart ripped out. Feeling Khávrinen in that other's hand was anguish – like feeling the sword of your sex held for idle examination in the hand of someone intent on your rape, or at least, on your use. No Fire leapt about it now; it was just grey steel with a faint blue sheen, a sword that in the thin pale light of the clearing looked clumsily made.

Herewiss knelt frozen there, held by Rian's will. 'Khávrinen!' he whispered: but the sword was captive as he was, and could not come to him.

'It might do,' Rian said, musing. He leaned Khávrinen against the arm of his chair with as much regard as if it were a broomstick. 'There's a fair amount of Fire trapped in the steel just keeping it alive, and as long as you're not touching it, it could be made amenable to use by another in no great time.'

Impossible! Herewiss thought – but to his own horror, he now wasn't sure that Rian couldn't do what he claimed. He struggled, but his body was not his own, and remained as still as stone. 'You've been thieving elsewhere, I see,' Herewiss gasped – at least he could still speak. 'Where is Cillmod?'

Rian shrugged. 'It doesn't matter. When Lionhall fell, I managed to rescue the one piece that was worth keeping, since an Initiate needs this silly stick to be acknowledged as King. Cillmod hardly matters, now that there *is* an Initiate. Freelorn will do as well as any other brat of Héalhra's blood, once his will is burnt out and he's tamed to our use. No great work, that, once my Lord is reborn.'

Herewiss thought he couldn't even shudder, and then found that he could, as Rian picked up Khávrinen again and bent his attention upon it. 'Let's see,' he said. Herewiss felt the draining start, as if the Fire and his soul were being pulled out of him in a thin, strong thread, cutting like wire. Darkness was gathering. A few more heartbeats, and Herewiss was afraid he would hear a breath drawn, hear the voice speak which it would be final madness to hear. *Khávrinen!!* he cried in mind. But no answer came. The darkness deepened—

Until the whole clearing flushed with light, and the deepening twilight that had filled it suddenly became dawn, with a vengeance. In the middle of the clearing stood a column of fire, licking up into the canopy overhead, and heat washed over Herewiss.

Now, Sunspark said. *You have someone of mine. I will have him back.*

Rian laughed at Sunspark. 'Oh,' he said to Herewiss, 'it's your pet. Didn't it learn the last time?'

Herewiss grinned. Rian had met Sunspark in its physical shapes in the real world, and had half-confirmed what Herewiss himself suspected – that the habit of living in a shape, trying to be human, had left it less fiery, more physical. But this was the otherworld, and freed of form as it was here, Sunspark was another story entirely.

Find out, manling, it said, and leapt: not at him, but into the trees, streaking into the depths of them unhindered, a firestorm on the run. All the great boles kindled, and the shadows beneath them were forced back. Out and out Sunspark spiralled, until all that could be seen in any direction was the darker smoking red of heavy growth burning, and the brighter fire of needles and branches exploding into flame.

Rian's concentration broke as he saw his sorceries, both the warfetter and the dark birth he was assisting, threatened by this destruction. Herewiss staggered to his feet, held out his hands: Khávrinen tore itself from Rian's grip and leapt into them. Sunspark came arrowing back into the clearing from behind Rian, and arched upwards. Its blinding flames fell and wreathed about Rian with devouring force. This time there was a scream, quickly cut off.

Sunspark flowed away from the centre of the clearing. Ashes drifted on the smoky, burning wind . . . nothing else.

Herewiss looked around at the inferno, the symbol of

Rian's sorcery going to pieces. That darkness, though, was unhurt, flowing among the burning trees: only the structure of the sorcery was destroyed. But it was enough for this moment. *Let's get out of here!*

Well enough. Herewiss clutched Khávrinen to him in relief and terror, and hurriedly took the long step backwards into his body.

'Lorn, oh Lorn, get up,' someone was begging him. Freelorn rolled over and moaned, and his head hit a rock. He blinked at blinding light. His eyes were dry, and even closing them was agony: the light itself was terrible after the black silence he'd been in, but he wouldn't have given it up for anything.

Blanis was trying to pull him up off the ground, and doing surprisingly well for one so small. 'Come on,' she was pleading with him, 'hurry up, the Queen needs you!'

He managed to roll to his knees. 'How long was it?' he said, and coughed: his throat was dry too.

Something shoved him hard in the side, so that he almost fell over. He clutched at what pushed him, but it was only Blackmane, nosing him worriedly, as he always did when Freelorn fell off, or down. Horses were not affected by warfetter spells: at the moment, Freelorn suspected this was simply because they were too stupid. Blanis helped him up, and Freelorn staggered. 'What's happening?'

'It was about twenty minutes,' Blanis said. 'We've got about a thousand dead, or in coma. The rest are like you.'

'Oh, that's just wonderful,' Freelorn said, and worked on remounting Blackmane through the dizziness. It took several tries.

Blanis was looking around her, confused. 'Where is she? Oh!' She caught sight of the Lion banner, lying on the ground.

'Disappeared,' Freelorn said wearily. 'She does that. Here, pick that up.' Blanis lifted up the banner, and Lorn shook his head as she offered it to him. 'Sorry,' he said, 'that's going to be your job until we can find someone else to carry it. I've got something else to carry.' He unsheathed Hergótha. 'Take the tack off her saddle. No, don't try riding Steelsheen! She's a one-woman horse. Just turn her loose. She may get killed, but no Arlene will ride her.'

Blanis worked at Segnbora's saddle breathlessly, while Steelsheen rolled her eyes and watched her suspiciously. 'The Arlenes are moving,' Blanis said. 'Herewiss did something, the Queen doesn't know what yet. Their main force is coming right at us.'

'Makes perfect sense,' Freelorn said. 'They think we're all lying on the ground, ripe to have our throats cut. If I were the Queen, I'd tell my front lines to stay lying right where they are. With their pikes ready. And when the first riders come through—'

Blanis's eyebrows went up at that, and her eyes went vague for a moment. 'The Queen says you have a nasty mind,' she said then, 'and she'll give order for that. There are some pikes down that way, nearest the road, and cavalry to support them.'

'How far has the main army come?' Freelorn said.

Blanis was working on her own saddle now. 'Their van is into the Ridings – their rear is still just passing the Vintners' Rise. Our foremost cavalry is putting itself back together in a hurry, what there is of it.'

'How many?'

Blanis mounted up and started wrestling the Lion banner into place. 'About nine hundred now,' she said. 'Some of the rear cavalry group have come up to fill in.'

'I take it the groups that were in front of the main march of Arlenes are scattered all over this part of the world by now,' he said.

Blanis nodded as they started to canter north. 'That lightning . . . I really *do* want to meet your friend. Yes, they're half of them about three miles north of Elsbede, and the other half somewhere south of Daharba on the near side, as far as we can tell. They're running. And who would blame them?'

'Not me,' Freelorn said. He stood up in his stirrups as they went, to see a bit more. The Brightwood's white banner was still up, far ahead and off to their right: the Eagle banner rode between them, pushing down the road much faster than the Brightwood levies were. Lorn looked at this, and said, 'She wants us to hang back too?'

'For the moment.'

Other riders were gathering around them now, a crowd of muddy surcoats, bloody swords. Freelorn held Hergótha up for them to see as he rode, and a kind of growl went up from the men and women who rode with him: appreciation, anticipation, anger. 'Our turn now,' Freelorn said. The growl got louder.

They were running parallel with the road now, about two miles from the Arlid. Prydon was visible, silhouetted against the late afternoon light. The ground they rode now was badly chopped up with earlier engagements, and the bodies of people and horses lay about, making their own mounts snort and shy. Soon they would be into the eastern townlands, and the going would be worse yet: not this open meadowland, but hedgerows, fences, people's houses . . .

Freelorn looked ahead and saw, on his left, the wood that comes curving down from the stony height of Esheh to within about half a mile of the road. 'There,' he said. 'Is that where she wants us to brace this wing?'

'Yes,' Blanis said. 'The Brightwood people will rest their battle across the road from you, against the northern slopes of the rise.'

'Right,' Freelorn said. To the riders around them, he called, 'In there, people! Among the trees, and as high up the slope as is safe for what you're riding.' He looked at the sheerer western side of Esheh, and added, 'Any of you riding goats?'

There was laughter at this, and some of the troops around who were on Steldenes or other mountain-breds went on ahead to secure the western side. Lorn watched them go, then stood in the stirrups again and looked

347

north. The Brightwood people were steady around the northern spur of the rise now, a great glitter of pikes in the low sunlight. Off westward was a great dark mass coming, horse and pikes behind, the Arlenes, pushing forward fast: very fast indeed—

In the centre, the Eagle banner had begun to slide backwards, the horse and pikes around it giving ground to the east. *What's the matter?* Lorn thought, his gut twisting with worry, as he watched the van of the Arlene army hurrying towards the Darthenes. *Why isn't Eftgan holding, there should be no problem, she has plenty of support there.* And the Arlene rear was moving much too fast. The mist was starting to rise early as it did in the autumn, and the ground behind the Arlenes was somewhat obscured: but, squinting, Lorn thought that he saw some other force coming up behind the Arlenes, but scattered, not formed up—

Someone cried out. Among the trees there was a crashing of branches, and a screech, not human: Freelorn saw a shadowy shape up there, and a horse toppled, screaming in pain. 'Fyrd!' he screamed, 'look out, there are Fyrd up there!'

And the tiny knot of organization and order went all to pieces again in a flurry of animal shapes that were suddenly all among them, dragging them down. *So that's why the Arlenes are in such a hurry. Rian is driving them into us.* One of the nadders came at Lorn, hissing. He swept Hergótha around and took its head off, punching Blackie in the side to take him out of the way of the nadder's still-writhing body and slashing claws. He wheeled to look for another foe, getting a quick glimpse of Blanis lashing out with her Rod, and Fire cracking from it like a whip-thong, burning out the brain of a maw three times her size. Over there, another keplian, looking around for a victim. He rode Blackie straight into it before the horse had a chance to see what he was heading at: he saw it, he screamed, the keplian reared and slashed with its claws, but Lorn went right in under them for what he wanted, the big artery on the side of the neck – chopped it sidewise and spurred away: the keplian fell, flailing.

There was a sharp pain in Lorn's leg. He looked down, surprised, and saw the slash across his thigh from the keplian's claws. He watched the blood ooze for a nasty moment – it was painful and ugly, but shallow, and he couldn't do anything about it. Freelorn got up in the stirrups again, saw the Brightwood levies holding their position through their own turmoil: frantic motion around the edges of their formation told him that the Fyrd were after them too. 'Hold it here!' he screamed to the people around him, 'don't lose it, we're going to have to charge!' He could see the Arlenes punching deep into the Darthene ranks, but the Darthenes were pulling back in order, letting them do it. A little deeper, and fully two thirds of the Arlenes would be past the rises where Freelorn and the Brightwood levies held. *Are they idiots, can't they see the trap?* But then, they had no choice. The Fyrd were driving them, poor creatures. Freelorn swore. *Why is Rian doing this?!*

The people around him were quieter now, the first wave of Fyrd that had hit them dead now. Sounds of weeping and swearing came to him, riders moaning with pain from their wounds. He headed among the pikers. Some were dead: more were pulling their own pikes, or others', out of dead Fyrd. 'Keep the line northward,' he said to them, 'they can't get up the back of this ridge without some warning. Horse, everybody up, form up with me, we're going to be moving in about three breaths! Blanis!'

'Here,' she said, coming up behind him, out of breath and bloody. 'Not mine,' she added, seeing his expression.

'Is she ready?'

'Just a bit more time. She wants to be sure.'

'You see what's coming behind them?'

'I saw.' Blanis turned a grim look on him. 'Someone wants bloodshed out here today. If not ours, his own people's—'

Freelorn shook his head. Then, 'Now!' Blanis shouted,

and bolted off down the hillside on her dun, with the Lion banner streaming wildly ahead of her in the south wind.

'Will you for pity's sake *wait for me*?!' Freelorn shouted. As he swept Hergótha in a great arc over his head, the mounted force looked down the hillside and saw every cavalryman's dream, a whole army moving so fast it had outrun its own rearguard, all its flank strung out and exposed, and a friendly force on the far side to be anvil to your own hammer. Freelorn kicked Blackmane, and the horse squealed and leaped down the hill, half running, half sliding sometimes, until the ground flattened out and they were tearing along towards the Arlenes at full gallop. The Arlenes were no more than a hundred yards away now, spilled well over the side of the road, and the terror rose up in him one more time, and Freelorn did the only thing he could think of as antidote: lifted his sword so that the setting sun caught it, and cried to those who followed him, *'Hergóthaaaaa!'*

The Arlenes heard, and turned: he saw shocked faces: too late for them to do anything now. CRASH! and it was happening again, arms, legs, the sharp end of a bloodied pike waving in his face, knocked aside, someone's sword, hacked out of her hand. Freelorn's force had caught the Arlene flank at open ranks. They pushed it far in, broke it in about five pieces, and then the light-armoured fighters went in through the openings, the pikes following to contain the fight. Caught unprepared this way, crushed against one another and hardly able to defend themselves at all, the Arlenes died in crowds. On the far side Freelorn could see the Phoenix banner pushing in towards him, could see the faces of the Brightwood people hacking their way through the Arlenes, climbing now over ground that was increasingly thick with bodies.

Off to the right came a roar, and a cry that carried even over all the shouting: 'The Eagle, the Eagle to the Lion at bay!' Freelorn grinned terribly. Many years since that battlecry had been heard. *What do they mean, 'at bay'?* Oh. He looked around frantically and realized that he had accidentally worked his way off to the side of his own people: only Blanis was nearby, and she was almost surrounded by Arlenes. Some of them were coming towards him now. Angry faces, frightened ones, and faces simply set grim: a spear poised for the cast—

'One more time,' he whispered to Blackmane, and spurred him to make sure. The horse leaped straight into the spearman, knocking him down. One sword Lorn saw raised, and took off the hand that held it at the wrist: another he kicked out of its owner's hands while its owner was staring at Hergótha, and then kicked the soldier's head, too, for good measure. Blackmane squealed and lashed out with his hooves, almost unseating Freelorn but knocking another Arlene down and out of the way. Then suddenly the Lion banner was right in front of him, and about forty Darthene riders were all around him, and Freelorn was sitting still, clutching his thigh and moaning. He had forgotten about the wound.

Blanis came pushing through, shaking the banner in her frustration at him. 'You don't listen, do you? Always off by yourself getting in trouble—'

Lorn, looking at her, had a sudden image of a young woman in a farmyard somewhere, shooing chickens with a broom, and he burst out laughing. 'That's what my name means,' he said, 'what do you expect? You just make yourself useful. Can't you fix this leg?'

'Leg?' She gave him a horrified look: he twitched the mailskirt aside, and Blanis looked at the wound. Her expression changed to relief. 'Oh, Goddess, I thought it was something worse. Here—' She stroked it quickly: the wound stopped bleeding, and closed. 'It won't be a strong scar for a while, don't strain it—'

'I'm in the middle of a battle, for pity's sake, of course I'll strain it,' Freelorn said. 'Never mind that now!' He stood up in the stirrups again, and the laughter left him. The Arlenes were utterly broken: the rearguard had split and was being hunted through the early evening mists, past the northern slopes of the rise and down south towards Daharba. But it was not Darthenes that were doing the hunting, and some of that dark force, new to the field, was coming towards them now. At least five thousand Fyrd, flowing towards the road.

'We might as well be facing a whole fresh army,' Freelorn whispered. 'And we're all over the place. Look at us!'

'The centre,' Blanis said hurriedly. 'The Queen thinks we can hold them there.'

Freelorn shook his head. 'She's out of her mind,' he said. 'There are as many Fyrd as we have people. And there are still the forces holding the fords, they'll cut us to pieces.'

'Come on!' Blanis said, and rode off towards the road.

Freelorn looked west, saw the mist, the unnatural way it was darkening: saw the great crowd of Fyrd coming towards them, running silent save for the occasional ugly beast-cry; saw Prydon behind it all with its walls and towers, a dark shape cut sharp against the sky: saw the sky itself, the long clouds reddening, great patches of darkness edged with fire. He knew the reality of his dream now. *This* evening, this falling darkness, with a force before them that would not be stopped by the fall of night, and something worse behind that, waiting Its moment.

He swallowed. *And what next?* he said – to whom, he wasn't sure. Possibly to the white shape that had hounded him through those dreams into this disastrous sunset, the image of fear and despair. *It's not Me you fear*, the Lion had said. *But what I represent: the price—*

He rode off hard after Blanis, and the twenty or thirty horse who had been following him closely went after. 'Break them!' she was shouting. 'She says, break them down the middle, split them into two groups and run them up against the hills!'

Freelorn looked at Hergótha in his hand as he rode, and considered how likely the tactic was to work. The odds were certainly no better than even. *But no worse*, said some stubborn part of him – the part that had spent too much time in rr'Virendir, reading old tales of the heroes, and falling in love with last stands and death-or-glory charges. And this sword had been in one of the greatest of those, and survived. So had its wielder. In different form—

He looked around him as he rode. Down below him the Darthenes were massing for the charge, and there was the Eagle banner, and the white banner of the Brightwood, and his own racing down to meet them: and at the head of everything, sudden, a flash of gold, burning in answer to the sunset, and a blade upflung and blazing blue – a rider with a lightningbolt in his hand, riding a horse whose mane and tail streamed fire. Freelorn's heart leaped. How long had it been since he had even seen Herewiss from a distance? He raced down after Blanis and lifted Hergótha as he went, not knowing who might be able to see it.

The Darthene van was already pushing forward, gathering speed. Herewiss rode near the head of it, and Lorn came in with his banner and his group of horse from one side, pushing towards the front of the group, determined to fight near Herewiss or die near him. It was getting dim enough, between the sunset and the dark mist, to make telling faces at a distance difficult: but Sunspark shone, and Khávrinen was impossible to miss, as were the Rods of the Rodmistresses riding around Herewiss, and of Eftgan not too far behind. The pace was increasing, past the canter now: horses were afraid of Fyrd, and the best thing to do was to hit them at the gallop. Freelorn saw Khávrinen raised, saw a great bolt of Fire break from it and strike out at the mass of Fyrd, only a hundred or so yards away now.

Then the two forces met. Snarling beast-voices, thick with a malice that no mere beast could know, went up all around: screams of horses and of humans answered them. At first Freelorn thought he could bear it, it was just one more battle – but his weariness was catching up with him now, and Hergótha began to weigh in his hand as it had not earlier. And the Fyrd came, and came, and kept on coming. No matter how many of them he killed, there were always more. And the horror of the combat wore on him. Inhuman, half-mad, these creatures hated all humanity: and they moved with terrible cunning and unison, like parts of a body run by one mind.

Freelorn fought and fought, and saw, between glimpses, the Darthene centre being pushed in. Soon the Darthenes would have no mobility left at all. Lorn could see his banner, just barely, but he had lost sight of the Eagle in the confusion, and as he looked for it, he saw the Phoenix totter and go down. Horrified, he looked to the front for Herewiss – just in time to see a shape vault up against Sunspark's brightness, take Khávrinen through its body, screaming, and fall again – but dragging Herewiss with it.

Freelorn's heart turned over in terror. He saw another wave of Fyrd push past where Herewiss had been, heading for something with awful purpose – he looked along their track, and saw the Eagle banner there, and just a glimpse of fair hair seen by the light of a blazing Rod. But the Queen could take care of herself. Freelorn spurred Blackmane towards where he had seen Herewiss go down.

The thunderclap, right overhead, was so loud it nearly struck him out of the saddle: and Blackie shied and reared, as did many of the other horses. Lorn looked up and saw what he at first could not understand. It was an arrow, or dart, shot high: so he thought at first, from its shape against the high dusk, and the way it flew. But no-one could now shoot an arrow so high that it still caught the sunlight, and this did, glancing it back blood-red and half-blinding through the dusk, like a star. But a star that fell. The arrow passed out of the light into darkness, but still showed against the sky, a black shape, falling at greater and greater speed: and it passed over the battlefield swifter than any eagle, with a roar like the angry sea.

The wind of the great shape's passing came after, but not before another of the terrible thunder-crashes, and a third and fifth and tenth as others dropped in its wake, the speed of their passage outraging the air into thunder again and again. Then a gale blew on the battlefield as the first dark form passed over once more, much lower this time. Even the Fyrd reacted to that, howling and hissing threat and rage at the sky. Many of them died in that moment's confusion, at the hands of those they had been attacking. The roar that the great shape made this time had nothing to do with speed. It was the sound of a great voice, singing in some unknown tongue, singing one word, dreadful and final. It sounded like *death*.

The dark shape flew on over the body of the group of Fyrd attacking the Darthenes, and landed. The Fyrd who were not crushed by it flung themselves on it, but the darkness shook itself, scattering them like leaves. It spread its great black wings, and arched its neck. In this darkness, Freelorn could see how preparatory lightnings flickered about the wing-barbs and sheeted down the membranes; and then the Dragon flamed.

Fyrd screamed and fled, but it did them no good. Down from the sky, in a hail of thunderclaps, more Dragons came at the same terrible speed. Fyrd began to run mad merely from their passing; the Darthenes began to pursue them, but Eftgan held them back, and wisely, for at first tens of the Dragons came down, then perhaps a hundred, and began hunting in earnest. Shortly Laeran's Ridings were a mass of fires or charred places. At the centre of it all, the first Dragon to fall from the sky reared up, watching his people about their hunting – a Dragon black with star-sapphires above, and pale with rough diamond below.

Freelorn laughed for joy, pushing closer. Another huge shape landed near Hasai, all star-emeralds and topaz, and vanished. Down near Hasai's hind foot she stood for a moment looking around her, then hurriedly made her way into the Darthene press, beyond the scorched ground. Freelorn went the way she did.

He made for Sunspark's light, and Skádhwë's, and found them both. Herewiss was sitting on the ground, dazed and hurt. His right leg was bitten to the bone, and Segnbora and one of the Rodmistresses were seeing to it, while Sunspark bent down over Herewiss, concerned.

A white radiance fell over everything. Freelorn looked up to see Hasai gazing down on them. '*Dhio'Aarhlehni*,' he sang in a downscaling chord of approval, '*aei'aeluehh.*' And the hair stood up on the back of Lorn's neck as he looked up into those huge burning eyes, for this much Dracon he found he understood. *King of Arlen, well met.*

'Not just yet,' said a soft voice that seemed very near. 'And maybe never.'

They looked around for the source of the voice, but it seemed to have none. 'We're ready now,' it said conversationally. 'It might have taken me a while longer, after your pet bonfire there ruined the structure I had already set up: but such structures can be re-erected. And you helped me, too. What was needed to finish was fresh death, a great deal of it. Fyrd are as good as anything for that: better, perhaps. They know their Master, their Creator, far better than you do . . .'

The leisurely form was looking at them calmly, as if it had been there the whole time. The dark mist lay thick over the ground, rising and falling slightly, as if something breathed underneath it, and Rian stood in it as if it were part of him. Herewiss, groaning with the pain of his half-healed wound, had managed to get to his feet and was leaning hard against Sunspark. 'You're dead,' he said.

'You mean you tried to kill me,' Rian said. 'But I'm one with my Master now. And even the Goddess, for all Her blindness in other matters, knows that He can't be sent out of the Worlds, not permanently. Nor can I, now.'

Hasai swung his head over to look down on Rian: and opened his mouth, and flamed. They all hid their eyes, but when the heat and the terrible light had died away again, Rian was still standing there, wearing a rueful smile.

'I shan't bother with you,' he said. 'My Lord has annoying memories of you and your people: you've chosen a bad day to become real, as you'll see. But more important matters first.'

The air was prickling with a terrible sense of dread. Almost as one, Herewiss and Segnbora lifted Khávrinen and Skádhwë – and then stared: for there was no Fire about either of them. Rian shook his head at their surprise. 'The Fire is merely His own power, stolen from Him and given to humans,' he said. 'What do you think He would take back first? No, indeed: no more of that while He rules.' He turned away from them, looking towards the fields between them and the river.

The mist thickened, deepened. It ate what light there was. The light of the rising full moon touched it, fell into it, was gone: the heat was being sucked out of what remained of the sunset. No Fire showed anywhere in the host, and Hasai crouched down and down as if forced that way by the mere sight of the rising blackness. All over the field, other Dragons did the same, the fire of their eyes going dim and cold, the fire of their throats choked off.

'Not just your fears, this time,' Rian said calmly. 'That has worked before, as a stopgap measure. This time – the fear itself, the cause itself. Death itself: the Dark itself: the real things, of which your little fears are poor images. He comes in His splendour, in His power, to take back His world.'

The darkness wavered, grew, towered up, blotting out the stars. Freelorn looked up at it, transfixed with terror, unable to look away. No-one else was doing any differently: all resistance or power seemed to have drained away, suddenly, in the face of this one. Sunspark was just a horse now, and a lean, frightened-looking one, with a bleeding man leaning against it on a crude sword. Next to him was a thin woman trembling and holding a sharp piece of shadow, the only thing blacker than the darkness that rose up before them. Near them was a carved statue of a flying lizard, frozen in the act of gazing upwards, impotent. There was a young woman on her knees nearby, weeping into her hands, next to a torn piece of cloth on a pole. And all around them, behind them, the bodies of the dead, the thin wails of the living and the dying, all lost in never-ending night.

Freelorn watched the blackness rise and struggle into shape. Utterly lightless, the essence of strife and hatred, It strove even with Itself, and the blackness of it hid Prydon, the whole western sky, the last vestiges of his sunset. All the dreams were right. Here it would end at last, as this shape refined itself into the one that would kill or drive insane all who saw it. It was the Dark, which the Dragons unaided had not been able to drive away, and could not now: and in that darkness were held ready all other fears, all gathered together and made real at once, as the Goddess was all joys. And no-one was going to be able to save them. Freelorn clutched Hergótha in trembling hands, and collapsed to his knees.

Will you pay the price? the voice said to him, very still and small.

His eyes ran with tears of pain as they tried not to see what he forced them to watch: the blackness now taking the shape of a man, the man he feared, and loved, and had tried to master: the man he had now brought to his death. *Can you love a mere mortal?* he had said. Now the darkness looked at him coolly and turned away.

You know the price, the voice said.

Freelorn fought for breath as the fear and bitterness sought to squeeze it out of him. *You brought him here*, the darkness said, starting to flow into some more terrible shape. *He will die now; all of them will. Your fault. None of this would ever have happened if you had not forced the issue.*

Freelorn caught a breath, held on to it as if it were to be his last one. *What price?* he thought.

You know, She said. *Saviour of your people you may be: but man again—*

Lorn tried to speak, but no words came out, only a kind of choked noise.

There is no hope. All of them will die, their souls destroyed:

*and your kingdom will die, and there will be no rising again,
for any of you. Despair*—

He clutched Hergótha, bent double over it.

Will you pay?

The pain tore him like a blade. Freelorn fell forward
and ground his face into the dirt.

Hercwiss saw him fall, but the sight of what was out there
held him immobile with terror. This was truly the Dark
risen again, come back to live here for ever. But the new
shape it was taking, as it towered up against the stars, was
the shape of madness. The Shadow had been the Goddess's Lover once, and had been fair. But It had long since
rejected that beauty along with all others, since they came
from Her. Now it shifted among countless mockeries of
everything She had made, gloating with its width of
choice; then slowly began to refine itself – winged like a
Dragon, but warped and hunched, all gross splayed limbs
and bloated body, monstrous. And a human face: but with
eyes empty of any human expression, any joy or interest or
even clean rage. This face wore a look of inane pleasure in
its own horror, of dreadful intelligence used merely as a
tool, and a loathsome one to be cast away as quickly as
possible. Delight in Its own malice, eternal spite, jealousy
that a universe was too small to contain: all these were
there. Before that face Herewiss felt the strength run out
of him like water. He fell, wishing he were dead . . . and
knowing it would be a long time yet.

The cry that came from his left was the only thing that
could have stirred him. It started as a moan, and scaled up
and up, a sound of final anguish that never quite became a
scream, though plainly it wanted to. *O my loved*, Herewiss
thought, and the tears ran down: but there was nothing he
could do. Still, he looked up, strained his eyes through the
darkness. If Lorn was finding his death, he would at least
wish him well on his way to the Shore—

The darkness was less. Some moonlight was somehow
not swallowed in the mists surrounding the shape of

despair before them. It shone on Lorn, crouched on his hands and knees on the ground. But then Herewiss shook his head to clear it, for this didn't look like Lorn, though it had a moment ago. It looked like someone on hands and knees, yes, heavy head hanging down. The moonlight clung about it, seemed to strengthen. The head lifted. White. Taller now, and it wasn't moonlight; it was light shed from the huge creature itself. It shook its mane, and light scattered from it. A long tail lashed about its flanks, and it lifted a heavy paw, took a step forward. A low growl rumbled in the air like thunder.

Herewiss dared the slightest glance at the black Beast's face, though doing so made him sick. Its expression of vacant hatred did not change, but It shuffled slightly backwards through the dark mist, and the black airs of certainty and damnation that had breathed from it now felt less sure. The White Lion looked at the Beast, and the growl grew louder as He took another step forward.

Héalhra! Herewiss thought – and then caught a sidewise glance of His eyes, and felt weak again, but from other causes.

This White Lion was not Héalhra.

No thought came to him through that glance, though, no sign of recognition: only a sense of tremendous rage and power, long-hoarded and now ready to be tremendously released, the way the earth grinds slowly and silently against itself until its force suddenly cracks the roots of mountains. The Beast coiled down on Itself at the sight and feel of this power, as if about to leap. In that moment the Lion lifted His head and roared. Not even the Dragons had been able to make such a sound; and it was more than a mere challenge, but a summons to whatever power might be in that place that was still unused, or free, to come to His aid. And He leapt at the Beast's throat.

They began to fight – if fight was the right word for something that felt and sounded more like an earthquake or an avalanche, some irresistible power of the world

360

venting itself in fury. The screams of the Beast were every sound of horror that had been heard since the world's creation, every keening of grief, every cry of the murdered; but the Lion's roaring kept blotting the horror out. And then came one scream that was not horrible, but clean and fierce, a sound of challenge. In a storm of white wings, as if the moon came flying, the Eagle came, and struck with talons of Fire, biting behind the Beast's head while the Lion held it down.

The darkness in the fields east of Arlid began to wash back and forth like water in a storm, as the Lion crushed the Beast's neck in his teeth, and threw Himself down on it, to kick it to death cat-fashion: and the Eagle's terrible talons ripped and tore, and black blood flowed. Now the Beast's screams were terror for itself – frustration and utter fear that It had invested too much of Its nature in this form, and might actually now die. It was struggling to escape. But the struggles were futile. When a god takes form in a physical world, even godlike form, there are rules that apply – chief of them, that other gods may affect that form. So it had been at Bluepeak, an age ago: so it was now. The Beast screamed for release and escape, and shrilled hatred that should have killed those on the field who watched the battle – already barely half-conscious themselves with direct experience of the awful intensity of the emotions of gods. But the Beast's screams made no difference. After a long time, they got fainter. After what seemed an eternity, they stopped altogether.

All who could looked up in that silence. The darkness was washing away, and the Beast's body, lying half-concealed in it, was beginning to be washed away by the dark mist as it retreated – the stuff of a bad dream, already half evaporated. The Eagle took wing and perched on Vintner's Rise: it looked at the Lion, called one last time, and faded away, like the moon going behind a cloud.

The White Lion stood looking at His city. Moonlight was bright on it again; but not as bright as His glory, reflected in the walls, and the waters of the Arlid. He turned then, already fading, and looked at Herewiss; and huge and fiery though they were, His eyes were Freelorn's. The look was a king's look, a conqueror's look: noble, benign, remote.

Loved— Herewiss thought, a last desperate cry of the mind.

No answer. The eyes closed, and the great form faded, became a ghost of itself in the moonlight: was gone.

It was a good while before anyone moved. Herewiss was one of the first to manage it. With Sunspark's help, he staggered out into the open space where the Beast had been. The mist had cleared away, and of the soul-killing thing that had fought there, there was no sign. Only one thing Herewiss found, and he and Sunspark stared down at it for a good while – the body of a tall, handsome man, with only one wound on him, where a sword had pierced his heart. He was otherwise unmarked, but there was a burnt, used look to him, and he was stiff already, as if he had been dead for a good while. His face in the moonlight wore a look that was difficult to decipher. It might have been doubt.

Segnbora came along after a while, with Hasai behind her. Hasai's eyes were aflame again, and so was Skádhwë. Herewiss was glad to see this, but had no heart to look at Khávrinen. Together they looked down at Rian's body in silence. Finally Segnbora said, 'What will we do with his body?'

'Take it back to Prydon,' Herewiss said dully, 'and give it the usual rites. He was a minister of the throne, after all. And his wife and child have a right to their grief.' His own grief would not even have that slight balm brought by the ceremonies with which a loved one is sent onwards. There would be nothing left to burn, as there had been nothing left of Héalhra. Herewiss knew as well as Freelorn had the price that had been required of the Lion.

And there all his self-control deserted him, and he turned away from Segnbora and Hasai, and buried his head against Sunspark's flank. It twitched at his tears, but didn't move. *Lorn!* he cried. *Oh, Lorn!*

'I wish you wouldn't do that,' Freelorn said from behind him, just a little crossly. 'My head hurts enough as it is.'

The shock was like being hit by a spent arrow, but much worse. Herewiss staggered around, and put his arms out as much to hold his loved as to keep himself from falling over. 'But you—'

Freelorn, though, was looking at him strangely. 'Wait a minute. Weren't you the Eagle?'

Herewiss blinked and wiped his eyes. The feeling of some ancient power, rooted in the earth and finally mastered, flowed off Lorn and left Herewiss feeling delighted and confused. Right now the confusion was winning. 'Me? Are you off your head? Why would I be?'

'I don't know – I just always thought that you would – you *are* of His line.'

Hasai lifted his head and looked north. 'If you are looking for the Eagle, then I believe she's walking down Vintner's Rise just now. And she's cursing, because on the way down she's found some kind of insect that's been eating the vines' roots.'

Herewiss laughed, though it came with difficulty: his throat was still choked with emotion. 'The descent in her line was direct, Lorn. The Brightwood people are just a cadet branch. Don't I have enough, with this, to keep me busy?' And he hefted Khávrinen, and didn't mind seeing its Fire now. Then he shook his head, and dropped the sword, and just held Freelorn again. 'Let her be the Eagle all she likes. What I don't understand is how *you* – how you *didn't*—'

Freelorn slipped his arms around Herewiss. 'It seems,' he whispered, 'that She doesn't care to repeat Herself – so She won't ask the same price twice. Or rather . . . She *asks.*' He smiled against Herewiss's neck, and said, 'It seems it's possible to bargain from a position of strength . . .'

They said little to one another for a long while. Finally, Segnbora said, 'Well, Lorn, are we going to stand here all night? What do we do now?'

'Go home?' Freelorn said, and looked across the river to Prydon, shining under the moon.

Epilogue

'A timely marriage': one made before your children
start nagging you about the subject.

s'Dathael, *Definitions*:
c. 1870 p.a.d.

They watched the King of Arlen come home, that night,
from the gates of Prydon, though at first they didn't know
it. The guards at the gates, and the people on the walls,
saw a group of people come walking and riding down the
road in the dark, up to the end of the old bridge, where it
had been broken. There they stood looking at it briefly,
and then, carefully, took their way down the path that led
to the small pier from which people went down to fish.
One of them let himself down, and the watchers on the
walls thought that perhaps there was a boat there, and that
the people would come across that way. But the single
figure, indistinct in the bright moonlight, simply walked
out across the water. No-one quite understood why he
stopped by one of the broken piers of the bridge, and
leaned against it. The sharper-eyed said that he was
hugging it. No-one argued. Stranger things had happened
tonight, as everyone knew who had been up on the walls –
nearly half the city, as it turned out.

The others who had come down with that single figure
walked across on a line of blue Fire that spread itself across
the water for them. While they did, a huge dark shape
came up out of the east, its wings wide, and soared up to
perch on one of the two towers that overlooked the great

gates. The sky had been full of those wheeling shapes for a while now; some of them settled on the walls or the higher towers, looking down curiously at the people, who looked back as curiously. Many lights had been put out for fear of attracting Something's attention, earlier that evening: now, encouraged possibly by the interested gaze of those huge eyes like lamps, the torches in the streets and the candles in the windows of the city were lit again.

The single figure who had walked across the water rejoined his friends, and together they walked down the road to the gates. The others fell back as they came to the gate itself, and the twelve guards there stood and looked at the young man who came up to them with Hergótha the Great in his hand. He paused for a moment, seemingly waiting for one of them to say something. None of them did. They knew what they saw, but what they *felt* was something that shone, something about thirty cubits long and ten high, Someone with solemn, amused eyes . . . and with claws.

'Well,' Freelorn said, 'I'm back.'

They stepped aside to let him in. He nodded to them, and walked on through, swinging Hergótha up so that the blade rested over his shoulder. The great red mantichore sapphire in the pommel shone like an eye in the torchlight. Up the dark street he went, looking from side to side, taking note of a lampstandard broken here, a paving-stone loose there: a man coming home after a long trip, noticing things that need to be fixed. His friends came after him, and the guards watched them go, seeing all the Flame pass them by, murmuring at the sight of the Rods and the strange weapons. But what drew their eyes again, until he was out of sight, was the indistinct form carrying the glint of red with it, the hint of moonlight on a pale form, sauntering along the street that led up towards Kynall, home at last.

Kingship in Arlen passes without much ceremony, as a rule. Once there's an Initiate, and the Stave comes to her

366

or him, then Arlen has a ruler again. Herewiss had his suspicions as to where it might be found, and a little searching in Freelorn's old room upstairs turned it up. The next morning, Freelorn took a while to sit in the throne again. Segnbora brought the Lion banner, and put it in its old accustomed place behind the throne: and Freelorn sat in the old white chair, looking down the length of the bright room, and smiled, just once, briefly. Then something caught his sleeve when he moved his arm. Freelorn looked down at the arm of the throne and said to Herewiss, 'What the Dark are these scratchmarks?'

Sunspark, back in one of its human-shapes again, that handsome red-haired young woman, abruptly became interested in something up the stairs, and headed that way. Herewiss chuckled.

'You'd better get up now and go somewhere else,' Herewiss said, 'if you don't want trouble.'

'What?' Freelorn stared at him. 'What kind of trouble could I get into here? This is where I belong.'

Herewiss smiled, and Freelorn soon found out what he meant . . . as the old ministers of the throne began arriving, all excuses and praise, to greet the new King and (they desperately hoped) to be reconfirmed in their offices. Herewiss turned and started to leave. 'Don't *you* go anywhere!' Freelorn said, rather sharply. Everyone in the room – ministers and their assistants, mostly – shivered slightly, as they heard the echo of a growl run down their nerves.

But Herewiss turned around, completely untroubled, though smiling wryly. 'It was worth a try,' he said, and went up to lounge on the steps leading up to the throne.

They spent the rest of the day there, and at the end of it Lorn heartily wished he had taken Herewiss's advice. *That'll teach you to listen to your counsellors*, said Herewiss's amused thought to him privately. There had been a few good moments – especially when first Moris, then Dritt and Harald, turned up, having made their way to Kynall from their various postings. There were embraces then, and healths drunk, while ministers stood and looked nervously on people whose loyalties had been with Freelorn when no-one else's were. But the rest of the day was a long list of hirings and firings, shuffling people (with Herewiss's advice) into positions better befitting their talents, or out of offices they had mishandled, or into ones where they could be politically useful but otherwise harmless. Mere loyalty to Cillmod was not a criterion for dismissal, as the ministers found to their relief and confusion. They were also surprised to find that Lorn would speak of him easily, when they were afraid to.

'Find him,' he said several times. 'He has nothing to fear from me. If he's dead, he'll be honourably sent onward. If he's alive, I want to see him.'

No-one seemed able to do anything about this, and finally Segnbora went out to see what could be found. Freelorn sat back and went about his business, only once finding himself stymied: when Herewiss refused to be his chief minister.

'You're off your head,' Herewiss said. 'You are not my master, nor are you going to be. But I do have a Mistress – and Her business to attend to. Find someone else.'

Freelorn put his eyebrows up at this, but knew the sound of Herewiss's mind being made up, and turned his attention to other matters, such as the army. The commanders had come in to offer their surrender, and Freelorn had burst out laughing. 'You can't surrender to me,' he said. 'You're on *my* side! Aren't you . . . ?'

The commanders hastily agreed. After a while, re-assured by Freelorn that the troops' pay would not be affected by the last week's work, they went away, relieved both to still have their jobs, and to get out of Kynall. The sense of something large, amused and white, watching them, was much with them all.

It was getting on towards evening when Freelorn stood up and said, 'No more of it. Tomorrow, ladies and gentlemen. Till then, good night.'

There were mutters from people who had unfinished business, but Lorn merely looked at them, and they left hurriedly, feeling other eyes than his resting on them. Freelorn sat back in the throne, rubbing his eyes wearily, and said to Herewiss, 'Is it always going to be like this, do you think?'

'You mean the work? You watched your father – you should know that better than me.'

'No, I mean – this.' Freelorn gestured over his shoulder with his thumb at the presence that hung about him, and which he suspected Herewiss could see perfectly clearly, Fire-gifted as he was. 'Not that I object, mind you,' he said hurriedly: for him, the Lion was Héalhra, as much a father figure as his own blood-father. 'It's just—'

'Oh. No, Lorn, I doubt it. I think you're in something like breakthrough. I think it'll get less . . . noticeable after a while, even for you: certainly for other people. But He'll always be there when you need Him.' And Herewiss chuckled. 'We won't be three in a bed, if that's what you're worried about.'

'I was meaning to talk to you about that,' Freelorn said.

Lorn, Segnbora said in their minds. *Lionhall, quickly. I've found him.*

It was only a few minutes' walk away, through the quietening streets. The city had come back to life today, at least partly. There had been a sense of holiday, people standing in doors talking about what they had seen the night before, a buzz of excitement, relief, and sorrow for those who had fallen. It was quieting again now, but there were still people standing around in the streets as if waiting for something: and they watched Freelorn pass by, and greeted him the way he remembered people in the old days greeting his father: 'Good evening, King.' The offhand sound of it was meat and drink to him.

Lionhall was not the massive pile of rubble it had been, for the simple reason that Hasai and several other Dragons had been carefully picking up the biggest pieces and

369

setting them out in order in what remained of the square, as delicately as children playing jackstones. The great crevasse down the middle had already been filled in with melted stone carefully smoothed over.

Freelorn and Herewiss made their way to the shattered portico, where Segnbora was kneeling over a supine form with Blanis, and two Rodmistresses from the army.

Cillmod lay on the ground, on a piece of board someone had brought. His legs were a welter of blood, but he was awake and alert, and in no pain, due to Segnbora's ministrations. He gazed up at Freelorn with an expression that looked strangely like relief, though there was unease in it too.

'This man was plainly being saved for something,' Segnbora said. 'Half a wall came down on him, but a fragment of the dome that had come down first kept the wall from falling flat, and it spared his chest and head. These are bad—' She looked dispassionately at his legs. 'But he'll walk again, though it may take us a while.'

Freelorn nodded.

Cillmod looked at him a moment. Then he said, 'Well, King, I would give you your Stave back, but it seems to be gone.'

'I have it,' Freelorn said. He returned the uneasy glance, and said what he had been thinking about for a while now. 'I am going to need a chief minister. A bit of a move downwards for you, it has to be admitted. But you kept this country running, however you could, when the rightful ruler was off acting the idiot. And you clearly have the talent, and you know the Four Hundred much better than I do. Will you help me now?'

'It will not be comfortable for you, I would think,' Cillmod said.

'I'm not here to be comfortable,' Freelorn said. 'I have work to do, that's all. Will you help me?'

Cillmod looked at him for a while. 'Yes,' he said at last.

Freelorn nodded. 'Go in Her care, then,' he said, 'and get better. If there's anything you need, let me know.'

Cillmod turned his head away. 'I'll see you at dinner,' Segnbora said. 'Come on, ladies.'

'Dinner,' Herewiss said. 'Not a bad idea. You haven't had anything all day. Not even at breakfast this morning.'

'Nothing for me yet,' Freelorn said. 'There's something I have to do fasting. I'll take care of it now.' He hugged Herewiss for a moment, one-armed, then turned and headed down the street, towards the city gates.

It was the oldest law, and almost the first one his father had taught him when he was old enough to understand such things. 'When Arlen goes to battle,' Ferrant said, 'it does so for safety, not for glory. It is for the people out on the fields, and in the little towns, that we go to war – because that battle will make them secure – not for our own aggrandizement. Now remember how Héalhra's son, when he could find nothing of his father to send to the fire, took up one of the people from the battlefield instead, one of Héalhra's townsmen who had come out to fight, honouring him as if he had been his father? So we do now. When a battle is over in which Arlene blood is shed, the ruler must find one of the people who fell, and send that person onward with his or her own hands, to remind them that we know their grief, and that it's ours, not just theirs. Not food nor drink may pass your lips until this is done. Remember it.'

Lorn made his way down to the battlefield, and walked through the trampled-up ground and mud under the early evening sky – just one more figure moving among the bodies, head bent, looking for someone.

No-one lying down moved. The wounded had been taken away by now: those who were left were healed of their wounds more thoroughly and finally than any leech or Rodmistress could do it. Lorn moved among them, numb, too numb even to weep. The bodies sprawled out on the ground in terrible relaxation, some blank-eyed, staring upwards, some curled up as if in sleep, but instead of quiet breath, their blood spread out around them, black and cold. Arms were stretched out to dropped weapons, to other dead; hands lay open and empty as if asking for something, ready to receive. But all their receiving was over.

Lorn stopped suddenly and knew he had found the one. She lay on her face, one arm twisted up under her, her fair hair all in wet strings, and the arrow that had killed her buried almost to the fletching in her back. The sword beside her was streaked amber and red-black with blood separating out, the remnant of her last kill.

He did not want to touch her, but slowly he crouched down and put a hand under one of her shoulders. She was stiff. It made him shudder, how like a heavy doll or a half-filled sack a human body felt with the life gone out of it: as if it had never been alive at all, had never ridden proud in the saddle or walked or laughed. She turned over too easily, the broken arm falling stiffly over her face as she did, like a sleeper's arm thrown over the eyes to shut the light away. And Lorn found himself looking at the face of the girl who had brought him Blackmane, the one who was rude to him, and willing to take his orders anyway: the one who rode off laughing him to scorn.

Now he wept indeed: his eyes blurred so they were hardly any use to him, he could not breathe, and the rage in him mixed with grief and the two of them strangling him. She would not be grinding any corn this time next year, or coming to him to complain about the lack of it. Freelorn swung her up in his arms. A long leggy bundle she was, not the light lithe creature who had laughed at him and thundered off fierce and furious, like the Maiden gone mad: dead weight in truth, sodden clay like the ground all around, clothes and mud and blood. He staggered as he tried to carry her away. Finally Freelorn had to throw her over his shoulder, like a sack, and that made him cry worst of all, so that he stumbled and fell, and swore at any hand that touched him to try to help. Finally he found his way back to the place where they were preparing to burn the dead, and laid her out on one of the pyres there, ordering her body as best he could, and saying the words of farewell. He waited until the pyre was ready, and put the torch to it himself, while the people around him watched and grieved. Then he made his way back towards the city. An hour, perhaps, the business had taken him. But in that hour he knew at last what all kings know sometimes – that any death of theirs that might prevent a war is worth it. But also that the great Death is loose in the world, and like the Goddess, sometimes one must live and wish to be dead, and go on regardless – with all the others' deaths slung over one's shoulder, the weight that is never wholly there, but never wholly gone, until the World end and be made again, and made aright . . .

He came to dinner in sombre mood, but it couldn't last long in the face of the others' merriment. All his own people were there, and Sunspark, in its young-woman shape: Eftgan had come in from putting her own army to rights, bringing Hearn with her. They all sat down to the meal together in one of the downstairs dining rooms, not the huge echoing state banqueting hall, but a cosy room with windows looking out westward. The evening was cool and still, the sunset clear and cloudless: the candles burned up straight, as if in a closed room. Outside the window, Hasai's head rested on a nearby wall, one eye looking in. Herewiss handed Freelorn a cup of wine when he came in, and Freelorn drank it straight off, and then stared into the cup, and at Herewiss, surprised.

'That's Brightwood white!'

'You're welcome,' Hearn said, dry as always, and gestured at a small firkin in the corner.

The cooks were evidently grateful for having been retained. Dinner was restrained, but splendid – the first roast goose of autumn, crisp and fragrant with peppercorns and red wine, and salt salmon, and beans baked in garlic cheese. Freelorn dived into it all with great enthusiasm.

'A leonine appetite,' Eftgan said, helping herself to a

second helping of goose. 'As regards work, too, I hear. You were at it already today. What will you do next?'

'Besides being King? Well, there was something else . . .' He blushed, then got embarrassed at his own embarrassment, and looked at Herewiss. 'Since we don't have to be running all over the place any more, I had thought we might get married.'

Herewiss chuckled, and then glanced over at Hearn, a sidewise look. 'You've been trying to get me to settle down for long enough!' he said. 'Would this make you happy?'

'Don't marry for *me*. And you settle down? Hopeless,' said Hearn, with the air of a man bidding farewell to a lost cause.

Herewiss rolled his eyes at his father, and turned back to Freelorn. 'But you know I won't be at home all the time, loved.'

Freelorn nodded. 'As if that matters particularly any more.' And it was true, for since last night, neither of them had been able to lose the sense of the other's presence within him, nearby, ready, committed. *How long has that feeling been there*, Freelorn wondered, *drowned out by our fears?* But it didn't matter now. 'You have your work to do,' he said, 'as I have mine. We'll make it work out somehow.'

'And certainly there'll be no lack of royal heirs,' Herewiss said, 'which will make the Four Hundred happy, if anything can.'

Freelorn made a wry face. After today's work, he was beginning to have his doubts. 'But that's another point,' he said. 'The princesses. 'Berend,' he said, 'how about it? Will you marry us, and make an honest man of me?'

Segnbora smiled, dimpling. 'Possibly this is a task beyond even the Goddess,' she said, 'but one must attempt the impossible, as She does. All right. But don't forget, I have a lifemate.'

'I wouldn't think of leaving Hasai out of it,' Freelorn said. 'Assuming he consents. What do Dragons do to get married?'

'Get pregnant,' Hasai sang, amused. 'And then, a bath in the valleys of the sun, to celebrate.'

'Oh, well then *that's* handled. Segnbora, take care of it.'

She burst out laughing, and Hasai went off into a bout of hissing like a lidded pot boiling over. Freelorn suspected he had just made some sort of dirty joke in Dracon, and let it lie. 'The more the merrier,' he said. 'But the Royal House of Arlen is going to be a very confused place. Sunspark, what about you? Will you marry in?'

She looked bemused for the moment. 'Why not?' she said finally. 'Maybe I'll understand this "progeny" thing eventually.'

Herewiss sat back grinning. 'In this family, I wouldn't bet on it.'

Segnbora laughed again. 'This is going to be one of those weddings where the participants outnumber the guests,' she said. 'But who cares? Is there anyone else we should have in the family? That's only five so far, not counting the children. What children there are so far, anyway.'

'I had thought about Eftgan,' Freelorn said. Herewiss and Segnbora looked at him with some surprise: but the Queen merely smiled. 'Well,' Lorn said, 'it's not as if she doesn't come of a good family. And there would seem to be certain – relationships – that might be more deeply explored.'

Eftgan laughed out loud. 'Don't ask me for help in being a demigod, lazybones! I'm having my own problems. But as for the business of uniting the two lines again, well, why not? It's good for a young king to marry an experienced queen, they say.' Freelorn leered at her hopefully. 'I don't mean *that*, you lecher! It also much reduces the chance of something like this interregnum happening to *either* of our lines again. I'm willing enough, if you all are. But don't ask me to be here much: I have my own row to hoe. And I'll have to ask Wyn, of course. But he always did like crowds . . .'

'Let it be so then.'

A tenday later, so it was. Who was to officiate was a problem, since normally for a royal wedding, the ruler of the other country came to do the honours in their capacity as the Goddess's high priest. Eftgan finally suggested that Kerim, the Chief Rodmistress, do the honours, and she agreed.

'Who are you going to invite?' Herewiss had asked Freelorn. Freelorn had looked at him in astonishment. 'Everyone,' he said. And so that came to pass as well. Most particularly he sent word south to Lalen and Nia. Five days before the wedding they arrived, Lalen quite astonished, but cheerful in an ironic way, and Nia overwhelmed. She was made much of, stuffed with treats, sat in the throne, and took to hanging about the rebuilding of Lionhall. Herewiss and the Dragons were managing this, and Nia shortly made common cause with Herewiss's sons, newly arrived from the Brightwood, who were also 'assisting' – that is to say, ordering the bemused Dragons around, and driving Herewiss half mad. Meanwhile, Lorn was busy with wedding arrangements. All the people of Prydon would not fit into Kynall at once, of course, so much of the wedding feast was staged outside in the squares and the main marketplace. So was the ceremony, since at least one of the participants, in common with his relatives, could not fit more than his head into Kynall.

They came out into the marketplace, two hours past noon, in a blaze of colour: Herewiss and Hearn in the white of the Phoenix livery, Segnbora blinding in the black glitter of dragonmail, Dritt and Harald and Moris in their best silks: and a sombre spot in the middle, the black of Arlen on Freelorn's surcoat, and the midnight blue of Darthen, both shadowed every now and then by Hasai, who was sitting on the fourth wall.

First of all that afternoon, Freelorn and Eftgan swore the Oath of Lion and Eagle again, briefly exchanging Hergótha and Fòrlennh, the hilts stained with their blood.

Then Kerim was called out, and the marriage began. The seven (for Wyn had arrived) took the vow, to share bodies and thoughts as pleasure and trust prompted, to live for and with one another and their children, to love while life lasted, though liking might come and go, and to do right by one another, as the Goddess would were She marrying in (which of course She was). Then they passed the cup of the sacral wine, and drank, pouring some over Hasai in lieu of actual drinking, so that everyone there burst out laughing at the sight of one of the bridegrooms being hallowed like a new-launched boat. And the whole crowd – four thousand people, it was later said – drank with them and wished them the truth of their vow. Then the fiddles and horns struck up, and the serious eating and drinking began.

The dancing started almost immediately, and didn't even slow down until a guard came riding into the square in some haste, a couple of hours later. She threw herself off her horse and hurried over to Freelorn, who was deep in a discussion of excise taxes with Wyn. 'Sir,' she said, 'there are Reavers at the gate!'

Freelorn blinked at her, a mild look. 'Here for the wedding, I would guess,' he said. 'I did invite *everybody*. How many of them are there?'

'Why, about four hundred—'

'Is that all? Plenty for them. Ask them to come in.'

The guard rode off, wearing an expression that suggested she thought Freelorn had taken leave of his kingly wits. But Freelorn finished his conversation with his husband, and waved Eftgan over. They had a few minutes to speak before the first company of Reavers rode into the market-place, looking around them with profound nervousness. The people in the marketplace looked back with exactly the same expression at the men and women on their little horses, all dressed in furs and roughspun: but there was a kind of splendour about them too, for they had dressed in their own best – ornaments of copper and carved bone, brooches of delicately interlaced wire, and wonderful copper-bound bows and spears. Freelorn looked at the man on the foremost horse as he came to a stand, and went forward. The man whom he had last seen down in south Darthen looked at him, and his expression changed. Almost a smile it became, though it was clear this was a laconic people who did not smile easily. Lorn went up to the horse, and bowed: the rider laid a fist to his breast.

'This is one of the chieftains of a people called Ladha,' Freelorn said to the crowd around him. 'We called them Reavers, because we didn't know any better. But now we do: now we both do. The Lion and the Eagle have made peace with the Reavers: they will war on us no more. In return, some of them will be living in the empty land down by Bluepeak and Barachael. They will guard our southern borders, and trade us horses that can walk right up walls.'

The crowd was muttering at this, but Freelorn was distracted, because the chieftain was holding out a skin bag to him. Freelorn raised his eyebrows, took it, uncorked it, sniffed. His eyebrows went much higher.

'Somebody bring this man a cup of wine,' he said. He waited until the chieftain had been handed someone's pottery cup, then saluted him. They drank together. Freelorn was hard put not to choke, and his eyes watered.

'What is it?' he said to the chieftain.

The man's eyes were glittering with amusement. He gestured at his horse, a mare.

Freelorn laughed and looked at the people around him. '*Thought* that was where they got that blond southern beer,' he said. The crowd burst out laughing.

Then everyone was offering the riders food and drink. Lorn drifted away, getting back to the business of being with his people again.

As soon as the horses were put back outside the city to pasture, the dancing started once more, and was still going on strong at dusk. Freelorn was having the legs danced off him by all comers, but that was part of a wedding, whether king's or commoner's. These were none of the stately dances of the court: these were country dances, stompers, thigh-slappers, circle dances with clapping and shouting. Freelorn was tiring out. *Nothing odd there*, he thought, *considering the last few days.* And he laughed at himself, for he was after all the Lion, better at short bursts of energy than long bouts of endurance. *I'm going to sleep for a week when this is over*, he thought as he finished a circuit of one of the circle dances, relinquished the hand of a young blond man from out in the country somewhere, and seized another hand that was held out to him, whirling the partner off.

The shock running up his arm, familiar, terrifying and wondrous, brought his head around with a snap. He looked at his partner. White linen blouse and heavier white skirt, soft boots, a countrywoman's attire: long, long dark hair, that flew with the turns and whirls of the dance. Her face he knew, having last seen it in the Ferry Tavern. Dusk was not quite well enough along yet to be certain, but in the folds of the dusty cloak, he thought he caught a glimpse of starlight.

She smiled at him, and kept him dancing when he might have stopped. 'What? So surprised?' She said, and chuckled. 'You did invite *everybody*.'

The rhythm changed, and Lorn got enough of his composure back to change the step with it, and let Her go for the side-by-side part of the dance. 'You're running yourself ragged, My dear,' She said, slightly breathless Herself with the stamping. 'I thought I'd better take My chance while I could. It's good luck to dance with a groom, they say . . .' Her eyes met his, and such a flow of Her power, and joy, and pride in him filled him, that the breathlessness was suddenly all his.

'Let's stop a moment,' he said, and pulled Her out of the dance. Off to one side was one of many trestle-tables with drink on it: Wyn had given the Throne an excellent discount. Freelorn reached out for a cup, but in the act someone tapped him on the shoulder from behind. He turned away from the tap, but it was only Segnbora, looking with astonishment at his partner. 'Oh!' she said.

'Lorn,' Herewiss said from behind him, holding their lovers'-cup out to him, 'why do you always— Oh!'

Sunspark peered out from under the table, in hunting-cat's shape. As it looked up, its eyes widened.

'A drink would be in order, I think,' She said. White radiance fell on Her from above, mingling with the moonlight that was already tangled in Her hair, though the moon had not risen yet. Low, and awed, and triumphant, the great voice sang: *'Sta-vhei'sduw rhdwae'Stihuw, hhwni-errhai'e!'*

She gazed up at Hasai. 'Oh, you are big,' She said, and chuckled again. 'Joy and honour to you too, dearest.' She reached out and took the cup that Herewiss handed her, his own hand trembling: She steadied it a moment before taking it. 'Thank you,' She said. 'I'm parched.'

She drank deep, and handed the cup to Herewiss, who drank as well and passed it on. 'Madam,' Segnbora said softly, taking it from him, 'what brings You here?'

The Goddess laughed. 'Every now and then, you know,' She said, 'something goes right.' She looked around at them. *'That* I thought I might come to see . . . since My law forbids me interfering otherwise.'

Sunspark lapped at the cup that Segnbora held for it . . . then looked surprised to find the wetness of the wine did it no harm: and Segnbora held the cup up to Hasai, and was surprised to see the golden light he supped from it at the end of his long forked tongue. The Goddess took it again, took one more drink, handed the cup back to Freelorn. 'It does say,' she said, '"as if She were marrying in . . ."'

They all gazed at Her, silent, in joy. It had become one of those times when hearts are suddenly so full, they will not admit of the spoken word, even among lovers and friends who have saved one another's lives. But in this company, none of them felt odd about it. 'I know,' She said to them at last. 'Never mind.'

'Lady,' Lorn said at last, 'a question?'

'From you, what else?' She said, laughing.

380

'Why did you forge us as we are?'

'To be weapons, Lorn. Surely you know that.'

'Surely. What this weapon wants to know is . . . will the battle *ever* be won?'

She looked at him with kindness, and rue. '"Not for ever; never for ever . . . the Shore makes sure of that."' She sighed. 'It will never wholly be won, child of Mine. Till time's end, no weapon I can forge will ever buy Me peace . . . or buy it for My worlds. That is My burden to bear. Mine, too, that I have caused you to be what you are . . . suffer what you suffer . . . in a lost cause.'

'Lost causes,' Lorn said gently, as if comforting Her, 'are what I was made for.'

'Beloved . . . that is exactly so.'

The stillness that fell then was mostly Hers. '*Hreiha*,' Hasai said, 'here is one place, *the* one place, where along with the Immanence, Your power fails . . . as in the humans' old stories, and our own. You cannot take away from us the responsibility, the desire, the will, that You gave us. Else Your worlds are truly hollow, and everything You've done has been vain. We did what we did – and would do it again, I know – whether you caused us to do it or not.'

'We might have done it slower,' Lorn muttered.

'But we would have done it nonetheless,' Segnbora said, looking Her directly in the eye, though she trembled with love as she did. 'Leave us our power, madam. And our love for You – which You could have forced – but in Your wisdom never did.'

The Goddess bowed Her head. 'So be it, then,' She said, in a voice hardly above a whisper; but the earth trembled with it, and the stars in their courses shook. 'As you give yourselves to Me . . . so I to you. Always.'

That we knew already, Sunspark said, its eyes glowing.

'Then go and rest,' She said. 'I have other weapons in the forge, and other loves to attend than you Five. Keep sharp, you were best. And sire children, or bear them, as the case may be: live, and love, and set My world on Fire.

As for the rest of it— The sword rarely has much warning, in a responsible warrior, if it's to be drawn. But it will be thanked afterwards . . . and made whole.'

She smiled at them. Then the woman in the long dusty cloak did Freelorn a curtsey, and turned, and strolled off among the dancers, into the dusk. Moonlight glimmered in Her hair. Noticing, the moon rose hurriedly behind Her, just before She vanished into the crowd.

Freelorn filled the cup again. 'To Our Lady of the Long Dance,' he said: 'who misses no step, and no partner.'

They all drank.

They danced the dawn in, as tradition requires. One of the dancers went missing, a while after the sun came up. Long and black his shadow could be seen, stretching out across the fields west of Kynall, tangling with the shadows of the trees of Orsmernin. He carried a sapling tree, and a spade. To a space on the eastern side of the circle he went, and on a small mound there, planted the tree. A number of breaths he stood there; then turned away. Behind him, the sapling's shadow got longer, and longer still, tangling with the shadows of the other trees in the Grove: seven years' growth done in seven breaths, and then stillness, and green leaves rustling in the wind.

The man in the field looked towards the city, and at the black banner cracking from the topmost pinnacle of the tower of Kynall's keep in the morning wind. Past the tower, flying, wheeled two great shapes, vanishing eastward: they flew, it seemed, into the sun.

Freelorn smiled, and gave his new allegiance to the dawn, and started walking back to town.

Here ends *The Door Into Sunset*. The fourth volume of this sequence, which tells the end of *The Tale of the Five*, will be called *The Door Into Starlight*.

On The Pronunciation Of Languages

For those interested:

Generally speaking, vowels in the Arlene and Darthene languages are pronounced as they are in the Romance languages of our world – the long vowels are 'pure' sounds (a=ah, e=ay, i=ee, o=oh, u=oo). There are no silent vowels in any language spoken in the Middle Kingdoms. Pairs of vowels may show up looking like English diphthongs, but they are almost never pronounced that way. The only exceptions are words derived (or apparently derived) from Dracon: Laihan (pr. lye-han), the *tai*- and *stai*- prefixes, etc.

Diacritical marks are therefore tucked in here and there to indicate that an apparent diphthong is actually meant to be split: as in Héalhra (pronounced HAY-al-hra). The diacriticals will also sometimes indicate where the stress in a word is meant to fall, in cases where there may be doubt. Sometimes they do both. If there are two diacritical marks in a word (Skádhwë), the second one is usually there to indicate that the vowel in question is not supposed to fall silent, or is unusually long: 'SKAHD-hway'. Or it may indicate a secondary stress, occasionally stronger than the (usual) first one in the word (Héalhrästi, As't'Raïd).

Consonants for the most part behave themselves and are all separately pronounced, though there is a tendency (common to the drawling North) to soften or elide some compound consonant structures, like the properly divided d-h compound in Skádhwë, into a breathed 'th' sound, *à la* the Welsh. This is sloppy pronunciation, but the author is hardly likely to carp at it, having fallen into the bad habit a long time ago while still learning Darthene. As regards words that seem to have been translated into English cognates from their native Arlene or Darthene (e.g. Freelorn, Herewiss, Britfell, etc.), they should be pronounced just as they look.

Dracon pronunciation is very different from that used for Arlene and Darthene, and has its own set of difficulties. Dracon has diphthongs after the manner of English – and tripthongs, and tetrathongs, and longer compounds not appearing in English or any other human tongue. But the diphthongs do not always run together as expected (*sdahaih*, for example, is pronounced 's-DAA-hay-ih'). With words containing multiple run-on vowels (*ohaiiw*) and longish consonantal combinations (such as *rhhw'Fvhr'ielhrnn*, the Dracon transcription of 'Freelorn'), the reader is encouraged to do exactly as he or she likes; the author, in mild desperation over her accent, has been doing the same for years. But there are a few general hints for the determined. The main stress of a word almost always goes on the first vowel or diphthong to make an appearance. In words beginning with one or more consonants (*nn's'raihle*), the rule remains the same, but all consonants preceding the diphthong or vowel must be separately pronounced. *Nn's'raihle* therefore has, not three syllables, but six: approximated for ease of human pronunciation, 'en-ne-s-R'EYE-heh-leh'. This last example demonstrates how it sometimes helps, when trying to speak Dracon, to 'fake' a vowel or two in a long string of consonants; even in a short one – like the honorific/species-descriptive *lhhw*, which can safely be pronounced 'lhew', as long as the sound is kept breathy. In the case of multiple vowels, the multiplicity is intended to indicate unusual length – of duration rather than sound. Singing the vowels in question may help, though it by no means makes them last as long as they're really supposed to. Dracon is a leisurely language, as might be expected when members of the species that speaks it can live a thousand years before shedding their skins for the last time and going *mdahaih*, at which time (free of the hectic demands of living bodies) they settle down to work on complete mastery of the tongue. Humans, who have less time, or more on their schedules, must just do the best they can.